THE
GONE
DEAD
TRAIN

THE
GONE
DEAD
TRAIN

LISA
TURNER

WM

WILLIAM MORROW
An Imprint of HarperCollins*Publishers*

THE GONE DEAD TRAIN. Copyright © 2014 by Lisa Turner. All rights reserved. Printed in the United States of America. No part of this book may be used or reproduced in any manner whatsoever without written permission except in the case of brief quotations embodied in critical articles and reviews. For information address HarperCollins Publishers, 195 Broadway, New York, NY 10007.

HarperCollins books may be purchased for educational, business, or sales promotional use. For information please e-mail the Special Department at SPsales@harpercollins .com.

FIRST EDITION

Designed by Diahann Sturge

Library of Congress Cataloging-in-Publication Data.
Turner, Lisa (Lisa Celeste)
  The gone dead train : a mystery / Lisa Turner.
    pages cm
  Summary: "After a time away to recover from the aftermath of a horrible case that left his partner dead, Billy's back in Memphis, drawn into an ever-widening murder mystery that focuses on flawed heroes: a disgraced major league baseball player, two legendary blues musicians on the lam, a straight-arrow lady cop tortured by a guilty conscience, and two iconic civil rights warriors with secrets so dark they'll shock the nation. Detective Billy Able is at a crossroads. His previous case left him questioning everything he believed about his abilities as a cop and as a friend. Even though he's considering leaving police work behind—he's unable to turn off the instincts he's honed after a decade on the force. But when he stops a crime he sees from being committed, he finds himself embroiled in a much bigger scandal. A murder that has just taken place has connections to a series of much older crimes and dates back to the civil rights movement. As he investigates, Billy uncovers so many layers of secrets he can barely keep the truth from the lies. And he knows the straight-laced cop assigned to the case is hiding something big. But is it connected to the case? And this time he's determined to make sure he finds out the truth before anything else can happen. But as the search for truth with the help of a Santeria Priest leads him deeper into the underbelly of Memphis, will Billy make it out alive?"—Provided by publisher.
  ISBN 978-0-06-213619-0 (paperback)
  1. Police—Tennessee—Memphis—Fiction. 2. Murder—Investigation—
Fiction. I. Title.
  PS3620.U76558G66 2014
  813'.6—dc23

                                                              2014008302

ISBN 978-0-06-213619-0

14 15 16 17 18 OV/RRD 10 9 8 7 6 5 4 3 2 1

For my friend Linda Kichline and my cousin James Flatter

THE

GONE

DEAD

TRAIN

Prologue

The sunset was a red slit of light like a devil's eye, hanging low and depraved over the Mississippi River bluff. Storm clouds thundered all around as Little Man Lacy ran for the river, his pants legs flapping, his long arms and big hands pumping as he moved up the street past the train depot. He was seventy-three years old, tall and skinny, his nose and earlobes giving way to gravity. He was meant to be a bluesman all his life, long as he could play. Instead, he'd dropped his music by the side of the road, abandoned his sax, like leaving an infant alone in a tub. Now fear was his instrument. His lips pressed together, and he hummed as he raced, searching for the pain that made his music real. But even the music couldn't help him now. He ran for the mighty Mississippi with all his heart, knowing water was his only salvation.

The Evils were upon him. He knew the power and the nature of the woman who'd released them. His breath whistled in his lungs, not because he was weak, but because the Evils were drying up everything strong inside. If he made it to the bridge, he might trick them into jumping in the water where they'd be trapped with no escape. Then he would stand on the bridge and laugh at their mistake, because everyone knows that once the Evils set out to take your soul, they'll have you one way or another. You can't shrug off fate, but he'd be damned if he wouldn't try.

The storm clouds hanging between him and the river saw him coming. They opened up, and the rain fell down. The water gave him hope that he wouldn't be taken, but the Evils just laughed, the sound buzzing in his ears like a thousand metal toys clicking.

By the time he reached the top of the hill, the street had filled with rain and mud that soaked his shoes. The mud was draining from the deep hole dug in the ground, deep as a cave. He saw DANGER signs and the neon sign for the Blue Monkey Club shining blue and yellow in the sky, which he took as a good omen. The river pulsed nearby, pounding in its banks. He heard its music.

He was a bluesman. He still had hope.

Then, around the corner came the woman carrying the Evils. She was tall and wearing golden hoops in her ears. She called out his name, "Little Man Lacy!" as she moved across the street like a viper on legs. She came at him with a small gray bag held high, a conjure bag made for carrying things only the Evils know.

His heart tore open. He turned to make a run for the river, but the mud was slick, and his feet went out from under him. He was falling.

The last thing Little Man Lacy saw as he tumbled into the pit was the woman's eyes shining in the dark.

Chapter 1

His first night back in Memphis, Sergeant Detective Billy Able hit G4 on the jukebox, "Me and the Devil Blues." He felt at home sitting on his favorite bar stool at Earnestine and Hazel's, drinking Miller High Life delivered by the bartender without his even having to ask. The music matched his mood for the evening—raw and personal.

He raised the cold Miller to his lips and let the liquid roll down his throat. Coming up the long way, the hard way, you lose track. You tell yourself, "Anything good comes natural. Give it time." You buy a bullshit line like that because slipping past a problem is less complicated than looking at it full on. At thirty-three years of age, Billy knew sliding past a problem was easier. You close the door and hear the click of the lock behind you.

He'd packed up that morning in Atlanta and walked out on the love of his life. After the eight-hour drive, he'd stopped at his place on the river to throw water on his face then had come directly to Earnestine and Hazel's, the most authentic piece of real estate in the city. Years ago, Otis Redding ate his lunch at Earnestine and Hazel's. Sam Cooke, Jackie Wilson, James Brown, Tina Turner—they all hung out with the ladies. Tonight, so would he.

The bar filled with purple light as the jukebox kicked in with a Red Davis classic, "You Ain't Enough for Me." The jukebox was famous for spontaneously singling out a man and speaking to his pain. Billy was that man tonight. He swigged more beer. *You ain't enough for me.* Maybe that's what Mercy had been trying to say all along, and he hadn't been listening.

What he wanted now was a few beers and some peace. He didn't want to get drunk, just comfortable. He considered the next few days to be a well-deserved vacation. A ten-dollar tip left on the bar would change all that.

He spotted the ten before the bartender did. They both watched the skinny punk in the motorcycle jacket snake the bill into his back pocket. His buddies laughed and slapped him on the back for his audacity.

Tonight Billy wasn't a Memphis cop. He'd been on leave for nine months. The ten bucks weren't his responsibility.

"Hey!" the bartender yelled at the guy's back.

The punk turned to make a smart-ass remark, stumbled into a table, and knocked a drink into a woman's lap. The two men at her table jumped to their feet and threw back their chairs.

Billy knew what would happen next. A brawl, then the bartender would come from around the bar with a sawed-off pool cue. Broken chairs, busted lips. He set his beer down and stood up. The bartender had a new baby at home. He needed the ten bucks. Besides, it was theft.

The jackass with the money strolled toward the door. Billy shot out his boot and tripped him. The guy went facedown, hard. His buddies took one look at Billy's face and cleared out. He picked the bill from the punk's back pocket and slapped it on the bar. The guy got to his feet and ran.

Law school students wandered in. Soul burgers hissed off the flat-top grill. Behind them came the "S and P" or "Stand and Pose" group—the men in their polo shirts and pressed khakis, their big-bosomed women in strapless sundresses that they had to constantly hike up like they were hauling two-pound bags of flour on their chests.

The bartender set Billy up with another brew, but it didn't taste as good as the first. This wasn't the homecoming he'd intended.

He checked his watch. Still time to catch Ruby Wilson at the speakeasy above B. B. King's Blues Club on Beale Street. He walked outside and stood at the curb. The night had a swelter on. He stepped into the street and felt gravity pulling through the soles of his boots. He was back in Memphis.

A Riverfront trolley with its square windows of light sat in front of Central Station. A young woman turned from the window to speak with the man seated beside her. They laughed. Billy felt Mercy's fingers wrap into his, even though she hadn't reached for his hand in weeks. Until that morning he believed they still had a chance.

The sound of a blues guitar lifted in the night, coming from the train station's main terminal. The evening still had potential. He decided to check it out.

He forgot that nothing good ever happens after midnight.

Chapter 2

Billy bounded up the steps of Central Station in search of the blues guitar. During World War II, the cavernous terminal had been packed with travelers, a hub for fifty passenger trains a day carrying thousands of troops and tons of cargo. Now, The City of New Orleans was the only train that looped between Chicago and New Orleans, stopping in Memphis, morning and evening.

The terminal was empty except for a young guy across the way, playing a Les Paul Goldtop through a mini amp. The kid wore alligator boots and high-dollar jeans with a manufactured rip in the knee. Had to be a college student with a rich daddy.

He was working his way through "The Gone Dead Train," a delta classic by King Solomon Hill. The notes bounced off the walls and flew straight to the top of the terminal like they were steel-winged birds. The kid's guitar chops weren't bad, but nothing in his young life could connect him to those heartbreaking lyrics. What he was, wasn't authentic.

Another man, old and brown-skinned, sat at the far end of the oak bench that ran the length of the terminal. His suit was stained and his tie hung askew. His legs were crossed at the knee, so a portion of one skinny calf showed above his sock. He'd twisted away from the kid and his guitar, head down and arms folded over the middle of his body as if he were being assaulted by the sound.

Billy recognized Red Davis, the bluesman whose song he'd just heard on the jukebox. Davis and his partner, Little Man Lacy, had come to Memphis in the aftermath of Katrina. He'd expected them to be the kings of Beale Street. Instead, they showcased at a couple of minor clubs and ended up living on the streets. Like so many other flood victims, Katrina had knocked the fight out of both men.

The kid's guitar screeched and wailed through the final bars, making Red's head jerk up. The old man glanced left, spotted Billy across the way, and came to his feet, eyes glistening with anxiety.

"What 'chu want from me?" he called in a hoarse voice.

Billy raised a hand. "Not a thing." He took a step back, thinking he could still make Ruby's set if he didn't get caught up in this.

The kid broke in. "Mr. Davis, did you like that last riff? I wondered if I could sit in with you guys." He beamed, apparently having heard the word "yes" all his life. "Mr. Davis?"

"Get out 'cheer, boy, you're bothering me," Red snapped. "I got a train to catch."

Billy knew the train for Chicago was two hours gone and wouldn't head back until tomorrow morning. He looked around, saw no bag and no guitar case for Red.

Still, the damned kid wouldn't back off. "No one blows a harp like you. No one plays bottleneck guitar like you either, not even Furry Lewis." He dug in his pocket and pulled out a wallet, held it up for Red to see. "I'll pay if you let me sit in."

Red swayed, the bulge of a pint showing through his suit pocket. "You can kiss my ass, son. That's what."

The kid's face reddened, then he smirked at Billy and nodded toward Red. "I saw him come in the terminal so I played 'The Gone Dead Train' as a send-off. But he's not going anywhere. He's drunk. Guess people get old and lose it."

Billy considered popping the kid for his insolence. "You heard Mr. Davis. He wants you out of here, so move it." The guy shot him a belligerent look but went ahead and packed up the Les Paul. He left by a side door.

Red looked around, rheumy-eyed and unsteady on his feet, patting his jacket pocket with his hand as if reassuring himself. Before leaving for Atlanta, Billy heard Davis and Lacy had checked into Robert House to dry out. Judging by the pint in Red's pocket, that was over. He'd like to get the old guy off the bench before security came along and booted him out of the terminal. Not what he'd had in mind for the evening, but it needed to be done.

"Nice night," he said, walking over and picking up the street odors clinging to Red's suit.

"You can kiss my ass too, Officer. I'm going to Chicago."

No surprise Red had made him for a cop. The man must have spent a lifetime being hassled by rednecks carrying badges. He might be drunk, but his instincts weren't far off.

"I'm Billy Able. We met the night you and Little Man show-cased on Riddle Street. We talked about Blues Alley, the old club on South Front. Remember?"

Red studied him, still suspicious. "I remember. Maybe."

"The jukebox at Earnestine and Hazel's played 'You Ain't Enough for Me' tonight. The crowd loved it."

Red met his gaze, coming out of himself at the compliment. "That song's about men making fools a theirselves over women. I had me a lot of women. Beautiful women. Now I'm just an old fool. Ain't nothing so strong as old fool love." He waved a finger at Billy. "Get old. You'll know."

"Ruby Wilson had a stroke a couple of years ago, and she still sings at Itta Bena. You and Little Man could play club dates any night of the week to keep your hand in. It'd be like picking up money off the ground." He tried to soften the tone of his criticism, but it didn't work.

Red reared back. "Ain't none a yo' damned business what I do. Me and Little Man worked twelve-hour days alongside grown men when we was kids. We got our reasons for not working now. And we ain't worried about the music. Every time we put it down, it comes back." He coughed and dragged his hand over his mouth. "It always comes back."

Billy pictured Little Man Lacy, tall and agile, a man without the power of speech but who could say all that needed to be said when he had a sax in his hand. Come to think of it, where was Little Man? The two men were always together.

"Where's your partner?"

Red coughed again and cut his eyes away.

Somewhere below the terminal, a door slammed. Red's body jerked, and a shadow overtook his face. Fishing out the bottle, he collapsed on the bench, his fingers shaking as he struggled with the cap. He took a long pull.

How had a man like Red Davis ended up creeping around a train station at midnight, looking spooked out of his mind?

Red lowered the bottle and wiped his mouth with his sleeve. "That damned kid over there. He's got no right playing that song. Shit. That song's about dying. Heaven and hell. I know which direction I'm going. It's not too late for me." He peered up at Billy. "You know which way you going, son? Is Jesus gonna save your soul?"

Chapter 3

Patrol Officer Frankie Malone began walking her shift at the south end of the downtown precinct. She looked in on the P. Wee Saloon, dead except for eight conventioneers who'd drifted down from Beale Street in search of a grittier scene. They were sitting with their backs to the bar, so tanked they needed to be strapped to their stools. A musician sat on the stage under a blue spot with his steel guitar laying across his thighs. He slid a bottle neck across the strings, his lips moving as he talked to himself, almost like he was playing at home alone. When the song ended, the out-of-towners whistled and stomped, breaking him out of his dream.

Frankie signaled the bartender. He nodded that he would call a couple of cabs rather than let the drunk tourists ride the trolley back to their hotel.

Two blocks up South Main she crossed the street to make a pass through Central Station, which closed in an hour. She would finish her foot patrol then pick up a cruiser and make her rounds in the rest of the ward.

Approaching the station, a metal door slammed open and a

scowling teenager carrying a guitar case and amp stalked across the street to the Arcade Restaurant. He didn't look like trouble, so she let him go and took the stairs up to the main terminal. At the top of the steps, her hands went cold despite the warm night. She stopped to check the crescents of her thumbnails. They were blue. Been that way all day. Been that way since the accident.

The terminal was empty except for an elderly man sitting on the bench and a younger white guy who was talking to him. She recognized the older man as the musician, Red Davis, but she'd never had a reason to speak to him. The other man, maybe in his early thirties, was standing in front of Davis, staring down with a look of concern. At the sound of her steps, the younger man's hand brushed the small of his back, the reflexive move of a cop feeling for his weapon. He turned in her direction. She saw it was Detective Billy Able, looking thinner than she remembered, and tired. His hair was too long for her taste, but he was still attractive in that bad-boy way.

"Evening, Detective," she called across the terminal.

"Evening, Officer," Able responded.

She remembered his voice, smooth and disarming, God's gift in an interview room. That's where Able had made his reputation. She heard he could charm the panties off a nun. Seemed like he'd been gone for months, then she remembered his partner had died under questionable circumstances, followed by that nasty case involving Judge Overton and a little girl. The case had dominated the local news for weeks. She heard Able had taken a leave of absence after that and left town.

Giving her hands a quick rub, she walked up. "Frankie Malone. Good to see you back in Memphis." They clasped hands. He blinked, most likely at the chill in her grip, and his gaze brushed her bruised cheek.

"This is Red Davis," he said. "We were discussing heaven and hell."

"And women," Davis added. "We're talking about women."

"Sorry for your loss, Mr. Davis." She noticed Able's puzzlement and realized he might not have heard the news. "Little Man Lacy fell into a construction dig by the Blue Monkey Thursday night. The crew found him the next morning. Cause of death hasn't been determined."

Able glanced at the old man, then back at her.

She'd been on the scene when the body came out of the hole. She left out the part about the whiskey bottle found beneath him. No reason to insult Davis by saying his friend got drunk, fell in a hole, and broke his neck.

She bent down to Red, seated on the bench, and spoke louder than she meant to. "I heard you checked into the ER on Thursday with chest pains. Are you feeling better?"

"I'm not deaf," Red shouted back, then swigged from the pint he was holding.

She straightened. He was drunk and grieving, probably broke. Able was staring at Red in silence.

"You're here mighty late, Mr. Davis," Able said.

"I was catching the train to Chicago, but the lady in the office said my New Orleans ticket wouldn't carry me all the way. I been sitting here cogitating on the situation. I got to get out of town."

"So catch the morning train to New Orleans," Frankie offered.

Red scratched his neck. "I got people in the burbs outside a Chicago. Don't want to go there and live down no rabbit trails, but I ain't got a choice."

"You lost your partner. Time with family is a good idea," Able said.

Red wiped his nose in a smooth motion of disdain. "You know about losing a partner. Lou Nevers talked to us regular when we was on the streets. I know what your partner did, and I know the reason he died. I'm gonna keep Lou and Little Man in my prayers every day." He sniffed. "It was that shit jacket. Snakebit, *ebbo*, voodoo. Hell."

Frankie heard "*ebbo*" and caught the reference. She could tell from Able's expression that the word meant nothing to him.

"What jacket?" he asked.

"Bought it at the Goodwill. It's cursed. I brought bad luck down on our heads. I should've been the one to pay, not Little Man."

Frankie glanced around. "You got this jacket in a suitcase somewhere?"

Red drew himself up. "You don't carry a cursed thing around with you. You don't talk about *mbua*. Evil draws its power from words."

A crackling sound spread across the ceiling. An echo boomed like artillery fire from the freight tunnels below. Red leaped to his feet, eyes bulging, and the bottle shattered on the floor. Weird sounds in the terminal didn't bother Frankie, but she understood why they bothered Red. The old man believed in Santería. He thought the Evils were after him. She glanced at Able, who had a mystified look on his face. He didn't understand Red's reaction, but he held out his hand anyway.

"Let me see your ticket," he said.

Red fumbled in his pocket, the alcohol already working through his brain. Able took the ticket and strode up the steps to where the cashier was closing out the register.

Frankie disapproved of what Able was about to do. Her first

year on the street she'd learned that handing out money didn't make a dent in people's desperation. Able was a veteran cop. His willingness to ante up for Red Davis surprised her.

He returned with a yellow ticket. "Next train for Chicago leaves at ten forty tomorrow night." He pulled five twenties out of his wallet. "This is for food and a cab when you get to Chicago. Not for booze."

Red's voice jumped to a higher register. "You ain't *hearing* me, son. I got responsibilities. I got to leave town *tonight*." He stared helplessly at the bills and the ticket in Able's hand.

"The terminal closes in twenty minutes," Frankie said. "I'll drive you over to Robert House. You can come back tomorrow."

Red shook his head, resigned. "Thank you, ma'am. I got a place to stay." He pocketed the money and the ticket. The side of his mouth twitched, and he eyed Able. "Lou Nevers told me about you. He said you're a smart cop, but you're too softhearted. Don't go believing every story you hear." He waved them away. "Go on now. I'll get myself outta here. I got some thinking to do."

They walked toward the stairs that led to the street-level entrance. She felt comfortable leaving Red. He had a pocket full of cash and a ticket to Chicago. Apparently, Able didn't see it that way. He paused at the steps and looked back at the old man now seated on the bench, his elbows resting on his knees and his long hands dangling. After a minute, Able followed her down the steps and out the door.

"See you around, Officer Malone," he said with a half smile.

He couldn't know that a month ago she'd aced the promotions exam. A position was opening up on the homicide squad. His squad. She desperately wanted the job.

"I hope so," she said under her breath, and waved.

They walked into the sultry night and went their separate ways.

Chapter 4

A persistent beeping jarred Billy out of a sound sleep. Opening one eye, he focused on the cheap paneled wall and the sunlight coming through the porthole, illuminating his unpacked suitcase. His shirt from the night before hung over the back of the chair. Somewhere on the slack water an outboard motor cranked until it caught.

He slapped the alarm's off button. It read 7:00 A.M. The damned thing must have been going off every morning for the last nine months. He rolled onto his back and closed his eyes, still able to feel Mercy as if she were curled against him while they slept.

He drifted off. The beeping started again. This time his feet hit the linoleum. Some jackass was honking his horn outside on the landing. He stomped through the barge to the front window and lifted the blind to see Frankie Malone standing beside her cruiser with her right arm stuck through the rolled-down window and her hand on the horn. She saw him at the window and stopped honking. He could tell she was agitated.

"Aw, hell, lady. What do you want now?" he mumbled and dropped the blind.

He wasn't about to get dragged into the personal drama of a woman he barely knew, but from the determined look on Officer Frankie's face, he was on her list. He went back for a shirt and to zip into his Levi's. He walked out on the deck, and let the door slam behind him, a signal that he wasn't at all happy with the situation.

He noticed she was inspecting his car with a slight smile, like she might know more about cars than most women and thought it was cool but couldn't quite place it. No wonder. Most 1986 Plymouth Turismos had been off the road for a while. This one had been stored in a barn down in Mississippi for seventeen years when he first saw it. He'd bought it on the spot and spent his summers between university semesters making it worth his ride.

He gave it a black matte finish and dropped in a rebuilt engine to replace the gutless four-banger that came standard. After that, he could outrun most street cars, surprising the hell out of them, especially on tight turns.

The Plymouth was the only car he'd ever fallen in love with. Maybe it was because it had no onboard computer and nothing on it ever broke. Or maybe it was because the damned car never let him down.

Frankie looked back across the barge's gangplank at him. Her cropped hair framed her classic good looks that contradicted the masculine cut of her uniform. A woman that attractive would be more effective working undercover or on plainclothes duty, which was probably where she was headed.

The bruise on her cheek he'd noticed the night before was even more visible now in the daylight.

"Good morning," she said. "We've got a problem."

"Maybe you do. I don't. I'm on vacation. You know what time it is?"

"Seven."

"Are you nuts, honking like that?"

"I couldn't knock." She pointed to the locked gate he'd installed at the foot of the ramp to keep tourists from boarding the barge.

He knew better than to ask, but he couldn't stop himself. "What's wrong?"

"Red Davis was found dead on the bench outside Central Station. He must have settled there for the night after we left. I caught the call a little before five. He was sitting up, chin on his chest, hands in his lap. Cold as a Popsicle."

She stared across the river as if weighing how best to continue. "There's something at the scene you're going to want to see."

He sighed inwardly. A dead body before breakfast means the whole day is going to be shit. "You said Red went to the ER a couple of days ago with chest pains."

She paused. "That's right."

"Did you check for bullet wounds or trauma?"

"Yes. There's nothing obvious."

"Then Red's DOA natural. I'm sorry he passed, but the case will be closed."

She gave him a long, loaded look. "Maybe. Maybe not."

"I'm on leave. I can't step into another detective's case. What do you want from me?"

"I didn't like what I saw at the scene. Before I could figure out why, Detective Dunsford showed up."

"Dunsford the Dud?" Billy laughed. "He's retiring in October. He's about as effective as a wet match."

"Precisely."

Behind them a tug running in the river's full current blasted its horn. He cleared his throat, wishing he'd kept his mouth shut. "He'll do all right."

"Dunsford's going to do a half-assed job. They'll close the case, throw Red in a trench at the Shelby County Cemetery, and push dirt over him. After you bought his ticket last night, I assumed you had some regard for the man."

He let that one pass. "Red has folks in Chicago. Did you find their names on him?"

"No one's meeting him in Chicago. He told you that story to shut you up."

She had him there. Something about Red's death had bothered her so much she'd gone to the trouble to track Billy down.

"What made you question the scene?" he asked.

She cocked her head. "You're the big-city detective. Take a look for yourself."

If she thought leaning on him would do the trick, she was wrong. It wasn't nearly as effective as knowing that he'd left Red alone last night when he was in trouble.

He ran his hand through his hair. "We'll get coffee on the way. You're buying."

Chapter 5

Frankie pulled over at Denny's on South Second for him to run in and grab a jolt of Mississippi Mud Coffee. Then she parked in front of Earnestine and Hazel's, around the corner from the crime scene. Billy could see Red's body already laid out on a gurney, encased in a white vinyl body bag.

While Frankie typed her report on the computer console, he drank coffee and tried to get his wits about him. He rolled down his window for some air. A prosperous-looking young couple, people from the new homes built on the bluff, waved as they walked past.

This part of town had been a different scene in the forties. Earnestine and Hazel's was a skinning joint back then with prostitutes working the warren of rooms over the bar. A variety of fools walked across the street from the train station, looking for a drink and some quick action from the ladies, only to regain consciousness with a knot on the back of their heads and their wallets emptied. A few blocks north, Beale Street had been home to gamblers, showgirls, street preachers, river men, blues players up from the Mississippi cotton fields, medicine men, voodoo priests, and housemaids. There was no more creative, stimulating, or dangerous fifteen square blocks in the country.

Billy noted the sun lighting up the peeled blue trim on the windows of E and H—the bar's nighttime potency having given way to exhaustion. What's enticing in the nighttime can look like hell in the morning. Daylight changes the nature of things.

He downed the last of his coffee and turned his attention to Frankie, who was speaking to him between rapid-fire keystrokes.

"Dispatch is pushing for this report on Davis. Dunsford isn't going to let me back on the scene, but he can't kick you out. Behind the bench you'll find a pile of plastic bottles. I dropped a small gray bag there, a conjure bag, used to transport *ebbos*." She glanced at him. "That means charms or spells. I'd say we're dealing with Santería."

She threw out *ebbos* as if she were comfortable with the word. Red had done the same. Billy knew almost nothing about the religion. Apparently Frankie did.

She read the text on the screen, tapped a key, and turned to him with the same earnest expression he'd had when he was a patrol cop.

"There's not much Santería activity in Memphis," he said. "The big evangelical churches rule the city."

"You'd be surprised by what's going on behind closed doors. I tried to explain the significance of the bag to Dunsford. He cut me off, told me it was trash and to throw it away. I couldn't let him toss evidence, so I squirreled it away behind the bench."

"I'm guessing there's a voodoo potion in the bag."

"Technically, it's not voodoo. The stuff looks like it came out of a vacuum cleaner bag: ground eggshell, pulverized coal, bits of a wasp nest, rock salt, guinea pepper. You knock it down in a blender then blow the dust into the face of the person you want to do away with." She flattened her palm and blew air in his direction. "Poof. You're dead."

"From eggshells?"

"In a believer's mind, it's a bona fide death curse. It could stop a person's heart."

"Did any of that devil dust show up on Red?"

"His jacket and face looked dusty when I checked him over. Then I found the bag, but before I could compare the two, Dunsford showed up."

Billy crumpled up his coffee cup. "I'm not saying you don't know what you're talking about, but I can't believe a savvy guy like Red is into that crap."

"He's wearing a necklace of green and yellow beads. That's a Santerían collar. I found rooster feathers, a red bandanna, and a red apple in his pocket—all elements of a charm meant to counteract a curse."

"No room for coincidence here?"

"Nope," she said with certainty.

"You don't believe in this stuff, do you?"

She made a face. "You know a lot about the Delta blues. That doesn't make you a sharecropper with a guitar. I saw evidence of Santería at a number of Key West crime scenes. This appears to be death by natural causes, but it's a mistake to take Santería off the table."

"Let's be clear. You got me out of bed to verify your theory that a voodoo curse killed Red Davis."

"Santería isn't voodoo, but yes, I'd like to hear your opinion."

He almost laughed at her cockiness. "You should take the promotions exam. You'd fit right in with the squad."

"I took it a month ago. Scored ninety-eight percent. Three

candidates are up for two positions in the investigative squads. I'm going to land one of them."

Her score impressed him, but her attitude put him off. "Look. Most times, a heart attack is just a heart attack. I haven't heard how you're going to connect Red's death to this bag of dust."

"Just take a look at his face." She handed him a pair of latex gloves. "I have to sign off my shift. Give me a call when you're done."

Chapter 6

Detective Don Dunsford was coasting through his final year on the force. The fact that his brother-in-law was a Memphis Police Association union rep along with Don's announcement that he would take early retirement at the end of the year had saved him from being slapped with probation for flunking the latest technical-training upgrade. He was never much of a cop. At this late stage, any case Dunsford caught was at serious risk of being underinvestigated. He had earned the nickname "the Dud."

Billy ducked under the tape and headed toward Dunsford. He was standing next to the bench where Red's body had been discovered, wagging a clipboard in his face to create a breeze. Dunsford was a low-oxygen type, a mouth breather.

"What's up, Don?" Billy said in a cheery voice.

Dunsford stared at him, a little blank. "Hey. You back in town?"

Billy shrugged.

Dunsford shrugged back. His mobile rang. He answered and walked away as if satisfied their conversation was over.

Billy located the gray bag Frankie had described and snapped on gloves to scoop out a handful of the concoction: fine dust with bits of eggshell and lumps of wasp nest.

Dunsford strolled over. "You hear about the hiring freeze? I got four cases running. Could use some help."

Billy dumped the dust in the bag and rolled off the gloves. "Any idea what happened here?"

Dunsford swatted the air. "Some Sambo named Davis died waiting for a train. Just another damned drunk."

Billy's jaw tightened. Davis's talent and emotional fortitude made him worth a thousand fools like Dunsford. "The man deserves more consideration than that."

"Naw. I didn't even call the ME's office. A waste of manpower. What's it to you?"

"My granddaddy was a black man. I'm thinking Mr. Davis might be my great-uncle."

Dunsford's face swelled with suspicion, then he sneered. "So that's why you're always standing up for the coloreds. You were bred to it."

He leaned into Dunsford's face. "My granddaddy got around. The white ladies loved him. I hope you and me aren't related."

Dunsford's lips parted so a whiff of sour breath escaped. Then he laughed, showing a gold tooth on the side. "You're good, Able. Had me going." He punched Billy on the bicep. Billy punched back harder and raised the conjure bag for Dunsford to see.

"You plan to use this in your investigation?"

"That little gal cop had her shorts in a wad over that thing. What's with you being so interested in trash?"

"I'm going to take a look at the body on the way out, see if I recognize a relative."

Dunsford's eyes went cold. "That's not necessary."

"I think it is."

"Oh, *yeah*," Dunsford retorted.

That response pretty much exhausted Dunsford's repertoire of comebacks, which meant he'd have to ante up or back down. But forcing Dunsford to assert his authority wouldn't get Billy a look at the body. What they needed was a distraction. He pointed toward the parking lot.

"Hey, Don. The tech with the camera over there has a question."

Dunsford's head swiveled toward a young woman with blocky shoulders and wide hips who was sorting through a camera bag. He ambled over, their near showdown having flown out of his head.

Billy tucked the conjure bag into his pocket and walked to the transfer-service driver who was standing next to his hearse. The driver apparently recognized him, because he stepped back from the gurney as a sign of compliance. Tech crews divide detectives into two groups—professionals and professional jerks. His partner Lou once said that only geniuses can get away with being sons of bitches on a daily basis. Lou had been a son of a bitch, but he'd pretty much kept a lid on it until the end. He wondered if Lou would've come here this morning with Frankie to check the scene or if he would've blown her off. He used to believe he could predict what Lou would do a hundred percent of the time. He'd been wrong.

The name "Davis" had been scrawled in black marker at the foot of Red's body bag. Billy put his hand on the zipper and glanced over at the driver.

"I got some paperwork," the driver said and walked to the front of the vehicle.

Billy ran the zipper down the side. Fermented alcohol wafted out of the airtight body bag as he folded back the edge. Instantly, he understood why Frankie had been so concerned. The expression on Red's face made his heart grip.

It's not unusual for a corpse that remains in a seated position for several hours to exhibit a dropped jaw, but he'd never seen anything like this gape-mouthed, Halloween mask of horror that was Red's face. Gravity couldn't create the distended eyeballs, the skin stretched tight around the eye sockets, or cause Red's lips to draw back and expose his gums.

Pain on the face of a dead man was nothing new, but he wasn't looking at pain. There was nothing natural or normal about the nature of Red Davis's death. This was pure terror.

He rocked the head to one side then the other to establish rigor and to check for blows around the face and skull. The fingers and nails of both hands showed no sign of trauma; however, a powdery film coated Red's face and dirt streaked the front of his shirt, something Billy didn't recall from the night before. Was it the same as the dust in the conjure bag? They would never know, because Dunsford wasn't going to include the bag's contents as evidence to be tested.

He heard a door slam and the service driver came around the side of the vehicle, giving a nod that it was time to load the body. Billy reached behind Red's head to straighten it before zipping the bag, noting the green and yellow necklace that Frankie had mentioned. As he withdrew his hand, a wad of organic material the size of a penny came away in his fingers. A piece of wasp nest.

"Hey, Don," he called. "You need to see this."

Dunsford broke off his conversation with the tech and came over, making grunting noises in the back of his throat at the sight of the unzipped bag. "What the hell? I told you to leave the body alone."

"Did you see Red's face?"

Dunsford gave him a sidelong look. "You know the deceased?"

"Everybody knows Red Davis." He held up the gummy wad. "I found this stuck between his neck and collar."

He brought out the conjure bag and poured some of the contents, including chunks of the nest, into his palm. "It looks like someone threw this crap in Red's face to make him believe he was cursed. A heart attack may have killed him, but this makes me think someone triggered it."

Dunsford stared at the dust in Billy's palm. His mouth puckered, and his eyes took on a sly certainty. "I get it. That little gal cop put you up to this. She talked you into coming down here to mess with me because I slapped her on the ass." He reached over and jerked the zipper closed. "I don't give a rat's ass what you think or what you've got to say, or how many cases you've closed, or who your granddaddy was. You're on leave, which means you're a neutered cop." He swatted the gurney. "Get going," he barked at the driver.

He turned back to Billy. "You act like you care about this bum. If you're so broken up, why didn't you get him off the street, huh? Now get outta my crime scene, pretty boy. And tell Mz. Thang to keep her nose and her tight little fanny out of my cases."

Chapter 7

Nine A.M. and his day already had a crust on top.

He phoned Frankie from the scene and caught her as she was leaving Confederate Park on North Front Street. While he'd been shadowboxing with Dunsford, Frankie had signed out with dispatch and located a woman who regularly shared a park bench with Davis and Lacy. The woman said they had recently taken rooms—a polite term for squatting—on the second floor, back side of an abandoned house on St. Paul Avenue. Another vagrant had taken over the first floor. Billy agreed to meet her at the house in thirty minutes.

He had no problem locating the vandalized Greek Revival mansion with busted-out windows on the second floor and a forest of weeds in the yard. An orange laminated sign tacked to the plywood that secured the front door read CITY OF MEMPHIS INSPECTION DIVISION—PLACARD OF CONDEMNATION.

"Condemnation" is a Bible word. Bible words are Memphis words. Words like "judgment" and "damnation" had been running through his mind since he'd seen that tortured expression on Red's corpse's face.

Last night he'd ignored his truer instincts and walked away

from Red. Now the man was dead. Maybe it had been his time to go, but that was impossible to know without looking into it further.

He walked around the side of the house. Someone had torn the plywood off a tall window on the side porch that was hidden from the street by overgrown boxwoods and was using the opening as an entrance. He peered in. Although the house had been abandoned long ago, the empty room retained an eerie elegance.

He left the porch, a mockingbird dive-bombing him from a pecan tree as he waded through the weeds to the sidewalk. Frankie had parked on the street and was leaning against the bumper of her blue Jeep Cherokee, laughing at the bird. Off duty, she'd changed into khakis and a cotton shirt.

They agreed that an inspection of the house was called for and walked together around to the side porch. Frankie pulled her duty weapon, a 9mm SIG Sauer, and ducked inside first. He followed.

Light filtered through dust-coated transoms, the room's stagnant air smelling of boiled hot dogs, urine, and feces. The odor nearly triggered his gag reflex, but he held back. No barfing in front of a girl, especially if she's not barfing, too.

Frankie stalked around the downstairs rooms while he stepped into the front hall. A door slammed. She joined him in time to catch sight of a large black man as he took off running through the trees in the side yard. They looked at each other and shrugged. No way to catch what had to be the house's downstairs tenant.

Upstairs, the plaster walls had been stripped down to the lath. Patches of light from downstairs shone through the rotting floorboards. At the end of the hall, they found the musicians' door held closed by a rusted hasp and an opened bicycle lock.

The windows of the large, square room were half boarded up, the ceiling buckled by water damage. Green and black mold streaked the walls. The air smelled of plaster dust, Irish Spring soap, and mildew. A crumbling brick fireplace and a battered armoire shoved in the corner marked this room as having once been the master bedroom.

Billy gave the space a quick once-over. What struck him more than the decay was the effort Red and Little Man had made to create order. A table pieced together out of scrap wood stood at the center of the room. On the table were two black candles. The men had cut holes in two pieces of paper and run the candles through them, the paper apparently meant to catch dripping wax. Lined against the wall was a pair of army cots, each with a neatly folded blanket and a metal pan turned upside down and placed in the middle of the mattress.

Red's guitar case stood at the foot of one cot and Little Man's sax case was at the foot of the other. What a relief. The instruments were safe. They represented the dead men's legacies.

Nothing about the room suggested the chaos of an alcoholic's lifestyle or that Red had died for any reason other than natural causes. Billy walked over to the fireplace where a white enameled pan with five eggs floating in oil sat on the hearth. One end of a cotton wick had been immersed in the oil. The other end hung off the side. A brown powder covered the top of the oil. He leaned in and sniffed. Cinnamon.

"Look at this," he said, expecting to find Frankie right behind him. Instead, she was standing in the doorway, rocking in her shoes like a kid about to take off running.

She pointed to a mildewed wall. "Those black patches are toxic mold."

"Are you sensitive to it?"

"No."

"Do you think the mold caused Red's heart attack?" he asked.

"No . . . I don't."

"Then why the hell are you standing in the hall?"

Her neck flushed. "Because I'm looking at curses. Bad ones."

She walked to the table and spread back the curled paper beneath one of the candles. "Take a look at this."

It was a promo shot of Red. Someone had cut a hole where his face should have been and run the candle through it. The base of the candle was sitting in a nest of gray hair. The same treatment had been given to the second candle, only the photo was of Little Man.

"Light the candle and the curse ignites on the person in the photo," she said. "Hair from the victim makes the curse even more powerful." She pointed to the pans turned upside down on the cots. "That over there is some really nasty stuff. People who believe in Santería keep a pan of water under their bed while they sleep to trap the evil spirits. The longer the water stays under the bed, the more concentrated the evil becomes. If the water is dumped on the mattress, the spirits are released."

"So get a new mattress."

"Doesn't work like that. The spirits track your scent, run you down like bloodhounds to possess your soul. Possession by evil spirits is the worst possible fate for a believer."

"How do you know this stuff?"

She huffed. "I told you, I worked with this in Key West. A neighbor of mine drove her car into a concrete wall rather than risk being possessed by the Evils."

"The Evils?"

"Evil spirits."

The seriousness of her tone surprised him. "Here's another explanation" he said. "Blues musicians set a tub of water beside them while they play. They like the sound as it passes over the water."

"Nice story, except these tubs of water have been dumped on the cots." She walked to the fireplace and studied the pan on the hearth. "I can tell you that the person who set up these curses knows something about *palo mayombe*. That's the black arts. I think someone cursed this room then hunted down Little Man and Red with the conjure bags and finished them off. The oil and eggs are evidence that they knew they were in trouble, but they couldn't light the wick soon enough. It has to burn for five days before a curse is displaced."

"They could have walked in and lighted the wick then stayed at Robert House for five days."

"No believer would enter a room this cursed. With Red's bad heart, I'm surprised he didn't drop dead in the doorway. No, they did the right thing. They ran with just the clothes on their backs."

He didn't want to hear any more about evil spells, and he sure as hell didn't believe it. He went over to shelves the men had constructed out of concrete blocks and boards. A box of saltines and twelve cans of Chef Boyardee ravioli were stored on the lower shelf. On the top shelf was a stack of staff paper for music notation. At one end stood a framed photo of a young woman seated at a baby grand piano. Beside the frame was a votive candle and a wilting daisy in a bud vase. At the other end were two clean washcloths. On one lay a beaded necklace similar to what Red had been wearing.

Frankie joined him and picked up the necklace. "This must've been for Little Man. The pattern of beads belongs to Obatala."

She slipped the white beads through her fingers and laid the necklace back on the cloth.

"Who is Obatala?"

"He's orisha, like a saint in the Catholic church only with a bit of Greek god thrown in. They eat, drink, have emotions. Every initiated believer has an orisha or, to be more accurate, is chosen by an orisha."

"You grew up around this crazy stuff?"

"It's not so crazy. Religious beliefs are powerful no matter who you worship. I've seen good and bad come from Santería just like any other religion."

He looked around the room. "Nothing I see here indicates intentional harm. It's more like pranks."

Frankie wiped sweat from her forehead, frustration on her face. "I guess whoever set this up is going to get away with murder."

She had him with that one. He didn't like it.

He picked up notated sheets of music. One appeared to be a completed song titled "Old Fool Love." Red had signed his name beside the title. The chorus read:

> Love at the door feeling bad,
> 'Cause love can't have what it needs to have.
> Old fool love. That old fool . . . love.

Red had used that phrase the night before. Billy could almost hear him singing it.

He put down the pages. "You probably don't know that Red and Little Man played big halls throughout Europe in the late eighties. In the nineties, they opened for major rock bands in Berlin, Paris, London. Red is an icon over there, a legend."

"I didn't realize," she said.

"Check out Red's guitar." He went over to the cot, laid the case flat, and flipped open the latches.

The guitar inside looked more like a cubist painting deconstructed into parts than a musical instrument. The neck had been stomped free of the body, the fingerboard fractured in two places, the head detached with only the strings holding it to the neck. The mahogany top had been smashed, flipped over, and the back crushed.

"What's wrong?" she asked, reading his shock.

He nodded toward the other case. "Check the sax." He watched as she popped the latch and looked the instrument over.

"Oh, my God. It's in pieces."

He stood and walked to the armoire, heartsick with the realization that Frankie had been right—something terrible had happened in this room. He opened the door to the armoire, his eyes moving over the dark suits that had been worn shiny, and the white shirts with stained collars. Among them he found a camel-colored sports jacket with a Goodwill price tag attached. He pulled it from the rest and held it up for Frankie to see.

"You think it's the cursed jacket?" she asked.

"I don't know. This setup stinks. We'll take the jacket, the instruments, and that sheet music, and the photograph of the girl on the shelf."

"And Little Man's necklace?"

"Yes, take that."

She looked away. He caught her tiniest smile of triumph.

On the way out he clicked the bicycle lock shut. The place would be stripped by sundown, but there was nothing he could do about it.

Coming down the stairs, a window on the landing gave them

a view of the street. An African-American man was on the sidewalk across from the house, arms crossed over his chest and his legs spread in a stance of defiance.

"Is that the guy we saw in the yard?" he asked.

"Not sure. And it's too late to find out. He just took off."

They ran downstairs but were slowed in the yard by the tangle of tall weeds. Tires squealed from around the corner. They pulled up. Billy looked at Frankie. "We need to find out who that was."

Chapter 8

Frankie dropped Billy at Court Square, an easy walk down the bluff to his place on the river. A noontime gospel concert had just started. People wandered the square, eating hot dogs and drinking Orange Crush underneath the giant shade trees. Moms brought lawn chairs and blankets so their kids could sprawl at their feet and listen to the concert. It was all so comfortably familiar.

He spotted a bicycle cop in a yellow shirt and helmet surveying the crowd. Bums typically staked out the benches on the square, but they had an unspoken agreement with the cops about noontime—no panhandling, no hogging the benches, and no peeing in the bushes.

Twenty members of the Tennessee Mass Gospel Choir were deep into a snappy version of "Joy to the World." The men and women, dressed in their summer whites, were lined up in front of the bandstand, singing and clapping to the beat. He wanted to stay for the music, but the sack of evidence from Red's room reminded him that he needed to work up a case file.

The choir hit the chorus. A middle-aged man in a ball cap jigged through the crowd and began to whirl around in a clearing in front of the bandstand like a child on a sugar high, his startling green eyes bright with mania. He wore plaid shorts that bagged at the butt and white athletic socks bunched at his ankles. People in the crowd hurled catcalls at him. Three kids sitting on a blanket at the edge of the clearing clapped and giggled.

"Oh, good God," Billy said under his breath as the man spun in his direction. It was Augie Poston, former all-star catcher for the St. Louis Cardinals, a onetime superstar and hero to millions of fans. At least that was true until mental illness had robbed Poston of his career. It was hard for Billy to stand there and watch a longtime friend like Augie make a fool of himself. Poston was a nice guy unless he dropped off his meds. Then he could turn volatile and run out of control. Like now.

The choir stepped it up a notch. Augie spun past Billy without seeing him. Waving wildly at the three kids, he flung his arms wide and lunged in their direction. Billy jumped into action and pushed through the crowd to grab Augie from behind, pulling him away from the kids and to the curb.

Augie shoved at Billy as a bicycle cop pulled alongside them.

"You idiot! You could've trampled those kids," the cop said. Furious, he stepped off the bike.

The cop would assume Augie was drunk or high, but Augie wasn't necessarily someone the cop would want to arrest.

"I got this, Officer," Billy said, and took Augie's arm. "I'll see that he gets home."

Augie yanked his arm away, then focused on Billy for the first time. "Oh, *hey*, man!" He threw his arms around Billy in a bear hug.

"Break it up," the cop said and jerked his thumb toward Main Street. "Beat it. Both of ya."

Augie took hold of Billy's arm. "Yes, sir, Officer, I'll take care of this."

They walked to the trolley line. Billy looked over at Augie, who bounced in his sneakers as the choir started up a new song. "The cop was right. You could've hurt those kids."

"Naw, man, I love kids. I just got carried away." Augie wiped sweat from his face with his sleeve. "You've been gone for months, haven't you?"

He'd never told Augie about Mercy or that he'd left Memphis to give Atlanta a try. "I've been doing a little traveling. How about if we pay Mr. Peanut a visit? We'll catch up."

Augie gave him a grin and a slap on the back. Augie had once commanded respect as one of the finest catchers to ever play the position for the Cards. No one in the major league could spot a hitter's weaknesses like Augie. He knew every batter, he knew his own pitchers, and he knew every major league field.

Then one day good-humored Augie became sullen. The next week he turned euphoric, driving his teammates crazy with nonstop chatter. During games, he would throw balls at rats running across the field. There were no rats. And there were no cameras in the air vents of his hotel rooms or people who wrote down everything he ate. Over the course of the season, he continued to call great games, but easygoing Augie had begun arguing with the umps and getting tossed to the clubhouse on a regular basis.

The psychiatrists said he was suffering from a mood disorder and paranoid psychosis—a loss of contact with reality. The meds they prescribed made him foggy headed on the field. His stats went down. His play suffered. When he dropped off the meds, the cycle would start over.

By the end of the third season, Augie's illness had taken over. The general manager exercised the club's buyout clause, which must have been valued in the millions. That left Augie a rich man but shut out of baseball for good. He'd moved back to hometown Memphis eight years ago.

Not long after, Billy met Auige at Bardog, a popular downtown watering hole. As a kid, Billy had dreamed of playing pro ball, so he got a kick out of knocking back a few brews with a major leaguer and talking up the game. They'd hung out together over the years, even catching a few Redbird games at the ballpark.

They took over a sidewalk table in front of the Peanut Shoppe with its sign of Mr. Peanut wearing a top hat and monocle. Augie bought a bag of fresh-roasted peanuts, shelling and tossing the nuts to the pigeons strutting at their feet. Billy bought a turkey sandwich and stowed the sack from Red's place in a seat under the table.

"Tell me some good news," he said, wolfing down his food.

Augie gave him a sidelong glance. "I have a new interest."

"A woman?"

"Oh, *hell* no. I asked my last blind date if I could call her. She said sure and gave me the number for dead animal pickup."

Billy laughed.

"Guess she was afraid of my love." Augie grinned and shook his head. "No love on the horizon. I spend my mornings selling sports memorabilia and photos on eBay. Afternoons, I shoot the shit with the guys at Bardog. Some days I'm so doped up on meds, I can't string two sentences together."

He rattled the bag and flung peanuts at a squirrel. "When I played ball, I had something to prove every day. The last few years there's been nothing. Now I've got a project. You wanna hear?"

Billy sensed a more involved story than he had time for, but what the hell. "Sure."

"My father passed away six months ago. I was cleaning out his house and found scrapbooks of news articles from the sixties, along with letters my mom had written to the editor. She was a vivacious woman, always had people over to the house. I told you she died when I was six, right?"

Billy nodded.

"My dad was a structural engineer on assignment in London. My mom grew up in London, a real smart cookie. She got her master's in education at Oxford. They met at a party. He was white, she was black, which didn't matter in London. They got married and moved to Memphis. Back then most whites in Memphis had never met an educated black person much less one with a British accent. She wasn't a maid, but they didn't consider her to be an equal either.

"My mom was big into the civil rights movement. Both my parents were. She taught English in a black high school. They promoted her to principal, but that wasn't enough for my mom. She ran for a seat on the school board, made a lot of speeches, wrote articles for the *Press-Scimitar*." He paused, smiled a little. "She scared the shit out of the racists. After she got elected, they couldn't shut her up. You following me?"

He was aware of the grief beginning to cloud Augie's face. This story wasn't going to be the good news he'd hoped for.

"Every Sunday, my mom left early to pick up an older couple who couldn't drive themselves to church. Dad always took me to Sunday school. Mom must have been backing out of the driveway when it happened. My father was in the shower. He didn't hear the explosion, but I did."

Augie swallowed. As he spoke, his eyes emptied as if he were staring into a black hole. "Mom drove a '64 Pontiac Tempest, white with red leather seats. It was a wedding gift from my dad.

When I got to the front door, she was . . ." His voice fell off. "The car was on fire."

Billy had witnessed people trapped in burning cars—the flailing, the screams. You try to wall off those memories and hope they won't follow you into your dreams. He couldn't imagine how a six-year-old would deal with it.

"I've never told anyone this," Augie said. "No point talking about what you can't change. But then things *did* change. I'm convinced now that she was murdered."

Billy's skepticism must have shown because Augie's hand went up.

"Just listen, okay? After she died, three men came to the house. My father was scared. He was fucking scared. I was a kid, but I saw it. Two of them took my dad into the living room. My dad let the other guy get me alone in the kitchen. The man grilled me about my mom's activities, like she'd been doing something illegal. He made me cry. After they left, my dad took me to an afternoon ball game. We never once talked about what was said. He pretended it didn't happen."

Augie grunted, wiped his mouth. "I was six. Just six. I found out later that the detectives spent one week investigating and then closed the case."

"But—"

"Let me finish. After the funeral, my dad dumped everyone he knew who was connected with the civil rights movement. He married a white woman from Tupelo. Court-ordered busing was starting up. White people were mad as hell. I could pass for white, so we became a white family. My dad must have thought 'white' was safer.

"Going through his house a few months back, I found a second box of letters addressed to my mom, personal attacks about her politics and her election to the school board. Eight were death threats, untraceable, of course. My folks must have expected blowback and hadn't taken the threats seriously."

A choking sound escaped his throat. He thrust himself out of the chair and took short laps up and down the sidewalk with his fists held tight at his sides. Billy looked away, giving his friend his privacy.

Augie sat down. "Sorry. It gets away from me." He cleared his throat. "The men who came to the house were FBI. I remember their badges. Mom died three months after Martin Luther King was assassinated. After reading those letters, I decided I had to find out why the FBI questioned us and why my mother died. So I'm investigating her death."

Billy took a breath. Cops develop the ability to emotionally distance themselves from victims and their families, a key to surviving the job. And as compelling as the story had been, Augie was sometimes delusional.

"How are you looking into this?" he asked.

Augie hunched his shoulders, defensive. "An investigative journalist approached me a few years back. He was working on a piece about mental illness in major league sports. He knew things about players I thought no one would ever find out. I declined to comment, but at the same time I was impressed by his research. I kept his card."

"So you called him."

"Yeah, after I found those letters. I asked him to look into my mom's case. He's writing a book. A lot of questionable shit happened in this city around the time of King's assassination. He said his book ties in with my questions about my mom's death, so we're collaborating. The book is going to be a real eye-opener. People in this city will be shocked."

Chapter 9

Augie leaned back in his chair—focused, reflective, a different man from the one who'd made a fool of himself in Court Square. "What do you think of my project?"

"I think your family went through hell. What was your mom's name?"

"Dahlia Poston."

"Beautiful name."

"She was a beautiful woman. Brave woman."

Billy balled up his sandwich wrapper, giving himself time to think. He wanted to know more about the journalist. "Does this guy write for local publications?"

"No, a big paper in the Northeast. He was investigating a dirty politician who got in bed with the paper's publisher. The politician managed to have my guy canned. This book is his comeback."

Of course Augie had believed the guy. Who can resist a good comeback story? "Any money passing between you?" Billy asked.

"I'm paying for research."

Augie's jaw tightened. He didn't want anyone poking around in his business, which was understandable. So tomorrow, after meeting with the chief about his reinstatement, he decided he would run down to central records and pull Dahlia Poston's file. If the journalist had visited records, his name should be on the checkout register. Billy would take it from there.

Augie yawned and pointed at the sack under the table. "What's that you're hauling around?"

Billy considered whether to bring up Red's and Little Man's deaths, then remembered he'd seen Augie talking with both men at a show they'd played in a club a couple of years ago.

"Did you know that Little Man Lacy fell into that construction dig next to the Blue Monkey the other night?"

"I heard. Rough luck."

"Red Davis died this morning on a bench outside of Central Station."

Augie's eyes widened. "Man! I hate that. Was it a stickup?"

"More like a heart attack. I ran into Red in the terminal last night. A cop named Frankie Malone came by on patrol. He was all right when we left him."

"Right. Mz. Police Goddess. She's intense. I wouldn't want to tangle with her."

"Mz. Police Goddess." That fit. "Frankie caught the call on Red this morning. The scene bothered her, so she asked me to take a look at the body. I didn't like what I saw, either. We searched a house where Davis and Lacy had been squatting. Red told us about a cursed jacket, some Santería thing. You know anything about Santería?"

Augie reared back. "Oh, buddy, that's strong stuff to the people who believe it. A lot of the Cuban players are into it."

Billy opened the bag and pulled out the photo of the girl sitting at the piano. Her waist-length hair, pulled to one side, revealed a backless gown cut to the base of her spine.

"We found this in their room. Have you ever seen this girl?"

Augie stared at the photo. "Wowee-wow. Is she related to one of the guys?"

"I don't know." He took out the staff paper with the song "Old Fool Love." "I figured the Blues Hall of Fame would want this song if we can't find his relatives."

Augie frowned. "A couple of weeks ago, I ran into Red at Confederate Park. He asked for a short-term loan of two thousand."

"Two thousand *dollars*?"

"He said he had a sure thing coming through. As collateral he offered to sign over the publishing rights to 'Burning Tree Blues.' We went to the bank, got papers notarized. I guess 'Burning Tree' is mine now."

Billy thought a moment. "He called it a sure thing?"

"Maybe he called it a business deal, I don't remember. He talked like it was solid." Augie shook his head. "This wasn't about booze and lost weekends. Red was kind of solemn when he asked. That's why I went ahead." His head dipped. "And I have to admit, I collect blues history. I wanted the publishing rights. I didn't care if he paid me back."

Billy pulled out the jacket, a camel-colored tropical-weight wool with wide lapels and stylized side pockets. They spread it on the table. He flipped back the right panel of the jacket and read the label: TAILORED BY BERNARD.

"Bernard had a shop on Main Street in the fifties," Augie said. "He dressed Elvis, Johnny Cash, Roy Orbison, B. B. King. If you wanted quality and style back then, you went to Bernard."

"Is he still around?"

"They closed the Main Street shop. Bernard would be in his late eighties."

Billy ran his hand across the right inside breast pocket and felt a lump. Slipping his fingers in, he pulled out a stack of three-by-five photos. He shuffled through them. The Chevy Impala and Ford Fairlane parked in the background suggested the photos had been taken decades ago. One of two men appeared in every shot, taking turns behind the camera. They both sported crew cuts and intense expressions. The taller one wore black-rimmed glasses. In every photo, they were talking with folks on the street. The majority of the people were black, some were white. Ages ranged from teenaged to elderly. Bell-bottoms and Afros put the photos in the mid- to late sixties.

He checked the left breast pocket. It was empty.

"May I see those?" Augie ran through the pictures slowly, frowning, and handed them back.

"Recognize anything?"

"Nope." Augie got to his feet, scratching his crotch. "I'm late."

"You're not late. What could you be late for? What did you see?"

"Got to go, my friend." Augie shot the crumpled Mr. Peanut bag into the can and took off walking across the trolley tracks.

Billy picked up the stack and flipped through them. This time he caught it. The tall guy, the one with the glasses, was wearing the Goodwill jacket.

Chapter 10

The tiny salon was tucked between a Speedy Cash store and an Exxon station on Summer Avenue, a formerly thriving thoroughfare whose remaining businesses were struggling to keep their doors open. The salon's sign read EL CORAZÓN DE FUEGO PELUQUERÍA, or Heart of Fire Hairdresser.

After dropping Billy off at Court Square, Frankie had driven there hoping to get a lead on the conjure bag and possibly the person who had made the spell.

A few months ago she'd noticed the word "*Botánica*" hand-lettered at the bottom of the salon's sign, a *botánica* being an herb shop that specializes in folk medicine and Santerían magical remedies. Curious, she'd stopped to see if the version of the religion she'd known in Key West had drifted up to Memphis.

In a small room at the back she'd found spiritual candles, packaged herbs, and potions that believers use regularly. The shop owner, a curvy young blonde named Mystica Arnaz, had explained that she was a new initiate and not qualified to make up complex *ebbos*, but that customers came in for the candles and remedies. It was a good business.

Frankie parked out front and made a list of fresh plants,

known by the Yoruba word *"ewe,"* that were needed to make a purifying bath. Santería is an earth religion. Its power to heal and defend against evil comes from plants that can be found in the tropical forests of the Antilles. She was pretty sure Mystica wouldn't stock the exotic plants, but a Santerían priest, a *santero,* would. A *santero* would also have the knowledge and means to make a death curse. Mystica might know such a person; however, getting the name from her wouldn't be easy. Every aspect of Santería is rooted in carefully guarded secrecy.

Frankie tweaked her short bangs in the mirror and checked her cheek. If she did manage to find the ingredients for a *ewe*, she would take a long soak tonight, something she hadn't done in years. The bath might calm her anxiety and help her get some sleep.

Inside, trance dance music pulsed and fluorescent lights shone on the emerald-green trim and glossy walls. Packets of herbs on a rack advertised the power to make "Your Husband Leave His Mistress" or "Chase Bill Collectors from Your Door." Neon prints of *The Last Supper* hung above shelves stacked with candles, statues of the Virgin of Guadalupe, and miniature skeletons draped in monks' robes.

The three stylists, all busy with clients, wore jewel-toned skirts, dramatic makeup, and their dark hair flowing down their backs, the opposite of Frankie's cropped style and preppy clothes. She could girl it up with the best of them, but as she walked past these women, she felt like a eunuch in a harem.

The exception was a stooped old woman at the back of the shop, who was wiping down a chair with a rag, her sharp nose and chin giving her head the flattened shape of a hatchet blade. She wore her gray hair knotted on top of her head and her apron tied with twine over her shapeless dress. Frankie got a whiff of cigar smoke as she walked by. The woman made a hissing sound as she dipped her rag in a bucket.

Mystica stood behind the counter, her heavy-lidded eyes focused on Frankie as she approached. Her last time in, the young woman had suggested hair extensions, making the assumption that Frankie's short cut had been a hairdresser's disaster.

"I'm so glad you've returned," Mystica said. "A beautiful lady should have long hair." She ran her fingers through her own blond mane, and her gaze passed lightly over Frankie's bruised cheek.

Frankie held up her list and started to speak, but Mystica was already hustling from behind the counter.

"Come have a seat," she said, attempting to herd Frankie toward a chair. "I will show you samples of extensions. Blond for you, I think, and below the shoulders like mine. Long hair is a woman's power. Men prefer it."

Frankie felt her cheeks flush. Brad McDaniel had made a similar comment about her hair the first time they'd met for lunch. It took a while for her to realize how well he'd mastered the off-handed comment meant to undermine a person's confidence. With any other man, she would have picked up on it, but for some reason Brad's slick routine had flown under her radar.

She stood her ground with Mystica and handed over the list. "I need these herbs for a *ewe*, not extensions."

Mystica instantly backed off the hard sales pitch. "You wish a purifying bath, yes? I understand."

She disappeared through a beaded curtain and returned minutes later with several items in a basket. "I do not have the *pata de gallina, romerillo,* and *salvadera*. Those herbs must be fresh. They will ship from Puerto Rico in three days."

"Maybe someone else in the city has them." Frankie pulled the conjure bag out of her purse. "Do you know anyone who carries this bag? They might stock fresh herbs."

Mystica turned the bag over and frowned. "It's possible Señor Sergio—"

At the name, the old woman erupted in Spanish and rushed over to Mystica, shaking her rag. Mystica fired back in rapid Spanish, both of them shouting over each other. Frankie caught "stranger," and she heard the woman call Mystica *una tonta*, a fool. The old woman wagged her finger at Frankie and stalked back to her bucket.

Mystica fumed and handed the bag back to Frankie. "I'm sorry. I cannot help you."

The conversation might have ended there, but Frankie picked up on Mystica's embarrassment at the reprimand. She leaned in and whispered, "I need this *ewe* today. It's important." She added a knowing nod, a silent communication between women.

"I understand," the young woman said, and flipped her hair in defiance as she went to the back room and returned with a cloth pouch. She touched her own cheek. "I see what your man has done. I've had the same. This spell is powerful. Your man will think twice before he hurts you again."

"That's not what I had in mind," Frankie said, stalling.

Mystica raised her voice for the shop full of women to hear, a surefire sales pitch. "We will teach a wife beater a lesson. His manhood will be limp as a flag on a calm day.

"Mix lemon juice, salt water, and cooking oil," she whispered to Frankie. "Fry a live scorpion in the oil until it disintegrates. Add what's in this bag. I will write instructions." She wrote quickly, glancing at the old woman, who was still throwing nasty looks in their direction.

"This isn't necessary," Frankie said, embarrassed by Mystica's pronouncement that she'd been beaten by her man.

Mystica folded the paper with a tight crease and shoved it in the bag. "Thank you for coming in. You will be pleased; I promise." She winked.

Frankie paid and waited until she was outside the salon to look at the instructions. On the paper, Mystica had written a name and an address: Señor Sergio Ramos. *Santero*.

Chapter 11

Walking from Court Square to the barge, Billy remembered there wasn't so much as a can of beans in the kitchen. He stopped at Jack's Food for staples along with some sourdough bread, lettuce and tomatoes, and a package of Wright's bacon—breakfast, lunch, and dinner in a bag.

Tomorrow he had a meeting at the Criminal Justice Complex, the CJC, with Deputy Chief of Investigative Services Bud Middlebrook. They were to discuss his return to duty. On the drive to Memphis, he'd decided to take a few days off before signing back on the force, give himself a chance to adjust to his sudden change in circumstances after the breakup.

He loved Mercy. He assumed she'd felt the same, but she'd lied to him. He was used to lies. People lie all the time to protect themselves or to get what they want. He should be able to forgive Mercy for that, but yesterday, when the truth came out, he'd found himself leaving so abruptly, so thoroughly, it made him wonder if she'd done them both a favor. Maybe leaving Atlanta had been in the back of his mind all along. Maybe he was the kind of guy who likes the concept of a relationship more than he likes being in one.

Some decisions you can't come back from. He was in the process of making one of those now. Or maybe the decision had already been made. He wasn't sure.

He put away the groceries and glanced around the living area of the barge. Whatever happened with Mercy, at least he was happy to see his place again.

The self-propelled barge had been bought by a speculator at auction and converted into the Old Man River Bar and Grill. Its new owner had tied up at the cobblestone landing next to the river tour paddle wheeler, the *Memphis Queen II*, a great location, but the bar had run into trouble from the start. The owner had put his son in charge and then left town. His son, who had a raging crank habit, cleaned out the cash drawer nightly. The owner returned to find the business sinking under debt and his son in the office, blacked out from a near overdose.

Disgusted, the owner closed the bar, added a shower, turned the small office into a bedroom, and put the place up for rent. The commercial kitchen with its stainless-steel counters stayed. The aft deck had a great view of the sunset. Billy had walked through and signed a two-year lease.

He thought about last August when Mercy had knocked on his door with a sack in her hand that contained potential evidence in her sister's disappearance. During the two-week investigation of her sister's case, their uneasy alliance had developed into trust, then love or at least the possibility of it. Her sister's case took a difficult turn. At the end, especially after Lou's death, he had wanted a fresh start.

Mercy owned a successful bakery in Atlanta. He moved

there, hoping to find work in law enforcement and make a go of it
with her. They had agreed that, if he didn't find a cop job before
his nine-month leave was up, she would consider relocating her
bakery to Memphis. When the time came, they would make the
decision together.

That hadn't happened. Yesterday she'd come home early from
the morning shift to tell him she had signed a contract a month
ago that expanded the bakery and tied her to Atlanta indefinitely.
She admitted she didn't want to live in Memphis and had never
intended to move. She wanted him to stay in Atlanta to help her
run her business.

He now took a six-pack from under the sink and shoved it into
the refrigerator. He was a cop, damn it. Did she expect him to
spend his life working in a cream-puff factory? He was getting
angry all over again. Best thing to do was check out the barge
and get his mind on something else.

The Internet connection worked, but his TV screen was blue.
The Cards played the Braves at seven P.M. He would walk to
Bardog, have a couple of beers and a plate of meatballs, and
catch the game. Until then, he had plenty of work to do setting
up a case file on Red.

First thing, he pulled out the staff paper and the photo of the
girl that looked to him like a promo shot someone had cut down
to fit the frame. The camera loved her. The profile shot revealed
a hint of full lips and pronounced cheekbones. Judging by the
slenderness of her back and the sheen of her long hair, she was in
her mid- to late teens.

The back of the frame popped off easily. He expected to find
the name of a club or a photographer's logo stamped on the back.
It was blank. She could be a model, Red's daughter, or possibly a
musician from a club where Red and Little Man ahd played. Or

the photo could have no meaning, a shot of a fantasy girl Davis and Lacy had kept to remind themselves of better days.

He searched around and found a large mailing envelope to slip the staff paper and photo inside for protection.

Next he spread the jacket on the table, a beautiful piece of goods with carved-bone buttons and a silk lining still in immaculate condition. Slipping the three-by-five photographs from the inner breast pocket, he noticed something he'd missed before— tiny curls of thread along the pocket's edge. Someone had stitched the pocket closed and then clipped it open. The pocket on the opposite side had been treated the same. Had there been a second batch of photos that were now missing, or had something else been hidden in the pocket?

Putting the pictures aside, he flipped up the jacket's collar. Monogrammed in gold thread were the initials L.G. He leafed through the photos to one of the man in the jacket. Bernard, who made the jacket, might recall the client if he were shown the photo and given the initials.

In a search of the *Commercial Appeal*'s archives, an article about the tailor's colorful career surfaced, but there was an obituary, too. Bernard had developed Alzheimer's disease and passed away recently.

He scanned his notes about the loan Augie had made to Red. Red used to be a big star. Was there a recording contract in the works and Red had planned to pay Augie back with the advance? He and Little man were living on canned ravioli. Red had been flat broke at the train depot. What had he done with the money? They'd fought poverty and racism and pretty much won that battle when Katrina hit. He understood that alcohol was a factor, but Red and Little Man could have recovered their sense of self-worth and some financial stability just by playing club dates. How had they ended up living in a condemned building, frightened to death by curses?

Everyone has weaknesses. Lou Nevers had a crack in him the size of the Grand Canyon. And what about Billy's own flaws? He'd seen people take a wrong turn, make a bad choice, and dig a hole they couldn't get out of. Mercy loved her bakery. She'd made a choice to get what she wanted. He was making a choice. He couldn't see himself doing anything but what he was doing right at that moment. Was walking away from Mercy showing a lack of character, or had he done the righteous thing for both of them?

Suddenly he wanted to call her, hear her voice. Instead, he walked out onto the aft deck, leaving his phone inside so he wouldn't be tempted. Across the water an enormous tree was being swept down the channel, its root system exposed. The tree looked healthy, but the river must have been more powerful and undermined its grip on the earth. Birds hung in the branches as it floated along, wondering what the hell had happened to their universe.

The urge to call Mercy passed. The light on the river turned gold. He went back inside. Back to work.

And ol' man river just kept rolling along.

Chapter 12

The brick houses with their oversize hardwood trees in the front yards made up the neighborhood, typical of the aging suburban tracts built in Memphis during the boom years following World War II. The homes beamed with the fastidiousness of retired couples who obsessively weed flower beds and sweep walks.

However, the ranch-style house that interested Frankie wasn't one of those. The bland house that had her attention had turned itself away from the neighborhood, its energy compressed behind shaded windows.

She pulled to the curb, engine left running in the late-afternoon humidity. A bank of clouds blocked the sun as it dropped toward the horizon. Frankie glanced through police reports concerning the owner of the house, a Señor Sergio Ramos. Complaints lodged by neighbors alleged loud parties in the backyard with drumming and chanting. Some reports hinted at animal sacrifice. Señor Ramos was a U.S. citizen of Cuban descent and a practicing *santero*. She knew what the neighbors thought were wild parties were actually initiations into the faith, rituals she had witnessed as a child in Key West. The complaints didn't interest her. She wanted to know if this Ramos character had the capability of making a death curse. If he did, she wanted the name of the person he'd sold it to. Ramos would be cautious. Posing as a customer was the only way she would get past his wariness.

In Key West she'd written a lot of parking tickets and handled dozens of domestic disputes. Investigating a possible homicide was a new experience for her. And while she was armed, she was walking into an unauthorized situation without backup. If Able knew what she was about to do, he'd stop her. If her watch commander found out, she could kiss her detective slot good-bye. She shut down the engine anyway and walked up the driveway.

Mimosa trees bordered the right side of the drive, their roots breaking up the concrete and making it almost impassable for vehicles. A breeze dropped pink blossoms, a carpet of them having accumulated into a decaying slick under her feet.

A traditional Cuban household only uses the front door for the delivery of monumental announcements such as the death of a family member. Having once made the mistake of knocking on a Cuban's front door, she had no intention of starting out on the wrong foot with this man.

The yard didn't appear to be fenced, so she continued along the side of the house and turned the corner. Trees shaded the backyard. At the far end of the property was a freestanding garage. In this setup, the garage would be the shrine to the orishas and the place where a *santero* performed the initiation rituals. If animals were sacrificed—a part of so many Santerían observances—that's where it would take place.

She stepped onto the terra-cotta patio that ran the length of the house. A potbellied cauldron sat in a fire pit at the center of the patio. The smell of rendered fat and cooling charcoal hung in the air. The odor would be one of the trouble spots for the neighbors. Concrete steps with an iron handrail led up to the back entrance of the house. Typical of a *santero*, a mirror hung in the eaves over the back door to keep the Evils from entering.

As she started for the steps, a white German shepherd, asleep beneath a tree across the yard, scrambled to its feet. It didn't bark, a bad sign. She wasn't afraid of dogs, but this one locked its eyes on her with an unnerving intelligence that stopped her in place. Suddenly the dog sprinted toward her, leaping onto the far side of the patio with the metal chain hooked to its collar clinking as it ran.

"Sit!" she yelled, standing her ground. She gave the "down" signal with her hand. The dog kept coming, head low, tongue lolling. Just as her resolve began to crumble, a man stepped out onto the porch.

"Dante . . . *para!*" he shouted.

The dog skidded to a halt a few feet from Frankie. It huffed and watched her with unreadable eyes. Frankie blew out a breath and regarded the man on the steps. He wore a loose white shirt, white pants, and dark glasses. He looked to be in his early forties, had a masculine jaw, and a lean, strong body, his forearms roped with muscle.

"Señor Ramos?" she said.

"I'm Ramos. Are you afraid of dogs?"

"Not at all." Then she realized her heart was pumping faster than usual.

Ramos padded down the steps, the mirror in the eaves flashing behind him, his fingers lightly touching the rail. "Dante means no harm. I promised her someone would take her for a car ride today. Come here, Dante." He bent to run his hand over the dog's coat and unclipped the chain from the collar. "Go apologize to the lady."

The big dog trotted to Frankie, sat at her feet, and lifted a thick paw. Frankie started to bend down to shake the dog's paw, then stopped. She hadn't come to participate in dog tricks.

"I'm Frankie Malone. Mystica Arnaz gave me your address. I didn't have a number, so I couldn't call. Is this a good time?"

"I'm expecting a client soon, but Mystica called ahead and described what you need. The cost is twenty dollars. Is that agreeable?"

"Fine," she said. The transaction was moving too fast. She needed time to look around the house. A gust of wind swept across the patio and raindrops the size of half-dollars smacked onto the tiles.

A drop struck Sergio's outstretched palm. "We must step inside, please."

He led the way up the steps and held the door for her and the dog as the rain pelted down. Her concern over entering the house had lessened. In fact, there was something vulnerable about Ramos that she couldn't place.

They walked through a spotless kitchen with stacks of oversize stainless-steel bowls on the counter and several knife blocks holding carving and butcher knives, a reminder of the rituals that must take place in the garage.

"Follow me," he said. His fingers brushed the door frames and chair backs as if he were keeping in touch with his surroundings as he showed her into the next room. His sunglasses stayed in place even though the storm had darkened the room.

Of course. The vulnerability she'd sensed was his eyesight.

The room off the kitchen was a *botánica* stocked with spiritual candles, fiberglass statues of Catholic saints, and wood-carved roosters. Shelves lined the walls with an array of ceramic and iron pots meant for collecting the blood of animals sacrificed during rituals. Blood feeds the saints of Santería, the orishas. Offerings of fresh flowers, candy, and lit candles flanked the urns and tureens used as shrines to the saints.

This wasn't the kitsch she'd seen at the salon. This was the real deal.

She noticed the hallway to the right. Somewhere in this house was a room similar to a pharmacy that would contain fresh herbs and sacred oils, along with strange items such as mules' teeth, owl feathers, and dirt from graveyards, all the elements needed to produce complex *ewes* and *ebbos*. As healers, *santeros* have extensive knowledge of plants and their powerful impact on the body. Unfortunately, some *santeros* use their position to fleece their "godchildren," or believers, to enrich themselves. It was dangerous business. Monies and gifts given to *santeros* are tributes that belong to the orishas. The saints are quick to punish anyone who would dare steal their fees.

"I'm so relieved you have the herbs," she said. "The woman who raised me practiced Santería. She made the *ewe* for me." Her throat closed with emotion. She hadn't spoken Amitee's name in years, the one person who had loved her unconditionally.

Sergio waved to a chair by the window. "Have a seat, watch the rainfall. I have Mystica's list. You were right to ask for this *ewe*. It will dispel the distress you've been experiencing."

His insight unnerved her until she remembered that the *ewe* she'd requested was meant to release negative energies. Naturally, he would assume she was stressed.

"It's been a long time since I've seen a *santero's farmacia*," she said.

His head cocked slightly. "Come along if you wish."

Chapter 13

S he followed him down a hallway lined with photos of tropical beaches along with several framed documents. She scanned them quickly until she came to two diplomas from the Universidad de la Habana—a Ph.D. in psychology and a master's in religious studies. Farther down the wall were commendations from international peer associations and a number of photos of people gathered for group shots. She passed the opened door of a sunny office with book-filled shelves and a desk with a large wicker chair pulled up in front. This man was a professional, not a witch doctor—a far more complex individual than she'd bargained for.

She joined him in a room with racks of apothecary jars and boxes she knew contained herbs; oils; powders; bat heads; quail heads; ashes; dried okra; Guinea, Chinese, and Indian pepper; charcoal; teeth from dogs, cats, and sharks; pieces of beehive; and all manner and forms of cotton. On a stainless-steel worktable were stone mortars and pestles for grinding and several Lucite containers holding small blue bottles with rubber stoppers. Beside the containers stood a large bottle packed with plants floating in a greenish liquid she knew was called Florida

Water. Every *santero* keeps a bottle for general use in spells and to dab on his forehead and limbs in order to dispel headaches or any type of psychic attack.

Next to the Florida Water lay a stack of gray conjure bags with a crosshatch pattern. The sight of the bags snapped her back to reality. She walked over and picked one up.

"Are there other *santeros* in Memphis?" she asked.

"None that I know of. Why?"

"I've seen a bag like this recently."

He glanced at her. "Where?"

"A man I met in passing had one."

Ramos opened the door of a small refrigerator and withdrew a handful of green herbs, water dripping from their roots. "That's a popular style of bag. It's sold on a number of Internet sites. Can you tell me about the man?"

"He was an African-American gentleman in his eighties."

"Why does this matter to you?"

"I wondered if you make *ebbos* and spells for people other than your godchildren. Like a special order."

"I see." He didn't look at her. He shook the water from the roots.

Her questions were too direct. Now he was suspicious. She changed the subject.

"I couldn't help noticing your doctorate from the University of Havana in the hallway."

He smiled. Behind his quiet formality, Sergio Ramos was a handsome man. "You notice many things. You're an inquisitive woman."

"I met a lot of Cubans when I lived in Key West. They risked everything to leave that country."

"So you're wondering why I was there for my training." He

bagged the herbs in plastic and wrapped it with a strip of raffia.

"I grew up in Little Havana, Miami. I was quite the romantic back then. I decided to attend university in Cuba to return to my roots, as it is said. When I graduated, I established a clinical practice in Havana and began research into the integration of the psyche with religious beliefs. Following that path, I became a practicing *santero*. I've now limited my role to *italero,* which means I specialize in the divination of the cowrie shells. This practice falls more in line with my training as a psychologist."

Frankie had learned from Amitee to trust *santeros,* that they function as moral authorities in their communities and as therapists by giving consultations using coconut shells or seashells to divine answers to life's problems. Ramos's background in psychology would make him highly effective in his practice as an *italero.* Or he could be a danger to the easily manipulated believers.

She saw him suppress a smile at what he must have thought was female curiosity.

"Shall I continue with my story?"

"No stone left unturned," she said, trying for charming, but the comment came off as brittle.

"You've noticed my failing eyesight. It's a genetic disorder that slowly damages the retina. I have no night vision and only a small amount of tunnel vision left. Two years ago I returned to the States to participate in a study offered in Memphis. My condition has stabilized. No more loss. I am very lucky. I miss Cuba, but this is my home now. I have an established clinical practice, and my work as a *santero* benefits the believers who live here."

He clasped his hands in front of him and smiled. "Now. Shall we discuss the true purpose of your visit?"

His tone was kind, not at all confrontational. He simply knew she had an ulterior motive, and he wanted to be told what that was.

She'd prepared for this.

"I do have a problem," she said quietly.

"A physical problem or a problem with your life?"

She cleared her throat. "Life." She touched her bruised cheek. "Both I guess." It was true. It was embarrassing; however, Ramos made a living by detecting the truth. He was more likely to respond to her if she was honest.

He picked up a small ceramic jar and held it flat on his palm for her to see. "Mystica mentioned the contusion. I took the liberty of making a plaster. I see the bone has been bruised. That is why the discoloration is taking so long to go away. The plaster will clear the discoloration and relieve the soreness. The *ewe* will work differently. It will dispel negative energies from your recent trauma. Boil the herbs in water and strain it. Soak in a tub of the mixture for three nights. Both remedies are meant to ease discomfort."

His expression clouded as he put the herbs and the ceramic jar into a sack. Like Mystica, he must assume she had been a victim of abuse.

"You asked if I make *ebbos* for people other than my godchildren. I assume you want me to make them to help you."

Ramos might be the only person in the city with the means and ability to make a death curse, but if she confronted him with what she knew, he would deny it. This wasn't an interview. It was more of a negotiation.

"I'm interested in the types of *ebbos* you make," she said. "I have questions."

"May I suggest a few sessions of therapy? Just talking. Then we can work with the *ebbos* if you feel it's necessary."

Let a powerful *santero* pry into her life? No way, too risky. "How about a few questions now?"

He felt the face of his watch for the time. "My next client arrives very soon. I believe I have a card in my office. You may call if you wish to make an appointment."

He ushered her into the hallway before going into his office. She waited, angry with herself for coming so close to getting the information and failing.

While he searched for the card, her gaze went to the series of photos she'd missed earlier, shots of people in groups, probably colleagues Ramos had met at conferences. It took a moment for one of the photos to register. It was an exterior shot of Robert House, the local center for homeless men and recovering addicts, a building she drove past every day. A group of about twenty men stood on the front steps. She spotted Sergio Ramos on the right. Little Man Lacy stood toward the back, towering over the rest. And there was Red Davis in the middle.

Adrenaline hit, followed by a chill. The conjure bag wasn't a guaranteed connection to Ramos, but this photo proved he had contact with the victims.

She'd come here expecting to find a *santero* and possibly a scam artist. Sergio Ramos was more than that. She'd been impressed, intrigued. Now she was seeing him with different eyes. He could be the source of the curse. He could also be the person who had delivered it.

Ramos appeared beside her with a card. "This will put you in touch with the person who books my appointments."

She took the card. "Thank you. I believe I'll take you up on that offer."

Chapter 14

Memphis sits on the Fourth Chickasaw Bluff, a ridge formed by buckling tectonic plates and the twisting course of the Mississippi River. The bluff is the highest point on the river's western bank between Natchez, Mississippi, and Cairo, Illinois. From the cobblestone landing in front of Billy's barge, the riverbank rises to Riverside Drive then ascends to Front Street.

Billy left the barge after sunset, the air thick with mosquitoes tracking him like tiny helicopters up the incline to the top of Monroe Avenue. He carried a copy of the *Memphis Flyer*, folded to protect the photos he'd discovered in Red's jacket. His plan was to go to Bardog, order Aldo's spicy four-meatball appetizer and a cold draft, and then work through the stack while watching a Cards game on TV.

Jesus Junior, or "J.J.," as he was known to every beat cop, stood on the sidewalk between Bardog and the Little Tea Shop. He was tall and brawny, an imposing figure in white track pants, a white jersey with HOLY GHOST written in rhinestones across the back, and spotless white sneakers. He made a living hustling tourists and selling the *Flyer* to people who didn't realize every downtown doorway had a rack full of free copies. His big money came from preaching Jesus. For a few extra bucks he'd throw in eyewitness accounts of Elvis riding his motorcycle around Memphis in the middle of the night while eating jelly doughnuts.

J.J. was a hit with the tourists. The city attracts the kind of people who want their stories about Elvis and Jesus told right together.

"Detective Cool," J.J. said, giving out his best glinty smile. "You been gone so long I thought the Rapture took you."

Billy nodded and kept moving. He didn't want to talk tonight.

"I hear Red Davis passed this morning, and you and Officer Frankie checked out their trap house." J.J. put his hand to his heart. "Sad day for us. A happy day for heaven."

Downtown residents know each other like it's a small town. News of death moves especially fast.

Billy stopped. "There's another guy living at that house."

"You mean Tyrese?"

"Yeah, Tyrese."

"That boy's been staying at his auntie's house in Yazoo City. She carried him back this morning."

"How do you know?"

"I seen 'em drive in." J.J. swung his head from side to side. "Tyrese don't know nothing about Red and Little Man, I can tell you that. People wears him out, know what I'm saying?" J.J. nodded. "Now I got a favor to ax you. I'm facing incarceration for lifting a bag of Cheetos out of Jack's Food Store."

J.J. was known for his high expectations and low accountability. His criminal sheet ran long with minor shoplifting charges.

"Just Cheetos?"

"Maybe a Colt 45. Maybe three. And some change off the counter. I got a court date. I'm axin' you to step up. Make it right."

"You need to speak to your buddy Jesus about this one," Billy said, reaching for the door. "I can't clean up your mess."

Inside, the bouncer sat to the right of the door, drinking a Red Bull. Amanda the bartender saw Billy coming and cued up Steve Earle's "Regular Guy" on the jukebox, one of his favorites. A few customers sat at tables, and there was that guy who always sat at the end of the bar next to the kitchen pass-through. Billy happened to know his name was James Freeman, a powerfully built man in his fifties with a face like a closed book. An untouched draft sat next to Freeman's half-empty mug, which meant he had company. Billy had never met Freeman and didn't care to tonight. He wanted supper and to watch the ball game in peace. He grabbed a big man bucket-style stool at the end of the bar near the door.

The regulars know about the stools. Avoid the ones called recliners you lean back and you'll wind up on your ass. The small man stools are two inches shorter than the big man stools. They make short men look shorter and tall men uncomfortable because they can't rest their elbows on the bar. The owner said he could afford to replace all the stools but thought competition for the big man stools gave the place a healthy edge.

Amanda brought over a draft. On the big screen, the Cards were playing at Atlanta, bottom of the eighth with the Braves at bat. With a 3–1 count, Rodriguez hit a towering pop-up in front of the plate. Brewer, the latest catcher for the Cards, lost the ball in the lights, fumbled, and fired it over the head of the first baseman covering home.

"That play has to be made," the TV commentator groaned.

"The Cards are in deep trouble. Augie Poston would never have made that kind of error."

"You can't replace a man like Augie Poston," his sidekick added.

Billy looked away from the screen. As bad as he felt about Augie losing his career, he could still have a decent life if he stayed on the meds, which he suspected Augie wasn't doing. Just like today, the possible consequences of that decision could be devastating.

Two years ago Augie had shown up late at Billy's apartment, paranoid as hell, claiming someone had rigged his car with a bomb. When Billy didn't buy it, Augie slammed out, hot-wired Billy's 1946 Chevy pickup, and crashed it through the front window of the former Welcome Wagon building at the corner of Court Avenue and North Second. Then he closed out the night by slugging a responding officer.

The incident had put Billy in a bind. Admit the pickup had been stolen, and Augie would be charged with a felony. Say he'd given Augie permission to take the truck while knowing he didn't have a license and Billy would have been responsible for damages.

As it turned out, the assistant DA had been a baseball fanatic. He reduced the charges to careless driving. Augie pled no contest to the charge of hitting the officer and was given a six-month suspended sentence. He paid for the damages, but the pickup, the only thing left to Billy in his uncle Kane's will, was totaled.

A week later, Augie showed up at his door and swore he'd never go off his meds again. Billy had taken a friend at his word.

Pushing Augie out of his mind, he ordered meatballs and another draft, then spread the stack of photos in front of him for inspection.

The time frame was definitely sixties or seventies in some southern city: Memphis, Jackson, Little Rock, Birmingham, Atlanta. The two men appeared to be FBI and the photos were surveillance shots. Even with the initials of the guy wearing the glasses, it would be hard to get a name.

Amanda delivered the meatballs and a side of kale she'd ordered for him. "Welcome back, Detective. Eat your greens."

Quite suddenly he felt Mercy sitting on the stool beside him, lifting her wineglass and giving him that sly glance that always kept him wondering. She was a puzzle, a mystery.

No, he told himself with a shake at his head. *Get the story straight.*

The relationship had been rocky for the last few months. He hadn't landed a job in law enforcement, and Mercy had begun keeping longer hours at the bakery. When they did get together, there was nothing to talk about. He'd thought it was a dry spell they could work out. Then yesterday, when he asked her to sit down and talk about their future, she'd sprung the new lease for the bakery on him.

He'd walked out. He'd heard the click of the lock behind him.

Someone yelled his name from across the bar and jerked him out of his thoughts.

"Hey, Able!" Augie strolled past the kitchen's pass-through window, drying his hands on a paper towel. He said a few words to Freeman, then reach for his draft and began sliding it down the bar.

Oh, for God's sake, Billy thought as he dragged the *Flyer* over the photos to hide them.

"You saved my ass today," Augie blared. "I was a damned idiot getting out there dancing." He still wore the plaid shorts and was now limping.

Billy picked up his fork. "Glad I could help. I'm eating right now."

Augie's green eyes glittered. "Freeman and I were discussing my book project. You and I talked about that, right?"

"Look. I'm sorry about your mom—"

Augie hauled a big man stool next to Billy. "The journalist got a copy of her file. He said the case was improperly handled. My mom was murdered." Augie stared at him, his face overheated and expectant, waiting for a response.

He wasn't about to go away.

Chapter 15

Billy put down his fork. "Okay. Give me details on those threatening letters you found at your dad's place."

"It's awful stuff. There was one postmarked three days after her death. The journalist said it wasn't on the file's documents list. It ended with a promise to pour gasoline on my head and light a match. I guess my dad believed it, because he never turned the letter over to the cops. If he had, maybe they would've taken her case more seriously."

"Holding back the letter wasn't smart, but I understand where your father was coming from. You said there's a connection between your mother's death and this journalist's project."

"*Our* project. Bad things happened in Memphis during the civil rights struggle. Law enforcement spied on black citizens, harassed them. The journalist says Calvin Carter is the key to proving that. You know about Carter the photographer?"

"He covered the 'I Am A Man' sanitation workers' strike and worked the trial of the men who murdered that kid, Emmett Till, the one who whistled at a white woman. And the Matt Parker incident, a young black guy who was dragged from jail, beaten, and shot. Carter took a chance covering those stories—a black man carrying a camera. But I'm told he was a cop before he was a photographer, so he knew how to handle himself in a crowd."

Augie gestured toward Freeman. "James's dad owned a bar on Beale Street in the sixties. James worked there as a kid. He has offices in that building now. He might be able to identify something in those photographs."

"Why do you care? You weren't interested this afternoon."

Augie picked at the skin on his arm. "You know I blank out sometimes, can't think straight. You were going through the stack when I came out of the can. Maybe I'll catch something this time."

Sighing inwardly, Billy handed over the photos.

Augie immediately pulled out a shot of the guy with the glasses. "He's wearing the jacket from Red's place."

"Yep. You think they were taken in Memphis?"

"James might know."

Two guys sitting at a table behind them jumped to their feet and cheered the Braves for having beaten the Cards by four. Freeman stood and threw bills on the bar. Well over six feet, he had a craggy face, salt-and-pepper hair, and carried himself with the physicality of a younger man.

"James," Augie called down the bar. "Able's got the pictures I told you about."

"You've already discussed this with Freeman?" Billy said. "Shit, man. They're potential evidence."

Augie slapped his shoulder. "It's all good. Think of Freeman as a consultant." Augie put up a hand when Freeman tried to maneuver past. "This is the detective with the pictures I told you about." He held out the stack of photos.

Freeman's gaze slid toward Billy. He waited for a reaction.

Billy nodded for Augie to hand over the photos. Freeman flipped through, stopped at one, and glanced at Augie.

"What is it?" Billy said.

"Nothing," Augie said, but guilt played over his face.

Freeman handed the stack back to Augie and fixed Billy with a cold stare. "Can't help you, Detective. And if I could, I wouldn't." Then Freeman turned on his heel and headed for the door.

"What the hell was that about?" Billy asked.

"Did I mention the guy hates cops?"

"No kidding. Why?"

"Something happened with his dad's bar on Beale Street. Something ugly."

He watched Freeman weave through a line of Parliament-smoking young women who were filing in. Behind the women, Jesus Junior strolled in. Ten steps inside the door, the bouncer grabbed J.J. and twisted his arm behind his back.

"Not tonight," the bouncer announced and marched him toward the door.

"Hey, Detective!" J.J. yelled over his shoulder.

"Shut up," the bouncer bellowed.

"Heelllp!" J.J. hollered.

"Help" isn't a word you want shouted in a bar. Billy walked over.

"I got this," he said and pulled J.J. outside into a greasy rain that was just beginning to coat the streets. They stood under the awning of the office building next door. "What the hell's wrong with you?"

"I tol' you my problem. Jesus said he wants us to look out for each other." J.J. reached out to pluck at Billy's sleeve.

He knocked the hand away. "What do you think I can do? I

got more rules on me than anyone else in the book. You created this. Fix it yourself."

"All right. Then give me twenty bucks."

"You should be selling used cars. You'd make a fortune," Billy said.

J.J.'s tone downgraded to contempt. "I *tol'* you about Tyrese. I figure you *owe* me."

Billy laughed and opened the door. "You think *everybody* owes you."

Inside, he found Augie still at the bar, focused on the post-game. He understood Augie's compulsion to look into his mother's death. His own mother had driven away on a cold night, leaving him so she could run off and marry a man who didn't want her kid included in the deal. She died on an icy curve five miles from the house.

Augie didn't understand that no matter how hard you try, you can't rescue the past.

He picked up the photos and folded them into the *Flyer.* "I'll look into your mother's case, but there's only so much I can do. You got that?"

Augie's attention never left the TV. "Sure, buddy. Thanks."

Billy stepped outside. The rain had picked up to a steady beat. J.J. was gone. He stood under the awning and phoned Frankie, got her voice mail, and left a message saying he'd found something interesting hidden in the jacket. He didn't give the details. Healthy speculation turns a patrol cop into a detective.

He tucked the *Flyer* under his arm and cut through a narrow alley across the street to shorten his walk—a risk, but he knew what to watch for.

But the light in the alley was out. As he passed the Dumpster, he felt a hand on his back. Before he could react, an arm came from his right and wrapped around his neck, cutting off his air. He grabbed the thick forearm with both hands but was dragged backward. *Break loose,* he thought, *or go down.* He drove his left elbow backward into the man's gut.

"Ughhh." The mugger's grip broke and he doubled over.

Billy nailed him with an uppercut to the chin. The man went down and rolled to hook Billy's left ankle with a leg swinging like a scythe. Billy fell on his ass, his shoe flying across the alley. He grabbed for the guy. Too late. The man was already up and running.

"Son of a bitch!" Billy yelled, mad at himself. First, he'd walked into a dangerous situation. Then he'd underestimated the dirtbag who had been waiting.

He watched the guy turn the corner, silhouetted in a curtain of rain. He was tall, solid, broad-shouldered. Bad luck that he'd picked a cop who knew how to fight. Beside Billy lay the *Flyer,* with the photos inside. He scooped them up. Thank God they were dry. He went after his shoe. No point in calling the cops with no real description to give them. He would call Bardog's manager from the barge and tell him about the mugger in the alley.

His phone pinged, signaling a text, probably from Frankie.

It was from Mercy.

> *I packed your belongings. 3 boxes arriving FedEx ground. Wish things had worked out. All the best. Mercy.*

Just like that. They were over.

Chapter 16

Frankie had leased the top floor of a two-story home in mid-town Memphis with its New Orleans–style garden, a sweeping staircase for her use alone, and sunlight that flooded the place through floor-to-ceiling windows. The giant pin oaks in the front yard grew so close to the windows, she felt like a forest creature living inside their branches.

She'd kept the furnishings spare with a few antiques, a couple of good paintings from her father's house, comfortable chairs, and good reading light. At first she'd thought the place was too big for her, then one night she'd danced from room to room, swaying to classic jazz on 91.7 FM. After that she'd danced through the rooms every day.

Back from Ramos's house, she boiled the herbs for the *ewe* and strained the liquid into the tub. After the soak, she wanted to do some research on Ramos, followed by a few hours of sleep before her final night shift. Exhausted, she removed her clothes, folding each piece to lay on the bedroom chair until she stood naked. She caught a glimpse of herself in the shadowed mirror—her splotched cheek and puffy eyelids, her body looking awkward and vulnerable. Her arms automatically wrapped around her stomach to stave off that feeling of being overwhelmed.

Shake it off, she reprimanded herself. Emotions accomplish nothing.

She applied the salve to her cheek, which smelled of menthol and flowers, then placed her hands on either side of the claw-foot tub and eased her body into the water. Lying back, she let the purifying warmth lap over her thighs and breasts. It was her nature to overthink things, rip down the walls of a problem and restack the boards. Once you've torn the romance out of something and replaced it with logic, there was no way to go back. Her eyes closed. Her shoulders dropped. She listened as the buzz of the cicada died off in the evening light. She wanted to search for comfort, but her mind wouldn't allow it. It constantly played the scene from the day she'd lost control.

It had been her day off. She stood in the parking lot of a Days Inn next to I-40 where tractor-trailer rigs rattled by twenty-four hours a day—a real classy setting for her first time with Brad. She'd been nervous. Brad pulled in and took his time getting out of the SUV, leaving her waiting and exposed to the truckers and other couples who were there for the same reason. What a club she was about to join. Cheaters on the Cheap.

Brad finally opened his door and set one foot on the pavement, half in and half out of the SUV, talking on the phone. That's when it hit her. There would be nothing romantic about what would happen in the next hour. Brad was working her into his schedule, a quick fuck on the side. She didn't like that word, but nothing else so completely described the situation she'd put herself in.

He slammed his car door and walked toward her with the phone pressed to his ear.

"Yes, sweetie. I know," she heard him say. "You're daddy's girl. Love you. See you tonight."

A *daughter.* Frankie had known Brad was married, but he said they were about to separate. She hadn't asked about kids. She'd justified their relationship by telling herself she was in love. Love, hell. This was sexual hunger. It's hard to think straight when you're hungry.

Brad strode toward her smiling, already loosening his tie. He reached into his pants pocket and flashed a package of condoms for her to see. What a good boy. He'd remembered her request.

She could tell by his grin he was about to say something lewd. She cut him off by announcing that she'd changed her mind, offering her hand for a let's-call-it-a-draw handshake. He stopped a foot in front of her and began to rant about the risk he was taking to be there—his family, his job. Everything he loved. What he might lose.

She knocked the condoms out of his hand. His face turned red. He looked away. Then he backhanded her, putting a lot of force behind it, his heavy class ring smashing into her cheekbone. No man had ever dared hit Frankie.

In the bathtub she bounced the flat of her palms on the surface to break the water's tension and to inhale the *ewe*'s fragrance. She drifted back to her childhood with her Jamaican nanny, Amitee, who used to drag a zinc basin into the backyard under the hibiscus trees. Amitee would pour in the *ewe*. Frankie would get in and lie back under hibiscus blossoms that smelled like honey. Amitee sat beside her and recited the names of the orishas. She would tell the stories about their passions and the blood of the animals each orisha preferred to drink. The stories were like African Grimms' fairy tales, not told to frighten her but to prepare her for life. There was no one else around to do it. Her mother was gone. Her father preferred losing himself in his work to avoid spending time with a daughter who was the spitting image of his cheating wife.

Amitee would say, "A problem confronts you, bathe in the *ewe*. When the Evils sit on your shoulder, drink the *ewe*. Clean your house, clean your body with the *ewe*."

Frankie rose from the tub now, water sliding off her compact body with its muscled biceps and strong legs. Durable. Not given to breakdowns.

She pulled the plug in the bath and got out. She needed focus. She had to control her thoughts. Toweled off, she put on yoga pants and a tank, reviewing in her mind the message Billy had left. He'd found something interesting in the jacket. He didn't say what. He'd left her wondering on purpose.

Still keyed up despite the *ewe*, she rummaged through the medicine cabinet for another bottle of tranquilizers. She took one pill, started to put the bottle back, then slipped it into her purse. She e-mailed Billy the notes from her interview with Ramos and included the doctor's credentials, published articles, awards from international peer groups, and his charity work.

She poured club soda in a wineglass and studied an Internet photograph of Ramos lecturing at a podium in a large auditorium. Her intuition did a war dance with her logic. She couldn't believe this educated man, apparently a compassionate man, had been complicit in a plot to terrify Red and Little Man. The conjure bag wasn't proof he'd been involved, but that photo in the hallway put him at the top of her suspects list. Ramos had the knowledge and the means. Did he have the malice?

His card listed a site where she could book online. His scheduling calendar showed a 1:00 P.M. appointment in two days. She had three days off after tonight's shift.

She went back to his photo—the intelligent gaze, the pleasant mouth. He didn't have a murderer's eyes. But she knew from experience that, despite appearances, doctors can be crazier than most people when they put their minds to it.

She booked the appointment.

Chapter 17

The next morning, Billy opened his eyes to a blurry realization. During the mugging there'd been no "give me your wallet" demand. The guy had used way too much muscle for the attack to have been random. The jolt he got from Mercy's text coming right after had kept him from making the connection between the mugger and the guy on the street outside Red's place. The two men were the same height and build. Something else was at play here.

He rolled over carefully, sore from being dumped on his ass in the alley. Dumped by Mercy, too. He handled the breakup pretty well while it had been his idea, but her text stole his illusion of control, like driving a car and suddenly having the steering wheel yanked away. What really burned him was her closing line. "All the best" sounded like a kiss-off for a guest who'd overstayed his welcome. She'd packed up his stuff and shipped it in one day. Maybe she'd planned the whole thing.

He took a hot shower, dressed, and scrambled eggs with cheese. While he ate, he found Frankie's e-mail saying she'd located a man named Sergio Ramos, a psychologist and a Santerían priest. She'd learned that Ramos had the knowledge and the components to make the curse, but then he had cut their interview short. Frankie was planning to go back and question him further. If Ramos had any sense, he wouldn't be available. However, Frankie was earnest and appealing. Even a smart man might drop his guard for that.

He took his second cup of coffee to the aft deck. Frankie made fast work of locating a possible source for the conjure bag. Aggressive, inquisitive, she appeared to have the temperament of a born homicide cop. She had the mind for the work. He hoped she had the judgment.

He switched to considering his upcoming meeting with the deputy chief of investigative services. The chief, Bud Middlebrook, had called him in Atlanta, fishing for information about his return to the force. He'd made a point of being evasive with the chief, not realizing that Mercy was already in negotiations for the new lease.

He stared across the water. Circumstances had beaten him up over the last year, but he damned sure wasn't beaten. Time to suck it up and reclaim his territory. He was signing back on, but the chief wasn't aware of that. If he played this right, he could get Middlebrook to make some concessions for things he wanted. This meeting was the only time he could make that happen.

He drove to the CJC an hour later to stand around in the squad room with the same detectives, the same stained carpet, and the same murder solve-rate charts that seemed to never resolve. Two changes hit him in the face. His desk had been shoved against the wall, and a copier now occupied the space where Lou once sat.

Billy left the squad with his reputation intact, but he guessed some of the guys had blamed him for being a ten-hour-a-day witness to Lou's disintegration without doing anything about it.

Easy for them to point a finger, but he couldn't fix what was happening with Lou when he hadn't seen it. Even the best cops don't notice their wives having affairs. They don't see their kids doing drugs. They all have blind spots, their minds shutting out what their hearts can't accept.

Roll back the calendar to the time before Lou's wife walked out, and maybe he could have affected the man's over-the-top reaction to losing her. Lou had replaced his obsession with his wife for an obsession with a child, Rebecca Jane Bellflower. In some kind of twisted belief that he was rescuing the girl from abusive parents, Lou had locked Rebecca Jane in an apartment and built a fantasy world for her. The world had included his abuse.

Lou committed suicide. Rebecca Jane nearly died.

An older detective, recently transferred from burglary to homicide, waved Billy over to break the ice. Detectives Nance and Vargas stopped by for a chat. The consistency of their dickish personalities was almost comforting. Then Dunsford trudged into the squad room like a forlorn cartoon character with his sloping shoulders and brown loafers that needed a good wipe-down. He scowled in their direction and went the long way around to get to his desk. Obviously, he was still pissed about Billy's intrusion into Red's crime scene. That meant he'd probably complained during the daily briefing and made sure it was flagged in Billy's file. Dunsford could become a problem.

At 10:55, he headed to the twelfth floor for his 11:00 with Middlebrook. On the way, his mobile rang. It was Augie, the last person he wanted to talk to. He turned off his phone.

Middlebrook's young assistant, Roxanne, was on a call. She mouthed "Hello," and pointed to the chief's door.

The chief moved from behind his desk to shake hands. In his fifties, he had the fit physique of a boss who worked hard to set a good example for his troops. He was a white-shirt, upper-management cop who never talked down to his men and was as forthright as his job allowed him to be.

The twelfth-floor offices were a major upgrade from the cramped quarters two floors below. On the window ledge behind the desk, the chief kept two Alabama Crimson Tide football trophies and three potted orchids—the finicky kind, not the grocery store variety. Some cops take up hobbies to keep the stress from killing them. Middlebrook had chosen orchids.

The chief put on a pleasant smile and leaned against the front edge of his desk. "Good to see you, Able. How did Atlanta suit you?"

"Nice city. Lots of opportunity there to grow."

"Yeah, it's bigger, faster. The traffic's a killer. And their department is suffering even worse budget cuts than the MPD."

"It's hard times everywhere," he said, playing along.

Middlebrook nodded as he worked to decipher the tone of the conversation. "And how's your lady? I'm told she bakes world-class pies."

"Mercy's great. Her business has really taken off in Atlanta."

"Are there wedding bells coming up?" Middlebrook raised his eyebrows.

"Not yet, sir."

"I see." The chief changed the subject. "You been following MPD crime stats?"

"I've kept tabs. Home invasions and domestics are through the roof. Solve rates are down sixteen percent."

"Half the city is afraid to leave their house. The other half check their semiautomatics to be sure they're loaded before they walk out the door. Over the next six months I'm going to lose three detectives. We're still badly shorthanded after losing you and Lou last year. You're one of our best, Able. You proved that last year with the Overton case. You handled yourself well in a bad situation. And we were all sorry to lose Lou."

Billy started to say he knew the chief had graduated from the academy with Lou and that the loss was just as hard on him. But being at the CJC had made Lou's death fresh all over again. All he could manage was a thank-you.

"I feel I should remind you that if your leave expires and you haven't signed on, you won't be able to rejoin the force in the future. It's department policy. Don't let that happen."

"Yes, I'm aware of that policy."

"And if you join Atlanta's department, or any other for that matter, you'll have to start over. You could be years working up to homicide."

"I hear you, sir. And I've been considering my options. There are a couple of things I would need to make up my mind."

"You know I can't give you a raise," Middlebrook said. He rubbed his chin. "What is it you need?"

"My old desk back. And I want it where it used to be."

Relief broke on the chief's face. "Good. Then I can count on—"

He cut in. "There's one more thing."

He spelled it out. Middlebrook started to argue, then reluctantly agreed. They shook on it.

"Glad you're coming back, Able," the chief said, and checked his watch. "Roxanne will get you started."

"I'd like a few days to settle in before I take on assignments."

"That won't be a problem. You've been on leave longer than six months, so there's more paperwork. Get a complete physical and an eye exam, and qualify on the range. No new health issues, right?"

"I'm in good shape."

"Then walk with me to the elevators."

A group of detectives from the economic crimes squad walked past them. Middlebrook waited until he and Billy were alone at the elevator to put his hand on Billy's shoulder. "I hope your return means Mercy is moving to Memphis with you."

"That's not going to happen, sir."

"I'm sorry. It's been a rough year. You had your horse shot out from under you with Lou, but you're back now. Time to move forward."

The elevator doors opened. "One thing, Able. Don't insert yourself in another detective's investigation. If it's not your case, stay out of it."

Middlebrook stepped into the elevator. "I don't want a second complaint to derail your reinstatement." The doors closed.

Round to Dunsford.

Chapter 18

The next elevator took Billy to tenth-floor central records where Edgar Kellogg was manning the counter. Lou and Edgar had been good buddies. Trading on that relationship, Billy had called ahead and asked Edgar to locate the case file on Dahlia Poston and to pull criminal sheets on Red and Little Man.

"Got your files right 'cheer," Edgar said as he walked in. Edgar was a wiry man, all Adam's apple and nervous energy. Billy had heard that as a young patrol officer Edgar developed a reputation as a badass with a billy club, breaking heads during the racial upheaval in Memphis in the late sixties. After a heart attack ten years ago, he'd lost forty pounds and chosen desk duty over retirement. Like Lou, Edgar knew where the political bodies were buried, so none of the bosses insisted he stand down.

Edgar gave him a register to sign and handed over the original file plus a stack of copies he'd made for Billy to take with him.

"Someone else requested the Poston file recently," Billy said. "Would you check for that name?"

Edgar disappeared into the stacks and came back, a disgusted look on his face. "You're right. It's been checked out, but there's no name. The guy must have paid cash."

"Did he sign the request register?"

Edgar cocked his head toward a round-hipped woman standing at a computer terminal. "I'm not the only person who works in this place, but I'm the only one who gets it right."

Billy sat at a table and opened the file, wincing at the horrific eight-by-tens taken of Mrs. Poston's charred corpse sitting behind the wheel. He studied each photo of the burned-out Pontiac, particularly the close-ups of the fuel line and gas tank.

Cause of death was clear—Dahlia Poston had burned alive. According to the interviews, her son witnessed it. That kind of trauma could start a grown man on the road to psychosis, much less a little kid.

Manner of death was less clear. There was a ruptured fuel line to consider and the three-inch piece of wire fused to the inside wall of the tank. The wire suggested that an assailant could have run an electrical charge from the brake lights to the gas tank. Hit the brakes and the tank blows the car to smithereens. Simple and effective.

According to the notes, a Detective Travis had been familiar with the wire trick and looked for additional wire running to the brakes. At that time, forensics was an evolving science with limited equipment, little testing, and no techs. The detectives did the work themselves. Judging by the devastation of the car, if there had been additional wires it could have easily been missed, or the extreme heat could have destroyed it beyond detection.

Travis had also looked into the ruptured fuel line. The fireball had been so intense it destroyed the entire fuel system, making it impossible to tell if a defect in the system had triggered the explosion. However, the ruptured line's survival of the fire left room for reasonable doubt that it had been the cause.

Billy read through the file again. Even though Dahlia Poston had angered a lot of people, he saw no proof of criminal intent. Neither had Detective Travis nor the medical examiner. The legal system requires proof. There was none. The examiner had ruled the death accidental. Billy couldn't argue with his conclusion.

If this journalist had any experience reading case files, he would know the facts as presented did not prove Dahlia Poston had been murdered. Therefore, he lied if he'd made that statement to Augie.

There was one possible weak point. Billy went back to Edgar, who was leafing through files at the counter.

"Did you know Travis, the detective in charge of this case?"

Edgar snorted. "Pain in the ass."

"Meaning?"

"Should've been a priest, not a cop. Never bent a rule in his life, never cracked a smile."

"But a good detective?"

"He was that all right."

"What about the medical examiner, Dr. Paul?"

Edgar's eyes rolled toward the ceiling. "Dr. Thomas Paul. Another pain in the ass, just like Travis."

"Is Travis dead?"

"Aneurysm. He collapsed on top of a corpse at a scene. Only time the guy ever fucked up." Edgar chuckled. "Dr. Paul is gone too, if that's your next question."

Billy would check the archives to verify Kellogg's opinion of Travis's track record. If Travis was that good at his job, his name would be all over the commendation lists.

"Do you remember the Poston case?"

"I remember the time. King had been shot, and we were all pulling double shifts. We put trouble down where we found it." He pantomimed whipping out a baton and whacking someone. "Bam, bam. Don't nobody move." He laughed and holstered his invisible baton. "The mayor, the director, the DA, the governor— all of them were trembling in their wingtips."

Edgar had been an eyewitness to the times, a primary source. Billy thought about the stack of photos and the possibility that Edgar could identify the locations, maybe even the two guys in the shots. He would try to come by with the photos this afternoon.

He sat down to summarize his notes. Could the medical examiner have designated the case "undetermined" instead of "accidental"? Absolutely. The ruptured fuel line provided reasonable doubt, but only by the slimmest margin. Had Dr. Paul made his choice out of political expediency? Probably, but impossible to know. Would the DA have pushed to avoid sensationalizing the death of a controversial black woman? No doubt about it. But Billy wouldn't go into all of that with Augie. It would only encourage him.

Billy turned his attention to Davis's and Lacy's sheets. They were clean except for a few offenses of public drunkenness and vagrancy. What surprised him was finding reports that predated Katrina. The guys had put it out that they'd been forced to leave New Orleans because of the storm. Tacking on the word "Katrina" added sympathy to any hard-luck story, but that didn't seem like Davis's and Lacy's style.

Frankie had texted that she planned to research the Davis and Lacy cases after signing off duty today. When she finished, she would call. That left him to contact a friend at the medical examiner's office who could check on their autopsy reports. The medical examiner was back in town. The ME's findings would dictate how involved he could be in either case. A closed case, which was what he expected Red's to be, made it available to anyone. An open investigation would be off-limits, even to him, until his reinstatement, which was several days off.

As he walked out, he checked for Frankie's call. What he found were thirteen texts and six voice mails from Augie. They added up to one message: "Meet me at Rock of Ages Funeral Home, midtown."

Chapter 19

Frankie's night shift dragged until dispatch notified her of shots fired during a home invasion. Turned out the burglar was the homeowner's soon-to-be ex-wife. After a girls' night out, the drunken woman had made the mistake of returning to her old address. When her key didn't fit, she crawled through the dog door. Her husband was waiting with an unlicensed Ruger .357.

Paramedics said the husband had only winged her. However, possession of the Ruger and the possibility that the man had seized an opportunity to shortcut an unhappy divorce put him in the back of Frankie's squad car. She transported the husband, still in his pajamas, to the Glamour Slammer, better known as the Criminal Justice Complex at 201 Poplar.

After processing him, she'd checked in as off duty with dispatch and took the elevator to the tenth-floor burglary squad room. Her friend, Detective Wayne Dixon, had offered to take a break so she could use his computer to do a search on Davis and Lacy and have her findings available for her meeting with Billy Able.

She yawned over the keyboard. Must be a buildup of the

tranquilizers she'd taken over the last couple of weeks plus the effect of the *ewe*. Normally she would go home after a ten-hour night shift, but this was her best opportunity to demonstrate to Able that she was good partner material. There was one opening coming available on the homicide squad for a new hire. If she impressed Able, maybe he'd go to bat for her with Middlebrook.

In three clicks she found twenty links to articles written by blues enthusiasts along with YouTube videos of club performances from Red's and Little Man's five-year-old European tour. Wikipedia listed four albums under Red's name. In the eighties, two of his songs made it into the top twenty of the R and B charts plus one crossover hit, "Burning Tree Blues." A few other artists covered Red's songs, so there had be royalties coming from publishing unless someone had managed to swindle him on his original contracts. She copied names to track the payments. If Red had family, the royalties would belong to them.

The archives for the New Orleans *Times-Picayune* carried a six-year-old profile on Davis and Lacy in the entertainment section. They had been mainstays in the Frenchmen Street entertainment district for years and were listed as regular players at the New Orleans Jazz and Heritage Festival and the French Quarter Festival.

Searching further, she dug out an old crime-beat article that reported an aggravated assault charge naming Davis and Lacy as the victims. In addition to the assault, which had put both men in the hospital, there were charges of burglary and criminal damage to property that were brought against their assailant, William Cooley, aka Cool Willy. The notorious pimp had attacked Davis and Lacy in an alley outside a nightclub. He later entered their home, where he'd damaged property including their instruments.

Pulling up the name William Cooley on NCIC, the National

Crime Information Center site, she found a history of arrests that began with shoplifting, assault, and solicitation of prostitution. Later he'd graduated to grand larceny and criminal assault. Yet Cooley's activities had paid well enough to hire lawyers who'd limited his jail time.

Her bruised cheek tingled. She touched it. A few more keystrokes brought up an article dated a year after the original crime-beat report:

> Orleans Parish prosecutors dismissed all charges against William Cooley, 27, accused of aggravated burglary and criminal damage to property in the beating case of Red Davis and Little Man Lacy. Instead of facing trial, Cooley, resident of Orleans Parish, was freed and the case closed at Orleans Parish Criminal District Court. District Attorney Armand "Bat" Bourque's office issued a statement that charges had been dropped because Davis and Lacy, two well-regarded musicians from the New Orleans area, had not appeared for trial. "Victims must make themselves available to the court in order for us to prosecute an aggravated assault case," Bourque said.

Davis and Lacy had left New Orleans, probably out of fear of reprisal from the pimp. Now they were dead.

Frankie clicked print and was standing to retrieve her reports just as she heard Wayne Dixon's voice coming down the hall.

"It's at my desk, Coral," Wayne said. "There are a few things you might want—photos of Brad hamming it up in the squad room, articles he clipped about cases he'd handled, and several commendation plaques."

Frankie froze. Coral McDaniel, Brad's wife, was here.

Wayne turned the corner with a sweet-faced woman of medium height walking behind him. She was thick through the waist with cushy upper arms exposed by her sleeveless blouse. Her drab skirt cut her off below the knees. An unhealthy pink stained the bridge of her nose and spread across her cheeks. She looked nothing like the woman Frankie had imagined Brad would marry.

Frankie glanced down at a cardboard box full of plaques that had been shoved under Wayne's desk. When she looked up, Coral was standing across from her, wearing the mildly shell-shocked expression every family member of a victim gets.

Frankie thought she might black out from the guilt.

"All done?" Wayne asked.

"All what?" Frankie asked numbly.

"Did you find what you needed?" He looked puzzled, then glanced from her to Coral. "Oh, sorry. You haven't met Coral McDaniel. This is Officer Frankie Malone, a coworker of Brad's."

Frankie had heard the rumors about Brad taking his wife to league ball games where he would introduce her to his "women friends." Coral must have known what he was up to and been humiliated by the snickers and sidelong looks.

"We were all stunned by Brad's passing," Frankie said, gathering her copies.

The sweetness had drained from Coral's face. "Your name used to come up on Brad's phone. He called you one night during dinner, said you were working together on a case."

Detectives don't call patrol cops about a case. Not from home. Not during dinner. Frankie was mortified. "I'll be out of your way in a sec," she said, projecting a calm she didn't feel.

"I have a daughter." Coral glared at her.

"A daughter!" Wayne's gaze darted from Coral to her. "I didn't realize. Did you know that, Frankie?"

"Not until recently."

"That's no excuse," Coral snapped.

Frankie gulped.

Wayne, a perceptive man, instantly got the picture. "Sorry, ladies. If you'll excuse me, I need to get back to work."

Frankie gathered her files and hustled toward the bathroom, the pressure in her chest blooming to the point of cutting off her air. She felt like she was dying. Or maybe she just wanted to die. She pushed through the door and ducked inside a stall.

Breathe, she ordered herself and pawed through her purse for the bottle of tranquilizers. Two pills rolled onto her palm. She downed both and took several deep breaths. Thank God she had the bathroom to herself. She needed time to pull it together before meeting with Billy.

The door whooshed open and thumped closed. Frankie heard a gasp then the tortured sound of air rasping into lungs. From under the door, she could see Coral McDaniel's flat shoes standing beside the sink. The sobbing stretched out. No one came through the door to comfort Coral, and Frankie had no right to do so. She stood there, soaked in Coral's pain, replaying Brad's death in her mind as she had done every hour of every day for the last two and a half weeks.

She had escaped Brad and the hotel parking lot, her Jeep merging with the heavy I-40 traffic. Her face hurt like hell, her cheek swelling where Brad's ring had cracked against the bone. Grimly she observed there was one small gain from Brad's assault—their affair had ended before it really heated up.

She'd checked her rearview mirror and seen Brad's black SUV booming up behind her. He passed her on the left then whipped in front of her, the sun sparking off his rear window as he tried to cut her off. She hit the brakes. He switched back to the left lane and dropped even with her window. She saw his mouth twisting with ugly words. Yelling, he waved his phone at her. He was furious that she'd turned hers off. Apparently, his ego couldn't stand a woman being the first to walk away.

They were doing ninety as they approached the overpass. Frankie remembered because she'd glanced at the speedometer and let up on the gas. Brad floored the SUV and moved ahead of her into the shadow of the overpass. He pulled the same stunt, swerving into her lane, trying to make her stop, only this time he overcorrected. The SUV tilted right and went into a clockwise spin. The front bumper clipped the last support. They flashed from beneath the overpass, the SUV in a flip with its passenger-side door smashing onto the asphalt. It rolled and righted itself on the shoulder. She thought it was over until she looked in her side mirror and realized momentum had continued to roll the SUV. She saw back wheels spinning in the air as it disappeared down an embankment.

Frankie slammed to a stop, called 911, and gave the mile marker. Then she was out of her Jeep, running, running.

In the bathroom she heard Coral blow her nose and the sink water running. The door opened and closed. She sucked in a shaky breath, aware that the meds were already filtering into her bloodstream. She felt detached, a little fuzzy headed. She'd never taken two pills at one time. Stupid thing to do. Billy was waiting for her call.

She stumbled out of the stall to the sink to splash water on her face. The woman who stared back at her in the mirror looked glassy eyed and unreliable. And unbruised.

Overnight, the bruise on her cheek had almost disappeared.

Chapter 20

Billy's mobile rang as the elevator doors opened onto the CJC's mezzanine floor.

"Where do you want to meet?" he said to Frankie, as he walked along the mezzanine railing. Below him people crowded the atrium, waiting for their court cases to be called.

"Something's come up," she said.

She sounded off her feet. A ten-hour night shift takes it out of you.

"You hungry? How about if you do what you have to do, and we'll meet at the Arcade. I have photos to show you."

"I can't. A friend had surgery and I may have to stay with her."

A kid ran through the atrium, screeching his head off. The sound bounced off the ceiling and fed back over the phone.

"Can't we—"

"It'll have to wait," she said, cutting him off.

A woman from below laughed and clapped her hands. He looked down as the echo amplified over the phone. Suddenly Frankie came into view, walking quickly away from the stairwell door and through the crowd, her phone to her ear.

"Where are you?" he asked, incredulous.

"At the Baptist East Hospital in the lobby. I'm about to take an elevator."

The elevator in the atrium binged. The doors opened, and people maneuvered their way out. The last person was a heavyset woman, her arms wrapped around a cardboard box. She glanced about as if uncertain of which way to go. Frankie, almost to the bank of elevators, stopped dead, as if poleaxed by the sight of the woman with the box.

"Hold on," she whispered and stepped behind a concrete pillar. The woman, casting about, got her bearings and made her way toward the main exit. She stopped briefly to speak to Dave Jansen, a detective Billy knew from the burglary squad.

Frankie peered from behind the column, tracking the woman's progress. Not only was she lying to him, she was acting weird as hell.

"Sorry to leave you hanging," she said in a husky voice.

"How about giving me a quick rundown on what you found on Davis and Lucy. We can get into the details later."

"I'll have to get back with you. Bye." She ducked from behind the pillar and headed for the back exit.

Mystified, he took out a pad and made a note of Jansen's name.

Chapter 21

The curved awning that shaded the Rock of Ages Funeral Home entrance rippled in the breeze as Billy pulled into the parking lot. Back in Memphis two days, he'd split with Mercy, Red and Little Man were dead, and Augie had dropped an unsolvable mystery in his lap concerning his mother's death. It hadn't been much of a vacation.

A couple of years ago he'd noticed a pair of high heels in a downtown crosswalk positioned as if the woman who'd been wearing them had stepped off the curb and was snatched away. He'd considered whether the Rapture had taken her, her shoes being the only parts of her that remained. He felt the same befuddlement now, as if cosmic forces were at work and he had not properly studied for the test.

Augie's messages asked him to come to the casket room, where he'd be making arrangements for Davis and Lucy. The only funeral arrangements Billy had ever made were for his uncle Kane, the man who'd raised him after his mother's car crash. Billy worked in his uncle's Mississippi roadside diner after school until he'd left for Ole Miss, graduating with a degree in criminal justice. At his uncle's urging, he'd entered law school.

After one semester, he'd known drafting briefs and representing creeps would not be his life's passion. An early brush with injustice and racism in a case concerning the murder of two little black girls had compelled him to become a cop. He wanted a career hunting down the bad guys. The last conversation he had with his uncle Kane was on the day he'd left law school and signed up for police academy training. His uncle never forgave him for failing to raise the family's standards by becoming a professional. Billy made a decision about what was right for his life that resulted in the last living member of his family cutting him off. He never had a chance to see his uncle again.

Walking down the hall, Augie's high-octane voice jarred against the mortuary's padded silence and guided Billy to the room full of backlit caskets. He found Augie talking with an angular young man in an ill-fitting suit and narrow glasses, who was scribbling on a clipboard. Augie flung his hand toward the heavy-gauge copper burial box that was showcased in the center of the room. Only the slight upcurve of the young man's mouth betrayed his pleasure at having such a big fish on the line. The copper casket would easily run eight thousand.

"Write it down," Augie said and jabbed the man's pad with his finger. He knocked the pad to the floor, swept it up, and handed it back. "Go on, write it, *write* it. I want forty dozen red roses. Not the cheap kind—long-stem, first-class." Augie's lips drew back in an exaggerated grin, his eyes blinking. He wore a suit jacket and faded shorts that had a rip in the seat the size of a fist. His neon-orange flip-flops screamed against the room's quiet setting.

Before leaving the barge that morning, Billy had read that the effectiveness of antipsychotics could decline over time and trigger a return of psychosis. At first he'd accepted that as a reason for Augie's behavior, but then changed his mind. It was more likely that Augie had dropped his meds, ignoring the paranoia and manic swings, in order to have the energy to investigate his mother's death. Yesterday he'd nearly trampled those kids. Today he looked like a madman. He was going to get hurt or hurt someone else if he didn't straighten up.

Inspecting the casket was an older man Billy recognized—Sid Garrett, a longtime civil rights trial lawyer and social activist. Used to the limelight, Garrett commanded attention with his silvery hair, swept back from his face, and a profile like the painting of George Washington crossing the Delaware. He'd written a *New York Times* best seller about the civil rights struggle, detailing the underhanded tactics J. Edgar Hoover had used against the movement's leaders. During his TV book tour, Garrett's skillful manipulation of other guests had turned his flyby interviews into regular commentary slots on the political talk show circuit.

Billy had first come into contact with Sid Garrett as a patrol cop when he'd been dispatched to a downtown parking lot for shots fired. He found Garrett lying facedown on the sidewalk with a bullet in his back. The shooter, a suicidal client, was sitting in a nearby car, a gun in his hand and the back of his head blown off.

The bullet in Garrett's spine left him with a pronounced limp and in constant pain. After recovering, he'd retired from his civil rights law practice and opened a refuge for homeless men with addiction issues. Garrett had dedicated Robert House to the memory of his older brother, Robert Garrett, who had been martyred during the civil rights upheaval.

Billy was aware of two muscular young men standing in the corner, watching Garrett with the intensity of Dobermans. After barely surviving the shooting, Garrett had recruited residents from the shelter's roster and trained them to watch his back.

Hiring bodyguards was extreme, but it was Garrett's way of dealing with the trauma of being shot. He certainly had the bucks to pay for it.

Augie grabbed Billy's hand and began pumping it at an alarming rate. "Good to see you. We're going to miss those two guys, huh?" he said, overbright and grinning. "Did you see the caskets we've picked out? Pieces of art."

Garrett, leaning heavily on a cane, angled himself between Billy and Augie as a way to prevent Billy's hand from being wrung off.

"Detective Able," Garrett said. "Pleasure to see you under better circumstances. The last time we met, I believe I was face-down on concrete." The corners of his mouth lifted, his dry wit covering his pain.

"I'm glad to see you've recovered, sir."

"Thank you, Detective. But this is a sadder story. Davis and Lacy lived at the shelter for a time. Fine men. Such a loss. I wanted to give Augie a hand with the arrangements."

"I'm curious. Are you aware of any problems Red or Little Man might have had with your residents?" Billy asked.

Garrett frowned. "Why? Is there a question concerning their manner of death?"

Typical defense lawyer. Garrett didn't like a cop asking questions about his residents.

He gave Garrett a disarming smile. "I just wondered why they would leave a clean bed and three squares a day at Robert House. Your shelter has a first-rate reputation."

"Our sobriety rule may have played into their decision." Garrett's closed expression told Billy that if he wanted more answers, he'd have to get them himself.

The funeral director hovered nearby. "Mr. Poston, we have a

fine selection of burial suits. Or are you bringing clothes for the deceased?"

"Tuxedoes," Augie blurted out. "We'll suit the guys up like Fred Astaire."

Garrett stole a glance at Billy.

"I'm sure they would appreciate this amazing send-off," Billy said, "but the New Orleans Musicians Relief Fund could sure use a hand. Have you considered picking less expensive caskets?"

Augie's euphoria evaporated. "We could play canned music. Bury the guys in pine boxes. Shit, man. I can afford ten of those copper caskets and still cover the musicians fund for a year."

Billy bit back a response and went for humor. "Okay, Augie, it's your funeral. By the way, I have some information for you. Let's find a quiet place to talk."

"Sure. Great. I'm about finished here."

"Go ahead," Garrett said with a subtle nod. "I'll take care of the suits."

Chapter 22

They found a sitting room awash in the rose-colored lighting that funeral homes use to flatter the dearly departed. Augie dropped into a wingback chair. His fingers compulsively brushed the face of one of his favorite watches—a vintage Bulova with a bright green band, its inner workings visible through the crystal.

Augie had always been meticulous about hygiene. Today his hair hung in greasy strands from under his cap, and he smelled like onions and dirty socks. He was definitely deteriorating. This conversation needed to be quick and gentle.

"We're dealing with two pertinent pieces of the physical evidence in your mom's case," Billy began. "There's the wire inside the gas tank, and there's the split fuel line. Either one could have caused the explosion."

"I know that," Augie said.

"Let's start with the wire. Number one. A screwup on the assembly line could have put the wire in the tank, but that's not likely. Number two. Someone dropped the wire in the tank and left part of it dangling outside to intimidate her. It's an old trick. Gangs still use it to make their target believe a car is booby-trapped. Number three. Someone ran the wire from the brake lights to the tank. Hit the brakes, the lights spark, the tank blows. Detective Travis specifically searched for evidence of the wire running to the tank. He found none."

"I don't believe that," Augie said.

"Let's keep moving and talk about the ruptured gas line. Any part of that Pontiac's fuel system could've been defective, caused the explosion, and split the line. Or the line could have split and blown the fuel system. Unfortunately, the fire destroyed the chassis, so we'll never know. There's no definitive proof that someone intentionally tried to kill your mother. I combed through that file. Let me repeat, there is no proof. If your journalist friend says there is, he's playing you."

"By that you mean he's after money." Augie's tone had turned poisonous.

"Try cutting off the money, see what you get."

"My guy has more evidence. I've seen it."

"Is it evidence about the fire or is it about your mom's politics?"

Augie puffed up. "Tell me this. If a white woman were barbecued on the front seat of her car, you think the cops would close the case after a week?"

That set him back a notch. If Red had been a white man, Dunsford would have handled the scene quite differently.

"Travis was a top investigator," he said. "After King's assassination, the brass might have tried to pressure him into fast-tracking the case, but the ME's conclusion would have been the same. There was no other way to rule it—accident due to mechanical failure."

He watched Augie shut down, disappear inside himself. No

doubt he'd heard insults and racial slurs thrown at his mom when he was a kid. He'd been powerless to do anything at the time. But he wasn't a kid now.

"You fucker," Augie muttered, coming back to himself. He turned a mean eye on Billy. "You're with them, aren't you?"

"I'm not with anyone. All I can do is interpret the contents of the file. I can't interview the principles in the case; they're all dead." His mobile rang. He checked the screen. It was Frankie.

"My guy says there's more," Augie barked, and thumped his fist on the chair's upholstered arm.

Billy was getting annoyed, and he didn't have the patience to watch Augie unravel again. "I need to take this," he said and strode down the hall to the rear entrance.

When he stepped outside, the heat hit him like exhaust out of the backside of a bus. He answered the call. "How's your sick friend?" He heard the slight intake of Frankie's breath.

"She's better. I've got information from New Orleans. When can we meet?" Her voice had a strange burr to it. He thought about the way she'd skulked behind the pillar, looking panicked.

"Come to the barge in a couple of hours. Call me when you get there."

They hung up. He was still pissed about her lying, even if she had a reason. Maybe she wanted to come by to explain. Still, she'd lied.

A black limousine pulled to a stop under the awning. A young woman with cappuccino-colored skin slipped out of the rear door. She wore a cream-colored suit with a brimmed hat pulled low so all he caught was a glimpse of high cheekbones, a slant of almond-shaped eye, and the corner of a rich mouth.

The woman spoke with the driver then moved up the walk

with the fluidity of youth, entering the mortuary, seeming to be oblivious to his presence. She brought to mind Mercy's lean, graceful body.

Then it hit him. The question he hadn't wanted to face. Was Mercy in love with another man? He squinted in the sun, the awning lifting in the breeze, the crape myrtles fanning themselves. Even the shadow of a possibility of another man irked him. He'd watched his mother walk out on him. His uncle Kane had cut him off. Lou committed suicide and left the job of discovering the body to him. Now Mercy. Had she betrayed him, too?

The last thing he wanted to do was deal with Augie, but there was no way around it. He followed the young woman inside and tracked down Augie, standing with Garrett among rows of folding chairs in a quietly formal viewing room. A tea table stood in the middle of the room with a caddie of china cups and a silver samovar for tea. Augie was waving a card about as he spoke to Garrett. Garrett was attempting to catch a glimpse of it, even reaching out to take the card as Augie slipped it into his pocket. Irritation flashed over Garrett's face. It was probably a quote Augie had requested of the astronomical funeral costs. Garrett may have let himself get roped into splitting them, not knowing what he was in for. It's always a risk to volunteer.

"Augie, I need to speak with you," Billy said as he walked in.

Garrett's expression neutralized the moment he realized they had an audience, but it was obvious he was still upset. His hand went to his silver hair, smoothing back the swoop from his forehead. "I must leave you now. I've called in a favor to get a mention on the next CBS's *Sunday Morning*'s hail and farewell list." Giving Billy a nod on his way out, he left.

Augie stood among the rows of chairs, shifting his weight side to side, his pupils jittering like an electrical storm was crackling through his brain. Billy knew this was a bad time to approach Augie, but he had to say his piece.

"You're off your meds. Don't deny it, because I know you are. It's a bad decision for you and everyone associated with you."

Augie's mouth jerked. "You're wrong. Wrong, wrong, wrong."

"Remember how you wrecked my truck? You almost went to jail. You promised me that you'd never drop off again."

"You bastard," Augie yelled. He kicked out, sending a chair flying into the wall. He kicked a second chair that closed on his foot and hopped until he flung it into the tea table, the samovar and teacups crashing to the floor.

"You searched my place! You stripped my bed, tore up my garbage," Augie wailed. "You're one of them." He regained his balance and dropped into an aggressive stance, teeth bared as if ready to attack.

Billy raised his fists. "You crazy jerk. Come at me and I'll knock your nutty ass into next week."

"Gentlemen," Sid Garrett barked from the doorway.

Augie wheeled to Garrett and pointed at Billy. "Throw this asshole out of the building. We can't trust him."

Garrett blinked with surprise, taking in the smashed table and teacups. He looked past Augie to Billy, expecting an explanation.

Billy threw up his hands and trudged by Garrett. "I've had it. Get a bucket of ice water and stick this lunatic's head in it."

As he passed the director's office, he noticed the young woman in the cream-colored suit now seated at the director's desk, her legs crossed and her head bowed beneath the hat.

The director was leaning forward, patting her hand.

Chapter 23

Frankie parked on the cobblestone landing as the eighty-foot stern-wheeler the *Memphis Queen II* passed behind Billy's barge. She pulled off her shades to watch the fifty or so people from kids to grannies, all wearing the same style of straw hat, as they lined up along the top deck's railing. They waved at no one in particular as the boat glided through the slack water with the Memphis skyline slipping by them. She turned off the engine and phoned Billy to let him know she was out front. A little disoriented, she gathered up her files, stepped onto the rocky cobblestones, and lost her balance. The pills. The damned pills had added a sheen to her vision. She'd taken a cold shower before driving over, drunk two espressos, and stuffed down turkey and cheese in an attempt to counteract the effects of the pills. Light-headed, disconnected, mortified, it was a ridiculous way to approach a meeting that could influence her entire career.

And she'd lied to Billy. She never lied. What was she going to do about that?

She shivered despite the heat.

When she was six, she'd stolen a necklace made of blue stones from her mother's jewelry box and hidden it under her pillow.

She reasoned that the tooth fairy would bring her mother back in exchange for the blue necklace. When the necklace was still under her pillow the next morning, she'd carried it to the ocean and thrown it in. A week later, her father had asked about the missing necklace. She said she knew nothing about it. That afternoon he paid the cook for the week and told her to never come back. The cook had begged for her job, cried; she had five kids, no husband. Frankie witnessed the whole thing, but she'd kept her mouth shut. After seeing that, she knew what her father would do if she admitted she'd lied.

She'd read that mistakes are made by people who have no talent for forethought. She believed that with her whole heart. Lying to Billy had been a mistake, a big one. She would like to change it by confessing, but if she explained what had happened, he would write her off. She needed his endorsement to get the spot on the homicide squad, and she couldn't take a chance of losing that.

She looked up at the sound of Billy's footsteps to see him trudging down the ramp, carrying a folder with Red's jacket over his arm. He wore wet cutoffs and a faded blue MPD T-shirt. The water dripping off the edge of the hull told her he'd been hosing down the decks and sweeping them. He had a sense of order. She liked that.

At six feet even, he wasn't an imposing figure, but he emanated a certain physical tension when he moved, like he knew who he was and nobody in their right mind would want to mess with him. He had a cool factor, too, a self-possession. A female detective could learn a lot from that.

He swung open the gate. "Welcome aboard," he said with a remote air she read as tired and a little angry.

Already there was a problem. She slipped on her shades to

cover her glassy eyes and followed him up the ramp. The pàssing riverboat had churned up slack water that smelled of mud and decay. She decided to start with something innocuous.

"The *Queen II* got under way," she said. "The passengers were all wearing the same hats."

He glanced back. "Tour boats book a lot of family reunions."

"All those people are in one family?"

"You must not have a lot of relatives."

"My dad died five years ago. I'm the end of the line."

"At least we've got one thing in common. No family."

One thing? What about they were both cops?

A teak table with a blue-striped umbrella and two glasses of ice water sweating in the heat waited for them on the aft deck. They sat down and swapped files, going over documents in silence. She looked up once and caught him watching her. He didn't look pleased.

He finished reviewing background information on Davis and Lacy then picked up the crime-beat article, rereading the part that covered the aggravated assault and property damage charges against the pimp. Toward the bottom was the part about the plaintiffs' no-show at Cool Willy's trial. He laid down the pages.

"Someone jumped me in an alley outside Bardog last night."

"You all right?"

"No harm done. He came from behind. I can't ID him, but he reminded me of the guy we saw outside the squatters' house yesterday."

"You think it was Cool Willy?" she asked.

"I don't know."

"At least we know the instruments were smashed in New Orleans and not here." She crunched some ice. "I don't understand why the guys carried busted instruments all the way up from New Orleans."

He looked at her like she was a member of the unredeemed. "Red had that guitar so long it was a wife to him. Little Man's sax kept him in grits and gravy for forty years. You don't throw away family."

That made no sense. Her dad had once told her, "People who live on train tracks get hit by trains." It seemed like a ridiculous statement at the time until she became a cop. Then she understood what he meant. She dealt with people all day long who made bad decisions, sometimes lethal decisions.

Billy was frowning at her. She decided to drop it.

"I know an ex-cop in New Orleans who does investigative work," she said. "I'll scan the photo of the girl at the piano and send it to him. He'll dig up more detail on Cool Willy and the guys."

"Ask him to check with the company that publishes Red's music. If he has family in Chicago, they deserve the royalties."

"I'm already on that."

Billy squinted at her.

"What? What's the matter?" she said.

"The bruise. It's almost gone."

She resisted putting her hand to her face. "I used a salve."

"What kind of salve does that?"

"It's . . . I got it from Ramos yesterday."

"The witch doctor?"

"He's a respected psychologist. I sent you his profile."

"He's a witch doctor."

She knew better than to take the bait. He wanted her to defend Ramos. Then he would toy with her.

"Look at this." She laid the conjure bag on the table between them and launched into an explanation of the bag's distribution on the Internet. Ramos used the same bags. From the size and depth of his pharmacy, she was willing to bet he stocked the simple components that would match the bag's contents. Billy shifted in his chair, listening. Next she told him about the shelter's group photo that had included Ramos, Davis, and Lacy. That got his attention.

"I've booked a therapy session with him tomorrow at one. It's the best way for me to go back in."

He sat silent for a moment. "While you're there, maybe you should talk out some of your own problems."

She lowered her sunglasses and stared at him over the tops. "That was a bullshit statement."

"When you called, you said you were at Baptist East Hospital with a sick friend. You were actually at the CJC."

He raised his eyebrows, expectant.

Her mouth went dry, but she held it together. She wasn't about to ask how he knew. "I had a confrontation with a woman in one of the squad rooms. No yelling, but it was intense. I was rattled."

"Was it connected to an arrest?"

"It was personal. I got away from her and took the stairs to the lobby. Then I called you. You answered as she came off the elevator. I was afraid that if she saw me, she'd start up again."

She felt sick with the memory of ducking behind a pillar. She'd told the story about a friend in the hospital as a means to gain sympathy. No way could she have faced Billy stoned on pills.

"So why lie about it?" he asked.

Because she'd messed around with another woman's husband, and now the man was dead. *Because she was ashamed down to her toenails.* She could never admit such a stupid mistake. She wondered if he knew that, too.

There was nothing else to do. She lied again. "I don't know why I did it. I guess I got flustered."

He looked surprised, then a grin escaped him. "What did you expect from the woman? Hair snatching? Fit pitching?"

Oh, Jesus, she thought. *Just like a man. Always up for a cat-fight.*

"No more trouble, I promise."

"How do you know?" he asked.

"It won't happen again."

He regarded her, elbows on the arms of his chair, his fingers steepled in front of his face. He left her hanging while a tugboat chugged by, its diesel engine a constant rumble across the water. On the new bridge, truck tires clicked across expansion joints.

She waited.

He pulled a small notebook from his pocket. "Let's get started."

He told her about Augie's two-thousand-dollar loan. A business deal, he'd called it. A recording contract? Maybe. Money and murder go together, but they didn't have enough facts to connect the two.

Next, he spread the jacket on the table and turned back the collar to point out the initials L.G. sewn into the felt backing. She flipped open the jacket's panel and ran her finger over the satiny label. She noticed that both breast pockets had been sewn closed and then clipped open.

"I found these inside the right pocket," he said, and handed her a stack of three-by-five images, all urban settings. Some of the black males had Afros. Some of the whites had muttonchops and mustaches. The women wore their hair parted down the middle and ironing-board straight. A few shots allowed for a glimpse of miniskirts.

Frankie passed through the photos a couple of times, focused on drawing conclusions. "The locations seem familiar." She pointed to a slice of an overhead sign. "That's a movie marquee." She shuffled through some more. "The fire hydrant is a good marker. I think I've seen that doorjamb."

She laid four photos in a square and put a fifth off to the right. "There's tension in these people's faces. Look at the body language. They don't want to be caught talking to these guys in suits who must be state or federal law enforcement. The one in glasses is wearing this jacket. Look at the slant of that outer pocket. Very distinctive."

"Good," he said.

She restacked the photos, pleased with herself, and started to count them out. "I get thirteen."

"No, there's fourteen total."

She counted again and got the same. He pawed through his file and shuffled papers. They looked under the table. He went inside then came out and walked to the rail. The tree line on the Arkansas side of the river had darkened into silhouette.

"No luck?" she asked.

He appeared to be watching traffic on the new bridge. By the set of his jaw, she knew he was furious.

"Do you know what happened to it?" she asked.

"I have a pretty good idea."

Chapter 24

"H ot as Hades out here, ya'll. Cold beer . . . cold Cokes." The hawker leaned in to snag the twenty being passed over to him. "You *know* what it is," he called. "You *know* what it is." The hawker had freckled skin and grizzled red hair, whale-shaped eyes shut tight at the corners. A scar ran beneath the pouch of his left eye. His upper arms were thick with muscle, and his body was agile, making it hard to pin down his age. He passed drinks over the heads of the fans in front of Billy.

Billy sat eight rows up and to the right of the visitors' dugout at AutoZone Park, home of the AAA minor league Redbirds. Whiffs of barbecued nachos floated through the stands. Overhead, the evening sky softened into a curved slice of pale blue.

In baseball there's a winner and a loser. You're safe, or you're out. Nothing in his life had been that clear-cut since Lou died.

The scoreboard showed the Tacoma Rainiers ahead by one. The Redbirds were at bat in the bottom of the second. The batter scuffed the dirt then spat in his batting gloves and clapped his hands together. He was putting on a show, more for the fans than for the left-handed pitcher. He swung late at the pitch and lifted the ball along the first-base line, a curving foul that arced into the

dugout section where Billy sat. Everyone, including Billy, jumped
to their feet with their hands up. In the aisle the hawker whipped
a glove from under his box, reached over a couple of people, and
snagged the ball. In one fluid motion, he fired the ball to the first
baseman as if completing a cutoff play. Then with a quiet smile
he stowed his glove under the box and continued down the steps.

"Cold beer . . . cold Cokes."

This guy was no fan, Billy thought. He knew his way around
a ball field.

In baseball you move up or you move on. The problem is,
some folks can't move on. Augie had made that point a couple
of hours ago at Rock of Ages. For the hawker, that meant selling
beer at the ballpark so he could still yell at the umps and catch
foul balls. Billy was afraid Augie wouldn't let go, either. He was
about to drive the good things out of his life in pursuit of answers
about his mother's death he could never find.

It was hard to believe Augie had stolen one of the photographs. He must have taken it when J.J. made that ruckus at the
door at Bardog. The photo was evidence in a possible homicide.
Augie knew that. Now Billy would have to confront him and get
the photograph back, which could be very messy depending on
Augie's state of mind at the time.

Warm air blew off the field and into the stands. Two solo
homers put the Redbirds up by one at the bottom of the third.
The crowd hooted and clapped, humiliating the Rainiers' ace
pitcher. He whipped one high and inside to the next batter, a
little chin music.

Billy preferred AAA ball to the animal-like proficiency of the
major league players. He liked watching these guys play their
hearts out for a chance to move up to the majors. AAA was still
a field of dreams.

He thought about Frankie. She wanted to skip the years in burglary and jump straight to homicide. She dreamed of moving to the majors and wanted him to help her get there.

But Mz. Police Goddess was sitting on a big damned secret and hadn't trusted him enough to bring it up. With one call to Dave Jansen, he could find out about the woman at the CJC, but what was the point? A partner who can't be honest with herself wouldn't be honest with him. He'd been down that road.

On the other hand, she had a damned fine detective's eye. Her analysis of the photos was impressive, and she'd thought to count the pictures. A touch of compulsion was valuable in this business. However, loyalty was essential.

The twenty-four-foot-tall digital screen flashed photos and stats of the players while the sound system switched between ballpark organ music and classic rock and roll. The kiss cam cut to the crowd, flashing live shots of couples on the screen. The announcer encouraged them to show a little love. Some couples kissed. One woman pointed at the man beside her and mouthed, "He's my brother."

The camera panned past a familiar face, swung back, and locked in. Billy's stomach lurched. Augie's sullen face loomed on the screen, his ball cap hanging cockeyed off his head. Billy scoured the stands and finally spotted him four rows up, at the club level. He was in the aisle, faced off with a teenage hawker who had a popcorn tray slung around his neck. The kid looked panicked, searching for a way to escape. Something bad was happening, and Billy couldn't get there in time to stop it.

"We have a celebrity here tonight," the announcer boomed. "The Redbirds' own Augie Poston, who went on to be the greatest catcher ever to play for the Saint Louis Cards."

The camera zoomed in. A cheer went up with the crowd's

recognition of their old hero, the man who'd led the Redbirds minor league team to three championships.

"Hey, hey, Augie," the announcer called.

"HEY, HEY, AUGIE," the crowd repeated.

"Hey, hey, Augie, give us a smile!" The camera pulled back as Augie shoved the kid's shoulders, upending him onto the laps of the people seated on the aisle. Popcorn flew everywhere, like a scene out of a slapstick movie. A burly guy grabbed Augie from behind to stop him from going after the kid a second time.

"Go to camera four," the announcer choked into his mike. "Cut to commercial, damn it. Now!"

Music blasted through the speakers as two security guards ran down the steps toward Augie. The screen flipped to blue, followed by the image of a Ford pickup flying through the air.

Dumbstruck fans watched as the guards wrestled Augie up the steps with him fighting all the way. Halfway up, a woman on the aisle threw her drink in Augie's face. Another dumped a bucket of popcorn on his head. The crowd erupted in whistles and catcalls.

Billy knew park management wouldn't escalate the situation by calling the cops, but they would toss Augie out on his ass. Augie would then go ballistic and do something else just as crazy.

Familiar with the ballpark's back corridors, he ran down a flight of steps to a side door that exited onto the street. A group of kids were out in front of the stadium, staring through the courtyard's iron bars. Billy hurried over, knowing they must be watching Augie.

One guard had a hand on Augie's shoulder while the other patted him down from behind for weapons. Satisfied, the second guard shoved Augie toward the gate and kept shoving until Augie staggered through the turnstile onto the brick apron in front of the ticket office and stood with his head hanging. He could've been a drunk. He could've been a pervert. He could've been a whack job. He looked like anything but a sports hero.

The guard hollered through the gate at his back. "Ya bum. You were great. Now you're an embarrassment."

"Ya bum," echoed one of the kids on the sidewalk.

"HEY, HEY, Augie. HEY, HEY, Augie, HEY, HEY, Augie," the gang jeered, and ran past him laughing.

Billy watched in horror as Augie came to life and took a roundhouse swing at the nearest kid. He barely missed. The kid jumped sideways and ran up the street, checking over his shoulder to see if Augie was coming after him.

Augie was still a powerful man. It would have been a hell of a wallop if he had connected.

He'd wrecked Billy's uncle's Chevy pickup and occasionally got out of hand in public, but Billy could live with those downsides of his condition. Taking a swing at a kid? That took Augie from mentally ill to dangerous.

Teeth gritted, he walked toward Augie. "What the hell? You just tried to deck a twelve-year-old."

Augie glanced around as if bewildered to find that he was standing on the street. "I didn't do that."

"You did, asshole," Billy shouted. Tourists walking by stopped to watch. "You're losing it. You're breaking down."

"Get off my back," Augie shouted, and stomped toward the taco cart stationed at the corner.

Billy yelled after him, "You'll never get back in this ballpark. Or any other park."

Augie turned around, stricken. "You've never screwed up? What about that little girl . . . Rebecca Jane? The judge almost beat her to death because of you."

The girl's name startled him into silence. Shame, adrenaline, cold outrage surged through him. "This is about you, jerk-ass, not me and not Lou. You're a nutcase, a waste of skin."

Augie's features sagged. He wheeled around to go and instead smashed into the side of the taco cart. The cart rocked. The vendor grabbed the handle and overcorrected it. Hot cheese sauce spilled down Augie's bare legs. He yelped in pain and snatched off his cap to squeegee the steaming cheese off his shins.

The vendor began yelling in Spanish and pointed at Augie. "*Su culpa! Su culpa!* His fault!"

"Oh, shit. Hang on, Poston," Billy said, rushing toward Augie.

"No," Augie spat. "No, no, no." He dropped his cap, reached for a Fanta bottle on the cart, and smashed the glass bottom on the cart's leg. Suddenly Augie was pointing the jagged end toward Billy, his eyes hooded and empty of awareness.

Billy stepped back, hands raised. "Put that down, bud," he said, struggling to keep his voice even.

Augie waved the bottle in front of him and lunged. Billy took a step back and felt for his SIG, forgetting he wasn't carrying.

Augie dropped low and charged. Billy sidestepped and shoved Augie hard as he passed. Augie tripped, barreled forward, and crashed headfirst into a lamppost. His knees collapsed under him, and he hit the ground, rolling onto his side. He pulled himself up to crawl to the curb and sat with his head in his hands.

The cop in Billy took over. He kicked the bottle out of reach and squatted on his heels beside Augie, examining under the streetlight the goose egg already beginning to bulge on his forehead. Could be a simple hematoma, could be an internal brain bleed.

"We're going to The MED and get you checked."

Augie leered. He swung a wild punch that caught Billy on the side of the mouth and knocked him on his butt.

Hand on his throbbing lip, he struggled to his feet, feeling like the parent of a self-destructive kid. At some point you can't protect them or yourself. You watch helplessly as they destroy everything reasonable in life.

"First stop is The MED," Billy said. "Then we're going to your place and get the photo you stole from me. Then you and me, we're done."

Augie got to his feet, suddenly seeming steady. He was swimming in his own waters now, a momentary return to sanity. "I may be a waste of skin, but I have something to prove. I'll do whatever it takes to get there."

A cab cruised up the street. Billy waved it down, but Augie was already striding away. He was having none of it.

Son of a bitch, Billy thought. *That's enough.* He wasn't about to drag Augie to the ER.

"This isn't over," he called out, thinking about the photo.

Augie turned and shot him the finger. "Like you said, Able, we're done. I got business to handle."

Augie's phone rang. He dug it out of his pocket and walked into the muggy darkness.

Chapter 25

At a quarter to eight the next morning, Billy parked the Turismo in the back parking lot of Augie's apartment building.

After years of obscurity, the DeVoy building had become a premier residence in downtown Memphis. Top architectural firm Kichline & Crockett had seen to the building's high-end renovation, starting with new glass facades and installing marble and mahogany flooring throughout the lobby. Several of John Torina's giant, moody agricultural landscapes hung in the public spaces, and handblown fixtures and wall sconces doubled as sculptural art. The building's opulence attracted couples eager to escape their mini-mansions in the suburbs, bond traders who were looking to upgrade their image, and Grizzlies basketball players on the prowl for downtown nightlife.

Augie had signed a three-year lease for a ninth-floor penthouse. He paid top dollar for the wall of windows in his living room with a skybox view of neighboring AutoZone Park and for the privacy of having only one other tenant on his floor.

Billy entered one of three elevators and tapped in the security code for the ninth floor. He carried with him two cups of coffee from Denny's and a bag of cathead biscuits with sausage—an excuse to drop by, apologize, and make sure Augie was all right. He had texted Augie twice the night before, asking if he was dizzy or nauseous. Augie had responded both times with "FU." This morning he hadn't responded at all.

Billy had a fat lip and a swollen cheek thanks to Augie's sucker punch, but he figured the knot on Augie's head looked worse. They both deserved a whooping for fighting like kids in a school yard. Augie wouldn't see it that way, but that was all right. They'd both been in the wrong. After a restless night, Billy knew he would stand by his friend no matter what.

And there was the photo Augie had lifted. An explanation would be good to hear, but if nothing else, he damn sure expected to get the photograph back.

The elevator door slid open. He walked down the quiet hall to Augie's apartment, surprised to find the door standing partially opened. He waited, not wanting to startle Augie, expecting him to walk into the entry at any moment. On the back wall, lights shone on the four-by-five-foot painting Augie had commissioned, a head-on portrait of him staring through a catcher's mask. His green eyes penetrated the bars of the mask with an expression as intense as a samurai warrior's. The painting was hanging crooked on the wall, as if someone had knocked it off-kilter.

Billy's heart began to thud. This felt wrong.

"Hey, Augie," he called. No answer.

He put the coffee and bag of biscuits on the floor of the entry, pulled his SIG and held it barrel up as he moved into the entrance. At the edge of the doorway that led into the living area, he peeked around the frame, checking for assailants or anything unusual in the room.

The place had been tossed—sofa cushions thrown around,

bookcase doors hanging open, a lamp knocked over, papers scattered, and drawers upended.

"Augie!" he called. The apartment was silent.

For half a second he tried to convince himself Augie had gotten drunk and torn up the place, but he knew better. He moved in quickly and began clearing the room.

"Augie. Hey, man, where are you?" he yelled, louder this time.

A granite-topped island separated the kitchen from the living area. There was a half-eaten sandwich on a plate beside the sink. Across the top of the counter he saw the refrigerator door standing open, the interior light glowing. On the tile floor to the left of the island he saw Augie's orange flip-flops.

Then he saw bare feet.

Stretched out on his side in front of the refrigerator, his right arm raised overhead like a swimmer's stroke, Augie's face was turned so his glazed eyes peered out from beneath his arm. The side of his face and back of his skull were caved in, hair matted with blood, white bone showing through. Blood spattered the cabinets and walls. Bloody handprints streaked the floor where he'd struggled to get up. The coagulated pool under his head and shoulders was dark and shiny, like blackberry jelly, its consistency and coppery smell indicating that Augie had been dead for hours. His body said, *Look at me. Look what was done to me.*

A buzz picked up inside Billy's head. His vision narrowed to a murky green light, as if he and Augie were floating at the bottom of a pond. He bent to touch Augie's fingers. They were cold.

Professional detachment slipped away. Augie was no anonymous victim. He was a member of Billy's tribe, and he had suffered. It took all of Billy's will to back away and tuck his weapon at his back.

He pulled his phone and was calling dispatch when he heard

footsteps coming down the apartment's back hall. With great purpose, he laid the phone on the counter, pulled his weapon, and trained it on the doorway. James Freeman walked in. His gaze went first to Billy then to the SIG.

"What the hell," Freeman said, his brain registering the sight of the weapon.

Billy leveled the gun at his chest. "Hands over your head. On the floor. *Now.*"

Freeman raised both hands, his own phone clutched in his right one. Reluctantly, he knelt on the tile floor. He was unshaven, wearing gray sweats and a shirt with the sleeves rolled up. He showed no evidence of blood spatter and no obvious wounds.

Freeman glared at Billy. "Don't shoot me, you son of a bitch. I've called the cops. They'll be here any minute."

"Shut up," he yelled and frisked Freeman one-handed, adrenaline fueling his movements. He yanked Freeman's hands behind his back, rougher than he had to be, and cuffed him with the flex cuffs he always carried, squeezing hard for the last notch. Freeman grunted as Billy dragged him over to the oven, yanked off his belt to run it through the oven's handle then through Freeman's arms, leaving him kneeling on the floor with his arms hiked up behind his back.

His training kicked in. He left the kitchen to move from room to room with his weapon drawn, checking closets, showers, and under the beds. An assailant could still be in the apartment. There could be more victims. He was responsible for securing the scene until someone on duty showed up. And strangely enough, he was responsible for Freeman's safety until relieved of it.

He went into Augie's bedroom. It had been ripped apart in the same haphazard manner as the living area. Pros don't jerk out drawers and throw clothes around. They work from the bottom drawer up, very neat and quiet. Only kids or amateurs would destroy a room in this manner. Or someone who wanted to create a cover.

The sheets on Augie's bed were white with red trim, the Cardinals' redbird with bat insignia embroidered in the middle of the pillowcases. One pillowcase had been stripped off, probably to carry loot. Billy noticed the empty watch trays on top of the dresser. Augie's vintage watches—every one of them was gone.

Augie was gone.

Grief flowed through him like anesthesia, leaving him addled and numb. He wanted to go to the kitchen, hold his friend and cry, but that would contaminate the scene. He leaned on the dresser, gathering his wits. Freeman was the obvious suspect, but he had to keep an open mind and work the scene, see the evidence for what it was. He wasn't on the force. Middlebrook wouldn't let him work the case. And after the fight with Augie last night, he would be a suspect, but once he got that cleared up, he could sign on and assist in the investigation.

In the kitchen, he found Freeman on his knees, sweat dripping from his forehead, his gaze fixed on Augie's battered corpse. Beneath the stubble his face had gone pallid. Was it grief, or guilt triggering the response?

He walked past Freeman to the body. He recognized the murder weapon, trapped between Augie and the refrigerator. It was the bat Augie had used when he hit his two hundredth homer. He had it bronzed and inscribed with the date. He kept it in his living room, leaning against the bookcase.

The bat had been a weapon of opportunity. Whatever else happened here, the murder had not been planned.

He forced himself to visualize the assault—Augie standing in front of the refrigerator, about to reach inside for a cold one. The first blow landed on the side of his head as he turned. The second shattered the back of his skull. Already going down, he'd raised his right arm to ward off the attack, evidenced by the compound fracture of the radius bone poking through the skin of his forearm. Out of a blind survival reflex, Augie had struggled to get up and slipped in his own blood. More blows. The attack had been overkill, fed by anger or passion.

He squatted by the body for a closer look, the lump from hitting the lamppost still visible. Augie's ghost floated in the kitchen, chiding him, his dead eye watching.

Billy moved to stand over Freeman, making him strain to look up.

"Did he suffer?" Freeman asked. A whiff of stale alcohol lifted off his sweating head.

"Yeah, Augie suffered. Turn around." He unbuckled the belt.

Freeman slumped to the floor with his back against the cabinet, the color returning to his face. "Augie came home last night around ten. We talked in the hallway."

"What were you doing in the hall?"

Freeman blinked. "I live here. I own the damned building." He gave Billy a superior look, letting the information sink in.

"What did you talk about?"

"The fight the two of you had in front of the ballpark. Augie's face looked bad, like he'd been rammed into a concrete wall."

"He ran into a lamppost."

"I think *you* ran him into a lamppost."

"We had a disagreement."

"Your fat lip makes it a fight. He said you got angry, called him names. Why were you so pissed off?"

Good question. Why had he been angry with a man who'd been clearly out of his head? Why hadn't he just dealt with it?

Sirens echoed off downtown buildings. Patrol cops and EMTs would come through the door any minute.

"What's your relationship with Augie?" Billy asked.

Freeman began struggling to his feet. "That's enough bullshit."

Billy pushed down hard on his shoulder. Freeman's ass thudded on the floor. "Answer the question."

Freeman cocked his head to look up. "We're neighbors, okay? Not buddies like the two of you. We didn't drink a six-pack and go out back for a fistfight." He thrust his chin toward the ransacked room. "Augie said you'd threatened him. I think you came here, killed him, then tore up the place to cover your tracks. Or were you looking for something?"

He sized up Freeman. If he took off the cuffs and Freeman tried to run, he'd have an excuse to beat the crap out of him. He'd get a lot of satisfaction out of that. The problem was, Freeman was close to being right. Billy had come here looking for something—the photograph. But he couldn't tell Freeman that. Not yet.

"Tell me about the front door," he said.

"I found it opened. Something is caught underneath. Or didn't you notice?"

Billy went to inspect the door. The lock had not been forced. He'd missed seeing the computer cord snaking across the white marble tiles, its USB connector wedging the door open. He'd seen Augie use a laptop to click through players' stats while he watched a game. Whoever took the laptop had jammed the door as he'd tried to close it.

The DeVoy's security cameras covered the entrance, the lobby, the public elevators, and the service elevators. None was posted in the residential hallways. Access to Augie's floor by elevator required a code. You could exit each floor onto the stairwell and walk down, but you couldn't enter a floor from the stairwell without setting off an alarm. It was as tight as an apartment building could be without compromising the privacy of the residents.

Then there was Freeman to consider. If he owned the building, he had access to Augie's apartment using the building's master key. He could have killed Augie last night and locked the door behind him. This morning he jammed the door open with the cord, creating an excuse to discover the body.

Besides the chaos of the room being tossed, Billy noticed that more than just the laptop and watches were missing. Eight picture hangers hung empty on the wall among a group of twenty photos, and the two brass stands in the bookcase that had held World Series game balls stood empty.

Who did this?

After a few beers at Bardog, Augie had a habit of bragging about buying and selling valuable memorabilia. Billy had noticed barflies listening in. The murder could have started as a simple heist by one of them or even by a casual acquaintance who used a bump key to unlock the door. If Augie had come home early, the guy would have felt trapped in the apartment and whacked Augie from behind. Then he tore up the place looking for loot, grabbed a few things, and ran.

This wasn't about escaping. Too much emotion had fueled the attack. This had been personal.

He walked back in the kitchen. Freeman sat cross-legged on the floor, leaning against the cabinet, his head down.

"Did Augie have clients come here to buy?" Billy asked.

Freeman's head snapped up, hostile. "How the hell would I know?"

"Have you touched anything, moved anything?"

"If you're asking about prints, mine are everywhere. I came last Thursday to watch a Redbirds game. We looked through his latest buys."

The elevator bell dinged. Billy heard heavy footsteps coming down the hall. He pulled his SIG and laid it on the floor.

"Lie facedown. Do whatever they say," he told Freeman.

"Police!" yelled a male voice in the entry.

"In here," Billy called.

Two patrol cops with concrete shoulders and shaved heads tromped through the living area, weapons drawn. Billy didn't know either of them.

He stretched out on the floor beside Freeman, hands over his head. A responding cop's job is to neutralize a scene and apologize later. Billy was in for some short-term humiliation.

He turned his head and found himself staring into Freeman's smirking face.

Chapter 26

The first cop's name tag read JAKES. He cuffed Billy where he lay, frisked him, and secured the SIG. The second cop, Ketty, frisked Freeman then knelt to check Augie for vital signs. He rose slowly, white faced, and shook his head at Jakes. They were young and gung ho. It was likely that neither of them had seen that level of violence taken out on a human being.

Ketty left to move through the apartment, securing the scene. Jakes paced the kitchen, his steel-toed boots clicking on the tiles. Protocol required their next step to be communication with their supervisor.

"I'm Sergeant Detective Billy Able. My MPD identification is in my back pocket," he said to Jakes. "I met with Deputy Chief Middlebrook yesterday. I suggest you make your first call to him."

Jakes pulled the ID. Billy gave him Middlebrook's office number from memory. Jakes called and explained the situation to Middlebrook. He listened, then uncuffed Billy and handed the phone to him.

"What the hell happened?" Middlebrook asked.

"Augie Poston was murdered in his apartment last night. His

neighbor claims to have found him about fifteen minutes ago. He called 911. I came in after him."

"Poston? The ballplayer?" Middlebrook went silent. "Why are you there?"

"We're friends. I stopped by to check on him."

"I assume you weren't involved in his death."

"That's correct, sir."

More silence. "Let me speak with Officer Jakes. I'll follow up with their supervisor and explain the situation."

Jakes took the phone, listened, and hung up. He took the cuffs off Freeman. "Sergeant Able, we need the two of you to sit at opposite ends of that dining table. Don't talk. Don't even look at each other until the investigative team gets here."

The EMTs checked Augie and left. No one to save on this run.

To Billy's dismay, the next person to shuffle in was Dunsford, grumbling and pissed off about catching another goddamn case. He had two flunky detectives from burglary with him. Dunsford saw Billy and came over.

"I heard you were here. I'll do my walk-through with Jakes and Ketty, then we'll talk." He turned to Freeman. "You called in the body. Did you or Able touch or move anything in this apartment?"

"I didn't, but I don't know about Able. He had me cuffed and on the kitchen floor. I couldn't see what he was doing."

"Son of a bitch, Able. You can't stay outta my business." Dunsford squinted at Billy's puffy lip but said nothing.

The CSU techs filed in the door with their kits. An Asian guy clicked off a couple of hundred digital photos. A young woman with a ponytail began dusting the frame on Augie's portrait in the entry. A third said he was going downstairs to process the elevators. During the walk-through, Dunsford shuttled between the back rooms of the apartment and Freeman to ask questions.

"My place is around the corner and down the hall on the left," Freeman told Dunsford. "You'll find two women there, probably still asleep. Thought I should mention it."

Dunsford's eyes rounded. "The hell you say. Two women?"

"It was a late night," Freeman said.

"Jakes, go wake up those broads," Dunsford said. "And keep them apart until we question them."

Dunsford made the right call. Freeman had discovered the body. That made him the number-one suspect. Having Jakes bang on the women's door would rattle them, and they wouldn't have time to match their stories. Their statements could implicate Freeman or themselves, or they might provide Freeman with a solid alibi.

Billy needed that information. As soon as he left the building, he would call a buddy in the squad who could gain access to Dunsford's interview notes and let him know what the women had to say.

He watched Freeman who was sitting at the other end of the table, his gaze scanning the living area, Augie's desk, the book-cases.

"What's missing?" he asked.

Freeman's gaze stayed with Augie's desk. "Augie had a draft of a manuscript written by some journalist. He kept it in a big envelope on his desk. Last night he said he planned to read through the manuscript this morning." Freeman glanced around. "I don't see that envelope, and those papers scattered on the floor aren't formatted like a book."

"Do you know the journalist's name?" Billy asked.

"Augie never would tell me."

"Did he say what the book's about?"

"Civil rights in the sixties. I assume you know Augie was wrapped up in his mother's death. He thought this journalist could help him. His laptop is gone, and look over there . . . his phone is off the charger. There's other stuff missing, valuable stuff. When I went to the back, I noticed his collection of watches is gone."

He wanted to bring up the photograph Augie had lifted at Bardog. Freeman might know where it was stashed, but Billy didn't want to take the risk of Dunsford walking in on the conversation.

The medical examiner arrived with an assistant and began recording the body's condition, the wounds, his clothes, and the bloodstain patterns. The ME mentioned that media was setting up outside the building. The story would go nationwide. There's nothing better for ratings than the flameout of a fallen star.

Supervisor Lieutenant John Carter arrived and took Dunsford aside, their gazes tracking from Freeman to Billy as they talked. He'd thought through his lack of an alibi. No one had seen him after he walked home from the stadium. At least the DeVoy's security cameras would prove he hadn't come here until this morning.

He began to make notes of his actions since he'd arrived. As he wrote, he found himself floating in the detached state exhibited by family members of victims—emotionally blank faces, calm questions asked with a need for precise details. The detached ones would later fall apart far worse than the loved ones who'd lost it at the scene.

The ME's assistants wrapped Augie in a white sheet, lifted

him into a bag, and zipped it closed. Billy checked his watch. Time was 10:22 A.M.

Dunsford came over and spoke to Freeman. "You're going to the CJC with the lieutenant to look through mug shots. Your women friends will come with me. When we're finished here, all three of you will give your statements." Dunsford cleared his throat and spoke to Billy. "Middlebrook let us know you were friends with Poston. Sorry for your loss, but you know the drill. We'll need your statement. I'll be backed up with these interviews the rest of the day. Come in tomorrow at ten. We'll get it out of the way."

Dunsford stuck his hands in his pockets and rocked on his heels. "And you should go . . . now. Leave. And take the stairs." His mouth twitched, getting a kick out of throwing Billy off the scene.

Billy stood. He was itching to work through the evidence, but saying even a word to Dunsford would be a mistake. He nodded to Freeman, then walked to the entry and stopped at Augie's portrait. Fingerprint powder coated the frame. The man in the painting stared at him through the catcher's mask, the warrior, the hero, Billy's friend. That was the Augie Poston he would remember.

"Don't worry, partner," he said quietly. "I'm going to make this right."

Chapter 27

The woman who answered the phone at Robert House spoke with a heavy Jamaican accent. She said Sid Garrett was attending a meeting at the Calvin Carter Museum on Beale Street and would be out the rest of the day. She could leave a message on his mobile. Billy declined and hung up. He wanted to tell Garrett about Augie in person. Death wasn't the kind of news you leave on voice mail. And with the Davis and Lacy funeral at eleven tomorrow, Garrett would have to pick up the slack for Augie.

He decided to leave his car and walk to Beale Street from the DeVoy. A breath of air might lift the heaviness that was beginning to settle in his chest.

Beale Street was once called the Main Street of Negro America. It was now cordoned off for the droves of beer-bellied Americans, the Brits, the Germans, and the Japanese tourists who come to Memphis in search of genuine Delta blues. A few of the original buildings had survived urban renewal, but not many. Beale had transitioned into a corridor crowded with flippers doing handsprings, hoochie-coochie souvenir hawkers, and burned-out bluesmen with their Crate amps set up on the sidewalk and their tip buckets out in front of their mike stands. Years had passed since those players had looked anyone in the eye.

Billy hated to see the street's culture being beaten down and ripped off, people showing up to capitalize on the low-down Delta blues. After hearing Augie's story about his mother and reading Dahlia Poston's file, he understood why Beale Street and its people were on Augie's mind.

It was midmorning. He turned the corner to find the street pretty much empty except for a few tourists loitering in front of store windows. After partying late in the clubs, they looked dazed, like accident victims who'd wandered in off the highway.

A pasty-faced horn player came out the side door of an all-night blues club, his tenor sax swinging from its neck strap. He was tall, boneless, rat-slender. He wore suspenders over a wife-beater T-shirt and dark glasses with small round lenses that made his eyes look like black holes. He leaned against a telephone pole, swung the mouthpiece to his lips, and blew hot blues riffs right out of the club. The sound echoed down the street and tore at Billy, reminding him of Little Man's soulful sax.

Little Man and Red were gone. Augie was lying in the morgue with the shit beat out of him. Not one of the three had been at the top of their game, but they'd all deserved a better end.

Cops learn to avoid the emotional wreckage of their jobs. Let a case get under your skin and a fuse ignites. The anger runs out of control. That's when mistakes happen. He could feel his anger building with every step and knew it was dangerous. These deaths were personal.

He opened the door to the museum, the space Calvin Carter

had used for decades as his studio. The museum had recently been established to preserve and display images that documented sixty years of African-American life when racism ruled the South. Carter and his camera had captured it all.

In 1968, two black Memphis sanitation workers were crushed to death by a garbage truck's faulty compacting mechanism. Outrage sparked the "I Am A Man" campaign that drew Dr. King to Memphis. Carter's photos recorded the public workers' strike. He also sat in on private meetings between Dr. King and his entourage before Dr. King's assassination. The King photographs were the centerpiece of the museum's collection.

The building had raw, wooden floors and a wide storefront window that provided plenty of natural light. Contractors had stripped away wallboard to expose the old brick, a perfect backdrop for the socially provocative photographs.

A prosperous-looking group was sitting around a conference table at the rear of the long, open space, watching a PowerPoint presentation. Garrett, seated at the far end of the table, noticed Billy standing inside the door. He whispered to the man on his left and came to his feet with some difficulty. The twist in his spine was more evident than it had been the day before. Survivors of catastrophic injuries—head trauma, spinal injuries, gunshot wounds—have their good days and bad. Garrett came forward, leaning heavily on his cane, his eyes reddened and his coordination slowed by pain meds. This was already a bad day for Garrett. It was about to get worse.

Garrett frowned as he approached and put out his hand. "Detective Able. What brings you here?"

"I have disturbing news. Augie Poston was murdered last night in his apartment."

"Jesus. Murdered?" The skin at Garrett's throat was slack,

his cheeks hollow. He rubbed the back of his neck and peered at Billy. "A home invasion?"

"That's to be determined."

"Was he shot?"

"I can't discuss it, sir."

He placed his hand on Billy's shoulder. "Forgive me. My condolences. Augie told me yesterday that you were the one friend who'd always stood by him."

Billy flashed on Augie's crushed skull, his fractured arm. No one was there to stand by Augie last night. Not even good ol' Billy.

The group at the table had gone quiet, listening, so the two men moved toward the window, and Garrett lowered his voice. "I'd like to offer an observation. Addicts come through Robert House all the time. I'm familiar with the signs of meth use. Augie was flying high yesterday. I even asked if he was on something." Garrett shrugged. "It's possible he had a habit and got involved with the wrong people."

The comment jolted Billy. Augie had denied being off his meds. He'd kicked over a chair to emphasize the point. But meth?

"Augie was no crackhead," he said.

"I saw what I saw. A drug element should be considered." Garrett squinted at Billy's swollen mouth. "The two of you were close to a fistfight at the funeral home. Did Augie do that?" Garrett raised both hands in apology. "Sorry, none of my business. Forgive the questions of a recovering lawyer. Now, tell me, is there anything I can do?"

"Handle the funeral tomorrow. Augie would appreciate it."

"I'll be happy to. By the way, James Freeman and Augie were friends. His office is across the street. I'll let him know."

Billy turned to look out the window at the building's black awning with the name FREEMAN PROPERTIES outlined in gold. "Freeman knows," he said.

"I have to get back to my meeting. Don't worry about the funeral. Again, I'm sorry about your friend." Garrett hobbled to the table and took his seat.

Billy remained by the window, feeling light-headed and off his feet. Could he have missed something as obvious as Augie doing crank? Augie talked about doping in baseball and how it was ruining the game. He hated drugs, especially the antipsychotics he was chained to. But what if he'd taken the chance of combining his regular meds with the high of meth in order to work on the book?

Dealers are a dangerous crowd. A wealthy ex-ballplayer would be red meat to them—prey to be taken down.

The sound of chairs scraping the floor told him the museum meeting was coming to an end. He wasn't in the mood to continue the conversation with Garrett. He started through the door just as a man with a shabby goatee came loping down the street with his arms flapping. When he got to the New Daisy Theatre, he stopped and stripped off his clothes. He was short, muscular, hairy, built like a fur-covered stump. He fell to his knees in front of the marquee and babbled at an older couple strolling by. They scurried away.

"Mr. Garrett, dial 911," Billy called over his shoulder. "Tell dispatch it's squirrel day out front of the New Daisy Theatre. Send a car to pick up a nut."

He stepped onto the sidewalk, wondering just when he'd become a magnet for the floridly psychotic. Crazy people are strong. Naked people are slippery. He hoped all he'd have to do was keep an eye on the guy until the cops showed up.

The man got to his feet. "Jehovah God! Destroyer of the world," he bellowed. He leered at Billy and galloped in his direction. It was Augie all over again.

"Stop! Police," he warned, but the guy kept coming.

A right cross sent the guy sprawling on the brick pavers. He rolled to his feet and shook his head. His fists came up. He charged again.

This time Billy grabbed his forearm and slung him to the ground. Stunned, the guy lay on his back, one hand on his head and the other cupping his balls.

The patrol car showed at the end of the block. While the officers cuffed Mr. No Pants, Billy noticed Garrett and his people lining the museum's window to watch the show. This was theater to them. People hate cops, but they can't get enough of what they do.

The patrol car pulled off. Billy went to sit on the curb in front of Freeman's place, his head in his hands, feeling shot out and disgusted. His gaze wandered over the buildings across the street. He'd never sat on this curb, but what he saw now was somehow familiar. Then it fell into place—the museum's facade, the cornice molding over the door, the fire hydrant Frankie had pointed out. He turned to look at Freeman's window behind him and the New Daisy marquee next door.

It was there, bits and pieces of the architecture he'd seen in the photos.

He was sitting at ground zero.

Chapter 28

Frankie's phone rang in the bedroom. She ignored it, standing in front of her bathroom mirror, mouth full of toothpaste, running late for an appointment with Ramos that was to begin in forty-five minutes. The outfit she'd chosen lay on the bed along with the copy of *To Kill a Mockingbird* that she'd planned to take with her. The book would serve as a plant if she failed to get the information she wanted today. She could return once more to pick up her forgotten book. Surprise visits can be revealing.

The phone continued to ring. *Shoot.* It might be Billy. She rinsed and ran to the bedroom to answer.

"Can you talk?" Billy's voice sounded strained.

"Yes. What's happened?"

"Augie Poston was murdered last night. You know who I'm talking about?"

"The ballplayer. He had some kind of breakdown." She sat on the edge of the bed. "What's that got to do with you?"

"Augie was a friend. I dropped by his apartment at the DeVoy this morning. A neighbor, James Freeman, claimed to have discovered the body a few minutes before I got there. I'm not convinced he wasn't involved."

"Freeman. He's a burly guy, real quiet. Some kind of real estate mogul."

"He's at the CJC now giving his statement. I'll give mine tomorrow."

A weed whacker buzzed in the yard below Frankie's bedroom window. The sharp smell of spring onions drifted through her window. Billy's friend had been murdered. Homicide wanted a statement from him. Not good.

"I'm sorry," she said quietly. "We'll catch the bastard who did this."

"I'm not so sure about that. Dunsford is lead on the case."

"Oh, fuck. Excuse me, but no fucking way. Really, I'm sorry." Dunsford would be the one to take his statement. Billy might strangle the guy.

Over the phone she heard the last notes of a sax solo followed by hoots and applause. "Where are you?"

"On Beale Street. I tracked down Sid Garrett at a meeting in the Calvin Carter Museum. Do you know Garrett?"

"The civil rights lawyer, shot in the back by a client."

"He was helping Augie with the arrangements for Red and Little Man's funeral. He's agreed to take over the service tomorrow."

Feedback from a guitar screeched through an amp and blasted Frankie's ear. "I can't hear you over that racket."

"Big Jerry is setting up in front of Eel-Etc. Hold on. I'll walk down the street." Seconds passed. The interference lessened. "You know those photos from Red's jacket? They were shot on Beale Street, some taken through the window of what's now James Freeman's offices."

"How do you know?"

"Freeman's offices are across the street from the museum. I was on the sidewalk after talking to Garrett. The setting clicked with me."

She tried to overlay what she knew of Beale Street onto the photographs. "I've walked that beat. I can't see it."

"Most of the buildings have been demolished. You pegged the movie marquee. It's the New Daisy Theatre."

He drew in a breath. She heard his exhaustion.

"A friend of mine is on duty at the CJC," he said. "He'll get a summary of Freeman's statement for me, and call when they've cut him loose. Freeman will want to check in at his office. I'll pick up the photographs to verify the location. Then I'll drop in on Freeman and ask a few questions."

"You've been through a hell of a shock. You might consider keeping your distance from Freeman. You're both witnesses in a murder investigation."

"I'll handle this," he said sharply. "You're meeting with Ramos today, right?"

He'd changed the subject so abruptly she backed off. "In about thirty minutes. I'll go in and push him to make a death curse. If he agrees, I'll confront him with the curse from Red's scene. He could be directly involved or he could have sold the curse to someone." She checked the time. "I have to go."

"Hold on. Don't move past his willingness to make the curse. Get the information and get out."

"I can handle a blind witch doctor."

"You don't know his game."

"He doesn't know mine. Besides, I carry a .22 Magnum pug in my handbag." She ran her hand over a warm patch of sunlight on the duvet. "Billy, I'm sorry you lost your friend."

Frankie settled into the comfy pillows of the large wicker chair that faced Sergio Ramos's desk. His office walls emanated a cool transparent green, a color found in many Cuban homes.

Shelves of books behind his desk included works of psychology, anthropology, world religions, and West African cultures. The collection was no intellectual prop. After reading his Internet biography, she was convinced he was legitimate. He could no longer read, but he may have kept the books with the hope of regaining his sight. Or maybe he just loved his books.

Ramos sat across the desk from her, wearing his dark glasses, a crisp navy shirt, and gray wool slacks. Looking at him, it was hard to believe this serene human being had the ability to concoct a spell that would drop a Santerían believer in his tracks.

She used her real name when she filled out his patient questionnaire. Under occupation she'd written the word "security." He asked her to read aloud the answers to questions that had stars beside them, personal information that mattered most in a therapy session.

He gestured toward the window. "Beautiful day. Memphis is a good city, but I do miss the sound of the ocean."

He knew she'd grown up in Key West. This simpatico opening was meant to establish a connection.

"I could hear the surf from my childhood home. When I got my own apartment, I had to stand on the toilet to look out a window and see the ocean."

He laughed. "The ocean views in Havana almost make up for the shortages of everything else."

She had chosen a scoop-necked, terra-cotta–colored shell that complemented her olive complexion; a pencil skirt; and beaded leather sandals, going for attractive without being obviously sexy. Almost out the door, she realized it didn't matter what she wore—he couldn't see. She went back to add a spritz of citrus cologne, the only feminine card she could play.

"You used the salve," he said.

"I'm amazed. The bruise is almost gone."

"And the *ewe*?"

"Not as successful."

"Change takes time." He folded his hands, one on top of the other. "When we met, you mentioned having some problems."

She cleared her throat. After talking with Mystica, he would believe the bruise came from an abusive relationship. It was true. Brad had been emotionally abusive. And he'd hit her. She didn't want to go into that, but she could give Ramos an experience from her past that would make the lie that followed all the more convincing.

"I'm having flashbacks from a childhood incident," she said. "I can't make it stop."

"Tell me, please."

"My mother left when I was four. I had a nanny named Amitee. She introduced me to Santería."

He nodded. This was a world he understood.

"Amitee and I went to the market every morning. A man spoke to her one day then followed us home. He did this several times over the next few weeks. At first he would sit in his car across the street. Then he began coming to the kitchen window and tapping the glass with his keys. He would bother her when she hung out the laundry. In that culture, the man would be considered a persistent admirer. Here we call them stalkers."

"Did she tell your father?"

"My father had just fired the cook because he thought she'd stolen a necklace. Amitee was afraid he would fire her, too." Frankie looked down at her hands clasped in her lap. "She didn't want to leave me, so she tried to handle the situation on her own."

Ramos sat very still. She sensed his displeasure. "Go on."

"One day we came back to find the man inside the house,

sitting in my father's chair. He started to pull Amitee toward the bedroom. I tried to block the doorway, which was ridiculous. He could have broken my neck."

"You were brave and foolish. And loyal."

"He let go of Amitee and broke a lamp. Then he left."

"Did the police catch him?" he asked.

"Amitee couldn't call them. He was a white man."

Ramos's mouth twitched with anger. "I understand."

"Amitee went to her *santero* for help. He made an *ebbo* of sweet cakes and fruit to persuade her orisha to protect her. He also made a curse of eggshell, coal, rock salt, guinea pepper, and wasp nest to drive the man away."

Sergio blinked at her description.

"You're familiar with that curse?" she asked.

"I am."

"It didn't work. The *santero* sacrificed chickens, pigeons, and a lamb. That didn't work, either." Frankie let her gaze drift to the window. She hadn't realized telling the story would bring up so much pain.

"Amitee came to work one morning with a scarf wrapped around her neck. It was a hot day. When I asked about the scarf, she showed me bruises where the man had choked her."

"I'm surprised her *santero* wasn't more effective."

"He was, in the end. He made a spell using a pumpkin leaf, ashes, a handkerchief the man had dropped, and a circle of paper with his name written on it. Amitee petitioned the patron saint Oshun to turn the man's life to ashes. Then she buried the curse in the ground."

"That's a powerful spell."

"The man ate roasted pork at a party. He got sick. No one else at the party got sick. He died a week later."

"Did you tell your father about this?"

She shook her head. "I was afraid he would fire Amitee. She changed after that. She believed the dead man was going to come for her. She kept the doors locked. One day she caught me walking home from school with a boy. She slapped me and dragged me into the house. I was eight." Frankie shifted in her chair. "A month later she had a heart attack and died."

"I'm sorry you lost your friend."

She'd just said those words to Billy. *I'm sorry you lost your friend*. For a moment she felt herself sinking once again into the vacuum of Amitee's decline.

After losing Amitee, she had avoided becoming close with anyone. Her father, a scientist, drummed into her the importance of being precise. Being right was better than having friends, he'd say. *Being right was better than winning*. She preferred to be right *and* to win. Brad had somehow gotten under that shield. Sadly, no one had won.

She cleared her throat. "History is repeating itself. A man I met at a party has been stalking me for months. I ignored him and then confronted him. He slashed my tires and kicked in my door. He says he can have me anytime he wants."

"You've reported this to the authorities?"

"He's a policeman. He's well regarded on the force."

Ramos straightened, taken by surprise.

"If I report him, he may kill me," she said.

"And you've come to me for help."

"Leaving town seemed to be my only option. Then Mystica told me about you. I remembered the *santero*'s spell. The death curse."

"You believe the spell killed Amitee's stalker?"

"Don't you?"

He glanced away. "What makes you think I would do this thing for you?"

"Because you can stop this man from hurting me."

"You're asking me to harm this person," he said softly.

"Before he harms me."

He regarded her through dark glasses. "I regret to say I don't believe this story about the stalker. I hear little conviction in your voice and no fear. Yet I know you're very upset. You can barely suppress your anxiety. Someone you cared about died recently in an accident. You blame yourself. I'm willing to help you with that."

Sunlight shifted in the window. The room seemed to fill with the scent of the bougainvillea that had draped her porch in Key West. She tried not to react.

How did he know about the accident?

"I've asked you to make a spell or a curse, whatever it takes, to stop this man."

He steepled his fingers and pressed them to his lips. "Death curses have unintended consequences. You saw what happened to Amitee."

She stood, suddenly feeling out of her depth. What made her think she could fool a *santero*? "Is there anyone else in the city who will help me?"

"No, there isn't. And I'm sorry, but I won't discuss the matter further. I'm afraid our time is at an end. If you wish to make another appointment, we'll explore your anxiety about the accident."

She walked out, leaving the book tucked under a pillow in the wicker chair.

Chapter 29

The black architectural awnings gave Freeman's ordinary building a contemporary edge. A shopkeeper's bell rang as Billy walked in. James Freeman was standing among empty desks with his back to the door, speaking with a young man and woman who were listening with rapt attention. Freeman turned at the sound of the bell, his smile shutting down as he recognized Billy. Freeman's staff frowned at him from around Freeman's back, then marched to offices at the rear of the building. Their doors closed, then the guy's door popped back open. Billy figured he must appear to be a threat.

According to the County Register of Deeds, James Freeman Sr. had owned this building and had run a small neighborhood bar during the sixties. After his death, a drugstore with a lunch counter took over the property. Soon after, urban renewal rolled through and flattened most of the historic structures on Beale, creating a ghost town. The building stood empty until Freeman Jr. bought it and opened his real estate offices.

Apparently, Freeman had gone home to shower and change into jeans and a starched shirt. Only the bags under his eyes betrayed the trauma of discovering Augie's battered body and the exhaustion he must be feeling from hours at the CJC, reliving every detail of the scene.

"How did you know I'd be here?" Freeman asked.

The only way to handle Freeman was by being direct. "I'm a cop. I know shit. I'm going after Augie's killer. I need your help."

"You should've thought of that before you hog-tied me to the oven door."

"There was a dead body in the room. That's the drill. And Dunsford—"

"I know. Dunsford is a sloppy cop." Freeman looked off, looked back. "Why ask me for help when you think I killed Augie?"

"Because the ladies in your apartment backed your story."

"You believe my lady friend and her sister? Just like that?"

"They have credibility. Linda Orsburn is the widow of the former Tennessee attorney general. Both women flew in from London last night. The sister says she watched TV all night. She reeled off the plot of every show on late-night HBO. Apparently, you snore, so she's willing to swear to your location. The department will run background checks on both ladies, but for now Middlebrook is taking their word."

Freeman folded his arms over his chest. "That's right, I'm in the clear. What about you?"

He didn't like Freeman turning the tables. "The DeVoy security videos show I arrived at seven forty-five this morning."

"That may be true, but I can't verify it. The cops confiscated the equipment. Where you were last night? All night."

"Home alone."

"Tell me again about the fight you had with Augie."

"He hit his head. I tried to help him. He busted me in the chops and took off. That was the last time I saw him until this morning."

"Augie told a different story. Now he's dead. That's suspicious as hell."

Down the street, Big Jerry's voice rang over the cheap mike. The tourists loved it, but the tinny sound was giving Billy a headache. And he didn't like to be pushed.

"What happened between Augie and me was personal, so get off my ass. Let's work together and find out who did this."

Freeman laughed. "So now you're the good guy, someone I can count on. That's bullshit. I've been screwed by cops before, just like my dad."

Augie pegged it. Freeman's hatred of cops was tied to his father. A kid losing a parent makes him bitter. Billy understood that.

"I'm sorry about your dad, but that doesn't make me a murderer."

Freeman searched his face, shook his head. "I don't know." He walked to a vintage Coca-Cola machine next to the door, dropped in a dime, and pulled the lever. A petite bottle plopped behind the door. He snapped off the metal cap and took a swig. "Ice cold. Nothing better." He dropped another dime into the machine and looked at Billy. "Buy you a Coke?"

"No thanks."

Freeman pulled the lever, popped off the cap and offered it. "Go on. It's been a rough day."

The Coke was a gesture, a peace offering. They drank their Cokes and watched through the storefront window as tourists filed in and out of the museum across the street.

"As I was leaving Augie's place, I saw two coffees and a bag of biscuits in the entry," Freeman said. "You know about that?"

"I brought the coffee and biscuits."

"I heard you calling out when I was in the back of the apartment. What were you saying?"

Billy looked over. "Where's this going?"

"Just answer the question."

His mind flashed to the opened door and the painting knocked off-kilter on the wall. He'd drawn his weapon. The image of Augie's corpse flared in his mind.

"I yelled Augie's name."

"You yelled it three times."

"I don't recall."

Freeman glanced over, then looked down, taking his time weighing the answers. "A smart cop might bring a cup of take-out coffee to the man he'd murdered as a way to cover his ass. But he wouldn't stand around yelling the victim's name if he thought he was alone. You didn't know I was in the apartment. You were so surprised when I walked into the kitchen, you almost shot me. But what I remember most was the way you examined the body. Nobody can fake that kind of grief and outrage.

"Bottom line, take-out coffee doesn't prove you're not the killer. But it's enough to make me step back for now." He looked at his watch. "I have a meeting that starts in twenty-five minutes. If you came here to ask questions, you'd better get to it."

Billy knew if he tried to bully Freeman he'd never get the straight of it. This was Freeman's game for now. Twenty-five minutes. He took out his memo book.

"Did Dunsford question you about Augie's eBay business?"

"Funny thing. He knew all about Augie's memorabilia collection. He's a NASCAR fan and bought slides off Augie's site a couple of months ago."

He made a note, surprised that Dunsford had an interest in collecting anything besides a paycheck.

"He asked if buyers came to the apartment," Freeman added.

"Did they?"

"Not that I've seen, but I'm gone all day."

"What else?"

"He asked how you and I know each other. I told him we'd met at Bardog a few days ago."

Billy knew Dunsford was opening the door for questions later about a murder conspiracy, a good strategy on his part. He needed to remember that Dunsford might not be as dumb as he let on.

"Anything else?" he asked, and kept writing.

"The ME told Dunsford the goose egg on Augie's forehead happened before the attack in his apartment. Dunsford wanted to know what I knew about it. That brought the fight between you and Augie into the conversation."

"And you said . . ."

Freeman spread his hands in front of him. "Exactly what Augie told me. That you said, 'This isn't over.' "

Oh, shit. He *had* said that. In this context, it sounded like a threat, which would be hard to explain without going into the missing photo.

"I also told him Augie was planning to work on the manuscript this morning, and it's now missing. He made notes, but he didn't follow up."

"What did you say about the journalist?"

Freeman shrugged. "Wasn't much I *could* say." A line rang on the desk. "That's the client I'm meeting. I need to get it." He picked up.

The break gave Billy time to jot down some notes about possible suspects.

I got business to handle. Augie had made that statement as his phone rang and he walked away. It was a critical point. The caller could have been a buyer, or it could've been the journalist or a drug dealer. Whoever it was, the caller's number was recorded on Augie's phone. If the caller was also the killer, he was organized enough to steal the phone in an attempt to conceal his identity. Same thing with the computer. But the manuscript had been stolen, too. A drug dealer wouldn't give a damn about the manuscript, but a buyer might mistake it for a memoir and think it had market value. If the journalist was the killer, he would definitely have taken the manuscript.

He wrote "journalist" at the top of the list and circled it.

Any one of the three could've grabbed the watches and other things around the apartment, either to sell or to make the murder look like a burglary.

Next, he focused on Garrett's drug theory. If the techs had found evidence of street drugs around Augie's place, Dunsford would have questioned Freeman about it.

Freeman hung up. "We done here?"

"Not quite. Augie's been really manic. I assumed he'd dropped off his meds. He's done it before. Garrett had a different take. He brought up street drugs."

"Where did that come from?"

"Garrett sees a lot of drug-related behavior at Robert House, so his opinion has some merit. Did Dunsford ask you if Augie was doing drugs?"

Freeman rubbed his jaw. "They had me look through mug shots for anyone who'd been hanging around the building. Maybe they were looking for dealers." Freeman stared at the floor. "It doesn't make sense. Augie hated drugs."

"I didn't buy it either until I thought about his obsession with his mother's death. The antipsychotics made him foggy-headed. He might have added some combination of speed or meth for a boost. Augie was so wired last night, if a dealer showed up, they could have gotten crosswise."

"I assume the medical examiner will test for drugs," Freeman said. "That should put the question to rest."

"A tox screen takes three to four weeks. Think hard. Did you notice evidence of drug use in Augie's place? I'd like to rule the possibility in or out."

"No drugs," Freeman said and checked his watch. "We're down to five minutes."

Billy pulled out the stack of surveillance photos. "When you looked at these the other night, you knew they were taken on Beale Street."

Freeman raised a hand. "Now you're talking about Red and Little Man. I'm not getting into that. Garrett knows more about those times. His brother was a civil rights worker."

"Augie stole one of the photos."

"Can't help you there," Freeman said, stone-faced.

"Did he show it to you?"

"Tell you what. I'll answer that question when you tell me the real reason you had a fight with Augie."

"That's not up for discussion."

Freeman called over his shoulder to the back office. "Diana, pack up the topo and spread sheets on the Moser property." He turned a professional smile on Billy. "You're right, Detective. Time to move on."

Billy shrugged. *All right, you son of a bitch. I'll give you the story.*

He told Freeman about Augie making an ass of himself at the ballpark and taking a swing at the kid in the street. He gave every detail of the fight. It sounded so pool hall parking lot—the name-calling, broken bottles, a friend busting up a friend over nothing. He felt ashamed just talking about it.

"I told Augie he'd be banned from the ballpark. I called him a waste of skin."

Freeman's eyebrows went up. "That's cold."

"It's the reason I went to his place this morning. I wanted to check on him and apologize."

"And get the photo."

"Right. Where is it?"

"I don't have a clue."

"Damn it, Freeman."

"What can I say? Augie told me about the photo. He knew you'd figure out he'd taken it." He looked at Billy full on. "Did you go to Augie's place last night?"

"No. And the security tapes will prove that."

Freeman grunted, stared at the ceiling, thinking. "Which entrance did you come in this morning?"

"The lobby. Why?"

"What about the back entrance?"

"What's the difference? You have cameras on both."

Freeman nodded as if he'd made a decision. "We both know Dunsford isn't smart enough to catch this bastard."

"Not unless the guy walks into the station house and confesses."

"I'll work with you, but I won't trust you."

"Not very flattering, but I'll go with it."

"Diana," Freeman yelled. "Cancel that appointment." He waved at a chair beside the desk. "Have a seat, Detective. I'm going to give you something. It may be true, or it may not. But I don't think you'll hear it anywhere else."

Chapter 30

Billy left Freeman's office and walked over to 757 Kentucky Street, his uncle Kane's favorite train-watching spot. In the seventies, you could see the Rock Island, Frisco, Illinois Central, Cotton Belt, Southern, Louisville & Nashville, and Missouri Pacific roll by, all in this one location. Now it was empty tracks and a ROAD CLOSED sign attached to the crossing bars.

Trains had romanced his uncle. Tracks cut through the cotton fields four hundred feet behind Kane's Kanteen, his uncle's roadside diner on a barren stretch of highway in Mississippi. His uncle would stand on the back stoop between the breakfast and lunch shifts, smoke curling from the cigarette tucked between his fingers, his eyes following the trains like they were beautiful women swaying down the tracks. He'd talk about the day he would book sleeper service on Amtrak's The City of New Orleans. He wanted to ride in the observation car, drink good scotch, and eat a New York strip steak at a table covered with a starched white cloth. He wanted to ride to Chicago, turn around, and ride back. That was his dream.

It never happened. A kid with a shaky hand who'd never

meant to shoot nobody killed his uncle while he'd been making change behind the cash register.

Billy had a cop's view of trains, very different from his uncle's sentiment. Trains take out dogs, cows, and witless drivers. Drunks stumble onto the tracks in the middle of the night and get mangled. Suicides lie down and wait for the engine to cut their bodies in half. There's nothing romantic about trains for a cop. Trains take people away.

He questioned how he'd handled himself today. A cop works a bad scene, he waits until the shift is over and goes someplace to lose his shit. He's no good to anyone if he can't control his emotions. Billy knew that from experience. When the flashbacks come, you think of something else.

Today was different. Augie's death was going to shadow him for a long, long time.

The sound of tires popping on gravel pulled him out of his thoughts. Frankie got out of her Jeep, wearing a skirt and sandals. She walked over to stand beside him.

"Thanks for picking me up," he said. "It's a long, hot walk back to my car." He turned his head so she could see his swollen lip. He thought his banged-up face would be the start of her questions, but she made no comment.

"I was coming from my appointment with Ramos when you called."

"How did it go?"

"I asked him to make a death curse to scare off a stalker who was going to kill me. He didn't buy it. But he confirmed that he was the only person in the city who could make that kind of curse. The session ended before I could get more."

"Sounds like it's time for me to have a talk with Dr. Voodoo."

She shook her head. "No, sir. This is my source. He'll call into the precinct if you show up and try to push him. That's the last thing we need. I've planted an excuse to stop by so I can get another look around."

He felt her gaze on the side of his face. She nodded at his lip. "You want to talk about that?"

A hatch of sparrows circled above the tracks then dropped into the switch grass beside the gravel. *Hell no, he didn't want to talk about it.* But she deserved to hear it. She was hanging out with a possible murder suspect. He'd be cleared of that tomorrow, but if somehow the shit got deep, it would get deep for her, too.

He told her all of it, starting with the fight at the ballpark. Disappointment was the biggest part of it, in himself and in Augie. He couldn't get past the fact that Augie had taken a swing at a kid.

Frankie listened until he was finished, her gaze fixed on the red-and-white railroad crossing bars in front of them. "You were trying to help a friend."

"Not really. I was angry. I provoked him. Augie deserved better."

Her expression clouded. "Cops are trained to deal with people at their worst. When it's a person we care about, training goes out the window. We make mistakes."

He glanced over. She'd gone pale. "You okay?"

"I'm fine."

He didn't prod. Taking the bruise into account, he assumed she'd had a rough time with somebody recently. Proof of damage. He couldn't let her see how well he understood.

"What's your next move?" she asked.

"I have to figure that out. Want to help?"

She dipped her head in agreement.

They covered Freeman's interview with Dunsford. Billy talked about Dahlia Poston and how Augie had witnessed the fire.

"Crap," she said. "No wonder he went off his rocker."

"Augie believed she was murdered. He tried to tell me there was more information, but I wasn't listening. Freeman filled in the blanks today.

"Augie told him that this journalist has obtained documents from the Justice Department through the Freedom of Information Act. It reveals FBI activity in Memphis during the garbage strike and after King's assassination. Augie's mother's name appeared in those documents."

"Jesus," she said.

"Dr. King was leading a protest march down Beale Street in support of the garbage workers when it turned violent—rock throwing, looting. Someone flagged down a woman who was driving by and commandeered her car to take Dr. King to the Lorraine Motel. Because of the riot, they couldn't get to the Lorraine, so a motorcycle cop directed them to the Rivermont, a posh hotel that used to be on the crest of the south bluff. You won't remember the Rivermont. It's condos now.

"The woman driving the car was Dahlia Poston. The motorcycle cop took down her license plate number and gave it to an agent. The FBI made the assumption that she worked for King or was his girlfriend. Dahlia Poston had never met Dr. King. Her involvement that day was a coincidence.

"Nothing came of it until King was assassinated. Soon after, the FBI showed up at the Postons' house with questions about Dahlia's relationship with Dr. King. Her car blew up not long after that."

"Why would the FBI bother the Postons?"

"King was a married man, but he liked the ladies. The agents were looking at jealous husbands as the possible shooter. They spoke with every woman who had even the slightest connection to Dr. King. Dahlia Poston was on that list.

"The bureau had a black eye over the assassination. It was no secret that Hoover despised Dr. King and thought he was stirring up militants. A segment of the population believed the bureau was involved. Three thousand agents worked overtime to solve his murder. They wanted to get it behind them. Augie believed his parents were swept up in the manhunt."

"Can you verify this?"

"It takes time. An FOIA request takes a minimum of a month. A warrant might speed things up, but I have no standing. This information could be solid or a con created by the journalist to keep Augie on the hook for money."

The heat of the day had coalesced around them, stealing the air. He took a breath. "A couple of weeks after King's assassination, *Time* magazine called Memphis a southern backwater. As one reporter put it, 'Blacks and women got their say. White men in suits got their way.' Not much has changed."

"What's this journalist's name?" Frankie asked.

"Augie refused to tell Freeman or me. Without his phone or computer, we're hamstrung until Dunsford subpoenas the records. When I go in tomorrow to give my statement, I'll ask Middlebrook if he can fast-track my reinstatement. Working from the inside, I'll be able to speed things up."

She thought for several seconds. "I'd like to start with some basic questions about Augie." She went to the Jeep and returned with a memo book. "A very smart cop once said that murder is about sex, money, or revenge. If you can't see one of those, you aren't looking hard enough, because it's there. Did Augie have a jealous girlfriend? Was he sleeping with someone's wife?"

"No women," he said.

"How about revenge, like a teammate holding a grudge."

"Augie hasn't seen those guys in years. I smell a dead end."

She nodded. "Okay. Let's talk about money. Augie loaned Red two thousand dollars. The night we saw Red, he couldn't rub two quarters together. He was scared, and he was running. Maybe he gambled and got in over his head. After Red died, whoever went after him might have gone after Augie."

"Bookies don't kill their marks. They break knees. Augie had the hell beat out of him. This was personal."

Frankie rolled her eyes. "I guess so, but Red should never have borrowed money. Personal loans always lead to trouble."

Growing up in Mississippi, Billy knew where Red was coming from, what he had endured. Red knew more about loan trouble than Frankie ever would. But Red had fought his way out. Billy remembered a press photo from Red's 1998 European tour— Red dressed in a silk suit with diamond cuff links, his shiny black hair swept back. The set of his jaw told the story. Red knew who he was back then. He had a place in the world.

That slick promotional photo was very different from the pack of photos in Red's jacket. After talking with Freeman, he'd begun to wonder if those photos were somehow connected to Augie's death. He rubbed his face, too tired to think it through. At some point he would discuss it with Frankie; however, there was one thing she needed to know right now.

"Remember that missing photo?" he asked.

"Number fourteen."

"Augie stole it. He took it the night I ran into him at Bardog. I was mad about it and went to his place this morning to get it back. The fight at the ballpark looks bad. Going there for the photo makes me look even worse."

She blinked several times but said nothing.

"I was home alone when Augie was murdered, so my only alibi is the security camera at the DeVoy showing I didn't arrive at the building until well after he was killed. Are you comfortable with that?"

"I'm okay with it, but Dunsford won't be satisfied." She stared at her shoes, frowning. "Are you going to tell him about the missing photo?"

"Only if he asks."

"Why would Augie steal it? I thought he was your friend."

"I don't know, but it has something to do with Freeman."

"Why?"

"The way Augie pushed for Freeman to see the photos at Bardog."

Frankie nodded. "When do you give your statement?"

"Tomorrow at ten, an hour before the funeral. At best, I'll get there at the end of the service."

"I'm off rotation for four days," she said. "I'll go to the funeral home early and check out the crowd. Maybe Cool Willy will put in an appearance. I have his mug shot. What else should I watch for?"

"Suspicious behavior. Trust your eyes, your gut."

"I prefer to know what I'm looking for," she said.

"Don't get too much in your head, you'll box yourself in."

"Instincts aren't my strong point."

"Don't fight me on this. You've got good instincts. Use them."

They walked to the Jeep. Frankie circled to the driver's door and stopped. "I just want to say . . . if I were in trouble, I'd want you on my side. You're a good friend."

He nodded, got in the Jeep. She started the engine. The sky was a pocket of blue, clean and normal. Traffic was distant even though this place was on the edge of downtown.

He appreciated her words more than she would ever know.

Chapter 31

They left Kentucky Street. Frankie dropped Billy at the DeVoy to pick up his car. Augie was dead. He was alive. Mercy was out of his life. The world changes just like that. His own existence chilled him, made him feel lost.

At the barge, he mopped the floors and wiped down the kitchen counters to stop himself from dwelling on the emptiness. After a hot shower, he collapsed in a chair on the deck with a plate of cheese and crackers. The sun bled orange into the river and slowly died. He went inside and poured a tall scotch from a bottle he kept in the back of the cabinet. He hated scotch. The liquor burned all the way down. He tossed back the last of it and went to bed. He was a long time falling asleep, listening to the night harmonics of the freight trains passing through the city.

He found himself riding a train that lunged through the moonless night. The cracked leather seat under his hand felt familiar. He smelled the accumulated odor of bodies that had ridden this train a hundred times, a thousand times. On the floor at his feet sat Red's guitar case. He lifted the case, felt the weight of the instrument inside.

Was Red riding this train?

The whistle blew, a sound like a blues harp, insistent and needy. The sound would leave its stamp on him, like Lou's sin, powdered glass working its way through his muscle and bone.

The dead leave their footprints on the living.

The windows filled with copper light. He realized a man was standing in the aisle beside him, dressed in a uniform with brass buttons. It was Lou.

"You can't ride this train," Lou said. "It's the gone dead train. Go on now, son."

Then he found himself standing outside on the tracks with the cold light of a locomotive coming at him, the whistle blowing deep in its throat.

He was alone. Nothing but the light bearing down.

The next morning he woke troubled and exhausted. He made coffee and pulled up news sites on the Internet that gave only the sketchiest details of the murder. The photo galleries showed Augie at his best, crouched behind the plate, his glove closing over a ball thrown low and away. Most of the articles focused on the loss of a superstar athlete. Only one delved into Augie's mental decline. Tomorrow they would come back with sensationalized accounts of Augie's mental illness and the brutality of his murder. It's what the public wants. You can't fight commerce.

He dressed for the funeral in a suit and a pressed shirt he found buried in the back of the closet. His statement with Dunsford was set for ten. Getting to the funeral afterward would be tight, but he wanted to make an appearance out of respect if at all possible.

He arrived at the CJC early, hoping to speak with the chief about moving up his reinstatement. If Middlebrook would let him sign on immediately, he'd be in a position to follow all three cases . . . after Dunsford cleared him, of course.

He stopped by Middlebrook's office. It was empty. His assistant, Roxanne, her bodacious curves muffled by a boxy tweed jacket, quit typing long enough to glance at his suit and buffed wingtips.

"You got dressed up to give Dunsford your statement?" she asked.

He shrugged. "When will the chief be back?"

"Around one. He'll be in the rest of the afternoon."

"Tell him I'd like to stop by. I'll check back with you for a time." He gestured at the exotic blooms packed into a crystal vase on her desk. "Nice flowers."

"From my new boyfriend. I'm in love." She gave him a wink. "Welcome back to the force, Sergeant. The ladies will be pleased."

Looking back, he only wished it had been that easy.

Dunsford sat in one of the interview rooms, leafing through files. In his rumpled jacket and polyester slacks, he looked more like an out-of-work bookkeeper than a cop. He even smelled of another generation—Pop-Tarts, Tang, and Aqua Velva aftershave.

It was unwise to write Dunsford off as a hack. He'd been trained to be a competent detective whether he was one or not. This case would be the last hurrah of his career, and he'd be heavily invested in making an arrest.

Dunsford got to his feet when he saw Billy in the doorway, but didn't offer to shake hands. "You're early."

Billy pulled the door closed. He knew better than to bring up the time pressure of the funeral. Dunsford would try to delay him out of spite. That was the thing that bothered him the most about Dunsford. He didn't care about anybody but himself.

Bright fluorescent tubes buzzed in the overhead fixture. The chairs, molded from thick vinyl, sported sturdy metal arms suitable for restraining agitated suspects with handcuffs. He was familiar with these chairs, almost like they were his first cousins. A sour odor perpetually wrapped itself around the room, the smell of guilt and sweat, an odor he typically ignored. Today the room smelled different. Maybe it was because he was the one who would sit on the other side of the table.

"I brought notes from the scene," Billy said, taking a seat and pulling his memo book from his jacket pocket.

"So you can keep your story straight?" Dunsford cracked a nasty smile.

"I'm not engaging in a pissing match, Don."

Irritation sparked across Dunsford's face. In this room, a good detective never lets a suspect get the upper hand, even if they're only joking around.

For the camera, Dunsford stated the date, time, and Billy's full name before shoving a legal pad and pen across the table. Billy wrote in chronological order every action he'd taken at the scene, every detail he could remember. He wrote four pages and read it over carefully. Once he signed the statement, he would be committed to facts that could be used against him in court. Everything in a statement has to be true, but not every truth has to be in that statement. Cops and lawyers know this. Regular citizens don't.

Cop 101: Everyone is a suspect until the lead investigator has good reason to rule them out. The burden would fall to Billy to provide Dunsford with a good reason to cut him loose. Before he left the barge, he'd decided to stuff his pride and work with Dunsford in every way to move the investigation forward. On the other hand, he'd be damned if he'd give up anything he didn't have to. This was no friendly chat.

He signed the statement and pushed the pad to the middle of the table. Dunsford sucked his teeth and read it through twice, jiggling his little finger in his ear and flicking away the earwax.

When he was done, he looked up with mock sympathy. "You seen the news footage of Poston shoving that hawker at the ballpark?"

"I was there when it happened."

"Rough way for a man to exit the public eye. A real nutso."

"Nutso" raised his hackles. Augie had been diagnosed with a mental illness, not a moral weakness. "He was a sick man."

"Touchy subject for you, I guess." Dunsford was enjoying himself.

The morning news had shown a clip of Augie's wild-eyed brawl, with stadium security hauling him off. The camera then switched to the entrance to the DeVoy and his corpse being wheeled out on a gurney. The footage was the final teardown of a sports hero's reputation. It made for great TV.

"I see you've opened your statement with the altercation between you and Poston on Monday night," Dunsford said.

"We both got pretty banged up. I wanted the details in the record. The next morning I went to his apartment to patch things up."

Guilt swamped him with the memory of the goose egg on Augie's forehead, but he didn't have the luxury of wallowing in it. The fight was the most damning evidence Dunsford had against him.

"You claim a taco vendor witnessed the fight," Dunsford said.

"He works the cart at the ballpark entrance, an Hispanic, in his forties."

Dunsford snorted. "That narrows it down. We'll try to locate him, but those guys switch jobs every other week. You have any business dealings with Poston?"

He knew where this was going. Soured business deals generated about 20 percent of the squad's homicide caseload. "Augie and I were friends. That's it."

"Fair enough." Dunsford flipped open his memo book and rubbed the side of his nose with his index finger. "You say Poston's door was open when you arrived. Was it cracked open, or did you turn the knob and find it unlocked?"

"I didn't touch the door. I made that clear on page one."

"You didn't break the door's seal, so we won't have to throw burglary into the pot. What did you do after you entered the victim's residence?"

"That's at the bottom of page two."

Dunsford laid down the statement and sighed as if he were dealing with a headstrong child. "You're here to give a statement and answer my questions. *All* my questions. If you don't cooperate, you know what will happen to your career." He leaned in. "There won't be one."

Jerk. Repeating questions already answered was within bounds, but Dunsford was going overboard. This was being recorded. If Dunsford was a big enough fool to risk reprimand, Billy would help him out.

"Whatever you need, Sergeant."

Dunsford's mouth twitched. "Cooperation. That's what I want. You say you went to Poston's apartment the morning after the fight to patch up your friendship. Tell me about that."

"Augie was out of control. He attacked me. It's there in the statement. I attempted to take him to The MED, but he refused help and walked away. I went home and texted him twice. I was worried about concussion. Both times he responded 'FU,' so I was less concerned. I went to bed. The next morning he didn't answer. I went to his apartment to check on him."

"We'll verify your phone records and the stop at Denny's," Dunsford said, and raised his gaze to make eye contact.

A smart detective's next question would be: *Did you have any other reason to go to Augie Poston's apartment yesterday morning?* To that question, Billy would be compelled to answer: *Augie stole a photograph from me. I went there to get it back.*

Once that line of questioning began, he would have to explain the photo from Red's jacket and give Dunsford the investigative work he and Frankie had done. That would tank both of their careers. On the other hand, if Dunsford asked the question and he flat-out lied, he could be charged criminally for giving false information to a law enforcement officer during an investigation.

As a distraction, he rapped his fingers on the edge of the table. "Something's bothering me. The last thing Augie said was that he had business to handle. His phone rang as he walked away."

Dunsford looked surprised, thrown off track. "Go on."

"You know about his eBay site. The call might have been a client wanting to meet at his apartment. You saw the expensive stuff at his place, the things people collect. The watches alone must have been worth twenty, maybe thirty grand. A collector would know the value of that inventory. It's a reasonable place to start."

Dunsford flipped through pages for his missing list. "Watches," he said under his breath. He had a reputation for letting files pile up on his desk. Cases had collapsed beneath his shoddy paperwork.

"You've got the subpoenas in process, right?" Billy prodded. "Phone records? Augie's e-mail server?"

Dunsford sneered to cover his confusion. He picked up Billy's statement and shook it. "We need to discuss what's *not* in this document. Four years ago Augie Poston totaled your truck."

That caught him off guard. "Everybody on the squad knows that story, including you."

"I remember you were so mad you drop-kicked the squad's coffeemaker."

"Yeah. What's the relevance?"

"You've been living in another state, answerable to nobody. You came back in town and beat this guy up. The next morning you're at his place in time to discover the body."

Dunsford jerked a file from the bottom of his pile and pushed it across the table. "Explain this."

Chapter 32

Clipped to the top of the file was the black-and-white of Dahlia Poston's torched Pontiac, her burned body wedged behind the steering wheel. Dahlia's back was arched against the seat in her attempt to escape the flames. Her right arm shielded her head, her face peeked out from underneath. The position was eerily similar to that of her son's body on the floor in front of the refrigerator.

How had Dunsford known about the file on Dahlia Poston?

"According to the sign-out sheet, you pulled this file the day before Poston was murdered." Dunsford settled back in his chair, contemptuous. "You may not see the relevance there either, but I do. It's damned relevant."

Billy slipped the photo inside the file. This was no flyby statement, this was turning into an interrogation. He'd underestimated Dunsford.

"I ran into Augie at the park my first day back. He talked about his mother's death. He believed she was murdered—"

"By whom?"

"He wasn't sure. He was paying a journalist to look into it. I figured the guy was hustling him, so I decided to take a look at the file myself."

"So you *did* have business with Poston."

"A favor for a friend. I take it you've looked through the file?"

"I did. There's no conclusive proof of homicide. It was correctly ruled as accidental."

"That's what I told Augie."

"And he believed you?"

"No."

"What I'm hearing is you looked into Augie's mother's death. He didn't like what you had to say, so he didn't want to pay you for your time. You showed up at his place with cuffs and a gun to get your money."

This wasn't good. Dunsford was working up a scenario. "I told you the reason I was there. I always carry cuffs, and I'm usually packing."

"What's this journalist's name?"

"I don't have a name."

Dunsford raised an eyebrow. "So we've got us a mystery man. Freeman didn't have a name, either."

Ah. There it was. Freeman must have mentioned Dahlia Poston's death and Augie's interest in the file when he told Dunsford about the manuscript. Dunsford pulled the file and saw Billy's name on the sign-out register.

"Freeman told you about the missing manuscript," he said. "That's how you made the connection to Dahlia Poston's death."

Dunsford flushed. "You've seen this manuscript?"

"No. But Augie talked about it."

"Let me get this straight. A delusional psychotic feeds you

and Freeman a story about a phantom journalist and a manuscript. Neither of you knows the journalist's name. Freeman believes there was a manuscript. He's seen a stack of papers, but he didn't actually get a look at it. Now it's gone. How's that not a wild-goose chase?"

Billy was tired of the runaround. He wanted to get down to the case. "Look, Don. The way I see it, you've got two ways to go."

Dunsford's hand went up. "Stop right there. You've been in town four days. I've seen you at two crime scenes. You're the primary suspect in the murder of a man you beat the hell out of in front of witnesses. For all I know—"

Billy pushed back from the table without a word, stood, and went into the hall, his chest tight and ears ringing. *Primary suspect, my foot.* Dunsford had no evidence against him. He was free to walk any time he wanted. If he did that, he could make the end of the funeral. He went down the hall for a drink of water from the fountain to think about it.

Of course, leaving would be colossally stupid. Middlebrook would review the tapes. So far, they were both coming off like idiots.

He went back to find Dunsford standing beside the table, his cheeks flushed and thinning hair ruffled out of place from running his hands through it. The man had the confused and angry look of a pinned bull.

Billy did a shoulder roll. "I needed to move around. Got a crick in my neck."

Dunsford spoke quietly. "If you're uncomfortable, we can go to my desk when we're finished, but right now I need you to sit down and look at me while we talk. Understand what I'm saying?" He cocked his head toward the camera.

Billy grabbed the back of the chair, swung it around, and straddled it with enough defiance to satisfy his ego.

"Let's get to it," he said.

Dunsford sat and pulled up to the table. "You're on the record as having walked home after the fight."

"That's correct. The next morning I picked up coffee and biscuits at Denny's. The DeVoy's security cameras will verify that I arrived at the building at approximately seven forty-five A.M."

"How did you gain access to the ninth floor?"

"I was at Augie's place last fall. I remembered the code for his floor."

"Can you verify that?"

A far-off alarm rang in his head, but he recited the code anyway: "44123."

Dunsford puffed air through his lips as he wrote. He was working up to something. "The DeVoy's security setup is the closest thing you have to an alibi. Is that correct?"

"I'd say it's pretty damned persuasive."

"Then you have a problem."

"How so?" Billy asked.

"Cameras cover the lobby and public elevators. The service elevator cameras are shells with blinking LED lights. They're dummies."

"I didn't know that, but it doesn't matter. You can't get to the service elevators without walking through the lobby."

"Unless you use the back entrance," Dunsford said.

"I'm sure the service entrance stays locked twenty-four hours a day."

"Of course it's locked. But the code you just gave also unlocks the back entrance. The building manager has it, and his assistant.

James Freeman has it. Augie Poston had it. No one else in the building has the code. But you have it. You could have gone to the ninth floor undetected on Monday night. There are no working cameras to say otherwise."

Dunsford put down his pen and fixed his gaze on Billy. His attempt to suppress a grin failed. His enthusiasm could have animated a corpse. He must have been envisioning reading Billy his rights, which would be the high point in his mediocre career.

For Billy, the turn was unexpected. It was bad. He needed to get the hell out. He looked at his watch. "I'm due upstairs for a meeting."

Dunsford ignored him and continued. "According to James Freeman, Poston claimed that after the fight you said to him, 'This isn't over.' Want to explain that?"

He'd thought about the phrase, knowing it would come up. Nothing to do but finesse it. "Augie and I were buddies. I wasn't going to let the friendship end because of a stupid fight. That's all I have to say for now."

Dunsford forced control into his voice. "All right. Go whine to Middlebrook. But remember. Your former position with this squad means squat. I'm the one who'll decide your status in this case." He spun a yellow pad across the table. "Give me your current address and contact information plus your address in Atlanta and the number for that girlfriend of yours. What's her name?"

"That's none of your business." He'd made it this far without blowing up, but his control was slipping.

Dunsford's lips thinned with spite. "That's all right. I'll have a conversation with Ms. Snow when the time is right."

He stood, wanting to put Dunsford on the ground. If he did that, the whole thing would fly in a direction he couldn't control. "We're done," he said.

Dunsford stood, too. "We're done. But keep in mind . . . the lack of evidence isn't the same thing as evidence. You might want to rethink your statement."

Billy hit the hallway and almost knocked over the guy pushing the mail cart. He was headed straight for central records. Edgar Kellogg owed him an explanation.

Edgar must have known he'd be coming, because he had a piece of paper folded and ready to push across the counter when Billy walked in.

The note read:

Seventh-floor break room. Five minutes.

Billy went to the break room and poured a cup of scorched coffee. He had to calm down so he could get what he needed from Edgar before the clerical staff straggled in with their boxed salads and microwavable meals.

Edgar pushed through the door, palms up and wagging, his tight potbelly poking off his skinny frame like a tumor on a twig. "I never said a word to nobody about that Poston file. But I'll tell you, that limp dick Dunsford will take you down if there's a way he can make it happen."

Billy wasn't going to explain it was dumb luck that Freeman had mentioned the file to Dunsford. Having Edgar on the defensive was useful. "Let's get past that. What I need now is a shortcut, and you're the man who can help me."

Edgar glanced at the door. "We only got a couple of minutes. What's up?"

Billy pulled out the stack of photos and pointed at the man wearing the jacket. "Do you recognize this guy?"

Edgar ran his thumb down the edge of the print. "These are from the sixties. That's a long time ago."

"Don't hedge, Edgar. You knew every blessed cop in the MPD back then."

The little man pointed at the picture. "This one's FBI."

"His name?"

"Leland Grant. He worked with the MPD during all that civil rights crap. COINTELPRO was their dirty-tricks program. They used special tactics to foul up radical movements."

"Can you identify the locations?"

Edgar fanned through the photos. "Mainly Beale Street. And that there is Grant's partner. He must have been standing inside Freeman's Bar to get the angle on that shot. The two of them were in charge of setting up listening posts in the colored neighborhoods. The FBI was keeping track of agitators and Communists coming down from up north—the ones registering the coloreds to vote."

"Something happened between Grant and Freeman," he said, hoping Edgar would bite.

Edgar hiked up his pants and rolled his tongue in his cheek. "Boy howdy. Freeman had this bar. It was a perfect setup to be one of Grant's listening posts, but Freeman wouldn't cooperate. The way I heard it, Grant warned Freeman he'd lose his liquor license if he didn't straighten up. Freeman got vocal about it, set a bad example for the other business owners. Grant got the liquor board to pull his license on some bogus charge."

"What happened to Freeman?"

"Lost the bar. Took it real personal. He hanged himself a year later."

Chapter 33

Refrigerated air blasted Frankie as she walked into the Rock of Ages Funeral Home. The cold set her teeth on edge despite the last half hour she'd spent in a hot car recording license plate numbers and photographing mourners as they entered the chapel. Two black Escalades, parked in the lot when she'd arrived, had Louisiana tags. She called a friend at the station house and asked to have the plates run.

She had a three-year-old mug shot of Cool Willy, aka William Cooley—six feet five and heavyset, with a shaved head and wearing a mask of sullenness meant to conceal either stupidity or cunning. If she couldn't pick him out during the service, she would go to the parking lot afterward and photograph the drivers as they stepped into their out-of-state cars.

The chapel, despite the fact that it was crowded with people, had walls draped in velvet that gave the room a cloistered atmosphere. Everyone wore shades, even some of the ladies in their church hats and pastel suits. Frankie slipped on hers so she could study the crowd without being too obvious. She was watching for anyone who was uncomfortable or hanging back from the crowd with a suppressed need to see how things played out. She had skipped Brad's funeral, choosing instead to donate money to the fund established for the family. She wondered, had she been there, whether a detective could have picked up on her distress. Even now her guilt festered like a spider bite poisoning her from within.

Did grief and guilt look the same? She scanned the crowd again, analyzing it this time with a different eye.

Among them were several tall, muscular African-American men who were sporting fades rather than hard-line beards. They wore diamond studs in their ears and Hugo Boss suits tailored to fit their vigorous bodies. They looked like athletes—Memphis Grizzlies or New Orleans Saints. Or they could have been connected with the music or film industry. Memphis attracted movie companies for its location shots and musicians who wanted to soak up some authenticity after having lived too long in L.A. If Cool Willy was among that group, he'd lost the baby fat, muscled up, and dropped the street swagger for a classier look.

She went to stand against the side wall, pinned against it, actually, by the throng. Men formed groups and sang a cappella in harmony. Women in long dresses the colors of parrots swayed around the chapel singing to themselves. It was, after all, a funeral for two musicians. She glanced down at her navy suit, concerned that her appearance screamed plainclothes cop.

Death had been so much a part of her job she preferred to skip funerals, so before leaving home this morning she'd researched funeral customs. If Billy knew that, he would laugh his head off. Trusting her instincts wasn't her style. She wanted facts. Everything else was drama.

She recognized street people, local musicians, a TV newscaster, and the residents from Robert House, who'd been bused in to fill two pews. The men wore jackets and ties, their hair shaved close at the backs of their necks. She picked up the acrid smell of alcohol and drugs emitted through their pores, vapors that followed addicts around, their kidneys and livers having worn out after years of abuse. She studied the men, aware that Red and Little Man had lived at the shelter and probably knew some of them.

At the far end of the pew sat an imposing woman, wearing a head wrap the colors of the Jamaican flag: black, yellow, and green. She held herself separate from the men, her posture as stiff as a headmistress in charge of a pew full of schoolboys. Some of the men appeared nervous, out of place. Frankie searched their features and took a few surreptitious shots with her phone.

An older man came down the aisle, wearing suspenders and carrying a beat-up acoustic guitar. He took the stage, filled with gorgeous red roses, and spoke in a deep, sad drawl with the authority of one who had seen too much.

"You all know that one of these days things are gonna change. Yes they will. And we will cry no more. This is for my friend, Red Davis."

He played "Burning Tree Blues," wearing it out on that old guitar, tearing the hearts right out of the mourners. Some of them raised their hands. Some cried and wailed. The emotion in the room rolled over Frankie, giving her chills through her jacket.

The man ended the song and left the stage. Then a trumpet sounded from the back of the chapel. A stately black man dressed in a white suit, a purple shirt, and a top hat with plumes sprouting out of the top stepped through the doorway. He blew the opening notes of "Nearer, My God, to Thee" and marched down the aisle followed by a trombone player, a brass tuba player, and another man with a snare drum. They proceeded to where pallbearers in straw boater hats were rolling the two caskets to the foot of the stage.

A preacher stepped to the podium to deliver an opening prayer. When he was done he gestured to a man with a cane limping down the aisle toward the stage. "Mr. Sid Garrett, a steadfast friend of our community, will now say a few words about the blessed departed."

Earlier, she'd noticed Garrett clasping hands with and receiving hugs from people in the crowd. He took the stage with halting steps, two young men positioning themselves on either side of the podium. Bodyguards? Were they window dressing to bolster Garrett's celebrity ego or did he actually need protection?

The audience stilled as he adjusted the mike and looked about, taking command of the room. "Late in the evening at Robert House, I often found Red Davis sitting alone in the lobby. He appeared to be watching the traffic, but I knew better. Red was pondering life. He was a poet and a philosopher, no stranger to the trials of the human spirit.

"I came to know Red Davis and Little Man Lacy during their stay at Robert House. Little Man was a gentle soul, mute from birth, but we knew him through every note he played."

"Tell it," someone called from the audience.

Garrett nodded. "Red told me once, 'People love the blues, but they don't want to remember why we sing it. Even the brothers despised us for coming out of the fields. Blues players remind them of everything they've tried hard to forget.'

"Red told the truth. He wrote what he loved and what he hated. He wrote about the adversity of life. No one ever held the door open for these two men. But even brave men can be brought low by nature. Katrina took their city. Broke their bodies and souls. We are saddened by their loss."

"Amen!" the crowd thundered. Garrett lowered his chin, obviously overwhelmed, or he was doing a good job of appearing so.

"Red and I sometimes sat up late at night, two old lions recalling the struggles of the civil rights era. I fought in the courtroom. Red lived the fight during the hardest of times. All his life he was refused lodging, transportation. He was refused a decent education. His manhood was challenged every day."

Garrett paused, seeming to reach back in his memory. "Red told me how they had performed on the night Dr. King was assassinated. He said that was the hardest blues they ever played in their lives. He talked about government agents harassing him and other citizens on Beale Street in the months before the assassination. After the loss of Dr. King, this city was afraid. The country was demoralized.

"The last time I spoke with Red he talked about making a change in one person's life. That's all he wanted, to make a difference. It was his final goal. I pray he was able to complete his task."

Garrett gestured toward the caskets. "At the end of this service, Red and Little Man will ride The City of New Orleans one last time. Their bodies will be laid to rest at Lafayette Cemetery in the city they loved."

Soft calls of "Hallelujah" came from the crowd.

"You may have heard on the news that Augie Poston has departed from us, too."

Shouts of surprised protest made Frankie jump. Garrett pointed to a man in the audience. "That's right, brother. Augie Poston left this world yesterday. All three men are home now, gone to their eternal rest."

Garrett raised his hands. "Let's bow our heads for a moment of silence in memory of these three fine men."

As soon as the people in the chapel settled, Frankie searched the faces in the room. Her gaze fell on a Hispanic man in dark glasses seated in the last pew. Sergio Ramos turned and nodded in her direction. Then he turned back to the stage and bowed his head. She was floored. How had he known she was standing there?

After the silence, Garrett raised his head and leaned into the mike. "God bless you all for coming. We are grateful for your presence. Now you may escort our departed friends in the time-honored, New Orleans style known as second line."

The trumpeter swung into an upbeat version of "I'll Fly Away." The mourners followed the caskets down the aisle, hand-kerchiefs waving.

Ramos made his way through the crowd to join Frankie as the chapel cleared. She should go to the parking lot to photo-graph the drivers of the Louisiana cars, but Ramos's presence seemed just as pressing. She decided to stay with Ramos. He extended his hand to squeeze hers.

"How did you know I was here?" she asked.

"My sight has dimmed, not my vision."

She noted the smaller man dressed in white and standing just behind Ramos. A driver. He could have pointed her out.

"I didn't realize you knew Davis and Lacy." She was lying, a cop's lie.

"I run a counseling program at Robert House. Some of the men are Santerían believers. I don't discuss my client list, of course. Did you know Mr. Davis and Mr. Lacy?"

She blinked, thinking fast. "I'm a blues fan."

His attention drifted toward the stage. He bent in close and spoke softly. "Ms. Malone, both men told me they had no family, yet there was a young woman seated in the area behind the panels reserved for family members."

She looked across the row of pews at the translucent panels. "How do you know someone was there?"

"I heard the door open. She was seated after the guitarist began to play. She's thin. The metal chair barely creaked as she sat. She was crying. She left shortly before the caskets went down the aisle. That's when I became aware of you standing against the wall." He smiled. "You are now curious as to how I knew it was you. With your background in Santería, you will understand. I was given a gift by my orisha when my sight began to fade. I feel a person's distinctive vibrations. It is as accurate as seeing them."

He reached for her hand again. "I'd very much like to speak with this young woman. I'm certain she's a relative. Could you find her?"

A dilemma. Should she chase the pimp or this woman? She had photos of the men and the tag numbers that she could follow up. The woman, if she existed, was an unknown.

"I'll see what I can do." She went to the paneled area and found a single folding chair that had been pulled forward for a better view of the podium. A door in the area opened onto a long hallway. She hurried down to the funeral director's office where a man in his twenties sat at a desk, talking on the phone. Frankie flashed her badge.

"I need to call you back," the man said and hung up. "May I help you, Officer?"

"A woman was seated in the family area during the Davis and Lacy funeral. Where is she?"

"She called a car service fifteen minutes ago."

"Which company?"

"I don't know."

"I need her name and contact information."

The man looked perplexed. "Our company policy won't allow me to give out that information without significant legal reasons or the family's written permission."

"So the woman is family."

"That's all I can say." He reached for the phone as an excuse to end their conversation. "Anything else?"

"Where would the car pick her up?"

She hurried down the back hall toward the sound of the brass band that had followed the caskets out of the building. She stepped out to see two hearses surrounded by people who were dancing and waving good-bye. The rest of the parking lot was empty.

She walked around the side of the building to the front parking lot. The Escalades with Louisiana tags were gone.

"Damn it," she muttered to herself. She'd made the wrong choice.

"Ms. Malone," Ramos called from the top of the front steps. "I assume you missed the young woman."

"Yes. I'm sorry."

"Possibly I can help," he said. "I believe I overheard the director use the name Jones."

Chapter 34

On the street, Billy shed his suit jacket and crossed over Poplar Avenue to the public parking lot. The smell of Dunsford's aftershave stayed with him all the way to his car. He got in and rolled down the window.

His future in law enforcement was on the line, and now a man who wouldn't make a decent dogcatcher had his fat fingers in it. Even if Billy was never charged with murder, the stigma of this case could damage his standing in the department. They might even refuse to reinstate him.

He loosened his tie, rubbed his eyes. To make this right he would have to work three homicides while knocking down the case Dunsford was so eagerly building against him. He'd taken the first step by talking with Kellogg. The Redbirds had a night game on the schedule, so this evening he would drive by to see if that taco vendor was on duty, the one witness who could testify that Augie had been the aggressor. He hated the sound of that, but it was true.

He flashed on Dunsford's satisfaction when he'd dropped the bomb about the security cameras. Freeman knew yesterday that the tapes were his only alibi, but Freeman hadn't mentioned that the rear entrance cameras were dummies. He had allowed Dunsford to spring his trap. Or Dunsford could be lying about the cameras. Only way to know was to check them, see if Freeman had been that big of an ass.

He phoned Roxanne at the chief's office to say he wouldn't be back in the afternoon. She sounded surprised, and then her voice had fallen off as if she'd put it together that he was on Dunsford's suspects list. No reinstatement papers for him until that status changed. He hoped Middlebrook would let it ride a day or two, give him time to turn Dunsford around before they had to drag in a union rep to discuss his rights.

Jesus, he had a lot of ground to cover.

Back at the barge, a light wind cooled the decks. He pulled on jeans and sat at the outside table with his laptop to make notes about the interview while it was fresh in his mind. There was no room for emotion in this. He was in a major jam, and needed a cool head.

The way Dunsford saw it, Billy had been hired by Augie to look into his mother's death. Then Dunsford jumped to the conclusion that they'd had a disagreement over money, which led to the fight outside the stadium. He believed Billy went through the rear entrance, killed Augie, and showed up the next morning to discover the body. If Dunsford learned about the scuffle at the funeral home, he'd make Billy his sole suspect.

Honestly, he saw how Dunsford could go there. The scenario had a lot of merit.

As he typed, he felt Lou Nevers reading over his shoulder, goading him, laughing at him, getting angry. Lou would say, "Stop flapping around like a ruptured duck and get on with it."

Right. *Get on with it.*

He called Garrett and caught him heading for the Carter museum to set up for the night's fund-raiser. Garrett agreed to answer a few questions afterward, suggesting they meet at Itta Bena where he'd be giving an after-party for donors.

Next he called Frankie, asking her to join him at the bar before his meeting with Garrett.

He washed dishes and jumped on the Internet. His last call before leaving the barge was to the home of retired FBI agent Leland Grant.

The back entrance of Itta Bena off South Second was an awning-covered staircase leading to the third floor. The bar was low-key, with exposed beams, wooden floors, and blue-tinted windows. During Beale's commercial heyday, the building housed black doctors and dentists. The space fell to disuse until B. B. King resurrected the entire building and turned the third floor into a blues club and restaurant with a speakeasy vibe. The club's name came from B.B.'s hometown, Itta Bena, Mississippi.

Frankie sat in a booth at the back of the bar, her hand wrapped around a club soda, a file laying on the table in front of her. On the wall behind her hung a private collection of Tina Turner photographs, spontaneous shots of Tina swinging her long hair and flexing her strong thighs.

Frankie wore a sky-blue cotton dress that showed off her legs and sparkly earrings that made her short haircut look sexy without being too obvious. It struck Billy that she'd never mentioned a man in her life, not that he was interested. But he was curious.

He took a seat across from Frankie and ordered a beer he didn't plan to drink. She opened the file and handed him two typed pages stapled at the top left.

"Notes from the funeral," she said.

Her clarity of detail impressed him as he read through it, but the punch line was missing. The report wasn't conclusive about Cool Willy's presence.

"You had a mug shot," he said, pointing to the photo in her file.

Perturbed, she handed over her iPhone for him to flip through shots of several black men who were all wearing similar suits.

"That looks like him isn't the same as *that's him,"* she said. "The mug shot is three years old. If he dropped a hundred pounds and cleaned up his act, Cool Willy could be one of those guys."

She took the phone, scrolled to a shot of a black Escalade with Louisiana plates, and handed it back to him. "This vehicle is registered to a limo service in New Orleans. The service has two owners. One is William Cooley, aka Cool Willy. The way I see it, someone leased the car to drive to the funeral. Or Cool Willy gave the car to a stand-in to check out the funeral for him."

"Or Cool Willy was there," he said.

"Or he was there, and I missed him."

She frowned, clearly upset at the possibility she'd screwed up. In this line of work, you are wrong 40 percent of the time. The secret is to know when to switch to the 60 percent side. Mz. Police Goddess, the complex human being that she was, needed a change of attitude if she was going to survive.

The server came by with another club soda and a coveted bowl of honey-roasted peanuts. Frankie ate a few nuts while he ran through the photos from the funeral, some of Sid Garrett giving the eulogy. Garrett looked drawn but in full command of the stage.

The last photo was of a Hispanic man wearing dark glasses who was standing at the back of the chapel. "Who's that?"

"Sergio Ramos. Nice looking for a witch doctor, don't you think?" Frankie took a sip of soda and batted her lashes.

"Did he give a reason for showing up?"

"He admitted that Red and Little Man were his clients. He offers pro bono counseling at Robert House. Several of the men are Santería believers."

"What's your read on this guy? Kindly doctor or killer showing up to gloat?"

She gave him an impassive look. "When I figure that out, I'll let you know. He did pick up on something useful . . . a possible family member showing up for the funeral."

She pulled another page from the file for him to read. As far as Billy was concerned, anything to do with Ramos was questionable, but he had to admit the vague description of the young woman he'd given Frankie sounded familiar.

He handed the report back. "A woman arrived at the funeral home by car service on Monday afternoon and went straight to the director's office. She was young, slender, well dressed. I walked by the office on my way out. She had the waterworks going. That mortuary is a busy place, so I didn't connect her to Davis and Lacy." He also didn't mention that he'd nearly come to blows with Augie moments before.

"Ramos said he thought he heard the name Jones."

He scoffed. "Jones. Yeah. That narrows it down."

"Didn't you work with a TBI agent named Jones?"

"No relation, I'm sure." The accuracy of Frankie's recall surprised him. Otis Jones had been on loan to the homicide squad by the Tennessee Bureau of Investigation last summer. Jones had partnered with him in the Overton investigation after Lou's death. It was a hard case and a difficult time. Jones had reined him in, kept him from overreacting.

"That's all I've got on the funeral," Frankie said and dug a handful of nuts out of the bowl. "Tell me what happened with Dunsford."

"The interview ran long. I hated having to miss the funeral," he said, hoping to put off her questions.

She nodded and focused on lining up peanuts on a cocktail napkin. "Did Dunsford push you?"

"What are you getting at?"

She looked up from the peanuts. "Your involvement in Poston's murder is troubling at best." Her gaze didn't waver. She wanted an answer.

"You're asking if Dunsford cleared me. He didn't. He'll stay on my back until he arrests me or the killer is caught. You're having drinks with a murder suspect. If you feel a need to cut ties, I'll understand."

"Before you kick me out of the booth, why don't you tell me what happened?"

He drained half the beer and gave her the rundown. The more he talked, the more her features darkened with concern.

"I went by the DeVoy to check the cameras," he said. "Dunsford was right, they're dummies. And the taco vendor who witnessed the fight is gone. My alibi has a big damned hole in it."

She opened the file and began to flip through pages.

"One last thing," he said.

She looked up.

"I went in early to ask Middlebrook for an immediate reinstate so I could help Dunsford with the case."

She gave a short laugh. "*That's* not going to happen." She pulled a sheet of graphs from the file. "I did a risk-benefit analysis of your situation. The percentages aren't great, but I'm willing to chance the exposure and hang in with you." She pushed the paper to him and chose a peanut from the middle of the line. "Take a look."

The graph meant nothing to him. He handed it back, wondering how a person could be so logical and so unpredictable at the same time. He would take her word that she was on board for now.

He went through his conversation with Edgar Kellogg about the FBI agent and Freeman's father's suicide. "They ruined the man. No wonder Freeman hates cops."

Frankie flinched. Good cops hate to hear about bad cops. "Go on," she said.

"I tracked down Leland Grant and called his house. His daughter answered. Grant died eight months ago of lung cancer. His wife had a stroke not long after. The daughter is getting the house ready to sell."

"And you had a sympathetic conversation with her about what it takes to clean a loved one's possessions out of a house. I'll bet you were good at that."

He grinned. "I got the information. She donated Grant's clothes to Goodwill two months ago. Red bought his jacket and found the photos."

"Is it possible Grant put them in the pocket years ago?"

"Doesn't sound like something an FBI agent would do. Chemo does funny things to a person's mind. Maybe he put them there during his illness."

"How about his partner, the one in the photos?" she asked.

"The daughter said he died twenty-seven years ago in a car accident."

"So that's the end of that." She frowned, thinking it through.

A server passed by carrying steaks and sides of fried green tomatoes and buttermilk grits. Downstairs, the house band was cranking up its first set. The bass and drums thumped through Itta Bena's floorboards. Across the room, Di Anne Price warmed up the crowd at the piano with a sweet jazz instrumental.

He'd been working through the idea that the photographs somehow connected Davis's and Lacy's deaths with Augie's murder. He wanted to hear what Garrett might add.

"Freeman said Garrett could give us background on the photos," he said. "He agreed to meet with me tonight."

"He had two bodyguards at the funeral. What's that about? You think it's post-traumatic stress from the shooting?"

"I'm sure. The guards chauffeur him around in a black Caddy with Garrett sitting in the back wearing Ray-Bans. Very Hollywood. He wrote a best seller about the civil rights era after the shooting. The book tour led to his TV commentator career."

"I heard him tear into a radio talk show host for getting the facts wrong," she said. "Impressive stuff. Why did he choose civil liberties for his law practice?"

"His brother got caught up in the Freedom Riders protest. Black and white students rode buses through southern states to force the issue of segregated public transportation. They were pulled off the buses, beaten, and jailed. One bus was burned in Alabama, but the riders kept coming. Robert joined them. He turned into a real crusader for the cause.

"After the Freedom Riders, he worked with sharecroppers in Mississippi who were being kicked off the property by their white bosses for registering to vote. Garrett's brother was smack in the middle of it."

"You've read Garrett's book," she said.

"I know people who were beaten because they tried to vote. Yeah, I read his book."

"Why didn't his brother write the book?"

"Robert went out one night to meet with a voter-registration worker in Mississippi. The next morning a farmer found his car on a back road. His body was never found."

"So little brother felt obliged to take up the cause," she said.

"With a vengeance. Garrett went to an all-black law school in Washington, D.C., then worked for the only black law firm on Beale Street. That gave him credibility and connections with the black community."

"What did their parents think about this?" she asked.

"They died early. When Robert disappeared, he left young Garrett an orphan."

"Jesus," she said and took a drink of her soda, thinking. "There was something about Garrett's eulogy that bothered me. He made it sound like he hung out with Red all the time, swapping stories. I don't know that I believed him. Could've been literary license. By the way, who footed the bill for that spectacle?"

"Augie did. Garrett may have agreed to pitch in. I saw him nearly choke when he got a look at what had to be an estimate. By the way, what's your general assessment of him?"

"He seemed really out of it. An addiction to scripts wouldn't surprise me. He's in a lot of pain."

"Yesterday, he insisted Augie was doing meth. He thinks a dealer may have killed him."

"Is that likely?" she asked.

"I'm looking into it, but I'm skeptical."

"I'd say Garrett is the one who's hooked." She ate another peanut. "Anyway, he knew a lot of people in the crowd. And he brought a busload of guys from the shelter with him. We'll take a look at those guys, right?"

Billy nodded. He heard laughter. Women in cocktail dresses and men in sports coats walked into the club with Sid Garrett leading the way. He spoke with the hostess, who ushered Garrett's guests to a secluded table tucked into a private room.

Frankie stood and picked up her soda. "I'll wait at the bar. Good luck."

Chapter 35

arrett raised a hand as he came over, gesturing toward Frankie, who now sat on a stool half turned from the bar. She really did look fantastic in that dress.

"Your friend over there was at the funeral this morning. Would she like to join us?"

He's fishing, Billy thought. *Wants to know Frankie's part in this.* "You have guests. We'll keep this simple."

"Fine by me." Garrett took a seat. "It just came to me that you were caught up in that mess last year with Buck Overton. You were partners with Lou Nevers. God, that was a shock. I never pegged Lou for . . ." He shook his head. "You left town, didn't you? So you're here in an unofficial capacity."

He wondered why Garrett was working so hard to bust his balls. Could be a lawyer's habit, or could be something else. "I've been on leave. I'll be reinstated in a couple of days." He placed the photos on the table between them. "I was curious what you might know about these."

Garrett picked up the photos and shuffled through them. His hands slowed as he went along. After close consideration, he laid the stack on the table and settled into the depths of the booth.

"James Freeman thought you'd find the photographs interesting," Billy said.

Garrett's chin lifted. "I just left Freeman at the museum fund-raiser."

"I wondered if you recognized anyone in these shots. Or if you have an opinion about why they were taken."

Garrett regarded him, his features shadowed by the club's blue lighting. "These were taken thirty feet from where you and I were standing yesterday." He separated out two photos, laying them side by side at an angle so Billy could see them, shots of a woman and a man, both African Americans.

"The men behind the camera are law enforcement," Garrett said. "I'd say FBI, but I'm sure you know that. The subjects are either informants or people who've been intimidated into giving information. Some of the people put in that position gave up trivial stuff to get the agents off their backs. Others were snitches, traitors to the cause, people who helped the FBI disrupt lives and destroy careers." He waved a finger over one photo. "You can see the difference between those who were snitches and those who were coerced. This woman appears to be angry, but her body language says she's frightened. The cops probably put her son in lockup as leverage. The man in this photo, you can see he's checking the street for anyone who might be watching him. But he looks confident, almost chummy. He's a paid informant."

Garrett spread the stack over the table. "These were taken to blackmail informants in the event they ever tried to step out of line. Times were difficult back then, dangerous. The cops were nervous. Bad things happened to people who didn't play along. The pictures were taken as insurance."

"And do you recognize anyone?"

Garrett shrugged. "I was a kid. Most of these folks have passed. But my brother told me stories of FBI intimidation of the black community, how they tried to get people to spy on each other. Hoover created an atmosphere of paranoia. The agents felt they could lean on people to get whatever they wanted. They were good Americans, doing their job."

"I heard what happened to Freeman's Bar," Billy said.

"My point exactly. The man killed himself."

"You may know about Dahlia Poston. Augie believed his mother was caught up in the investigation after King's assassination. She died under questionable circumstances. A fire."

"I wasn't aware of that." Garrett grew still. "The Klan murdered my brother a year before Dr. King's assassination. We never found his body."

"I read your book. A compelling story."

"Robert's disappearance was front-page news in every major publication for two weeks. He gave a victim's face to the atrocities in Mississippi." Garrett's eyes dimmed. "At least his death made a difference." He touched the photos. "Are there more?"

"Why do you ask?" Billy wanted to avoid the subject of Augie stealing one of them.

Garrett nodded. "I have no interest in how you came by these photos, but I will ask that you donate them to the museum, all of them, if there are more. We have nothing like them in the collection. And please, if it works out, let me handle the transfer. An intern might not understand their importance."

"I can't promise, but I'll try to make it happen."

Laughter came from the private lounge, the voices of women in Garrett's group cutting through the noise in the bar. Garrett glanced in that direction. "Well, my friend." He braced both hands on the tabletop, preparing to stand.

"A manuscript was taken from Augie's apartment the night he

was murdered," Billy said. "It concerns the civil rights era. I wondered if Augie told you about it or mentioned the author's name."

Garrett sat back down. "You think this person was involved in Augie's murder?"

"Let's say I'd like to have a conversation with him."

"You're well aware that Augie was in bad shape at the funeral home that day. We didn't discuss books."

Billy nodded, remembering Augie's out-of-control behavior. "By the way, I wasn't able to attend the funeral, but my friend said it was quite a send-off."

Garrett rolled his eyes. "Unfortunately, I'm responsible for the costs until Augie's estate is settled. He died intestate. His assets are frozen."

They rose together and shook hands. "It's been interesting, Detective. Here's my card. My mobile number is on the back. When you're ready to release those photos, please give me a call."

Billy took the business card and stared down at it. A light clicked on in his brain. He kept his voice even. "You said Freeman was at the fund-raiser tonight. Did he mention having any plans afterward?"

"He was in the company of a beautiful woman. I'd say he has plans. When I left the museum I saw a light on in his office across the street."

Billy glanced across the room at Frankie. She caught his eye and slipped off the bar stool. "Thanks for your time. I'll get back to you about the photos for the museum."

Frankie jostled through the crowd at the bar to meet Billy in the hallway entrance.

"From where I sat, Garrett was stunned by those photographs," she said.

"They brought up memories of his brother's disappearance. Otherwise, he didn't add much to what we already know." He pointed toward the door. "Right now I have to find James Freeman. I have a hunch to pursue."

"Let's go," she said as they eased through people waiting to be seated. She had that scent-in-the-wind look cops get when they're up for the chase.

"It's better if you don't come," he said, moving ahead of her. "I'll explain later."

He walked to the door and realized she wasn't behind him. He turned to see her glaring at him, not pouting—no way a cop like Frankie would pout—but her arms were crossed over her middle and her back was pressed against the wall. An older couple brushed past. The woman giggled, aware of a spat in progress. He walked back.

"You're not leaving me out of this," she said.

He moved in and spoke quietly. "I think I know a way to find the journalist. I'm going to need Freeman's help to pull it off. It's illegal, but it has to be done."

"I didn't just hear that."

"No, you didn't."

He led the way down the outside stairs onto the sidewalk. They stepped into a stream of people who were out for the evening, the air smelling of smoked ribs and beer-soaked concrete. Two bike cops sat in front of the barricade at the head of the street, their eyes searching for pickpockets and D & Ds, drunk and disorderlies.

A breeze lifted the edges of Frankie's hair like down on a baby duck's back. It would be fun to hit a few clubs with her, hear some Memphis music. Maybe later, when all this was over.

He checked his watch. "I'll have to find Freeman and convince him to cooperate. I'll text if we're successful. Tomorrow you and I will line up our next move."

Her mouth twisted in dissatisfaction. "Text me no matter what."

Before he could answer, a thick male voice called out from behind them. "Hey! Hey you!"

They turned to see a powerfully built black man standing next to a row of parked cars farther down South Second. He had the bill of his cap pulled down to shadow his face under the streetlight.

He waved them over. "Come 'ere. I gotta talk to you."

Billy's jaw tightened. Damned hucksters want to be paid to go away.

"Beat it," he yelled.

The guy pointed at Frankie. "You, lady. You were at the funeral."

Frankie squinted at the man, then whispered, "Second car back. Escalade with Louisiana plates. The engine's running."

The man flung his arms wide, stumbled back, and caught himself. "Where's my bitch?" he slurred.

"That's Cool Willy," Frankie murmured. "He's stinko."

Billy waved and ambled forward in a loose gait. Willy wasn't fooled. His street smarts kicked in. He bolted for the Escalade, threw himself behind the wheel, and slammed the door. Billy ran behind, smashing his fist into the tailgate as the Escalade squealed away.

"You got the plates?" he yelled to Frankie.

She held up her iPhone.

He walked back, fist aching. "That's the guy we saw outside the squatter's house. He may have been the one who jumped me in the alley."

"How did he find us?"

"He followed you home from the funeral then here."

"That's creepy."

He gestured toward the bike cops. "Ask one of them to call in the plates. If we're lucky, he'll be hauled in for a DUI before he goes underground."

She took off.

He walked to the corner just as a full moon broke through the clouds. The door to B. B. King's downstairs club swung open. The house band's brass section was pushing out a sound like the Memphis Horns. It blasted into the night's warm air.

Across the street, an officer leaned his elbow on the counter of an outside bar. He was talking to a big-bosomed lady bartender wearing a low-cut tank top. The cop had a can of Coke in his hand. He leaned his head back and drained it, then looked at the bartender, who laughed.

Billy's mobile pinged with a text.

> *Three boxes arriving tomorrow. I've sent another package overnight.*
>
> *Mercy*

Billy stared at the text, the music and the full moon working on him. He waited for the pain to hit. Frankie walked up. He pocketed the phone.

"I'm heading to Freeman's office," he said.

"You sure you don't want me along?"

He gave her a stern look. She raised a hand. "Got it, I got it. I'll expect to hear from you."

Chapter 36

Light showed from beneath the window shades at Freeman Properties. Billy knocked and waited, being polite.

He got no response, so he pounded on the door. "Freeman. It's Billy Able. Open up."

The shade's slats moved. Freeman jerked the door open. Soft jazz escaped as he stepped outside and pulled the door closed. It bounced open a crack. Billy saw a flash of bare arm and long hair.

"Did you pick up a piece of art at the fund-raiser tonight?" Billy asked.

"I'm getting a restraining order to get you off my back," Freeman said as he tucked in his shirt.

"Got a question. Did you see Dunsford or the techs remove any business cards from Augie's place?"

"You're shittin' me."

"It's important."

"I'll give it some thought. Call you later."

"I need this tonight," he said.

"I'm catching a flight at six A.M. I'm back tomorrow evening. We'll discuss it then. Good night." Freeman turned to go.

He wanted to put Freeman in a hammerlock, but that would really piss him off.

"Listen. The journalist gave Augie a business card with his phone number. If we find the card tonight, I can get to this guy before Dunsford does. I guarantee once Dunsford gets hold of him, he'll lawyer up and we'll have nothing."

Freeman looked back into the room. "Damn it, Able. You've got god-awful timing."

"It'll take an hour, tops." He gestured toward the door. "She'll wait."

"You can't go digging around Augie's apartment; it's a crime scene. And I'm sure as hell not letting you in there on your own."

"Then come with me. It'll take less time."

The door opened. A leggy redhead holding a pair of heels in her right hand stepped out to stand beside Freeman.

"Let's *all* go," she said. Freeman glared at her. She smiled obligingly. "I'll make myself comfortable at your place until you're finished." She looked at Billy. "Right?"

He stifled a grin. "The lady wants to get comfortable at your place."

She extended her hand. "I'm Linda Orsburn. Based on what I just overheard, you probably shouldn't introduce yourself, Detective."

"Yes, ma'am." He was shaking the hand of the widow of former state attorney general Chuck Orsburn. She appeared to know a great deal about the law.

"The cops are going to notice if the seal on Augie's door has been breached," Freeman said.

He shrugged. "Shit happens. We'll find the card. You'll call the main MPD number and tell them you thought you heard water running in the apartment. You had to break the seal to check because of potential damage to the apartments below. If we're lucky, the message will get lost. Worst case, Dunsford will want an explanation."

"You don't ask for much," Freeman said.

"This guy could skip town. You got a better idea?"

"Son of a bitch, I don't know." Freeman shook his head. "Every time I close my eyes, I see Augie's body." He fumed, glanced at Linda. "All right. My key works as a passkey to every lock in the building."

"And while we're there, we'll look for the photo," Billy said.

Linda bent to slip on her heels. "I just love a good detective story."

The stadium lights still blazed through Augie's window even though the game was over and the stands were empty. Billy had already been over the room twice, working a grid, checking every conceivable nook where Augie could have slipped a card. In the process he noticed what he'd missed before—the cracked glass on the table between the two lounge chairs, the edge of the desk deeply scarred, all signs the assailant had searched for something, his adrenaline out of control.

Freeman came from the back of the apartment and stepped over the sofa cushions still lying on the floor. "Augie's bedroom and closets are clean. So are the second and third bedrooms. Not much furniture in those rooms. No one ever came to visit Augie." He shook his head. "I hate to think about those vintage watches going for five bucks on some street corner. I tried to buy that Rolex Submariner. Augie turned down seven grand."

"My favorite was the Bulova Accutron with the yellow dots

and the gears showing underneath the crystal," Billy said. "He wore it for good luck anytime the Cards played on TV."

He opened a desk drawer with hanging files. "I've been through every hidey-hole in this room, even his coat pockets. No card, no photo. There's almost no paperwork in the drawers. He must have scanned everything onto his computer. If he scanned the card, we're out of luck."

Freeman checked his watch. "What's it been, forty minutes?"

"The lady will wait. She thinks this is exciting. You poured her a glass of wine?"

"And put on a movie."

Billy nodded toward the kitchen. "Check the drawers by the phone, will you?"

They both worked in silence, ignoring the blood spatter on the wall by the refrigerator and Augie's half-eaten sandwich by the sink. They were there to do a job. Regret would accomplish nothing.

Ten minutes later Freeman slammed a kitchen drawer shut. "There are a couple of store coupons and some take-out menus. No cards. The kitchen's clean. Maybe Dunsford's crew took the cards with them."

Billy went to stand by the island. "The techs weren't looking for an old business card. Odds are they wouldn't pick it up." He did a sweep of the room, looking for anyplace he might have missed. His focus went to the bookcases of hardbacks. "I saved the books for last. Did you notice the bottom two shelves are packed solid with books about civil rights in the sixties and seventies? A copy of Garrett's book is there."

"Research for the manuscript," Freeman said. "Augie was really into it. We even discussed Garrett's book a couple of times."

"Did you see the technicians go through the books?" he asked.

"They pulled books down then checked the shelves."

"Contraband search," he said.

"They flipped through a few of them, but I didn't see them remove anything."

"All right. Let's get to it," he said.

Freeman frowned. "I hope Linda likes James Bond movies."

They both took a shelf, working from opposite ends, fanning through pages, removing dust jackets, shaking the books and then replacing them. It seemed like a futile gesture, but they stayed with it.

After a while Billy glanced up. "By the way, thanks for—"

Freeman raised a hand, his face suddenly angry. "Let's get something straight. I've bought into the premise that you're looking for Augie's killer. But I'm not your friend. I was Augie's friend. So don't thank me."

Billy slammed a book shut. "If you believe I'm after Augie's killer, why did you let me walk into Dunsford's ambush over those dummy cameras?"

"That was for you and Dunsford to work out. We're in the middle of a murder investigation. I'm not the one to judge how it's handled."

"I planned to sign back on with the department so I could get involved with the investigation. Between the fight and my screwed-up alibi, Dunsford's got me down as a suspect. If I'd known about the cameras, I could have dealt with it. Now I'm working blind. And what's with using dummy cameras in your building, anyway?"

"My security experts assured me even the pros can't tell the difference."

"And you took their word for it?"

"No one gets to the service elevators without going through the lobby," Freeman said.

"What about the back entrance?"

"There's a coded lock. A manager has to open up for the residents and deliveries."

"Who has the code?"

"Only me, my two managers—"

"And Augie," Billy said.

Freeman flushed. "He's the only tenant with the code. He wasn't always in the best shape to walk through the lobby. At the rent I charged him, Augie deserved a private entrance."

"He could have taken the killer up the back way to his place unobserved. Or he could have given him the code. The guy could've gotten in and out of the building without ever being recorded."

"I know. You think I don't feel bad about that?" Freeman said. "Somebody beat my neighbor with a baseball bat while I was sleeping down the hall. That's why I'm breaking the law to help you search for a damned business card that probably doesn't exist. I'm putting my faith in you—a damned cop, because I don't have *any* faith in Dunsford."

"I understand why you hate cops. I know what happened to your dad."

"You think you know. Two men used to come to my dad's bar and try to push him around. They were FBI agents. Sometimes they brought the cops with them to run off customers at a time when my dad was barely making ends meet. They wanted him to eavesdrop on conversations, report on who was talking to whom. My dad refused."

Freeman walked to the window, the glow from the stadium

lights gone. "My mother worked afternoons and evenings at Goldsmith's department store for a regular paycheck coming in. With her at work, I had to go to the bar at night. I washed glasses, wiped down tables. One of the agents must have noticed me.

"Grant was his name. He showed up one afternoon. Dad thought I was out back, but I had a hidden nook under the bar where I liked to read in the afternoons. I heard this guy say he'd seen me working in the bar, and he could use that to shut us down unless my dad cooperated. Dad threw him out. A week later a woman from the liquor board tacked a notice on the door that closed the bar."

Freeman turned away from the window. "That's what law enforcement has done for me and my family."

He couldn't change Freeman's mind, and sympathy would only make him angrier. "Your family got a rotten deal. I'm sorry. I'll try to do better for Augie."

Freeman's face went stiff. "Sure. Fair enough. Let's keep looking."

Chapter 37

Billy pulled another book, Hampton Sides's *Hellhound on His Trail,* held it by the covers, and shook it. A card fell out. He picked it up, read it, and handed it to Freeman. Freeman ran his thumb over the raised symbol at the top of the card.

"That's an embossed press corps emblem," Billy said. "It's not so obvious. A reporter can hand a card like that to a possible source without spooking them."

"'Walker Pryce,'" Freeman said, reading the name out loud. He flipped the card over and flipped it back. "That's a Chicago area code on the front. There's another number on the back."

Using his mobile, Billy Googled Walker Pryce and Chicago then scrolled down. "Walker Pryce had a byline at the *Tribune* a few years ago. He wrote a book on politics, journalism, and corruption. This has to be the guy."

"Call the number," Freeman said.

"It's too soon." He did a reverse phone lookup and got a Memphis address.

"I want to get my hands on that leech," Freeman said.

"You're leaving town tomorrow, remember?"

Freeman's expression flattened. "It took me six months to get that meeting."

"I'll handle this guy." Billy locked in the address and glanced around. "We found Pryce, but the photo's not here."

"Augie told me he had it."

"Did he show it to you?"

Freeman flexed his hands. "No."

"What the hell are you saying?"

"I ran into Augie the other night at Bardog. He was telling me about the photos when you walked in. He got so excited, he went into the bathroom to calm down. He came out with a plan to convince you to let me see the pictures."

Billy recalled Augie's buddy-buddy exuberance and how he'd pushed to show them to Freeman. "You were such a jerk," he said.

"I know. I was looking at a picture of the man who caused my father's death. I signaled to Augie that Grant was in the pictures. I was angry all over again about my dad. I was ready to punch somebody. You were my first choice."

"Did you point out a specific picture to Augie?"

"Not specific."

"Do you know which photo Augie took?"

"I never saw it. He offered to make a copy for me, but I didn't want it. I think he took it to Pryce."

"But you're not sure."

"It's an assumption. Augie ran his tail all over town to help that guy. Those photos are gold to someone writing about civil rights. Maybe Pryce has the original."

"I met with Garrett tonight. He gave me some historical context, but his real focus was on acquiring the photos for the museum. Pryce and Garrett have the same interest."

"Where does that leave you?"

He didn't answer. He sensed something underneath all this,

an undersmell. So far he'd been the only one aware of it. If he opened up, told Freeman about Red and Little Man, there was no guarantee Freeman wouldn't run to Dunsford with the information. But there wasn't much choice.

"I'm thinking Augie's murder is connected to Red's and Little Man's deaths."

Freeman nodded. "How?"

"Red bought Grant's jacket. Little Man died. Red blamed the jacket, but he was talking about the photographs. then Red died."

"I thought Red died of a heart attack."

"I'm sure he did. Somebody scared the shit out of him."

"You're saying Davis and Lacy were murdered?"

"Their deaths are somehow tied to the photos. Augie had a photograph. Now he's dead too, and the photograph is missing."

"Have you got the rest of the photos with you?" Freeman asked.

"Oh. So now you're interested."

"Shut up. Give me the pictures," Freeman said.

Billy handed them over. Freeman started through them.

"What are you looking for?" Billy asked.

"I don't know. I was so angry when we were at Bardog, I wasn't paying close enough attention." Freeman pulled out photos of two women. "Here's something. Dad told me these ladies were feeding lies to the cops to make a little cash on the side."

"Counterintelligence. No harm done."

Freeman shuffled through more and stopped. "This can't be right." He turned the picture for Billy to see.

A young black man with a heavy jaw and wearing a wide-brimmed hat with a conical crown was deep in conversation with Grant. The young man was listening, head inclined, shoulders relaxed. Grant had one hand up, making a point.

"I saw that one," Billy said. "An interior shot. No shadows from the sun."

"It's Calvin Carter. There's one of him at the museum standing beside a woodie station wagon. I recognize the face and the hat. You're telling me Garrett saw this picture and didn't ID Carter?"

"I asked if he recognized anyone. He said everyone in the photos was probably dead. Then he jumped into the story about his brother."

"That's Garrett. Hell of a player. No way he wouldn't recognize Carter." He handed back the stack. "Maybe Carter was pulling the agent's leg for a little cash the way the ladies were. He had eight kids. That's a lot of mouths to feed."

"But why didn't Garrett point him out? He made a play for me donating the photos to the museum. He emphasized *all* the photos."

Freeman laughed. "That son of a bitch is worried there might be more shots of Carter. Even a hint that Carter was an informant could dry up funding for the museum. Did Garrett know Augie had one of the photos?"

"I didn't tell him, and I don't think Augie would have brought it up."

Freeman shook his head.

"This may be important, or it may be a distraction," Billy said. "What are you going to do?"

"Deal with it later. Right now I'm going after Pryce."

Walker Pryce's address took Billy south along the river toward an industrial section recently rezoned for residential use. A California developer bought the property, knocked down the old brick and tin warehouses that were once used to store cotton bales, and stripped the five-acre site of both plant life and history. After the developer went bust, the work had stopped, and the project went into receivership.

He drove past the stone posts at the subdivision's entrance marked WATERS TRACE. The city had installed the required curbs, but the building lots were devoid of construction, nothing but raw dirt and weeds. Had Pryce falsified his address?

The only structure in the desolate space was at the center of the property. By moonlight, he read the sign in the front yard: MODEL HOME/SALES OFFICE. It was a white clapboard house with tall green shutters and a porch flanked by narrow columns. A light burned in a window to the left of the front door. In the driveway sat what looked like a brand-new red Porsche Boxster—sixty thousand on the hoof.

Billy pulled to the curb thirty yards short of the house, killed his lights, and sent a text to Frankie.

Success. Found journalist's name. Walker Pryce, from Chicago. Please run NCIC. Send results ASAP. THNX.

Pryce had enough money to drive a new Porsche. Could be he'd received a big advance on the book. Could be he was a trust-fund baby. The idea that the money for the car had come from Augie made Billy's blood run hot.

He'd like to knock on the door and punch this guy Pryce in the mouth, but even a conversation with him would be a mistake. He had no authority to question Pryce. He'd have to lie to get his foot in the door. Pryce was no idiot, which made this a one-shot deal.

Frankie would check Pryce for a criminal history and outstanding warrants. He'd go home and do his own research.

Tomorrow, he'd show up at Pryce's house with some excuse to look around for evidence. Then he'd start with the questions. It wouldn't take long for Pryce to figure out he was being looked at for Augie's murder, but in the meantime, something interesting might come up.

The meeting had to happen in the morning. By tomorrow afternoon, Dunsford would have Augie's phone records and Pryce's number. If Pryce showed up for an interview with Dunsford, he'd most likely bring a lawyer who would shut things down five minutes into the conversation. Dunsford would then switch his focus back where he wanted it in the first place—on Billy.

He drove home along the banks of the Mississippi, the river running dark and unknown beside him. At the barge he threw his keys in the bowl on the counter, cracked a longneck Bud, and listened to the vibrations coming from the tracks across the road. The rails rattled under the weight of the freight cars, a grinding, booming sound.

He drank some beer and thought about the way he should handle Pryce. He was on leave, so the restraints of standard procedure didn't apply. Nine months was a long time to be away. He wondered if the lack of oversight had changed him. The memory of Augie's crime scene burned constantly in his mind. That had certainly changed him. So had Red Davis's terrorized face. If anything else had changed, it was his disappointment in the people he'd cared for the most. Mercy had only been the most recent.

As he settled his computer on his lap and typed "Walker Pryce" into search, the deep, broad wail of the passing train took hold.

Chapter 38

Frankie found herself standing outside B. B. King's Blues Club just after ten P.M. Billy was on a quest, and he hadn't invited her along. Actually, that wasn't fair. He was about to do something illegal and wanted to shield her from culpability. But still, she felt like a kid left standing on the curb.

She watched him edge through the overheated crowd, the kind of cop who gambled it all in the pursuit of justice. He'd been lucky in his career, pushed it to the brink, had some close calls, but now he was a murder suspect, and she was the only one in his corner.

Moments ago, she'd caught a stricken expression on his face while he was reading a text. He'd tried to blow it off, but she knew the look. Last year, she overheard cop gossip about him falling for a woman who lived in Atlanta, the reason for his long leave of absence. The woman was also the likely reason for his return. Frankie hoped that wounded look didn't mean he was carrying a torch.

Plenty of female officers had been disappointed when Billy Able left town. The same ladies would be glad to see him back, especially without a ring on his finger.

After her involvement with Brad, she was suspicious of love, going so far as to consider romance a near-death experience. Speaking for herself, one more bad relationship, and she was going to start keeping cats.

She searched the crowd. It had swallowed Billy whole. Whatever he was up to, she hoped she wouldn't have to bail out Freeman and him later tonight.

Driving home, the full moon threw light between the limbs of the giant hardwoods that lined the streets. She remembered another full moon on an evening when she'd ridden beside Brad McDaniel for what she thought was their first date, starry-eyed fool that she was. He'd taken her to a little restaurant out Highway 64 near Bolivar where she had the best fried catfish and hush puppies she'd ever eaten. It was a funky, out-of-the-way place. She'd been too smitten at the time to realize it was also a safe harbor for a married man to take his girlfriend. Driving back, the moon had set fire to the frozen fields, sparking off the blanket of late frost.

She never imagined Brad would end up dead because of their relationship or that she would need tranquilizers to make it through the day. There was no way she could rationalize falling for a married man. It didn't matter that he'd lied about being separated. She wasn't supposed to make that kind of mistake.

She pushed away sad thoughts as she turned into her driveway, realizing she hadn't eaten all day. A glass of chardonnay and some comfort food would take her mind off Brad while she waited to hear from Billy.

She went upstairs, undressed, and walked barefoot to the kitchen to crank the oven to 400. Earlier tonight at the bar, a server had passed by with a skillet of low-country shrimp and cheese grits. She remembered the Gulf shrimp in her freezer and some leftover grits soufflé in the fridge from the day before. She took out the grits, spooned them into a heavy iron skillet, and pushed it to the back of the hot oven.

Her thoughts turned to the way Garrett's face had collapsed as he leafed through the photographs. Billy explained away Garrett's reaction by saying he was having flashbacks of his brother's death. From her seat at the bar, the man looked more panicked than sad. What had he seen? She mentally flipped through the photos while pushing the shrimp around in a pan of melted butter. What did he know that they'd missed?

She opened the oven door to check on the grits. Her mind was on the photos when she reached in with a pot holder for the heavy skillet. As she lifted it out, her wrist seared against the red-hot heating element.

"Damn it," she yelled, dropped the skillet, and ran to the sink to turn on the cold-water tap. A dry sob broke from her throat. Somehow the blistering pain got mixed up with the jolt of Brad's slap. She remembered the ugliness on his face as he screamed at her through his car window. Then he was chasing her. Then his car rolled.

She felt the steel bands tightening around her chest. She wanted a pill. Two pills. Three.

Slumped over the sink, her heart began racing. *Goddamn you, Brad, Coral's a widow. Your daughter has no father. And all I want is to feel numb. You bastard, you died because you couldn't have your way.*

Heart thudding, she turned off the tap and inspected the raw patch on her wrist. Her neighbor kept an aloe vera plant on the back porch, the best treatment for burns. She cut some gauze strips and crept downstairs to break off a leaf. The dripping goo cooled the sting of the burn, and she wrapped her wrist in a bandage.

In the back garden, a small fountain bubbled beside a concrete bench. Lights peeked from under the hydrangea bushes. She walked barefoot across the grass and sat on the bench to try and calm down. She'd been reading up on post-traumatic stress, but understanding the response wasn't the same as controlling it. That had been the worst. She had no control.

She unwrapped the gauze. Even in the low light of the garden, she could tell the burn was going to leave a scar. So would Brad's death if she let it. She could change that by talking to someone about the accident and these damned anxiety attacks, but first she had to come clean with Billy, at least about the anxiety. He already knew something was wrong. He had to trust her if there was any hope of their working together. She would talk to him and then find a therapist to work through what had happened to Brad.

Decision made, she went upstairs to check her mobile. Billy had texted with a request for an NCIC search on the name Walker Pryce. His quest had paid off. She scanned her e-mails and found the New Orleans PI report.

She printed the report and went to the kitchen to clean up the grits she'd spilled on the floor. With the work she had ahead of her, an apple with peanut butter would do fine for supper.

On her way back to her desk, she passed her handbag. She dug out the bottle of pills and poured the capsules into her palm. She'd thought the pills would be good for her. She'd thought the same about her relationship with Brad. She dumped the pills into the garbage and went to work.

Chapter 39

*T*he coming storm whipped trash across Billy's feet. He *heard the snap of the ballpark flags. He smelled the packing clay of the pitcher's mound under his cleats. Augie stood a couple of feet away in a Redbirds' uniform and catcher's gear. He passed a ball back and forth between his hands, his eyes straying toward home plate where a batter stood. Billy looked down. He had a pitcher's glove on his hand.*

"How you want to handle this guy?" Augie asked, expectation on his young rookie's face. He wiped his brow with his sleeve. A red line opened above his brow bone. Blood spilled into his eyes.

Lightning struck the field.

Billy jerked awake. He pulled himself upright on the sofa and scrubbed his face with his hands. What if Augie had gone home the other night to meet with Pryce? What if the questions Billy raised about Pryce scamming Augie had gotten Augie killed?

It was morning. He stumbled into the kitchen. The sun through the porthole made a perfect circle of light on the counter. He opened the refrigerator door, not seeing food, only remembering Augie's face in his dream. He poured orange juice and made coffee to pull himself together. Frankie's check into the NCIC database had arrived last night. It produced no criminal record on Pryce, not even a parking ticket. He thought through his own research into Pryce's Chicago career: discovery of contaminated food served in school lunch programs, the exposure of two pharmacies that were cutting dosages on patients' meds to increase profits, four Cook County Sheriff's Department deputies who had successfully robbed banks while working the CSI unit. Pryce had caught a bullet in the shoulder for that one.

Billy showered and shaved, puzzling over what happened next to Pryce. He'd written a three-part series on a candidate running for the governorship of Illinois. A week after the first article came out, Pryce resigned, and the paper retracted the article. After that, Pryce was either shunned by the industry or got caught up in the mass downsizing of print media, because his byline never appeared in another major publication.

His self-published book blasted crony capitalism and corporations that owned print media while they were in bed with state politicians. Pryce didn't name his former employer or the elected governor, but Illinois readers would know. *Publishers Weekly* reviewed the book. It won critical acclaim.

Sales were nonexistent. Pryce had fallen off the payroll grid. No income equals desperation.

Billy read through the *Commercial Appeal*'s online crime report to find out if media relations had managed to keep a lid on the details of Augie's case. First, he wanted to know what Pryce might have learned about the murder by reading the paper. Second, he wanted to know if he'd been named a suspect.

Notorious investigations leak like rotten hoses. If his name appeared on Dunsford's confidential suspects list, it would eventually get out to the press. The department would pay hell walking back his reputation, guilty or not. Articles that appear above the fold, accurate or not, break careers. He was surprised to realize he would do anything to stop that from happening. Whatever it took.

The only article covering the investigation gave few details. He was relieved.

He ate toast. Drank coffee. Just after eight, he called Pryce.

The voice that answered sounded abrupt. "Pryce."

"Walker Pryce?" he asked.

"Who is this?"

"Billy Able. I was a friend of Augie Poston. I understand you were, too."

"Your name is familiar."

What had Augie told this guy? Give an investigative reporter your name, and he'll have your shoe size in ten minutes. "You know Augie died two days ago."

"Yeah. He was murdered."

"I want to come by and talk with you about the manuscript the two of you were putting together."

Pryce paused. "How did you get this number?"

"Augie gave it to me."

Silence.

"You there?" Billy asked.

"When do you want to come?"

"How about twenty minutes?"

The development looked even more desolate than it had last night. Billy cruised up to the house expecting to see the Porsche. Instead, the grille of a black tow truck faced out of the driveway. The name "Bob's Recovery and Towing Service" was written in curlicue script on the driver's door. A guy in his late twenties stood off to the side with a mug of coffee in his hand, watching the truck driver hook a cable to the Porsche's frame. Walker Pryce was tall and fit, with shaggy blond hair and the kind of boyish features everyone loves to give in to. He exuded entitlement, the kind that comes from a solid start with two parents who are willing to spring for the best of everything for their kids.

Billy pulled to the curb. He was familiar with Bob's Recovery and Towing. They did the majority of the repo work in town, not the tow work for the top-end Porsche dealership in the city. He walked up the drive.

Walker Pryce extended his hand. They shook and stepped back to watch the driver winch the Porsche onto the tilted flatbed.

"Beautiful car," Billy said.

Pryce glanced over with a grin. "My dreams got bigger than my wallet."

Billy nodded. *You mean your meal ticket died.*

They watched the truck pull out of the drive with the Porsche riding piggyback. Then they headed into the house.

He scanned Pryce from behind for a weapon although his jeans and shirt were cut too close to hide much. Even though Pryce looked more like an out-of-work actor than a guy who spent weekends on the firing range, if he was Augie's killer, another victim would be that much easier to take down.

They walked into a living room with a cluttered desk, a wall covered in sticky notes, and binders stacked from floor to ceiling. The house showed well with polished wood floors and stone countertops, but the general construction of the place felt slipshod.

"Great place," Billy said. "How did you end up living in a model home?"

"The developer set me up. My presence keeps their insurance costs low."

Every light in the place burned, and the air was running full blast. He suspected Pryce wasn't responsible for the utility bill.

"I'm thinking about buying a condo downtown," he said. "I hadn't considered a house. Mind if I look around?"

"Go ahead." Pryce settled on a bar stool next to the kitchen island. Billy wandered around but kept his eye on Pryce.

Freeman had provided a list of items stolen from the apartment: the watches; laptop and phone; rare photographs of blues musicians; candid shots of Dr. King, Medgar Evers, and Robert Garrett, all martyrs to the civil rights cause. Augie's two autographed World Series baseballs had been taken from the bookshelves, also two blues harmonicas, one belonging to Little Walter and the other to Sonny Boy Williamson.

Any of those items left in plain sight would be picked up with a warrant search. That would be incredibly easy. But after reading Pryce's background and having met him, he didn't think the journalist would make that kind of mistake.

He stopped at a partially opened doorway and glanced in Pryce's direction. "Bedroom?"

"Be my guest."

The room was bare except for a bed and a chair in the corner with a standing lamp. He noticed a pair of platform heels tucked beneath the chair. Apparently, he had a girlfriend who sometimes stayed over.

He returned to the kitchen. Pryce sipped coffee, his voice casual. "Remind me of the purpose of your visit."

"I want to talk about Augie. I can't get my mind around someone having reason to kill him." He shook his head as if bewildered. It wasn't a question; it was an opened door. Whatever Pryce said, he could then respond, and they'd have a dialogue going.

"Augie had his demons. His mother's murder haunted him," Pryce said.

"I thought it was an accident."

"As a journalist, I'm allowed to speculate about a case. But we'll never know the truth, will we?" Pryce went to the sink to dump his coffee and rinse the cup. "You wanted to discuss the manuscript," he said over his shoulder.

"Augie paid you to look into his mother's death. Your manuscript is all the better for the research and, from the looks of your car selection, you were thriving with Augie's support. His estate should be reimbursed from the royalties. I'm sure the two of you got something about that on paper."

"My financial arrangement with Augie is none of your business. Anything else?"

"You're aware that whoever murdered Augie stole his copy of your manuscript?"

Pryce returned to the bar stool next to the island. "I couldn't know the manuscript was stolen unless I was the murderer. But then you're not here to talk about money, are you?"

Billy noted his change in tone. The house suddenly felt isolated, surrounded by so much empty acreage. He wondered whether Pryce might try something. "I wanted to run a scenario by you, see if it has merit."

"All right." Pryce rested his chin on his fist. "Shoot."

"Let's say Augie asked you to come by on Monday night. You showed up. He lowered the boom, said he was dropping you from the payroll. Things got heated. Augie turned aggressive.

You were afraid for your life. You hit him. Then you panicked. You decided to grab stuff, make it look like a robbery. On the way out the door, you saw your manuscript. Couldn't leave that, now could you?"

Pryce didn't flinch. "I'll do you the favor of addressing you as Detective. However, my source at the CJC says you have no authority to question me, particularly now that you're the primary suspect in this investigation. I'll admit the scenario you posed is something Detective Dunsford might consider. Therefore, I'll be contacting my attorney before Dunsford contacts me." Pryce gave him a look that conveyed, *Your move.*

Pryce was threatening to lawyer up, the exact mistake Billy predicted Dunsford would make.

Pryce straightened off the counter and continued. "I have a scenario for you. There's a furloughed cop who had a very public fight with the victim the night he was murdered. According to the cop's statement, the victim walked away. Let's say the cop followed the victim to his apartment. The victim died. To get out from under suspicion, the cop shows up at the house of the next-best suspect a couple of days later. The cop kills the poor bastard and plants evidence he took from the first victim's apartment. The cop claims self-defense was the reason for the homicide. Naturally, the cop's buddies at the station house will want to believe him."

Billy barked a laugh. "You must not be too worried. You let me in the door."

"I'm not the one carrying a weapon."

The pretty-boy act was gone. Billy was now seeing the man who'd brought down four sheriff's deputies.

"Change of subject," Pryce said. "I got a call from Augie on Monday. He was enthusiastic about a pack of photos a friend had found in a jacket. He wanted to come by and show me one of the photos."

"Do you have it?"

"Augie kept the original. I have a copy."

"It's evidence in another investigation. Go get it."

Pryce threw back his head in a false laugh. "We both know copies aren't admissible in court."

He felt the heat rise in his face. "It's evidence. Go . . . get . . . it."

"You want a look at that photo? I need proof you're the person who has the rest."

Now he understood. Pryce was so eager to see those photos he'd risked letting a possible killer in the door. Unless he *was* the killer and therefore knew Billy was no threat.

"Dunsford will fumble around and waste time, but eventually he'll clear me," Pryce said. "We can make a deal now. I'll give you my alibi and turn over the copy of Augie's photo in exchange for copies of the other pictures."

"I can't agree to anything based on an unverified alibi."

"You're worried about my alibi? I know about the glitch in the DeVoy's security system. You don't *have* an alibi. Dunsford will get Augie's phone records today. I'll be his first call. After that, our deal's off."

Good God, he thought. *How did this guy know about the dummy cameras?* And he was right. Once Dunsford called, any contact between Pryce and him—discussing case details or swapping evidence like the photos—would be considered working at cross-purposes with the investigation. Pryce was in the clear for now, but with this interview, Billy was already skirting the line.

"Where were you Monday night?" he asked.

"A club. I was there until three in the morning. Plenty of witnesses will back me up."

"The club's name?"

Pryce shook his head. "You said the photos are connected to an investigation. I need proof they're not locked up in the evidence room."

"We'll get to that after I contact your witnesses."

"Then we're dead out of the gate." Pryce looked at his watch. "We have to wrap this up."

The entire conversation had been about Pryce's obsession with the photographs. No sorrow, no grief over Augie. No questions. Pryce's avoidance was either guilt, or a measure of the man's narcissism. It turned Billy's stomach.

"Celebrities sell books," he said. "Augie's murder will put your book at the top of the *New York Times* best seller list."

Pryce's face hardened. "You believe I killed Augie. I know better than to ask questions about how or why he died. I'm proud of the work Augie and I did together. The book will honor him. Your work is turning you into a cynic, Detective."

It was difficult to say which of them was angrier. Billy was surprised to realize that, up to this point, they'd been evenly matched. He decided to flip the spotlight back on Pryce.

"What's with the platform heels under the chair in your bedroom?"

Pryce brushed hair out of his eyes and looked off. "I had hoped to finesse that detail." He exhaled. "You're familiar with the midtown club called the Devil's Sentiment?"

Sweet Jesus. "Yeah, I know the place."

Pryce went to the bookcase and returned with a binder of glossy publicity shots. The first was of a woman in theatrical makeup with long blond hair, wearing short shorts and stiletto heels. She posed in a three-quarter turn with an expression of pure, animal challenge.

After ten years on the force, nothing about human sexuality surprised Billy. But this one got to him. The profile. The smile. It was Pryce.

Pryce closed the binder. "On Monday nights I perform in drag. I sing the blues like Etta James, not lip-synching, I really can sing. I was performing the night Augie was murdered. I was either backstage, onstage, or talking to customers. I have witnesses."

His mind ran through the information he'd read about Pryce. "Did the gubernatorial candidate use your sexual preference to get you fired?"

Pryce gave him a tired look. "I'm not gay. Actually, that would be easier. An out gay man working in media isn't a big deal anymore. But I'm straight. A straight investigative journalist who dresses up like a woman and performs on stage . . ." He shook his head.

"I only performed in clubs outside of Chicago. After my first article on the candidate went to print, someone from his staff followed me. He sent a video to my paper's corporate office demanding retraction of the article and an end to the series. Otherwise, they would expose me and the paper to ridicule. Corporate couldn't stomach the fight. They caved on the series. I wouldn't retract, so I had to hit the road."

"You could have slipped out of the club at any time and killed Augie."

"Get real, Detective." Pryce smiled and pulled a piece of paper from his back pocket. "Here's a list of names and numbers. These three guys will swear I never left the club the night Augie was murdered. It's a solid alibi. End of story."

Billy had dealt with a lot of players. Pryce didn't sound like he was bluffing. A strong alibi would take him off the suspects list. If the alibi fell through, he could always call Pryce's hand.

Pryce's phone rang. He checked the screen. "I'm counting on you to solve Augie's murder before I have to explain the drag queen thing to Dunsford. We don't have a lot of time." He held up his phone. "This isn't Dunsford, but I have to take the call. You need to go."

"I want that photo," he said.

"Make those three calls first. I'll be here all day." Pryce gestured for Billy to leave and headed for his desk.

Billy didn't budge. "Hey, Pryce."

Pryce turned around, perturbed.

"Do you believe in coincidence?"

"Not at all."

"Neither do I. It's no coincidence that your manuscript disappeared from Augie's apartment. There's a reason it's missing."

He stood on the porch outside Pryce's house with his hands in his pockets. In most interviews you get a conversation going. Once that happens, people have a hard time shutting up, even if the subject turns threatening. But not this guy. Not Pryce. He'd made no attempt to impress Billy with his innocence. Guilty men have a hard time maintaining a level of confidence throughout an interview. It's one thing to lie. It's another to lie consistently.

Pryce had not behaved like a suspect.

He could hear Pryce on the phone, pacing the room, probably talking to his damned source at the CJC. Pryce stopped near the window. His words came through clearly.

"Yeah, my car's in the shop. Good. Drop by before noon. I'm looking forward to it." He hung up.

Chapter 40

Frankie fought the rush-hour traffic to turn onto Ramos's shaded street. She wanted to catch him early—before he met with clients if possible. She'd stayed awake until two, forming questions meant to extract the answers she needed. No fooling around this time. Was Ramos involved in Red's death? If not, then did he know who was?

Halfway down the block a black Nissan sedan rolled past her. Ramos was in the passenger's seat, his dark glasses making him recognizable.

Was she too early or too late?

At the end of the block, she turned around and drove back slowly, trying to decide what to do. As she pulled even with the house, the front door opened and the grim-faced woman from the *botánica* stepped out with a broom in her hand.

Frankie stopped and slumped in her seat, watching the old woman sweep the porch like she was mad at it. Her moss-green dress swung in counterpoint, her skin the color of dust. A stub of a cigar protruded from her clamped teeth.

Now it made sense. The old woman was Ramos's house-keeper, maybe even a relative. At the salon, she'd jumped on

Mystica because she was protective of Ramos and didn't want Frankie near him.

A VW bus with duct tape securing a side window turned into the driveway and sputtered to a halt. A young woman wearing skinny jeans and heels climbed out. Frankie recognized her as one of the hairdressers from the salon.

The housekeeper threw the cigar stub into the bushes and walked to the edge of the porch.

"*Presura*," she demanded, signaling for the young woman to hurry.

"I'm coming, I'm coming," the woman called as she picked her way through the broken concrete of the driveway. They met at the corner of the house and disappeared around back, the broom left leaning against a column on the porch.

Frankie wrote down the VW's tag number and took money from her purse to fold in her pocket. She let three minutes pass before starting up the driveway for the back of the house.

This time she was prepared for Dante the dog to come galloping at her. Instead, the patio was silent. Live animal cages had been stacked in the shade of an elm tree on the far side of the patio, the cages holding two red roosters, four pairs of white doves, and five hamsters huddled into tight fur balls. A goat, in the largest cage on the bottom, was weaving from side to side with anxiety, only stopping to rub its forehead against the bars. None of the animals made a sound.

Smoke curled from under the cook pot sitting in the patio's fire pit. Memories flooded back to her—blood and feathers, hooves and horns, and the smell of rendered fat and boiled meat.

Santería had been part of her childhood, but she'd blocked the blood sacrifices from her mind. She couldn't imagine charming, educated Sergio Ramos slitting the throats of these struggling animals. The sacrifices were meant to absorb the problems and negative vibrations of troubled people. Most of the animals would be consumed as meat consecrated by the orishas. But she didn't like it. She'd begun to think of Ramos as a renowned psychologist, not a pagan priest. There was no contradiction in the bloodletting for him. She hated it.

A little rattled, she took the porch steps and peered through the door's window at the two women who were standing beside the kitchen counter. The hairdresser was counting out bills into the old woman's hand. A conjure bag lay on the counter between them, the same kind Frankie had discovered near Red's body.

This was no surprise. It had dawned on her that the old woman's cigar wasn't a bad habit; it was a clue that she was a practitioner of *palo mayombe*. Bad magic. Amitee used to shake her finger in Frankie's face and warn against the *paleros judios*. They cast spells by controlling the spirits of dead witches, criminals, and suicides who reside inside a special cauldron. The pot contains bones of the dead, crossroad dust, animal carcasses, and hot spices. During ceremonies, the *paleros judios* blow cigar smoke and spew rum at the cauldron to invoke the spirits and command them to obey. Their magic works faster than that of a *santero* because the spirits are compelled to obey. A *santero* works within the wishes of the orishas, who ultimately have the control.

Frankie had to make a move. She opened the door and breezed in. "Oh, hi. Sorry to interrupt. I left my book, um . . . *mi libro*, in the doctor's office." The room stank of moldy leaves and dog excrement. She pointed to the bag on the counter. "Hey, cool. That's a great pouch, right?"

The hairdresser went wide eyed and snatched up the bag. "It's mine."

Frankie reached for it. "Can I see?"

The young woman curled her nails around the bag. "Ovia will make whatever you need." She nodded to the old woman and whipped out the door, heels clattering.

The old woman slipped the money in her bra and eyed Frankie. "*No tenemos su libro*," she said, waving Frankie toward the door.

Frankie slipped two twenties from her pocket and held them for Ovia to see.

"But I have a terrible problem. Will you help me?"

The woman sneered. "A spirit follows you. His hand is at your throat. He blames you . . . an accident."

"Is he here now?" she asked, trying not to be a little spooked. Ramos had mentioned the accident, too.

Ovia's eyes roved over the room. "I will send him away."

"Great. Do that. But this is a different problem. I want to give a man *un gran susto*, a big scare, with a curse. Can you do this? Make this live man go away? Never come back?"

Ovia jutted her chin out with pride. "I can make him go away. Sure."

"Can you make him leave this world? *El ebo muerte*?"

The woman's gaze rested on the money. "It will cost much more."

"I asked Dr. Ramos to make a death spell, but now I see that you control the cauldron and the spirits. I'm impressed."

Ovia stepped closer. The odor of stale cigar smoke wafted from her dress. "I am Tata Nkisi, a *mayombero*. You know this."

"And your death spells work."

Ovia nodded. "I made two spells last week."

"I'd like to speak with the person who bought the spells."

Ovia showed her teeth, shook her head. *"No sé el nombre."*

"You don't have a name? Was this a man or a woman?"

"A woman came to *la botánica.*"

Frankie handed one of the twenties to her. "Tell me about the woman."

Ovia stashed the money inside her dress then stretched to hold her hand high above Frankie's head, indicating height. *"Una iniciado en la Santería. Seis necklaces."*

Tall, a Santerían believer, and she wears six necklaces, Frankie thought. Five for the necklace initiation ceremony, one for a specific orisha.

"Is she black or white?"

"Mulatto," Ovia said.

"From the islands?"

Ovia waved away the question. "You want my help? No more questions."

"How much money for the *ebbo* I described?"

"Fifty dollars."

"And if Dr. Ramos makes the curse? Is it more?"

Ovia flattened her hands and moved them back and forth. "Ramos cannot help you." She pointed to her chest. "Only me."

She was selling black magic out the back door. She picked up clients at the salon and got her supplies from Mystica. Rare items she must take from Ramos's pharmacy and replace them before he missed them.

If she were to believe Ovia, Sergio Ramos did not practice the black arts. But was he aware that his housekeeper did?

Voices came from the backyard, then footsteps on the porch. Ovia snatched the second bill from Frankie's hand.

"You want *el ebo muerte*? The doctor cannot know." She drew a strange pattern in the air over Frankie's head and stepped back as if satisfied.

Ramos came through the door. His hair was damp-combed off his face, and the aroma of aftershave followed him into the room. Of course. He would need a barber's help.

"My driver recognized your car, Ms. Malone," he said. "Have I forgotten an appointment?" He extended his hand then frowned and touched her bandaged wrist. "You've hurt yourself."

"She came for a book," Ovia said. "I told her to go."

"The book is on my desk," Ramos said. "*To Kill a Mockingbird* is a favorite of mine, an attorney who stands for justice when no one else will."

"I considered practicing law because of Atticus Finch, but I chose to be a police officer instead."

She laid her badge wallet in his hand. Presenting her badge in an unofficial investigation was a risk, but it put muscle behind the questions she wanted to ask.

Ramos thumbed the shield, his eyes coming up, hidden by the glasses, but she could tell he was gazing at her. "Now I understand why you always carry a gun. I recognized the smell of the cleaning oil for your weapon."

"You and I attended a funeral for two men." She pulled the plastic-wrapped conjure bag from her back pocket and pressed it into his hand. "Someone used their belief in Santería to scare them to death."

Ovia reached to snatch the bag away, but Ramos clamped his hand on her wrist. "Do not speak, Ovia. And do not leave the room." He opened the conjure bag, dumped its contents, and ran his fingers over the dust. "Eggshell. Coal dust. Wasp nest. Guinea pepper. Rock salt," he recited quietly.

"I found the bag near Red Davis's body," Frankie said. "He suffered a heart attack on the spot. We believe someone chased Little Man. He broke his neck in a fall. Both men died in terror. I saw it on their faces."

Ovia spat at Frankie's feet. "This one is bad. You've seen her spirit man. *Está furioso.*"

Ramos spoke to Ovia in heated Spanish. They went back and forth for a while, Ovia gesturing at Frankie in an attempt to shift blame. Ramos pointed at a chair, his voice thick with emotion. *"Siéntese y no hable con la señorita."*

Ovia collapsed in the chair, defeated.

Ramos turned back to Frankie, stiff with formality. His conversation with Ovia had unnerved him.

"You were counseling both men," Frankie said. "The conjure bag and unusual components that you keep in your home were found near the body. This looks bad for you."

Ramos tilted his head, impassive. "I was not involved in these deaths, but I am responsible for the members of my household. To that end, I may be culpable."

"Were you involved in the making of this curse?"

"No."

"Did Ovia make it?"

He looked over at the old woman. "She won't say."

"She claims to have sold curses to a woman last week. I need that name. And I need anything Mr. Davis told you that might lead to his killer."

"I will speak to Ovia when you are gone. And I hold Mr. Davis's privilege to confidentiality, so I can tell you nothing."

"Red and Little Man had their lives taken from them. As professionals, you and I have a duty to stand up for them. Tell me. What do you think Atticus Finch would do in this situation?"

Ramos looked surprised. He thought a moment, then a smile played over his lips. "You would have been a gifted attorney, Ms. Malone. Please, join me in my office. We have things to discuss."

He took her hand. "But first we must treat this burn."

"What makes you think it's a burn?"

"I'm a witch doctor, am I not?"

Chapter 41

Talk to witnesses at the scene of an accident, and every one of them gives you a different version of events. There are as many sides to a story as there are people involved.

Billy sat in his car near the stone entrance to the Waters Trace subdivision wanting to get out of the car and kick the shit out of one of those pillars. He smacked the dashboard instead. Everyone he talked to was working their own agenda. Take Pryce, a man Augie had helped in every way he could, but to hell with Augie Poston. Pryce didn't give a damn about his murder. In the meantime, the killer was slipping away.

He pulled himself together and started down the list of Pryce's witnesses. He got voice mail on all three. He called Frankie. She answered on the first ring.

"I met with Walker Pryce," he said before she could speak. "If you're driving, pull over." He heard the click of her blinker.

"Let me guess," she said. "Pryce was performing open-heart surgery onstage at the Met. He has witnesses, and you're angry about it."

"I just knew Pryce was our guy. And he's mixed up in this somehow, but it's possible he's not the killer."

"What happened?"

He watched a dump truck rumble along the highway beside the subdivison. He was gripping the steering wheel, needing to cool off.

"I called and suggested I stop by. Before I got there, he had his hands on my work history and the detail of Augie's investigation, including the fake cameras at the DeVoy. He was so far ahead of me I choked on his dust. We had our talk. I didn't get much. On the way out, he gave me the numbers for three alibi witnesses and said not to get back in touch until I was satisfied he wasn't Augie's killer."

"Cocky son of a bitch."

He started to tell her about Pryce's drag queen drama but decided to give out that information on a need-to-know basis. "The only reason he agreed to talk to me was to get his hands on the rest of the surveillance shots. He claims to have a copy of the one Augie stole from me but says Augie kept the original."

He heard Frankie breathing into the phone, thinking. "Is it time to pull Dunsford in on this?"

Oh hell, he thought. *The voice of reason is stepping in to save our careers.* "We're in the clear except for my interview with Pryce, which is borderline. Neither of us has broken the law."

"Let me think. What were you and Freeman doing last night that was so illegal you couldn't tell me about it?"

"That was different. If we find real evidence . . . material evidence, we'll put it in Dunsford's hands."

"The photographs *are* material evidence."

"*Got damn it*, Frankie. If we give Dunsford those pictures before we prove he's mishandling these cases, we'll lose our leverage and both of our jobs." His tone was nasty, demeaning.

"Watch it," she said then stopped. "No, you're right. Absolutely right. Where are you now?"

"Near Pryce's house. He's expecting someone to come by. I'm hanging around to see who it is. Frankie?"

"Yes."

"Sorry about the bad attitude."

"Understood. We're both under pressure. By the way, the PI report came in while I was doing that NCIC check on Pryce."

"Anything significant?" he asked.

"Hold on."

He heard her unclip the seat belt and the sound of papers rustling.

"He contacted Red's music publisher. Red's manager worked the early contracts, so the manager got the biggest cut. There're still royalties coming in, but a couple of years ago the publisher lost track of Red. No forwarding address. He was probably afraid Cool Willy would find him."

"Is there a new recording contract in the works?"

"They said fans want original recordings from the older artists, not new music."

That tanked his explanation for the business deal Red had bragged about. He heard more paper shuffling on Frankie's end.

"Here's something. Cool Willy is rebranding himself with his legal name, 'William Cooley.' The limousine service is legit. He claims he's walking away from drugs and hookers."

"Nice try. You can dress up street trash, but it's still street trash."

"The PI thinks he's setting up a money-laundering operation."

"That sounds right. What else?"

"The girl seated at the piano is Theda Jones, the daughter of one of Cool Willy's chippies. Her mother is African-American, her father, a Japanese tourist. The girl's a stunner, with real talent at the keyboard. At fourteen she won a partial scholarship to the

Montague School, outside Baton Rouge, a prep school for musical prodigies. To make the program, she had to come up with ten grand of her own money. Instead of helping, Mom let Willy get his hooks into her. He set her up as a call girl for the johns who roll into the Quarter for medical and corporate conferences. Theda was his off-the-menu specialty, very high dollar. The girl realized he was making too much money to let her go back to school, so she tried to get away. She played piano in the cocktail lounge of the blues club where Red and Little Man headlined. The club owner said Cool Willy started pressuring him to fire her. When things got heated, she disappeared."

"Any idea where she went?" he asked.

"I think I know. Ramos let me review Red's file this morning."

"You went to Ramos's today without telling me?"

"You went to Pryce's by yourself. I can handle myself, Billy."

She explained how the housekeeper had been selling black magic out the back door.

"What's Ramos's part in this?" he asked.

"The old woman acted guilty as hell. Ramos appeared to be shocked."

"What's your gut say. Is he involved?"

"You're always bringing up my gut," she said.

"Instinct is a big part of this work."

"We've been over this. And quit being such a jerk."

He gritted his teeth. Pryce had taken a bite out of his ego, and he was unloading on her.

"Ramos took responsibility for his housekeeper's actions, but said he wasn't involved. Even the housekeeper said he wouldn't make a death curse. I saw no indication in Red's file of a problem between them. Deductive reasoning says Ramos isn't the killer. No guts involved in that thought process, I might add."

He grinned into the phone.

"Red told Ramos he was supporting someone in Boston. He used the phrase 'old fool love.' "

"Now it's coming together," he said. "Red and Little Man sent the Jones girl to Boston. Cool Willy found out, beat the crap out of them, and broke up their instruments. They ran to Memphis and stayed under the radar by not playing on Beale Street so Cool Willy couldn't track them down."

"You think Cool Willy and Jones are tied into their deaths?"

"Willy is a contender. Jones, I don't know. It doesn't make sense. Red spent every cent to keep her in piano strings. But I'd still like to question her."

The young woman he'd seen getting out of the car at the funeral home had to be Jones. The hat she wore blocked her profile. He could kick himself for not recognizing her. He might have made the connection if he hadn't been so focused on Augie at the time.

He realized Frankie was silent on the other end. "What's up?"

"I was thinking about something Garrett said during the eulogy. I'd like to talk with him about Ramos's relationship with Davis and Lacy."

"That's another thing. Garrett skirted the issue when I asked if he knew anyone in the surveillance shots. I showed the photos to Freeman last night. He recognized Carter as one of the informants."

"Calvin Carter?" she asked.

"Freeman and I figure Garrett didn't point him out because he's shielding Carter's reputation for the sake of the museum. It's not a big point, but I'd like to follow up."

"I'll talk to Garrett and cover both questions. He won't feel as threatened by me."

"No, I'll handle it," he said in a gruff tone.

"You owe me one after shutting me out with Freeman last night. I'll report back when I'm done." She hung up before he could protest.

He started the car and headed downtown for City Market.

"All right, Mz. Police Goddess," he muttered. "You'd better not screw this up."

Chapter 42

Frankie drove to Robert House, a three-story rectangular building straight out of the seventies urban renewal project. She parked in front of the entrance, remembering the concrete steps and Ramos's group photo hanging in the hallway. She sat there, thinking and jotting notes about her conversations with Ovia and Ramos. She was certain Ovia had made the curses, but she didn't get nearly enough information about who had bought them. Ramos had cooperated by opening Red's file, but in her mind, he was still on the hook.

Bringing her badge into the confrontation had been a mistake. If Ramos called the station house to follow up, there would be ramifications even though Red's case was closed and she had the right to investigate on her own. Her approach with Garrett would have to be more subtle. Flashing a badge wouldn't intimidate Garrett. It would end the conversation.

She'd pushed Billy hard for this interview, partly because he had taken his frustration about Pryce out on her. If they were going to work together, they had to start up the way they could keep up. She was no girl Friday. She wanted to get this right. Garrett might have information that would tip the balance on whether Ramos remained on her suspects list. And there was Garrett's evasion about identifying Carter's photograph.

She thought about the day she'd watched an MPD tracking dog work a field. He followed the scent through mud and wet grass, onto a playground, and across a busy highway. His handler couldn't slow him down.

She hoped these cases would boost her career, but they could also be the reason she might end up at the mall selling jeans. She was willing to take that risk. Like that tracking dog, she wasn't about to quit.

She fluffed her hair, got out, and locked her Jeep.

The reception area had two digital screens flipping through shots of vegetable gardens, men sitting in classrooms, and men in chefs' hats cooking on commercial-grade stoves. Glancing around, she was struck by the contrast of the fresh images on the screen with the two exhausted-looking men in the waiting area, necks bent forward, elbows resting on their knees. The incongruence made her a little uncomfortable.

She caught up with Garrett on his way out of his office. His wet-combed hair looked a little greasy, and his pupils had shrunk to black pinpoints. As she approached, his tongue flicked out to lick his lips. His breath had a chemical smell to it.

She introduced herself as Frankie Malone and explained that she was assisting Detective Able with an investigation. She didn't say she was a cop, and he didn't ask.

"Could you spare a few minutes?" she asked.

He leaned heavily on his cane, something elusive going on behind his eyes. "I remember you from Itta Bena last night. And from the funeral." His voice retained a deep resonance even though he was in rough shape. "You should have called first. I gave Detective Able plenty of time for questions last night."

"These are different questions." She gave him a broad smile. "We really need your help."

"We're transplanting strawberries to the rooftop garden right now. I'm on my way to an appointment, but I should check their progress before I leave. Come with me."

They took an elevator to the roof where two men were using hooked knives to split open bags and dump topsoil on long, raised beds. Garrett moved among the rows with his broken gait, ending up at the railing at the roof's edge. Below were at least two acres of gardens where men were wrapping the roots of strawberry plants in wet paper towels and placing them in cardboard boxes.

"We're moving those plants to the roof to preserve the first crop we put into our garden. They were the beginning of our culinary program. You can't imagine the positive impact it has on a man to harvest and cook the vegetables he's planted."

Garrett swept his hand over the garden, much like on aging monarch. "Tomorrow we break ground for a new building. We'll add forty-five beds, six classrooms, and a state-of-the-art commercial kitchen. Fifteen of our culinary graduates currently work full-time in restaurants. Our program receives a lot of donor support. I'm expecting a good turnout for the ceremony tomorrow, including media coverage."

"You've given a great deal of yourself to Robert House," she said.

Garrett lightened up on his cane, some of his fire coming back. "Last night we launched a fund-raising campaign for the Carter museum. We're matching a two-hundred-thousand-dollar federal grant. Calvin's photographs brought international attention to the civil rights struggle even before President Kennedy became involved. That's how the world learned there were two Americas. One white and one black.

"My brother was murdered because he was passionate about civil rights. He appeared in some of Calvin's most compelling photographs. I've invested my time in the museum to be sure his life is properly memorialized. Last night at the fund-raiser, the board announced that a display will be dedicated to Robert's story."

He smiled graciously. "Enough about the museum. You have questions."

She took a breath. "Detective Able has concerns about the circumstances surrounding Red Davis's and Little Man Lacy's deaths. I've spoken with Dr. Ramos about his counseling sessions with Red Davis. Both men were believers in Santería. I was surprised to learn that Dr. Ramos is a *santero*."

Garrett blinked. "Are you familiar with Santería?"

"I grew up with it in Key West."

"Santería is common in the Gulf Coast area. After Katrina hit, the shelter had an influx of people from that region. Dr. Ramos has been very effective."

"He mentioned private sessions with Red Davis."

Garrett's pupils flared then diminished. "I won't confirm or deny that. All sessions are confidential."

"The doctor holds Red's right to confidentiality, but he was willing to discuss the sessions with me because of Detective Able's concerns."

"Little Man fell and broke his neck. Red had a heart attack. Both men were alcoholics. Why is Able pursuing this?"

"We believe someone used their religious beliefs to terrorize them."

Garrett's lips compressed. "You're suggesting that Dr. Ramos was involved?"

"I didn't say that. But I want to know if there were problems between Ramos and the two men."

Garrett smoothed his palm over his hair. "I did hear shouting during some of their sessions."

"Can you be more specific?"

"I don't recall the details. Emotional outbursts are common during therapy."

His statement puzzled her. Neither Ramos nor Davis seemed like shouters. "Do you recall either man having disagreements with other residents?"

Garrett's nostrils flared. "We don't spy on our residents. In fact, I barely knew Davis and Lacy."

"Forgive me, but your eulogy gave the impression that you'd spent a great deal of time talking with Davis."

"We had a few conversations, but let's go back to your questions about the doctor. The safety and privacy of our residents is my responsibility. If you believe Ramos was involved in the deaths of these men, you need to tell me now."

He glared at her. They weren't sitting in an interview room, but the same rules applied. She was asking the questions, not Garrett. She ignored his demand and went on.

"Dr. Ramos confirmed something you mentioned in the eulogy, that Davis was interested in making a change in a particular person's life. Davis told Ramos he was sending money to someone living in Boston. Shortly before he died, Davis borrowed two thousand dollars from Augie Poston. He claimed to have a locked-in business deal that would enable him to pay Poston back. Can you tell me anything about that?"

Spots of color appeared on Garrett's cheeks. "Red Davis

was a drunk. He was in no shape to make any kind of deal." He stopped. "Did Red get the two grand?"

"Yes."

"I doubt you'll find out where the money went." Garrett raised his hand in farewell. "With that, I must leave you. Feel free to look around the property. There's a donation box at the door."

She noticed the raised hand was trembling. Perspiration had broken out on Garrett's brow. "A final question before you go. Last night when you looked through the photographs with Detective Able, you failed to point out Calvin Carter among the informants. Able specifically asked if you could identify anyone. Carter was a young man at the time, but certainly you must have recognized him."

Garrett fixed her with the stare she'd seen him use to intimidate guests on talk shows. "Possibly my eyes were tired. Or the lighting was poor. Maybe I was distracted by the full moon. Or maybe it's none of your goddamned business.

"You come here with bullshit questions, wasting my time. The last thing my brother said before he walked out the door of our house was, 'Know what's important. Protect it.'"

Frankie blinked. *Protect what's important?* What did that mean? Billy had said this wasn't a big point, but obviously it was to Garrett. She decided to push a little harder.

"If those photographs prove that Carter was an FBI informant, the museum's future will be damaged. Isn't that right?"

Garrett focused on the men in the garden below. Something strange moved across his face, then his professional mask slipped back into place. "Believe what you wish. I'm late for an appointment."

"We're not finished, sir."

He swatted the air. "Go to hell, Miss Malone."

She watched Garrett go. His claim that Davis and Ramos were shouting at each other wasn't credible. He'd recognized Carter in the photograph, but his speech about poor lighting and being distracted by the moon was ridiculous. Then he'd brought up his brother's last words. *Protect what's important.* Maybe it was the drugs, but the end of their conversation had bordered on madness.

She started to leave, aware that the two men who'd been prepping the beds were watching Garrett hobble to the elevator. They looked back at her, knocking loam from their gloves, their gazes vaguely aggressive as they positioned themselves between her and the elevator.

Don't screw with me, guys, she thought. *I'm the one with the gun.*

To avoid a confrontation, she chose the metal staircase that ran down the side of the building and would put her into the back parking lot. At the bottom, she walked along the building, past a row of windows at the ground level that let onto the basement kitchen. Through an open window, she heard a woman singing a Jamaican folk song that she recognized. She stopped and squatted on her heels to look through the half window. A woman, probably the one who'd been singing, had her back turned and was wielding a cleaver, breaking down a whole chicken on a butcher block. She used her thumb to deftly split the chicken's keel bone from either side of the breasts.

A bandanna in black, green, and gold, the colors of the Jamaican flag, covered her hair. Hoop earrings swung in rhythm with the cleaver. From beneath her shirtsleeve, Frankie saw flashes of a green watchband on her left wrist.

The woman was tall, with broad shoulders underneath her chef's apron. Her muscular arms moved as gracefully as snakes, glistening in the kitchen's heat as she swept the chicken parts onto a tray and reached for a new carcass.

On the shelf above her head stood two statues representing orishas—Ochosi, the divine hunter with his bow, and Ogun, the protector with his shield and sword. A red candle, symbolizing strength and domination, burned between the statues.

Frankie recognized the woman as the stern mistress who'd been seated with the men from the shelter at the funeral. She didn't trust hunches, but she was having one now. Ovia had described the woman who bought the curses as a Santerían worshipper who was unusually tall. This woman stood six feet in her sneakers.

Frankie gathered her courage and took the steps down to the kitchen. The woman looked up as she came through the door.

"We take no visitors in the kitchen, miss. Thank you very much." She waved her cleaver in dismissal and continued working.

"I heard you singing 'Linstead Market.'"

The woman stopped. "You know Jamaican folk songs?"

"I've spent time in the islands." Frankie approached the butcher block for a closer look, aware of the cleaver in the woman's hand. The name "Dominique" had been scrawled across the top of her apron with a laundry marker. Five signature necklaces of the Santería necklace initiation hung at her throat along with a sixth necklace for Ogun, just as Ovia had described.

"Sid Garrett suggested I look around the kitchen," she said.

"Ahh. You must be an angelfish then. The bossman calls people angelfish when they give money to the shelter."

The image of a delicate fish wriggling on Garrett's hook flashed through Frankie's mind. "He might consider me an angelfish of sorts."

Dominique's head-to-toe appraisal reminded Frankie that she didn't look anything like an angelfish. She shopped at Target, not Bergdorf Goodman.

"My family owns a nursery," she said. "Mr. Garrett wants our help with the roof garden." She inclined her head toward the statues on the shelf. "I see you honor the orishas. Are you a believer?"

Dominique gave her a sidelong glance. "You know Santería?"

"Enough to place *ebbos* in my home for good luck, but not enough to solve my problem," she said in a plaintive tone.

Dominique selected a boning knife and ran the thin blade down the chicken's backbone. Frankie recognized the high-end Japanese chef's knife, far more expensive than she could afford.

"Strong money got no problems in America," Dominique said. "You an angelfish, you got strong money. I'm busy now, forty chickens to break down for bossman's bashy party tomorrow." She cocked her head toward the door.

The conversation was over unless Frankie could hook her interest. In the Jamaican culture, family matters most. She put on a downcast face. "You talk strong money, but money won't stop the man who wants to steal my family's land."

Dominique's gaze darted up. "This man takes your gardens?"

"A judge will give him our land next week unless I stop him."

The knife hovered over the chicken. Dominique's eyes cut at Frankie. "A *mayombero* will make *guzum* curse for you. You know Santería, you know this is true."

"Are you talking about Dr. Ramos?"

"Nah. Ramos is no *obeah* man, no voodoo. I know *mayombero* who will send this *gravalishus* man away." Dominique tilted her head in consideration. "Or this man could die. I have seen it happen with my own eyes."

This had to be the woman Ovia described. And from the sound of it, she'd watched Red die. "How can I find this *may-ombero*?"

"She trusts no one. I will get the curse for you."

"For how much?"

"Eight hundred dollars." Dominique put down the knife, her sleeves riding up while she crossed her arms as if this was her final word.

Her watch was different from anything Frankie had ever seen. How had Billy described Augie's stolen watch? Green band. Vintage. Valuable.

"Eight hundred dollars. Too much for a curse." She nodded at Dominique's arm. "Tell me about your watch."

Realization that there was more to this deal crossed the woman's face. Her fingers brushed the watch face. "My family passed this down to me. You like it?"

"I do."

"My grandmother leaves me watches and more things. Very rare." Dominique let her words dangle, meant to entice.

"You're willing to part with these things?"

Male laughter came from beyond the kitchen. Two gangly young men banged open the door and swaggered over to pull aprons off a hook and tie them around their waists. A smaller dark-skinned man came in behind them. He tucked himself into a corner and began reading a book, glancing up on occasion at Dominique.

One of the other men gestured at Frankie. "Hey, Jamaica. We got us a new girlie cook?"

"Outside with deez box of potatoes. Peel and wash." Dominique pointed at the door.

She turned to Frankie, angrily shaking her head. "I'm done

over with this kitchen. My auntie has a California job for me four days from tomorrow. I will wear a chef's coat with my name sewn in red. And I take my Jamaican friend with me over there. He's always with a book." She spoke to the little man in the corner. "Go to the cooler and bring more chickens. You and me have work to do."

He nodded and stepped inside the walk-in cooler.

A stocky man with a mangled nose shuffled into the kitchen. "Hey, Domino. You want help with them chickens?"

She brandished the cleaver. "I'm no Domino," she hissed.

"Shit, lady, forget it." He slung a box of potatoes onto his shoulder and walked outside with the other men.

"You see?" she said to Frankie. "I sleep here; I work here. Bossman makes me come to his house twice a week to scrub his toilets and iron his shirts." Her eyes flashed. "He works me like I'm his property. No respect for Dominique. But I show Mr. Bossman. I show him."

The woman paused, running her tongue over her lips, thinking. "Yes. I have decided. We meet at the bus station. I'll bring the curse and things to sell. You bring cash. We both get away from these bad men."

Frankie nodded. Dominique had just laid out a classic sting operation for her own takedown. "I'll see the man who wants to steal our land tomorrow. I need that curse tonight."

"I'm in the kitchen till eight o'clock. We throw a bashy party tomorrow for TV people. You and me, we will meet at the bus station tonight at nine."

Frankie wrote her number on a piece of paper and laid it on the counter. "You call when you're on your way."

"Yes. Good-bye now."

The Jamaican man returned with the chickens. Dominique's cleaver came down to severe a chicken leg, as if both their troubles had been resolved.

Frankie left the kitchen, hardly able to resist going back to clamp cuffs on Dominique. The woman's tough act would break down in the interrogation room. But if she was right and that watch was part of Augie's property, arresting Dominique now could mean the rest of the stolen items might never be found. Dominique could claim she'd bought the watch on the street. They would have no reason to hold her. Billy needed more persuasive evidence than that to get Dunsford off his back.

She found the lobby where an old man in an oversize Stetson was sitting behind the desk. He grinned at her approach.

"Welcome, welcome, welcome," he said and shoved the hat brim back with his thumb.

"Wonderful place you have here. By the way, I didn't catch the name of the Jamaican chef."

"You mean Dominique Powell?"

"That's it. Has she worked here long?"

"Couple of years. Long enough to think she runs the place." He laughed.

"Thanks." She slipped a ten in the donation box on her way out the door.

Chapter 43

At City Market Billy picked up his tuna sandwich with a side of fried okra and a giant iced tea. He sat at a sidewalk table in the shade of a spreading oak across from a Main Street trolley stop. Four days ago he'd shared a similar table with Augie in front of the Peanut Shoppe. Only four days.

He thought about Augie's mental illness and how Lou's obsession with Rebecca Jane had brought him down. Can we sense our hidden flaws before the damage is done, or will they take us from behind? Augie deserved to round the bases and coast into home plate. Instead, his flaw stole his dignity. Someone else stole his life.

He shut down those thoughts and focused on his food. The tuna was chilled and delicious. The fried okra still sizzled with hot oil. A breeze from the river swept up the bluff, carrying the sound of carriage-horse hooves echoing down the corridor of granite buildings.

This felt like home. His shoulders dropped, and he inhabited his own skin for the first time in weeks.

The trolley crossed the intersection and rolled to a stop. Doors whooshed open. A young woman in skinny jeans and ankle boots stepped off.

He instantly recognized her honey complexion and the classic planes of her face. Theda Jones walked to his table, languorous, hypnotic, never breaking eye contact as she approached. He knew the type, comfortable with the power she held over men. Her confidence made her even more provocative.

"May I join you, Detective Able?" she said. The timbre of her voice sounded polished beyond her years.

"Of course." He stood and angled the second chair away from the table.

She smiled and took a seat. "I'm Theda Jones. I met Augie Poston the day before the funeral for Daddy Davis and Little Man. Augie told me about you."

"We crossed paths outside of the funeral home."

She rested her elbows on the table, interlacing her long fingers. "When I saw you sitting here, I knew God had brought us together."

"I don't believe you tracked me down through divine intervention, Miss Jones."

Her smile stiffened. "Forgive my subterfuge. Augie told me about your home on the river. I was on my way there when I saw you from the trolley. But I still believe there's a touch of the divine involved. That's how I live my life."

He didn't buy that last bit. According to the New Orleans PI, he was gazing into the eyes of a call girl and gifted con artist. He avoided the word "whore," because Theda Jones had been pushed into the business. She had supposedly made a break from it.

"What's on your mind, Miss Jones?"

Her lips pursed. "I'm frightened, and I don't know anyone in this city who can help me."

"Go on."

"Last week everything changed. I found out Little Man had

died. By the time I got to Memphis, Daddy Davis was gone, too. That young man at the mortuary was kind enough to introduce me to Augie. He told me you were looking into their deaths." She paused, picking up on his skepticism. "I know. Augie said too much, but men do that. They like to tell me things."

He remembered how bowled over Augie had been by the photo of Theda seated at the piano. It was a miracle he hadn't given her his credit card and pin number. "You said you're frightened."

"The man at the mortuary told me they died of natural causes. I think there's more to it. Daddy Davis sent a letter and a package to me a few weeks ago. He asked me to keep them safe. He hinted there might be trouble."

Her eyebrows rose, looking for his acceptance. A letter, a mysterious package. She must think he was an idiot.

"Is Red Davis your father?"

"He's the only man who's ever been good to me. I met Red and Little Man at a club in the Quarter where we were performing. They thought I had talent. There was some trouble, so Red arranged a scholarship at a conservatory in Boston. He bought my ticket, bought my clothes. They were like two angels flying me away."

He wondered if she knew she was the reason they ended up homeless. "Did Red keep in touch?"

"He sent letters and some pocket money. Red always signed his name Daddy Davis. The letter and package were the last. I didn't hear from him for a couple of weeks. Then I read about Little Man. I spent every cent I had to get here."

Theda's story ran close to the PI's report except for the part about turning tricks for Cool Willy. Couldn't blame her for leaving that out. The real discrepancy was that she claimed to be flat broke. She'd shown up at the Rock of Ages Funeral Home in a hired car and dressed like a million bucks.

She looked past him, her gaze becoming fixed. She reached into her handbag and slipped on a pair of sunglasses. "There's a man watching us," she whispered.

Billy turned for a look. "Ah, hell," he muttered.

J.J. eased off the wall and sauntered over, same spotless sneakers, only this time his jersey read GOT JESUS? with a fat question mark printed in gold. He stood outside of Billy's reach while cocking his head at Theda, giving her a big, gummy smile.

"Morning, lovely lady. May I recommend a downtown carriage ride? I'll arrange a better tour than the detective here can ever give you. No charge."

"Beat it," he said to J.J. "Now."

Theda removed her glasses. "That's a nice offer, but I'm sure a gentleman like you knows when not to intrude." She gave him a finger-wave good-bye that drew an even broader grin from J.J. but didn't send him on his way.

Billy got to his feet.

J.J. stepped back. "It's a free sidewalk, Detective. And I'm a free man, no thanks to you." He made a show of stomping down the sidewalk as best he could while wearing sneakers.

Billy took his seat again and looked across the table at Theda, knowing she was a hustler far more skilled than J.J. At least she was beautiful to look at. "Tell me about this package."

"It's a box about ten inches square. The letter said to keep it safe and not to open it. I've wondered if what's in the box got them killed."

"Did you open it?"

She shook her head. "Red believed in Santería. I'm from New Orleans, so I know it could be something awful like human remains or animal entrails. I brought it with me to give back to him."

Her gaze moved to the pot of pansies next to the station, the flowers ruffling in the breeze. He heard a mix of abandonment and sadness as she continued.

"I went to the school office to sign out for a family emergency. They asked me to remind Mr. Davis that his check for the balance of my final semester was late. That's when I learned there never had been a grant. Red has been paying my tuition all along. Thousands of dollars."

Her hand brushed her neck. "The unpaid tuition is fifteen thousand. I hate to bring this up, it sounds so crass. The school has nominated me for an international piano competition at the end of the next session. If I win, I'll be signed by a talent management group and have a debut recital in New York plus a recording contract."

"That's quite a prize," he said.

"It won't happen if I get kicked out of school."

"Maybe there's money in the box."

"His letter implied that it's extremely important, and possibly dangerous. That doesn't sound like money."

"It doesn't sound like a curse, either."

"I was wondering . . ." She gave him a pleading look. "If what's inside is so valuable, a collector might be interested in buying it. Like I said, I don't know anyone here. If it turns out that the package is valuable, maybe you could help me find a buyer and keep half the proceeds."

He settled in his chair, comfortable that he knew what was coming—you provide up-front money and we'll share in the larger profits later. "That's very generous. What would you need from me?"

She brightened. "Money to get me back to school. Four hundred dollars will buy my train ticket to Boston."

"I can't give you money when I don't know what's in the box."

"I understand. We'll open the box together before you give me the four hundred."

She was proposing a classic Nigerian letter scam, but what if she had a legitimate letter and package from Red? Both could be important to the investigation. Or was this a con coming from an intelligent, beautiful call girl who killed the only two people who had ever cared for her?

"Before we go on, I have a question," he said. "You played the Quarter, right? You must have run into a pimp named Cool Willy."

Theda's lids fluttered. She grimaced, coughed. "He's a bad man. That's all I know."

He paused, allowing her discomfort to soak through. "This guy attacked Red and Little Man in New Orleans. Put them in the hospital. Then he went to their house and destroyed their instruments. A lot of emotion went into that. Do you know why he did it?"

Her chin lifted. "No, I don't."

"Neither do I. This pimp showed up at their funeral. You saw him there, isn't that right?"

Her features grew strained. Was she holding back a lie or holding back the truth?

"Cool Willy put them in the hospital for a week with multiple injuries." This wasn't exactly true, but he wanted to push it.

She coughed again, covered her mouth. She gasped and glanced at his empty tea glass. Tears swam in her eyes.

"Are you choking?" He stood, alarmed.

She nodded, fanned her face with the flat of her hand, and struggled to draw in a breath.

He ran for the market's door and squeezed through the crowd at the counter. "Water," he barked. Someone stuck a bottle in his hand. He flung bills at the counter and hit the door, twisting the cap as he ran.

The truth dawned on him at the sight of their empty table. He stopped, looked about. The sidewalk thronged with people. In front of him, the trolley was rolling south, ringing its bell. A city bus pulled off in the opposite direction. He could see the driver wiping his face with the end of a rose-patterned towel that he kept draped around his neck. Billy took a swig of the water.

There was no way to know which way Theda had gone. He'd been played for a second time that day.

"Lose something, Detective?" J.J. stood with his back pressed against the granite wall. He held up a twenty that flipped in the breeze. "The lady axed me to say she'd be in touch." His face beamed with satisfaction. He tucked the money in his track pants. "By the way, you planning to tap that? She sho' is fine."

"Clean it up, J.J. You got more class than that."

J.J.'s lips bunched, and he drew air through his nostrils. "The other night at Bardog . . . you hit me in the feels, bro. You and me got history. You let me down."

Billy's phone buzzed in his pocket. "Sorry about the feels, brother. I have to take this."

"That's all right, man. Jesus Junior forgives." J.J. walked off.

Billy figured it was Frankie reporting on her meeting with Garrett.

Chief Middlebrook came on the line. "I need to see you in my office. Now."

Chapter 44

Crossing the crowded CJC atrium, Billy shouldered through clerks, cops, and defendants returning with their take-out burgers, boxed fried chicken, and turnip greens. Several uniformed cops gave him a nod. A couple of detectives shook his hand. That meant the news that he was a suspect in the Poston investigation had not leaked to the ranks. But it would. He felt bad about that, like he was letting down people who depended on him.

Across the atrium, the doors of the express elevator to the upper floors opened. He saw Middlebrook's assistant step inside and turn to press the button.

"Hey, Roxanne!" he called and picked up his pace toward the elevators. She searched the crowd with an expectant smile, but when she saw it was him, her eyes went cold. Still looking at him, the doors slid closed.

What the hell? Roxanne had always been friendly, even a little flirty. Now she was giving him attitude. Maybe she knew something about his meeting coming up with Middlebrook. That worried him. The chief was a pro at protecting his men. He had counted on Middlebrook being in his corner through this.

He punched the button for another elevator and thought back to his phone conversation from Augie's apartment with Middlebrook. The chief had taken him at his word, but since then Middlebrook would have watched the interview tape and seen his consternation when Dunsford brought up the dummy cameras. He'd have to be ready to handle that and whatever else the chief threw at him.

He assumed Middlebrook called this meeting to decide which horse to back—Dunsford or him. Nothing personal. In the politics of the department, a murder charge filed against one of their own would smear the department's reputation, even if he were eventually cleared. If he was found guilty, it would be worse. But the real scandal would be if it came out later that the department had stepped in to cover for him.

He put his phone into silent mode as he left the elevator and rounded the corner to the chief's office. Roxanne was already seated at her desk. Her chin lifted at his approach and her eyes stayed on her computer screen. He was tempted to stop and speak with her, but the chief's door was open, and he could see Middlebrook sitting at his desk. One confrontation at a time. After the meeting, he would find out what was going on.

Middlebrook was reading a newspaper when Billy walked in, his face sagging with anxiety. When he saw Billy at the door, he came to his feet.

"Able. Close the door. Sit." He gestured toward a small conference table in the corner and came around the desk. He laid a copy of *USA Today* on the table and positioned it so that Billy could read the headline below the fold: "Augie Poston: Murder Under Wraps."

Middlebrook sat down and tapped his finger on the article.

"A sports hero beaten to death in his own home. People want to know what the hell we're doing about it."

The media wanted a person of interest or at least sordid details of the murder. Anything to keep the story hot. A homicide detective suspected of that murder would send the pack into a frenzy. Billy scanned the article, aware of Middlebrook watching him. He glanced up and caught the chief switching to a sympathetic expression.

"Poston was a friend of yours. Tough that you had to see him like that."

Middlebrook was playing the role of the commiserating cop. Under different circumstances, he would have assumed the chief's comment was sincere, but this was no normal conversation.

He folded the paper. "You asked me to come in so you can decide if I murdered Augie Poston. I didn't do it. I want to help catch the bastard who did."

Middlebrook's face stiffened. "Guess my interview techniques are a little rusty. But you're right. I read your statement and watched the interview. You fought with the victim. You have no alibi."

"Let's establish a few facts. The footage from the stadium proves Augie was out of his mind. I didn't start the fight, he attacked me. And I didn't threaten him. He mistook my meaning and reported it to Freeman as a threat."

"I saw the footage on the news. Damned shame Poston had to go out that way." Middlebrook paused. "I want to set that investigation aside for a moment. Dunsford reported that you stuck your nose into the Davis case. You want to tell me about that?"

The switch took him by surprise. What was Middlebrook up

to? "Don Dunsford is a racist, which is the reason Red Davis's case was getting a flyby examination. I wanted to take a look at the body myself."

"Did you pick up on anything?"

"What I saw concerned me," he said.

"The ME ruled the case natural causes."

Billy looked away. Introducing death curses at this point would shut down his credibility.

"I know that, sir."

"All right, Able. That leads to my next question. Have you been attempting to investigate the Poston case?"

With the door closed, the office was soundproof, which meant Billy could hear his own heart beating. He could tell Middlebrook had settled in to wait an his answer. This was dangerous territory.

"I'm a cop. I have a duty to find my friend's killer."

"Ah, Jesus. I knew it." Middlebrook rubbed his eyes. "Dunsford is digging like hell to prove you did this, and you're helping him."

"What would you do, Chief? Sit on your ass?"

Middlebrook walked heavily to his desk and returned with a pad and pen. "Who did you talk to?"

"After you cleared Freeman, he and I discussed possible suspects."

Middlebrook wrote, looked up. "And?"

"Sid Garrett. He worked with Augie on the funeral arrangements for Davis and Lacy the day before the murder. I contacted Garrett so he could pick up the slack at the service. Garrett made a comment about Augie's erratic behavior the day before."

"Sid Garrett is a sharp guy. What did he have to say?"

"His opinion? Augie was hopped up on crack. His murder

was a result of a drug buy gone south. I don't agree. Neither does Freeman."

"Is that it?"

Oh, shit. A leading question. He had grounds for discussing the murder with Freeman and Garrett. Pryce was different. Pryce was a suspect. He hesitated.

The chief got to his feet and paced in front of his desk. "You've talked to someone else. Who was it?"

If he didn't answer, he risked charges of obstruction later on. "I located the journalist who's been working with Poston on a book. The manuscript is missing from the apartment."

Middlebrook stopped pacing. "Has this journalist given Dunsford a statement?"

Billy shook his head.

"God as my witness, Able, this could take you down."

"Yes, sir."

Roxanne knocked and stuck her head in the door. "Chief, Detective Dunsford is here."

Dunsford pushed past Roxanne, holding a sheaf of reports in front of him like a Labrador carrying a dead pigeon in its mouth. In his eagerness, he failed to notice Billy seated at the table off to the side.

"Sorry to barge in, Chief. Sid Garrett just called and said Able got in a fight with Poston at the funeral home on Monday. He saw the whole thing. A couple of hours later the son of a bitch went after Poston in front of the ballpark. The way I see it, Able followed Poston home and finished him off. Garrett said the next day he'd witnessed Able punching a man's lights out in front of the Carter museum. We need to drag Able's ass in here, get him off the street before he kills somebody else."

Middlebrook looked over at Billy. Dunsford followed his gaze.

Billy stood. "Story of your career, Dunsford. Always a step behind."

Dunsford's mouth clamped shut.

"I asked Able to come in," the chief said evenly.

"You called my suspect in without telling me?"

"Don't question my judgment," Middlebrook stated flatly.

Dunsford shot daggers at Billy. "Sorry, Chief."

"Calm down, Don. Tell me what you've got."

"In front of Able?"

"Tell it. Now."

Dunsford huffed, shaking the papers in his hand. "Information on Poston came in last night. His eBay account and social media networks gave us nothing. Poston's done very little business over the last four months. Phone records show he's been in constant contact with one Walker Pryce over those same months, and with you, Able." He gave Billy a long look.

"Augie left messages asking me to meet him at the funeral home," he said.

"The record shows Poston called you umpteen times the day he died. We're also looking into this Walker Pryce's background, a former journalist out of Chicago, recently moved to Memphis. He's my next call." Dunsford slapped the papers with the back of his hand. "Got his number right 'cheer."

Billy risked a glance at the chief, who was giving nothing away.

"Call him," Middlebrook said. "Use my phone."

Dunsford sneered at no one in particular, tapped in the number, and waited.

"Yeah, this is Detective Don Dunsford, Memphis Police Department. Is this Walker Pryce?" He listened. "Can't hear you. Say again." He frowned at Middlebrook. "Officer Tate, Chief

Middlebrook is standing here with me. I'm about to repeat what you just said. You were on patrol. You saw fire trucks at the Waters Trace development. You stopped to investigate. There's one male victim, breathing but unconscious. You're talking to me on the victim's mobile phone because it rang and the EMT saw Memphis Police Department on the screen. He handed it to you."

Holy God, Billy thought. *It's Pryce.*

Chapter 45

Middlebrook signaled Dunsford to put the phone on speaker.

"Okay, Tate, give us the details."

Billy heard men shouting, the squawk of two-way radios, and the chugging sound of the diesel engine on the water-pump truck.

"There's a gash on the back of this guy's head," the voice said over the speaker. "A lot of blood. And he's got a snootful of smoke."

"Tate, this is Chief Middlebrook. Have you identified the victim?"

"A wallet was on him. Driver's license says Walker Pryce."

"What caused the head injury?" Dunsford asked.

"Hold on." They heard Tate call out then he came back on the line. "Sir, this is the fireman who went in the house after Pryce."

A different voice came on. "Wilson here. I'd say somebody whacked him from behind. He wasn't beat up, but there weren't nothing around him coulda caused that kind of injury."

"Where did the fire start?"

"The bedroom. Somebody wants a house to go up, he sets a smoldering fire on a mattress and opens two windows in opposite rooms. Then he skedaddles before the cross ventilation flares the fire and torches the house."

"Did you find opened windows?"

"Yes, sir. And the smoke-alarm system didn't ring into the station. I'll bet the inspector's going to find it was tampered with. A truck driver on the highway spotted smoke coming out the front window and called it in. Otherwise, this fellow would be cooked. Got to go, sir."

Tate came back on. "Pryce is being transported to The MED. Anything else?"

"Lieutenant Markus and Detective Dunsford will be there shortly. Good job, Tate." Dunsford hung up.

Middlebrook glanced over at Billy. The chief knew he'd talked to a journalist, but he hadn't given Pryce's name, the time, or the location. If the facts came out now, Middlebrook would doubt everything he'd said, including his declaration of innocence of Augie's murder.

This could get ugly.

"Roxanne, get in here," Middlebrook called. She appeared at the door with a notepad. "There's a fire victim en route to The MED with a head injury and smoke inhalation. I want a status report from the ER. The name is Walker Pryce."

"Walker?" Roxanne said.

"Walker Pryce. What's wrong, Roxy?"

Billy saw it, too. The blood had drained from her face, and her mouth worked without making a sound.

She ran to Middlebrook, waving her notepad in Billy's direction. "He was at Walker's house this morning. He hurt Walker, I know it."

Middlebrook gripped her shoulders. "Calm down. How do you know Pryce?"

She started sobbing. "He's my boyfriend. He called this morning and asked questions about Detective Able and the Poston case. He said Able had insisted on coming over to talk. Walker seemed nervous about the meeting, said he needed to be prepared."

She made a high sound in the back of her throat like a cat and rushed at Billy, her hands balled into fists. Before she reached him, Dunsford grabbed her around the waist and hauled her back.

"Roxanne! Get hold of yourself," Middlebrook barked.

She jerked away from Dunsford and glared at Billy, breathing hard.

Now he understood why she'd been so rude at the elevator. Pryce had made her believe he was a threat and tricked her into giving restricted information without considering whether it would get her fired.

Her emotions were very real, very convincing, and more than enough to persuade Middlebrook.

The chief guided Roxanne toward the door, patting her shoulder and calling for another secretary. "Tina, help Roxanne pull herself together. Drive her to The MED. And Roxanne, keep me updated on Pryce's condition. I'm so sorry this happened."

Middlebrook turned back. "Able, sit at the table. Dunsford, take the chair in front of my desk." The chief sat behind his desk and squared the papers in front of him, organizing his thoughts.

"Able, tell me if you went to Pryce's house this morning. If so, tell me why and what happened."

He was screwed. J.J. and the cashier could swear he was at City Market an hour ago, but if the fire started before then, their affidavits would be useless. Giving Middlebrook that information would be digging his own grave, especially with Roxanne crying outside the door and Dunsford ready to pounce. Surviving this meant he had to bluff the chief into backing off.

"You're asking if I set that house on fire. I resent the hell out of your question, Chief. You practically twisted my arm to sign back on, and now look at this mess."

"Sign back on the force? The way I see, you're trying to kill everybody in reach," Dunsford said.

Middlebrook shot Dunsford a look that shut him up, then he turned to Billy and in an ominous tone said, "If you don't convince me you're clean, I will personally end your career in law enforcement. And I will recommend that you be charged with attempted murder. Now. Do I need to repeat the question, Sergeant Able?"

"What do you want from me? Your assistant gave confidential information about a high-profile case to her boyfriend, a journalist no less. That's all you've got. Roxanne's opinion about anything else isn't proof, it's emotion. I say let's back off, wait to see what Pryce can tell us. He knows who tried to kill him."

"You haven't answered my question," Middlebrook said.

Billy stood. "Chief, I would like to comply, I really would. But I can't answer your question at this time."

"Then Detective Dunsford will read you your rights."

Dunsford hopped out of the chair. "You have the right to remain silent. Anything you say can and will be used against you . . ."

Billy talked over Dunsford's head to Middlebrook. "You're fucking charging me?"

Middlebrook thrust his chin at Dunsford. "It's his case. I'm done."

Dunsford completed the required warning, licking his lips at the end as if he were tasting blood. He eyed Billy. "We're going to the interview room now. Time we cleared up a few things."

Unbelievable. Middlebrook was moving ahead when they didn't have a thing they could use to prosecute. And Dunsford was delusional enough to think he could trick another detective into incriminating himself. Time to shove the bullshit back at both of them.

He held up his hands. "Unless you charge me, I'm not going anywhere. Do what you need to. I'll be more than happy to respond."

"Cool down, Able. It's just a conversation," Dunsford said, backing off. He slicked his hand over his hair and glanced at the chief, nervous about what to do next.

"Forget it. I'm not going to help you investigate me." Billy pointed a finger at Middlebrook. "A little while ago I looked you in the eye and told you I didn't kill Augie Poston. Now I'm telling you I didn't set Pryce's house on fire, either. Charge me or I'm out of here."

He waited, looking from Dunsford to the chief and back again. "Yeah. I didn't think so."

He strode out of the office, feeling angry and betrayed. Middlebrook let that rat terrier Dunsford try and push him around. At least Roxanne had left for The MED, and he didn't have to see her accusatory eyes.

He took the express elevator and walked into the atrium, half expecting a uniform to come around the corner and arrest him. Dunsford might try to trump up a minor charge to hold him, but Middlebrook would do the reverse—get more information, then make the decision whether to come after him or not.

Outside, he crossed Poplar and stood on the sidewalk in front of the parking lot. Before he got behind the wheel, he needed to calm down. Son of a bitch. He'd skated out this time, but he was in real trouble.

The motive for the fire had been murder. Professional arsonists know how to set that kind of fire. So did the Chicago cops that Pryce had taken down. Unfortunately, so did he. Two years ago he'd investigated a near perfect murder where a man used a similar method to kill his wife. The man set the fire but couldn't bear letting his expensive fishing rods burn, so he took them out of the house. It never occurred to him that the cops would notice that the two rod stands in his study were empty. The man went down for second-degree murder.

Dunsford and Middlebrook would remember that case.

To make it worse, Garrett had called Dunsford with a slanted version of the brawl at the funeral home, failing to mention that Augie had been over-the-top crazy. Garrett also knew Billy had handled the naked guy when he didn't have to. Looking back, he wished he'd invited the dude into the museum to swing his nuts at the board of directors.

What had prompted Garrett to make that call?

It was all breaking against him. He'd lost Middlebrook. Dunsford was gaining on him. None of it should be happening. He wasn't guilty of a damned thing.

A car slowed behind him and honked as it passed. He turned and saw James Freeman driving a red Corvette convertible. Freeman took a right at the light and turned into the west entrance of the lot. He got out and cut across the parking lot, coming straight for Billy, looking mad as hell.

He felt his own steam rise. His hand went up in Freeman's face. "Don't you say one damned word."

Freeman stopped. "You bastard. You used me to get to Pryce. You burned down his house."

The scene in Middlebrook's office left him feeling raw. He wasn't about to put up with more accusations. "Don't be an ass. I told you I intended to see Pryce this morning. I wouldn't broadcast that if I'd planned to kill him."

"That's bullshit. Whether you planned it or not, that's what happened. I heard the call go out on the police scanner at my office. I figured you were involved. I'm here to tell Dunsford about our going into Augie's apartment last night to look for Pryce's number."

"I already told Chief Middlebrook about Pryce." He pulled out his phone and held it up to Freeman. "I'll dial the number. You can talk to him yourself."

Freeman hesitated.

Billy pocketed his phone. "I didn't kill Augie. I sure as hell didn't try to kill Pryce. While I was at his house, he got a call. He arranged for someone to come over. I guarantee that's who set the fire."

They stood toe to toe in the parking lot, sweating out a classic stare-down.

Freeman blinked first. "You got an alibi this time?"

"As soon as I round up my witnesses."

Freeman chewed his lip, studying Billy. "I canceled my meeting. It felt wrong to leave town. I wanted to do something, so I checked eBay and Craigslist for Augie's stolen stuff. Nothing showed. Do you know anything about Pryce's condition?"

"He was hit from behind and took in some smoke. He's unconscious. There's evidence of arson."

"Do you still consider him a primary suspect?"

"Not anymore. He gave me a list of people he claims will

swear he was with them the night of the murder. I talked briefly to the owner of a club where Pryce performs, and got hold of one other guy." He handed Freeman the list. "If their stories hold up under questioning, Pryce is off the hook."

Freeman studied the list. "What's the name of the club?"

"The Devil's Sentiment."

"That gay club in midtown?"

"Pryce performs there. He's a drag queen. The club owner says he really draws a crowd."

Freeman handed back the list. "Maybe someone from the club got jealous and set the fire. Did Pryce have the photo Augie stole from you?"

"No. He claims to have a copy, but he wouldn't show it to me. We agreed that once I've confirmed his alibi, he'll turn it over. He wants copies of the rest of the shots. Of course, his copy of the photo has been destroyed."

"And we still don't have the original," Freeman said.

"Whoever killed Augie probably took that photo from the apartment."

Freeman ran his hand over his mouth. "I want to be clear on this. Exactly where were you when the fire started?"

"Eating a tuna sandwich at City Market. Now get off my back about that."

Freeman studied him, shook his head. "How did I get in the position of trusting a cop who's about to be charged with two counts of murder?" He took out his phone. "Give me your mobile number. I'll go to The MED and see what I can learn about Pryce's condition."

Chapter 46

Billy drove through the downtown Pinch District, heading nowhere. He thought about the guys he knew in high school who'd matured early, made the football team, and dated the prettiest girls in the county. After graduation, they picked up good money during the casino construction boom in Tunica. They blew their paychecks on muscle cars, darts tournaments, and cheap women in the bars.

Then the boom died, and the football heroes were forced into minimum-wage jobs at Fred's and AutoZone. Their wives grew fat and dissatisfied. Their kids didn't have a chance in hell of doing any better than their folks.

He'd been the lucky one. The money his uncle had scraped together along with a string of jobs he worked put him through four years at the University of Mississippi and a year of law school. The course of his life changed when he'd walked away from the idea of practicing law after learning that two little girls he knew from church had been kidnapped. Despite credible leads, the sheriff never questioned an upstanding member of the community. A couple of months later the man died in his sleep. Family members discovered the girls' bodies in his basement the day after the funeral.

After hearing about the girls' murders, he'd quit school, attended the police academy, and worked his way up to sergeant detective in homicide. He loved the hunt. It was unthinkable that he could have his job jerked out from under him by the likes of Don Dunsford; however, that appeared to be what was happening.

He tuned the radio to WEVL 89.9 for the *Deep Blues Show* and rolled past a tiny brick building known as Effie's Lounge. The sign with its hand-painted martini glass had almost faded away. Foot-high weeds grew in front of the iron security door. A white pit bull trotted from behind the building and lifted his leg on the fire hydrant. The dog looked more resentful than mean.

Billy felt the same.

He pulled under the shade trees in Washington Park across the street from the carriage-horse stable where he could watch the draft horses turned out in the pasture. Two grays and a black munched on flakes of alfalfa while switching flies off their hocks with their tails. Their coats held a subtle gleam.

He checked his phone. A text from Frankie said she wanted to get together. After his meeting with Middlebrook he was radioactive, and he was angry with her. Garrett's call to Dunsford made him think her talk with Garrett had sparked his hostile attitude. What other reason was there?

He called. "Got your text," he said.

"I'm at the CJC. Where can we meet?" She sounded excited.

Most of what he had to tell her was bad news, and, at this point, he wasn't sure he could control his reactions. "That's not a good idea. Let's do it over the phone."

"Seriously?" Now she sounded resentful.

"Tell me how it went with Garrett."

"He was shaky, unkempt. His pupils are pinpoints. He's definitely addicted to pain meds."

"Did he have anything to say about the Carter surveillance photo?"

"He admitted everything and nothing. He's a master at blowing smoke."

"I don't know what happened between the you of two, but an hour ago, Garrett called Dunsford about my confrontation with Augie at the funeral home."

He told her about going by Middlebrook's office, and Dunsford barging in with Garrett's incriminating evidence.

She was quiet for a long time. "They set you up. A detective doesn't push his way into the deputy chief's office with case information, right? He goes to the shift commander. Middlebrook used Dunsford to rattle your cage."

Her insight surprised him. "I don't think Middlebrook is the one setting me up. The scuffle at the funeral home looks bad, but Dunsford made it sound worse than it was. He's trying to push Middlebrook into releasing my name as a suspect."

"You trust Middlebrook," she said.

"I do."

"I'm just saying . . . maybe you shouldn't. Any more happy news?"

He told her about Pryce and the fire.

"Good God," she said.

"I ran into Freeman at the CJC. He'd heard about the fire and decided he should confess to Dunsford that we'd broken into Augie's place. I talked him out of it. That's all Dunsford needs to lock me up."

"You broke into a crime scene?"

"To find Pryce's number. Now they're looking at me for the fire. Dunsford even read me my rights, trying to bluff me into incriminating myself. But they can't charge me. They have no proof."

"Billy, this shit's getting deep. You need to quit making it worse."

"Great advice, sweetheart. You want to tell me how that's done?"

She paused, clearly taken aback. "You're right, you can't sit around and hope for the best."

"Nope. Not an option."

He watched a skinny teenager walk to the pasture gate and whistle. The horses ignored him until he rattled the chain on the gate and unlocked it. The two grays swung around and ambled toward him. The black horse turned its rump toward the boy and continued to eat hay.

Billy realized his teeth were clenched. He'd been undermined from every direction. He told Frankie about Theda Jones stepping off the trolley and her story about Red and the mystery package.

"That's crazy," she exclaimed. "You think it's true?"

"The package may exist, but here's my problem. With this fire, I'm convinced Pryce didn't kill Augie. Dunsford is hell-bent on locking me up. I have to figure out who the killer is, and I mean *now*. The Davis/Lacy investigation will have to wait."

"What if we prove the three cases are linked?" she said.

"With the photographs?"

"Not the photos. I met a woman in the kitchen at Robert House. She worked there when Red and Little Man were residents. She fits the description of the person who bought the curses—tall, wearing six necklaces, and she's into Santería. *And* she was wearing a watch with an emerald green-band."

"A Bulova?"

"I couldn't tell. Her sleeve kept covering it. But it's definitely not a watch you'd pick up at Target. She said she inherited it from her grandmother along with other things she wants to sell. She's supposed to meet me at the bus station tonight at nine. I pitched a story about needing a death curse. She's bringing a conjure bag and the watches. Call me crazy, but she could be fencing Augie's stolen stuff."

"What's her name?" he asked.

"Dominique Powell. She's Jamaican. Built like a shot-putter."

"You've run a background?"

"She's got a history. A woman accused her of trying to steal an umbrella. Dominique got mad and hit her over the head with it. She was charged with battery, got community service that she served at Robert House. She stayed on to run the kitchen. From what I've seen, she runs most of the men there, too. What I can't figure out is how she could have ended up with Augie's stuff."

"Give me a minute." He turned on the engine, clicked the air-conditioning on high, and closed his eyes so he could concentrate. "Okay, I'm winging it here. Let's start at the beginning. Red borrows two thousand from Augie. According to Theda Jones, he needs a fast fifteen thousand or she'll be kicked out of school."

"Two grand doesn't help much," Frankie said.

"It's seed money to buy scripts. You don't need a dealer to do that. You find people who've been in car wrecks or have cancer—street people, addicts who doctor-shop, even old people with bad knees and bad backs. If they need cash, they'll get by on half their meds and sell the rest for ten bucks a pill. The profit margin is huge. Oxycodone goes for fifty bucks a pop in the downtown clubs.

"Red needs scripts fast, so he hires some guys from the shelter to round them up. He sells them in the clubs. The cash piles up. Greed sets in. His helpers decide they want a bigger slice, like a hundred percent. They assume he's keeping the money in the house where he and Little Man were squatting."

"Where does Dominique come in?" she asked.

"She hears the men shooting the shit about Red and the cash. She knows that Red and Little Man believe in curses, so she says, 'Give me a cut, and I'll hex that house so bad they won't go back in. In fact, I'll run them out of town.'"

"That sounds like Dominique. She's tough."

"Let's suppose Red let it slip that Augie had given him money. After Red's gone, one of the men from the shelter breaks into Augie's place. Augie comes home, goes to the kitchen to make a sandwich. The guy sneaks up with Augie's bronzed bat and swings it."

"That's quite a story," she said.

He thought a moment. "It doesn't explain how the killer got onto Augie's floor without the code. Augie would have to have given it to him."

"What if Dominique went in? You said Augie had problems with women. Maybe Dominique came on to him. He invited her up and gave her the code to keep things discreet. She went to his apartment looking for the money but ended up killing him. She's strong enough. She tossed the place looking for cash but didn't find any, so she stole his stuff."

"Why steal the manuscript?" he asked.

"It's your story. I'm just helping out."

"I don't know. This scenario is a big 'what if.' I'm guessing Dominique doesn't have Augie's watch. She'll show up tonight with her granny's old Timex. The curse is different. I agree she's good for that."

He shouldered the phone, put the car in gear, and turned toward the river. "You said she's meeting you at nine?"

"Yep."

"We'll both be there," he said.

"How about if I come to the barge around eight thirty?"

"Fine. By the way. Good job finding Dominique and spotting the watch."

He could almost hear her grinning over the phone.

He went to the barge where it was cool and dark, he dug around in a drawer for a pen and a legal pad, and he dropped on the sofa. He hunted killers for a living. This time he had a personal incentive.

First, he recorded the story line he and Frankie had put together. Right off, he saw that the scenario had big damned holes in it. First, Red didn't have the stamina to sell scripts in the clubs. Second, the staff members at Robert House weren't fools. They would spot unusual activity among the residents and bust them. Third, no credible connection existed between Dominique and Augie, nothing that would put his stolen property in her hands. She may very well have caused Red's and Little Man's deaths, but he didn't believe she was involved in Augie's murder.

Why had Augie been murdered? What was the killer after?

He flipped the page and noted his original suspect list: Freeman, Pryce, Cool Willy, Augie's clientele, a drug dealer, Augie's former teammates, some bar rat who'd pegged Augie as an easy mark, and the least likely, a random intruder. Reluctantly, he crossed out his top choices. He circled Augie's clients, still a possibility, but he didn't have the information he needed to investigate. Cool Willy and Theda Jones were both from the world of prostitution and violence. Theda had met Augie at the funeral home the afternoon he was murdered. Maybe he invited her to his apartment, gave her the code, and Cool Willy had come along with her. Money would be their motive, but that didn't ring true for Billy.

Then there were people who become fixated on celebrities. Maybe Augie befriended a homicidal fan and never mentioned the person to Freeman or him. What about his neighbors? They could easily gain access to Augie's floor. Surely Dunsford had detectives canvass that entire building. As an investigative reporter, Pryce moved in dangerous circles. Had one of Pryce's contacts killed Augie and then tried to kill Pryce?

He tapped his pen on the paper and wrote his name at the bottom of the page. A high percentage of murder victims know their killer, maybe even care about that person—a business partner, a lover, a family member, a friend like Billy.

He rested his head on the back of the sofa. Nothing accomplished. While he followed blind leads, the killer was staying one jump ahead.

He must've slept. The next thing he heard was the beep of a horn and the sound of a truck engine revving into reverse. He went to the window as a FedEx delivery truck accelerated up the cobblestone landing into the evening light. Walking outside on the deck, he saw the driver had stacked the boxes, three large and one small, inside the gate at the foot of the ramp. The air had turned dank. Folds of gray clouds, still distant to the south, were moving in quickly. He brought the boxes up the ramp and piled the three large ones in the corner of the living room. The smaller box marked next-day delivery, the one Mercy had texted about the night before, he put on the coffee table. While searching for a pad, he'd seen an unopened pack of Camels in the drawer. He got the pack and sat on the sofa for a smoke, knocking ashes into a coffee cup while he thought about the package and what might be inside. He stubbed out the cigarette and opened the box.

It was a sweet potato pie. He knew from the aroma of the spices that it was the recipe they had created together. His throat tightened. He picked up the pie and took it to the kitchen. Then he walked into the bedroom to keep from losing it. Frankie would be showing up soon.

He dug out of the closet the loose gray shirt he used for undercover work. His black Stevie Ray Vaughan T-shirt and Redbirds ball cap, the one with the long bill, he kept in a drawer. He laid the two shirts and the cap on the bed, fighting to shift his focus from the hole in his heart to the job coming up. He stripped off his T-shirt and pulled on the black one. He slipped his SIG in his waistband at his back and pulled on the gray shirt.

Thunder rumbled.

Shortly before eight thirty P.M. he heard a car pull up at the foot of the ramp.

Chapter 47

The rain began the moment Frankie pulled up to the barge. Fat drops slapped the windshield like mud daubs. Pecking sounds followed, hail bouncing off the hood.

Billy tromped down the ramp and through the gate, his shoulders hunched against the rain and the darkness. He jerked open the passenger door and slid in as the storm cut loose in earnest. He didn't look at her.

"You got your gear?" he asked.

"Gun, cuffs, badge, and a pack of fake money I made up out of printer paper."

He flipped on the courtesy light and leaned forward, trying to get a look at her feet. "You're not wearing street shoes, are you? You could slip."

"Back off, I'm good with the shoes."

He settled in the seat, the pale courtesy light touching his forehead, the side of his nose, the down-turned corner of his mouth.

"Something wrong?" she asked.

He took a while responding. "I'm focused on what's coming up." He glanced over at her. "What's up with you?"

Whether he was in the mood to hear it or not, she had something to say, like a confession, before they went out on this operation.

"The other day when we talked, you said trust between partners is everything in this business." She swallowed hard. "I have something to say about that. An incident not long ago had an impact on me and not in a good way. I've tried to deal with it on my own, but like you said, I should have gotten professional help to get past the trauma."

She looked over to gauge his reaction, but the light was too dim. "The thing is, I've been having anxiety attacks. I've been self-medicating. It's not working out."

"What are you using?"

"Tranquilizers. I had a prescription from when my dad died. It's supposed to take the edge off, help me sleep. They worked at first, but this week things started getting out of hand."

The rain began to pound the Jeep's roof. She stopped talking. She wanted him to respond, say something.

"Was the incident work related?"

Oh, God. His tone was so flat it made her nervous.

"I'd rather not go into—"

"Did it involve the woman who got off the elevator at the CJC?"

"Um. Yes, but that's beside the point. The day I called to cancel our meeting I was having my worst anxiety attack. I overreacted, took two pills. All I can say is, I'm working through this. I apologize for my behavior. It won't happen again."

Maybe it was a trick of the light, but he looked like he was taking this personally. Something was happening.

"Are you still using?" he asked.

Still using? "For God's sake. I don't have a habit. I threw the pills away. I'm solid tonight, don't worry. Look, Billy. I enjoy working with you. I hope we'll do more together in the future." She brushed her hair off her face. "This was poor timing, but I couldn't go forward without being honest with you."

"You lied. The day it happened, I gave you an opportunity to clear it up and you didn't. Why should I trust you now?"

She started the engine. "You're going to have to trust me. We're in this too deep. Besides, you need me." She reached into the backseat for the grocery store bouquet of carnations she'd bought and dropped them in his lap. "Here's your cover for the bus station. You're meeting your girlfriend coming in from Little Rock."

He took the flowers. She turned off the light. She'd said her piece. The other conversation would have to wait.

They drove to the bus station with the rain coming down in sheets. She lucked out on a parking spot at the curb fifteen feet from the entrance. The Greyhound sign—blue and red neon—shone watery and indistinct through the windshield. A couple running down the sidewalk, holding plastic bags above their heads, ducked inside the station to take shelter from the storm.

"Dominique is supposed to call when she's on the way, but we should go in separately in case she's early. I'll take a position in the southeast corner beside the ticket counter to draw her in. When she arrives, you circle behind in case she tries to bolt."

She was in this now, the hunt. She looked over. He seemed focused on a point far down the street instead of listening to her.

"You with me?"

He nodded.

"If she's got the goods, I'll run my hand through my hair. Be ready to use some muscle. This woman is six feet and built like Serena Williams."

He pulled an envelope from inside his shirt. "Freeman e-mailed these examples of Augie's watches to make the identification easier."

She took a penlight off the console and shone it on the photos.

He tapped the first photo. "That's the Bulova with the green band."

"Swear to God, that's the watch. I told Dominique to bring it with her."

"He also followed up on Pryce. They've moved him to a room. Maybe he'll wake up and remember who tried to kill him. Simplify things."

She stole a glance at him. He had a lot riding on the next thirty minutes. If Dominique showed up with Augie's property and they could take her down, they would either have Augie's killer or be just one step away from him.

"You ready?" she asked.

He popped open his door and went in first. She followed a minute later, sloshing through puddles at the entrance. Someone had taped a handwritten sign on the inside of the glass door: NO GUNS.

The crowded terminal smelled like wet dog and popcorn. The big room felt worn-out and tired of struggling, waiting for the roof to collapse and end its misery. The single remnant left of its pride was the classic GREYHOUND insignia hanging above the ticket counter, five feet of sleek chrome greyhound stretched out in a full racing sprint.

Mothers with screaming kids on their laps took up most of the front-row seats. In the back rows, overweight seniors sat with their swollen legs stretched out, blocking the aisles. The people standing around were folks waiting to meet someone or to board a bus themselves. Others were less benign. Scattered throughout the terminal, loners leaned against the walls with their arms crossed over their chests and their heads hanging, eyes averted. These were the felons, the losers, the opportunists—the guys you don't want to be seated next to on the bus.

J.J. the street hustler brushed past her, looking like a tall Mr. Clean in his white jersey that read JESUS IS COMING. LOOK BUSY. He glanced her way and nodded but kept moving toward the restroom. He was soaked to the skin and obviously irritated.

Three guys in their twenties wearing motorcycle boots and leather vests over bare chests clomped up and down the terminal's center aisle as if patrolling it. Their attention roved over a knot of four teenage black guys wearing NBA jerseys. The boys had staked out territory by the water fountain, milling around and cutting their eyes at the crowd. Both groups looked pissed off, as if the rain had driven them into the terminal against their will.

The arrivals/departures board hung high on a wall to her left. Incoming buses from St. Louis and Little Rock were overdue. Those scheduled to leave for Nashville and Louisville had been delayed. Frankie overheard a woman say the storm had skirted Memphis, but flash floods had shut down parts of Highway 40. The delays explained the overcrowding with passengers brushing against each other, trying to make room.

She watched Billy move along the far wall, slapping the flowers against his leg like they were a rolled-up newspaper. He was scanning the packed space the same way she was. He stopped, took out his phone, and tapped in a text:

Tough place for a takedown.

Sure was, but Dominique already had one foot out the door for California.

She texted back:

Too risky?

Her phone rang while she still had it in her hand. It was Dominique.

"Angelfish, you at the station?"

"I'm here." She glanced at Billy and nodded. He drifted midway down the side of the terminal into position.

"Lord, God, this rain. We outside the station."

We? Did that mean a cabby or a friend with a car? A second person would complicate the takedown.

"You brought the curse and the watch and your family things?" Frankie asked.

"I got that stuff, Angelfish. You buying my things tonight?"

She heard the need in Dominique's voice. "I'm still interested. Meet me in the back corner, past the ticket counter."

She hung up. Her heart pounded as she scanned the terminal for any last-minute problems. And there was one. The teenagers were moving as a group from their position to the center aisle where the bikers were pacing. One of the kids pointed at the nearest biker. He must have made a wisecrack because the biker, a big guy with swastika tattoos on both forearms, lunged forward to pop the kid in the chest, knocking him into the other three.

Not now, she thought as she moved into a group of people who were grabbing their luggage and bustling away from the fight. Billy caught her eye and shook his head as he strode toward the skirmish, meaning for her to stay in position. She stepped back, agreeing that she shouldn't intervene in a flare-up that would probably burn out fast.

The boys shoved their friend forward like he was a prizefighter they were pushing back into the ring. The biker flexed his neck and showed gapped teeth when he smiled. The kid raised his fists. The biker stepped in and dropped him with a left hook to the jaw. The teenagers shouted. Everyone in the terminal turned, their attention now taken by the fight.

Frankie looked around. Where the hell was the security guard?

Just then Dominique sailed through the door, carrying a box she'd wrapped in a garbage bag to protect it from the rain. She had on a black dress to her ankles and the same yellow, black, and green bandanna she'd worn in her kitchen. The noise and the press of the crowd didn't seem to faze her as she searched the faces for Frankie.

They made eye contact. Frankie waved for Dominique to come up the side aisle to keep her out of the ruckus. Dominique edged through the crowd then slowed, her attention drawn to the ring of people that had formed in the center aisle.

The kids were at the center, taunting the bikers and pulling their friend to his feet. A wiry biker elbowed aside the bigger guy. Frankie saw a shiv appear in his left hand. He pressed it against his thigh so the kids wouldn't see it coming.

But Billy saw it coming.

"How 'bout it," he shouted and rammed the biker with his shoulder, the jolt knocking the weapon from his hand.

Both groups froze and watched as Billy scooped up the knife and pocketed it.

Dominique cocked her head toward the group and rolled her eyes. Frankie shrugged. Thank God she didn't have to step in. Billy was damned good at his job.

Dominique began to move again. She was twenty feet away when Frankie picked up in her peripheral vision the third biker easing up on Billy's right. Brass knuckles appeared in his right fist.

"Behind!" she yelled. Billy twisted left, but the biker's fist chopped down and caught him on the back, knocking him to his knees. The crowd closed in, hiding him from her sight.

She ripped out the SIG strapped to her ankle and raced toward the fight. The biker raised the brass knuckles above his head, prepared to slam down with lethal force. From out of no-where, J.J. pushed through the ring of people, bellowing like a madman. He grabbed a fistful of the biker's hair and yanked him backward.

"Police!" Frankie shouted, coming in behind him. The other two bikers and the kids took off running. Billy scrambled to his feet, lunged at the biker who'd slugged him, and snagged his vest from the back. The biker wriggled free of the vest and sped toward the door.

Frankie was furious. The bastard could've killed Billy. She raised her gun, but held her fire. The sight of a gun set the crowd bumping and pushing for the exits. She whirled and locked eyes with Dominique, who had gotten the picture and was clearly outraged about being conned. She flipped Frankie the bird, and pushed through the crowd for the door, the box still in her grip.

"Go," Billy shouted.

Frankie shoved her way through the crowd that had slowed Dominique long enough for her to leap from behind and make a grab at the dress. Her hand had closed over the black cloth when a huge woman in a Graceland T-shirt broadsided them both. Frankie's feet slid on the wet floor. She went down hard on her ass with the dress still clutched in her hand. Dominique stayed on her feet and twisted around to swat her dress free, which sent the box tumbling across the floor. Dominique screamed some-thing unintelligible before bolting out the door.

Frankie knew if she didn't get to the box, quick hands would make it disappear. Billy blew past her and was out the door as she grabbed for the box. She got to her feet and followed him with it in her arms.

Outside, the rain hit her in the face like buckshot. Billy directed her left. He ran right. She dodged cars in the parking lot, careful to keep her feet under her and not fall on the box. She searched up and down the cross street for Dominique, then ran through the departure bays on the right side of the terminal. The Little Rock bus rolled in, its headlights revealing that Dominique was nowhere in sight. Frankie had retraced her steps to the covered entrance just as Billy got there.

"Are you okay?" she asked.

"I'm fine. How could a big woman like that disappear so fast?"

"She said someone dropped her at the station. They must have been waiting in the parking lot. She could be holed up anywhere."

He slammed his fist into his palm. "Damn it!"

"At least we got the box."

J.J. pushed through the door and stuck his head out. "You guys working with no backup? Cause you damn near got jacked up."

"Good play, J.J. I owe you," Billy said.

J.J. grinned. "Like I always say, Jesus saves."

Frankie held the box out to Billy. "You want to go inside and open this?"

"Heads up," J.J. said and gestured toward the street behind them. An MPD patrol car, blue lights rolling, was two blocks away and cruising in their direction.

Chapter 48

We'd better open it at the barge," Billy said, knowing they had already pushed their luck.

She handed him the keys. "You drive."

He stowed the box in the back of the Jeep. Frankie used callback on Dominique's number and got the "not accepting calls at this time" message. Dominique had either turned off the phone or removed the battery so her phone couldn't be tracked. He suggested Frankie call cab company dispatchers and the ticket agent at the bus station, giving them Dominique's description. After she did that, she checked with the night manager at Robert House who said that Dominique had left there around eight thirty P.M., carrying a suitcase and a box wrapped in plastic. She had not returned.

The rain stopped. The sidewalks became crowded again, making it unlikely they would spot Dominique. They considered calling in patrol officers for help, but that would require explanations they didn't want to make. Dominique didn't have money for a plane ticket, there was no passenger train until midmorning, and she wouldn't dare go back to the bus station. They'd done what they could to contain her within the city. Most likely, she'd found a place to stay for the night. The only thing left was to head to the barge and open the box.

When they got inside, he gathered gloves, scissors, tape, and his laptop. He made coffee while Frankie wiped down the stainless-steel counters, the best surface in the place to deal with evidence. If she noticed the pie sitting on the cutting board, she didn't mention it.

They snapped on gloves and cut away the green plastic, revealing a packing box with pictures of jumbo cans of tomatoes on the side. Dominique would have picked up the box in the shelter's kitchen. Frankie popped open the flaps. On top was a soft, gray conjure bag. Beneath that was a white pillowcase with red trim and the Cardinal's insignia.

Billy's heart jumped at the sight. They looked at each other and grinned. He'd felt the three deaths were connected. Here was the first evidence pointing in that direction.

Frankie unfolded the pillowcase and began lifting out watches zipped into plastic bags, their crystal faces showing through. She laid everything on the counter: eighteen watches, two worn baseballs covered with signatures, two blues harmonicas, and seven framed photographs of civil rights martyrs. The Bulova with the green band was missing. No phone, no laptop. At the bottom of the box lay a large mailing envelope bulging with pages. Frankie slipped the manuscript out. A USB flash drive tumbled out with it.

She picked it up. "I'll bet Pryce gave this to Augie so he could upload the manuscript."

"Is the missing photo in there?"

She shook the envelope. No photo. He tried to not let his disappointment show.

"Let's start with the conjure bag," he said.

He handed Frankie a plate and a spoon. She poured some of the bag's contents on the plate and used the spoon to spread the mixture.

"Dried herbs, sand, dust balls, peppercorns, and some bug legs," she said. "The white thing in the middle is a tooth, probably bought out of the mouth of someone at the shelter." She spooned the contents back into the bag. "It's fake. Dominique thought I wouldn't know the difference. Of course that doesn't mean she's in the clear. It would help if we could get Ovia to make an identification, but there's no way in hell she'll do that unless Ramos pushes her."

"You've convinced me Dominique planted the curses in the rooms and triggered Red's and Little Man's deaths," he said. "But why? What was her motive?"

"She's hot-tempered and might hold a grudge, but I don't think she's the kind of person who could pull this off by herself."

"Then someone threatened her or paid her," he said. "Either way, someone else is involved."

"Let's start with the theory we talked out earlier."

He shook his head. "It doesn't hold up. Red was in no shape to wander around selling scripts to raise cash. And no one from the shelter, especially a six-foot Jamaican cook, could have gotten into the DeVoy and killed Augie."

Frankie stared at the evidence on the counter. "Okay. We'll start over."

"How about if you catalog the evidence on my laptop while I scan through this manuscript?"

"I'll do that, but why stop to read it now?" she asked.

"Because I'm stumped. When that happens, I look past the obvious."

He sat in his reading chair in the living room with the stack of pages on his lap while Frankie worked on the evidence in the kitchen. He flipped through, looking for Pryce's name. It didn't appear anywhere on the manuscript. Then he read the introduction. Halfway down the page he read: *There came a time when, for one brief moment, God turned his back on the people and the devil had his way. Dr. King was murdered right here in our city. Dedicated people paid with their lives. Others have worked since then to prove the devil hasn't won . . .*

It was a powerful statement, more passionate than he would have expected from Pryce. He scanned more pages until chapter five stopped him cold. He read every line. Twenty minutes later he went into the kitchen and laid the manuscript on the counter.

Frankie looked up from the computer. "I'm almost finished. Did you find anything?"

"According to this, Calvin Carter was on the FBI payroll for years."

She blinked. "He was a *paid* informant?"

"Like Garrett said, all kinds of people were talking to the cops or FBI agents. This book claims Carter did more than that. He gave up information about civil rights leaders who were risking their lives, and regular folks, in the movement. Even a priest who ran an outreach ministry."

He thumped the manuscript. "Carter attended meetings with top civil rights leaders. While they discussed strategic planning, he snapped photos and listened. Then he met with agents and turned over the names of the people present and the dates of marches and demonstrations with their locations. That gave agents plenty of notice to setup street fights that would turn peaceful demonstrations violent. They made it look like the organizers were behind it."

He paused. "Carter gave the agents personal information

to leak to the press. They contacted employers to get ordinary people fired for being involved in the movement.

"You remember what I told you about Grant putting pressure on Freeman's dad? Pryce focuses on that kind of surveillance. Some say the NSA is doing that now.

"Pryce got his hands on Dahlia Poston's FBI file. She was the type of activist who scared the pants off Hoover and the white establishment. She was educated, outspoken, and black. The FBI was keeping an eye on her. I'm sure Augie must have read this. He told me there was more to his mother's case, but he never explained what he meant. Now I see why he was so obsessed with her death. Pryce must have given him a copy of her file and maybe even one on Carter. They're probably on his laptop."

"Speaking of that, I should upload whatever is on that flash drive," she said, feeling around behind the computer for it.

"I have to hand it to Pryce," he said. "He's uncovered a block-buster story. Carter was a hero in this city for forty years. Old warriors in the movement, especially the people who trusted him, will be heartbroken. Some will be outraged. Some will con-demn him. Others will deny he did it."

"Outing Carter as an informant will crush Sid Garrett," she said. "The museum just won a big grant. Garrett's in charge of fund-raising, and the board promised to dedicate a wall honoring his brother. The revelation about Carter will kill donations."

They looked at each other. Frankie's eyes narrowed.

"Garrett's got a lot to lose," he said.

Chapter 49

'll get my case file," he said. "Let's meet in the living room, and we'll start at square one."

He returned with the expandable folder he'd been using to store the case information. He sat on the sofa beside Frankie and brought out the stack of photo, handing her the one of Carter talking with Grant.

"Garrett saw this photo of Carter at Itta Bena," he said.

"Do you remember if there was a second Carter?"

"I don't, but if Augie had a shot of Carter, it would definitely have gotten Pryce's attention. The promise of more pictures like it would make him take the risk of meeting with me. So we'll have to assume Augie stole one similar to this." He picked up a pad and made a note. "We'll start with Red buying the jacket and finding the photos. He would have recognized Carter right off the bat."

"Why?"

"Red and Little Man played the clubs on Beale Street off and on for forty years. Carter had a studio on Beale. A big part of his income came from taking promo shots of musicians. The three men had to have crossed paths. The question is whether Red knew these were surveillance shots and understood what that meant."

"I may have an answer to that," she said. "In Garrett's eulogy, he said Red talked about agents hanging around Beale at the time of Dr. King's assassination. Maybe he recognized Grant."

"So it's reasonable to assume Red knew Carter was talking to an agent and was pretty convinced Carter was an informant. Red wouldn't have cared until he thought about the one person who'd be devastated by that piece of news—Sid Garrett. The photo suddenly became valuable if he could collect on it."

"Red didn't seem to be the kind of guy who'd go for blackmail," she said.

"Except that he was obsessed with Jones, desperate to keep her in school. Remember 'Old Fool Love'? He was hooked. It would make sense for him to approach Garrett and offer to sell the photograph. Fifteen thousand for Theda's tuition. Or maybe he asked for more. Garrett's loaded. Red might even have threatened to find another buyer. If he said he had more pictures, Garrett would know he was going to be on the hook for thousands."

"If Red was working a deal with Garrett, why borrow money from Augie?" she asked.

"I don't know. Possibly a payment on Theda's tuition or for living expenses. She looks like she could go through a couple of grand a month."

Frankie stood and began pacing. "How do you think it went down?"

"Red went to Garrett and made his pitch. Garrett probably pretended to accept but stalled for time to figure out what to do. That could be the reason Red had to ask Augie for the money. In the meantime, Garrett was looking to stop Red, but in a way that wouldn't dirty his hands. He remembered Red and Little Man were into Santería, so he lined up Dominique to put curses in their rooms. He wanted to scare them bad enough to leave Memphis and never come back. He couldn't know the curses would kill them. But after it happened, he was okay with it. Problem solved."

"We've put Red and Garrett together using the Carter photograph," she said. "Robert House connects Garrett with Dominique, and the death curses. But what about Dominique and Augie? They didn't know each other. You said you don't believe she could've killed Augie and gotten in and out of the building. If that's true, how did she end up with his stuff?"

Billy said nothing for a time. He'd believed the photographs were a common thread between the three murders. Now the answer was coming to him.

"Let's go at it from another direction. Who stole Augie's stuff in the first place? At the stadium Augie said that he had business to take care of. Pryce's book was serious business to him, but we know Pryce isn't the killer. However, on the afternoon before Augie was murdered, he spent several hours with Garrett, making funeral arrangements. Augie was angry with me. I wouldn't be surprised if he talked to Garrett about his mom and brought up the manuscript. I saw Garrett's book at Augie's place, so Augie knew they had a common interest in the civil rights era. Maybe Augie invited Garrett over, or Garrett invited himself."

"Lots of people have that book. It proves nothing."

He raised a hand. "Hear me out. We know the parking lot for the DeVoy is behind the building. With Garrett's disability, it would be hard for him to walk around to the front entrance. It's reasonable to imagine that Augie would give him the pass code for the door and the elevator. Even if he came through the main entrance, I doubt the cop who reviewed the tapes would flag him as a person of interest."

"Okay. That's reasonable."

"In the course of the conversation, Augie went into more detail about the manuscript and about Carter's involvement with the FBI."

"But wait," she said. "If the manuscript set Garrett off, shouldn't he have gone after the author instead of Augie?"

"He didn't have a name. It's not on the manuscript, and Augie wasn't giving it out. When Garrett *did* find Pryce, he tried to burn him and his book."

Frankie threw up her hands. "I don't buy this. Garrett's not the violent type. He may have indirectly caused Red's and Little Man's deaths, but he's too sophisticated to resort to bludgeoning a man when he had other alternatives."

"You're the one who pointed out that he may be a drug addict. If it's true, his impulse control is shot. Augie showed him a photo of Carter and Grant. The blackmail scheme was back to haunt him. Garrett thought he'd never get out from under. Everything he cared about was at risk. He snapped. He killed Augie in a rage. Then his rational side kicked in. To keep anyone from finding the manuscript, the photo, the phone, or the laptop, he tossed the place. He took the watches and the rest of the stuff to make it look like a burglary."

"You really think Garrett is responsible for three murders?" she asked.

"I'm convinced he set in motion events that led to Red's and Little Man's deaths. Concerning Augie, I saw Garrett at the museum the day after the murder. First, he was in a lot of pain, which you'd expect if he swung that bat. Second, he pushed hard to persuade me that Augie had a drug habit and was involved with dealers. He did a good job putting out a phony lead, good enough to have me considering it."

Frankie thought about that. "If your scenario is right, we're back to the question of how Dominique got her hands on the stolen stuff."

He shrugged. "I haven't gotten that far. Garrett's too smart to keep incriminating evidence at Robert House. And he wouldn't have given Dominique the watch."

Frankie sucked in her breath. "Oh, God. She complained about having to scrub Garrett's toilets and iron his shirts. She was mad as hell about it. She said, 'I show him.'"

"That makes sense. As his housekeeper, she could snoop around. She found the box and knew it was valuable stuff. Since she was ready to skip town, she went there today and took it. But she didn't get to the phone and laptop because he has them locked up."

"Speaking of laptop, we need to check that flash drive," she said.

He brought the computer from the kitchen and set it on the table. The dialogue box on the screen gave them the option of showing all files. The flash drive contained a docx folder and a jpg file. He clicked the folder first. It contained a copy of the manuscript. Then he clicked the jpg file.

A photograph of Agent Leland Grant opened. He was facing the camera and talking to a teenage boy whose head was tilted up, squinting against the sun. Frankie and Billy stared at the screen.

"Where did this come from?" she asked. "Did Augie steal *two* photos?"

"No, just the one." He fell silent, thinking. "The reason Augie stole the photo was to give Freeman a picture of Grant. This is the best shot of Grant in the bunch. The others are in profile. This has to be the one Augie stole and showed to Pryce. It's on the flash drive because Pryce scanned it for him."

"Then Augie never had a photo of Carter." She leaned closer to the screen. "You think this kid is significant?"

He shook his head. "I don't know. We've missed something. I was sold on Garrett for all three murders because I thought seeing the photo of Carter had sent him over the edge. Now I'm not sure."

In his mind's eye, he'd seen Augie at the refrigerator, his back turned, having offered Garrett a beer. And there was Garrett, panicked and raging, picking up the bronzed bat. Augie half turned, catching the first blow on his temple. Stunned, he stayed on his feet long enough for Garrett to deliver the second, crushing blow to the back of his head. Then he went down.

The images sickened him. He wanted Garrett to not be the guy, but he couldn't let that sway him.

"You with me?" Frankie said.

She'd been speaking to him.

"You said, 'If Garrett didn't do it, who do we have?'"

He rubbed the back of his neck. They stared at the screen, trying to come up with something.

"Look," she said. "We have some compelling evidence, but we need more. There's a ground-breaking ceremony at Robert House tomorrow. You should take some of this stuff with you and wave it in Garrett's face. Maybe if you shake him up in public, he'll incriminate himself."

"I can't use the actual evidence. I'll have to go to the Redbirds store tomorrow for a pillowcase and make up a dummy manuscript. Here's the dilemma. If I don't hand over this evidence immediately, Dunsford can charge me with obstruction of justice for withholding it. And if I *do* turn it over, he'll claim I had possession all along, which for Dunsford is proof I killed Augie."

Frankie furrowed her brow. "Actually, I've got that covered. In case the loot turned out to be real, I took the precaution of dropping by the station house to pick up a copy of the squad's major offense summary with the list of stolen property. That gives me a legitimate reason for being familiar with Augie's list. I can truthfully say I met Dominique at Robert House and noticed the watch she was wearing. She offered to sell the watch to me along with several other items. I was skeptical that it was Augie's stolen property, but I agreed to meet her at the bus station to find out. In the course of the evening, I got my hands on the evidence, but the woman escaped. Once I verified it was stolen, I turned it into the evidence room . . . which I will do after I leave here." She shrugged. "Nothing more than a rookie's dumb luck."

He let out a low whistle. "Impressive."

"Every word is true. I only left out the bits about you. I'm usually very honest."

The barge shifted in the water. Frankie got a funny look on her face. "We didn't finish the conversation we were having in the car."

And now's not the time, he thought. But she was staring at the counter with a numb look he knew all too well. There was no getting around it.

"You did fine tonight," he told her. "What I said about not trusting you . . . that wasn't fair. I was angry about something else."

Her cheeks flushed. "There's more to it. You may not have heard what happened to Brad McDaniel."

"I know. I read about the accident."

"You don't know."

"I know enough. The woman on the elevator, the one with the box you freaked out about? She's Brad's widow, Coral."

Frankie stilled.

"I saw her speak to Dave Jansen after she got off the elevator. I called him, asked who she was. I didn't know Brad's wife, but I sure as hell knew about his history with women. He couldn't keep his mouth shut for bragging."

Her eyebrows lifted, lips parted. He knew she considered herself to be a tough cookie, but the circumstances of Brad's death would be hard to get past.

"We can discuss this, but you have to promise there'll be no crying," he said.

"No crying," she said.

"You mentioned a trauma. I thought about your bruise, the way you flipped out when Coral McDaniel came off the elevator. I figured you'd been involved with Brad, got caught up in the accident. You weren't in the car, were you?"

"He was chasing me. He lost control."

"Sounds like Brad."

"I've never done anything . . ." Her mouth spasmed. "Anything like that in my life. He told me—"

"You don't have to explain. Like I said, I know about Brad. We can go into the details if you want, but whatever happened, you should let it go. And forget about those damned pills."

"I screwed up," she said.

"I've screwed up many times. Nobody in this world is perfect."

She managed a strained smile. "You asked why you should trust me after I lied. I've been completely honest now. You know it all."

She waited, wanting to be absolved. For some reason, he couldn't give her that. Might have been something to do with

Mercy. Might have been the pie he could see on the cutting board over her shoulder.

He nodded toward the evidence on the counter. "Let's wind this up. We'll sort out the rest tomorrow."

He copied ten pages of the manuscript and put it on top of a ream of blank paper. She packed the evidence in the box and taped it in the original plastic. The CJC evidence room was open 24/7.

At the foot of the ramp, she promised to call him if she ran into a problem. Otherwise, she would be in touch early. They almost shook on it, but she had the box in her arms and the moment turned clumsy. They nodded and she was gone.

He walked around to the aft deck to get some air. Somewhere on the bluff a dog barked. Downriver another dog responded. Then there was a different sound, a growl coming off the water, as primitive as anything living in the backwoods. He'd heard about sightings of bobcats not far from the bridge near where the Wolf River flowed into the Mississippi. And there were older stories about panthers that once slipped through the shadows of the ancient swamps of the Delta.

The growl died. The gentrified dogs fell silent.

He thought about tonight, Frankie's revelation about Brad and the confrontation with Garrett tomorrow.

Which pack did he belong to—the kept dogs or the wild ones?

He went inside to think about that. Over a piece of pie.

Chapter 50

B illy woke at first light. Walker Pryce was on his mind, so he called the ER nurses' station. He was friendly with the nurses at The MED, having spent endless hours there questioning gunshot and stab-wound victims. He asked if someone would get a status report on Pryce.

Vicky at the desk called back. During the night, Pryce's intracranial pressure had increased. They'd moved him to the neuro ICU. Bad news. The murder count could easily rise to four.

He hit the streets in search of Dominique. If he lucked out, he would turn her over to Dunsford and pray the man handled it right—sweat her with threats of a felony-theft charge then offer to reduce to misdemeanor possession of stolen goods if she would confirm where she got the stuff. If she brought Garrett into it, her statement would connect him to Augie's murder. That would blow the doors off the investigation.

For all that, even with Dominique's testimony, convincing Dunsford that Sid Garrett was a murderer wasn't going to be easy. Dunsford had spent his career fitting crimes into boxes. If they didn't fit, they weren't real crimes. Billy had compelling evidence, but the possibility that Garrett had killed Augie was still hard for him to accept.

Frankie had called to say she was on her way to Ramos's house to question Ovia about locating Dominique's hideout. It was a long shot but worth the try. She would call when the interview was over.

On his fifth run down Union Avenue, his mobile rang.

"The old bitch admitted she sold the curses to Dominique, but that's as far as she'd go. I pushed pretty hard. She was madder than a wet cat. She spit on me."

He could hear that she was wired up after interrogating Ovia.

"And catch this," she said. "Garrett called Ramos and banned him from Robert House because he'd given me access to Red's file. He went off about Red's privacy rights, then claimed his own privacy had been violated. Then he rambled on about his dead brother and the NSA taking over the world."

"He's right about the NSA," he said.

"No, listen, Billy. Ramos thinks Garrett is out of control. A week ago he confronted Garrett about his script addiction. Garrett's response was to have the lock changed on Ramos's office."

"Sounds like you nailed Garrett's addiction."

"I think he's losing it. Maybe we can wrap up this case by supper time."

"When will you talk to Dunsford about the evidence?" he asked.

"I called the squad. He hasn't come in."

"Lazy bastard."

"Maybe he picked up another case," she said.

"Bullshit. He's eating pancakes at Perkins."

She laughed. "You really can't stand that guy."

"I know Dunsford. He likes his pancakes. Extra butter and syrup." He thought for a minute. "Go in, give your statement to anyone sitting around the squad. That puts you on record without giving Dunsford a chance to question you. And try to get an ATL issued on Dominique. We need to find her. Handle this right, and it could be a win for you."

"I'll settle for not being fired," she said.

"You'll be fine. I'm heading to Robert House for the groundbreaking ceremony. I bought the Cards' pillowcase and put the dummy manuscript in an envelope that makes it look like the original. Maybe I'll catch Garrett off guard, and he'll do something stupid like confess."

"God. No telling what he'll do. This sounded like a good idea last night, but I forgot to mention there will be media present. Should we rethink this?"

"I'm going to show up. I want to look Garrett in the eye before we push this any further."

He thought about Lou Nevers. He never got to look Lou in the eye and ask why he'd made his choices. Lou didn't even leave a note.

Frankie's engine cut off. "I'm at the CJC. Good luck."

A Channel 3 News van pulled up to the curb as he turned into the Robert House parking lot. Reporter Jasmine Cooper flashed some leg as she climbed out of the passenger side. She was young and hungry to move up to the anchor desk. She expected a boring assignment, a puff piece. Today might surprise Ms. Cooper, might even be her big break.

He thought about secrets, how cops catch people at their worst, even solid citizens like Garrett. War stories come in three tiers: funny stuff sanitized to entertain the general public; stories shared only with people who work in public safety—cops, fire-fighters, ER doctors and nurses. And then there's the untellable. Every cop has stories that he'll take to the grave. Some he's proud of. Some hurt too much to repeat.

He backed into a space at the corner of the lot, got out, and leaned against the fender. Shallow pools of rain from last night's storm spread in low spots on the asphalt. A crowd of about a hundred was milling around at the front of the building. He picked out city officials, clergymen, and several attorneys from top-tier firms. It was common knowledge that Garrett wasn't a favorite in the legal community, but people showed up because he was a celebrity and because they admired his dedication to civil liberties.

Billy had a clear view of Garrett standing halfway up the steps. A young woman was clipping a microphone to his jacket. Garrett patted the woman's arm as if he were a kindly old man. Unlike a few days ago, Garrett looked relaxed and moved as if pain free, although the circles under his eyes were spreading across his face like a mask.

Ten of the Robert House residents stood around on the steps behind Garrett, shirts pressed, hair combed. The scene looked staged at the expense of the men's dignity, but then he noticed the way they were joking with Garrett. They clearly liked him. Money alone doesn't build that kind of bond, especially with men who've had their pride kicked out from under them.

Billy glanced back at the pillowcase and manuscript lying on the passenger's seat. He wondered if Garrett had convinced him-self his actions were justified because he was saving the museum. Even the decision to kill can be defended by a murderer as his highest and best choice.

A couple of steps up from Garrett his bodyguards stood with legs apart and hands clasped, looking like extras out of *Men in*

Black II. Billy gave the guys a hard second look. He'd dismissed them as ass hats with the cushy job of following a man who was paranoid about being shot when there was no real threat. All they needed to keep their jobs was to put up a good front and to know when to keep their mouths shut.

However, these two were far more capable of swinging a bat than Garrett. Sneaking into the DeVoy would have been tricky, but Pryce's place had been an open opportunity. Garrett could have waited in the back of his Caddy while they ambushed Pryce and torched his house. Or they could have learned of their boss's problems and gone after Augie and Pryce on their own. That didn't seem likely, but still.

He pushed off the fender and walked through the crowd. If he was going after Garrett in public, he needed a sense of conviction to pull it off. He could count on one hand the number of men in his life he'd respected. Garrett had been one of those men up till now. He'd like to speak to Garrett before he made a final decision.

He stopped in front of the podium. "Excuse me, Mr. Garrett," he said.

Garrett ignored him, pretending to study his notes. Finally, he spoke without looking up.

"What is it, Detective?"

"You've got a big problem. When you're done here, we need to talk."

Garrett placed his hand over the mike on his lapel and nodded toward a group of five men working their way toward the podium. "See those people? They're my board members. Big contributors."

"This is important. It's about the investigation."

Garrett leaned down in Billy's face. "You and your bitch girlfriend have already wasted my time. Walk away or I'll have you escorted off the premises." He straightened, waved at the approaching group, and gave Billy a genial smile. "Thank you. Glad you could stop by." He spoke loudly enough to make the front row of people believe Billy had handed him the best news of the week.

In no mood to fight with Garrett's goons, he walked back to the car, took out the pillowcase and dummy manuscript, and resumed his position against the fender. He'd given the man his chance. Time to let the shit fly.

Garrett tapped his lapel mike and slipped his hands in his pockets, projecting folksy sincerity.

"I'm grateful to all of you who've made the expansion of Robert House and the Carter museum possible. My brother Robert believed it was the duty of every American to defend the freedom of those least able to do so for themselves. He stepped up during the darkest days of the civil rights struggle and fought to make his beliefs a reality. After my brother disappeared, I pledged I would carry his torch. In that tradition, our goal at Robert House has been to help and heal. In the same tradition, our goal at the Calvin Carter Museum is to remind and educate.

"We must never forget the past when, for one brief moment, God turned his back on his people. The devil had his way. Dr. King was murdered right here in our city. My brother Robert paid with his life because he dared to stand up for what he believed. Many of us have worked since that time to defeat that kind of evil and prove the devil hasn't won."

Billy opened the manuscript and flipped to the second page: *God turned his back on his people. The devil had his way . . .* Garrett's words struck him like juice off a frayed electrical cord. Garrett had lifted words straight out of the introduction.

Son of a bitch. Garrett did it. He killed Augie and stole the manuscript.

Billy walked around to the car door, hands shaking so badly he could hardly hold on to the pillowcase and manuscript as he laid them on the car seat. He didn't need props to set off Garrett. He had the truth. His vision tunneled down to Garrett's face as he walked through the crowd to the podium.

"The residents of Robert House thank you," Garrett was saying, "and the museum thanks you. We'll now gather in the west garden for our ground-breaking ceremony. After last night's rain, that should be easy work, even for us old folks."

Everyone laughed politely.

"The culinary students have prepared lunch—"

"Stop there," Billy said, standing a few feet in front of Garrett. "I have a question." He waited a moment until he had people's attention. "Did Augie Poston beg for his life before you crushed his skull or did you kill him with the first blow?"

The woman beside him gasped. Others shrank away as if he were a felon with a knife. The bodyguards sprang down the steps to flank Garrett.

Garrett's reaction was immediate. His head dropped forward, his fingers wrapped the edge of the podium for support. Then his head came up slowly, eyes narrowed like the slits of a cottonmouth. He wasn't done.

"Do *not* interrupt me," Garrett said, power rising in his voice.

Billy held up his hand. "Sir, you've spoken lines from Walker Pryce's unpublished manuscript, a man who nearly died in a house fire yesterday. Pryce allowed only one person to read that manuscript. That was Augie Poston. Poston was murdered and the manuscript stolen from his home. I'm going to prove that you not only have that manuscript, but that you killed Augie Poston."

Garrett stabbed a finger at Billy. "Detective Able, according to the police, you're the number-one suspect for Poston's murder. You are a renegade cop, possibly delusional, most likely dangerous. Whatever you think you're going to do, it will be done from a jail cell. I'll make sure of that. My friends and I have seen all we want to see of you today. Leave now. If you refuse, I will have you hauled out of here in handcuffs."

Garrett then swept the crowd with his gaze. "Ladies and gentlemen, I apologize for this unpleasant interruption. I will curtail my speech and ask you to step to the gardens where I will join you shortly."

He clipped off his mike and churned up the steps with amazing quickness, disappearing through the doors.

Behind Billy, Jasmine Cooper and her cameraman were elbowing their way toward him. He was pissed off, realizing too late the mistake he'd made. Only part of the crowd heard his accusation, but because Garrett had a mike, everyone heard what he had to say, including the TV cameras. Jasmine would verify with Middlebrook the accusation Garrett had made. The chief would have no choice but to confirm it. Within hours, every local station would name Billy Able, former detective for the MPD homicide squad, as a person of interest in Augie's murder. He'd dug himself a deep, damned hole. Middlebrook was going to be furious over this.

Jasmine stuck the microphone in his face. "Detective Able, how do you respond to the allegation that you're the prime suspect in the Poston murder case?"

The camera lens stared at him from behind Jasmine's shoulder.

"No comment," he said, and started for the car.

Chapter 51

etective, Detective." Jasmine Cooper's heels clopped on
the asphalt behind him.

Billy stayed ahead of her, keeping his stride regular
so he wouldn't appear hurried on camera. He could walk like
Mother Teresa and Middlebrook was still going to be all over him
when this footage hit the news. Dunsford must have told Garrett
he was their primary suspect. Or Garrett made the story up on
the spot. The old guy could have done it. He was that good on
his feet.

The phone in his pocket vibrated. Probably Frankie. He'd let
it go while the camera was trained on him. He got in the car and
cranked the engine. Jasmine stood with the cameraman thirty
feet away, waiting. She wanted a cutaway shot—guilty cop flee-
ing the showdown. *Not this time, lady.*

He rested his hands on the steering wheel then waved to her.
Jasmine got the message. She made a beeline for the building to
go after Garrett.

He took out his mobile and checked the call.

This is Teri Selby, ICU nurse at The MED. Vicky in ER gave me
your number. Walker Pryce has asked that you come speak
with him. Come as soon as you can. Give my name at the
desk. I'll take you back to see him.

He texted Frankie to meet him at The MED, then drove out
of the parking lot.

appreciate you coming so quickly, Detective," Nurse Teri said.
She was blond, pretty, dressed in blue scrubs, and had that
pleasant but no-nonsense air he admired in the ICU nurses.
They walked past several glass-wrapped rooms.

"The doctor inserted a catheter through his skull to monitor
intracranial pressure," she said. "Mr. Pryce is lucid, but he might
go in and out while you're talking." She fixed him with a steady
gaze. "He's in serious condition. I realize you're here on a police
matter, but don't press him."

They entered the room. Walker Pryce looked rough—head
shaved, face swollen, eyelids bruised, IV tubing draped over the
bed rails and into both arms. Compression boots pumped away,
forcing the blood in his legs to circulate. The blood pressure
monitor and infusion pumps beeped. The catheter sticking out
of Pryce's head looked like a meat thermometer.

Billy knew about brain trauma—bodies thrown through
windshields, heads cracked open on concrete. The brain swells
and the skull cuts off blood and oxygen. If the pressure becomes
too great, a surgeon has to remove a chunk of skull to let the
brain expand. Some survive it, some don't.

He felt bad for Pryce, but he hadn't come to the ICU to hold
the man's hand. He would keep it simple, a couple of questions.

The nurse moved to the bedside to adjust the saline drip. Pryce stirred and looked around. It took a few moments for him to realize Billy was standing at the foot of the bed.

"Hey, Detective."

"Hey, Pryce. You look like shit."

Pryce tried to grin.

"Need some aspirin?" he asked.

"More like a martini."

Billy took a breath to let his anger with Garrett recede and tried to look reassuring. "You're going to beat this. In the meantime, I'm going to catch who did this and kick the crap out of them. Are you up for a couple of questions?"

"Sure."

"Do you remember what happened?"

Pryce frowned, his eyes fixed on a spot near the window. "Is the house gone?"

The house had been gutted. A man this sick didn't need to hear that news. "I'll look into it and let you know."

Pryce swallowed. "There's a draft of my manuscript in the Cloud."

"Great. Then it's safe. Listen. Someone called you yesterday as I was leaving. Do you remember?"

Nurse Teri cleared her throat. *Ease off.*

"My book comes first," Pryce said. "That's why I called you here."

"What about it?"

"You have to promise you'll get my manuscript published if I don't make it. Bird-dog the project until it's in print."

"You have Roxanne to handle that."

Pryce was watching him. "You're thinking I manipulate

people. Roxanne, Augie. I admit it. But this book's important. It's my job to expose the bad guys whatever it takes. I won't apologize for that."

Pryce looked at the nurse. "Would you step out a moment?"

"Ten minutes," she said. She gave Billy a dark look and left.

"Roxanne can't handle it. Swear you'll get the book out, or this conversation is over." Pryce was slurring. One pupil was more dilated than the other and the whites of his eyes were blood-red.

Billy knew this might be his last chance to get information. If Pryce needed help with the book, he'd ask Freeman to step in. "All right, I swear. I'll do it for Augie if for no other reason."

"Deal. My password is . . ." Pryce looked puzzled. "Umm. My name with my birthday backward."

Billy took out his memo book and recorded it. "Got it. Do you remember who did this?"

"I remember a knock at the door."

"Have you talked to Dunsford?"

"Who?"

Billy reminded himself to keep it simple. "The detective in charge of Augie's case is named Dunsford. He may have stopped by to talk to you."

"Dunsford. Oh, got it. No, I'll put him off. What I'm about to tell you isn't recorded anywhere, so get this down."

Nurse Teri stuck her head in the door. "Gentlemen, Mr. Pryce needs his rest."

Pryce waved her off. "Most of the Department of Justice documents I've read were redacted. I had pieces, but not the whole story. Then Augie brought over that surveillance photo with the agent talking to the kid. The kid's face was familiar. I pulled a file and went back through FBI reports related to an incident outside of Greenwood, Mississippi. The reports indicated an agent had screwed up badly. It didn't say how."

Pryce pointed to the water glass. Billy gave him a sip through a straw.

"Thanks. You getting this down? I said that already, right?" He swallowed. "This involved an FBI agent named Grant, the guy in the picture, one of his informants, and an agent in Mississippi who had infiltrated the KKK. Grant's informant had information on a voter-registration drive about to take place in Greenwood. He had the names of workers, meeting places, and how funds were to be distributed. In exchange, this informant wanted extra protection for one person. Grant was eager to get his hands on specifics, so he agreed."

Billy stopped writing. *God almighty.* He had an idea of where this was going but didn't want to interrupt.

"The informant told Grant that a civil rights worker from Memphis was to meet with Oswell Carley, a black leader in Mississippi, a very militant dude. The FBI and the KKK had been trying to track Carley, but he'd managed to stay out of sight most of the time.

"The meeting was to take place at night at an abandoned cotton barn off Highway 82. The Memphis guy was delivering nine hundred dollars to fund the ground game for the registration. You know what I mean. They paid people to knock on doors, for transportation and the occasional bottle of whiskey."

"Hold on," Billy said, writing.

"Would you read some of that back?" Pryce asked. "I lost my place." He listened as Billy read, and nodded. "Right, so Grant told the Mississippi agent about the meeting and that he should watch for trouble. Grant didn't know the Klan had become suspicious of the agent. This guy was looking for a way to prop up his cover. You know, maintain his credibility.

"The Klan wanted to get their hands on Carley, so the agent blabbed about the meeting at the cotton barn. He thought they would beat Carley up, scare him out of the state. He assumed it would be over and done with before the Memphis guy arrived. The agent asked to be posted as lookout on the highway so he could wave the Memphis guy off if he showed up early. But it all went to hell. The Memphis guy was already at the barn with Carley when the Klan got there."

Billy stopped writing. He knew what was coming next. "The Mississippi agent was standing on the highway while the Klan was at the barn killing Robert Garrett."

Pryce gave him a lopsided smile. "I figured you'd get it. The Klan hated Garrett even more than Carley, because they saw him as a traitor to the white race. When they found Robert with Carley, they shot him. The agent never learned what happened to the body. They hauled Carley a couple of miles away and lynched him. No one was prosecuted for the lynching, and the two murders were never connected."

Pryce closed his eyes. "Hang on," he slurred.

Billy was acutely aware the nurse would throw him out at any minute. He waited for Pryce to open his eyes before he spoke.

"When Augie showed you the photo, he had no idea the kid was significant," Billy said. "But you knew it was a young Sid Garrett talking with an FBI agent."

"That's right. I kept a file on the Garrett disappearance. The papers ran several photos of Robert posing with his kid brother, Sid. The face didn't click with me right away, but when it did, I realized it had been Sid who demanded special protection for someone. He was exchanging information because he was afraid for Robert's safety. Poor kid, the whole thing backfired."

Pryce continued. "I called Garrett a couple of days after Augie died and told him I had a photo of him as a teenager talking with his FBI handler. I wanted an interview. Pure arrogance on my part. He called when you were there to say he was coming over. I don't remember what happened, only the knock at the door."

"I saw Augie and Garrett talking at the mortuary," Billy said. "Augie had a piece of paper in his hand. Garrett looked upset. I assumed they were discussing the estimate for Red and Little Man's funeral. Augie must have shown Garrett the photo. Later that night, Garrett must have gone to Augie's apartment and killed him. He tore the place up looking for the photo."

Pryce nodded. He made a grunting noise, trying to clear his throat to speak. The blood pressure monitor sounded an alarm. He sighed, closed his eyes.

Shaken, Billy stepped back as Nurse Teri came through the door and brushed past him.

In the hallway, he quickly reviewed his notes to make sure he'd gotten it all down. From the look of things, he might not get another chance to speak to Pryce. He checked for a text. Frankie was waiting for him in the lobby. He took the elevator down.

She was leaning against the wall across from the bank of elevators, arms crossed over her chest. She straightened when she saw him. "Dominique called. She wants us to pick her up."

"Where is she?"

"The library."

"The library?"

"Come on. I'm parked out front." She talked as they wove through the crowded hallway. "Dominique forgot to pack her good knives last night. She called this young Jamaican guy she trusts and asked him to bring them to the library after the ceremony."

"Why call you?"

"She got wind that Garrett knows she stole Augie's stuff. She's frightened. She wants immunity for trying to fence the watches, and she wants protection from Garrett. In exchange she'll testify about Garrett asking her to scare Red and Little Man with the curses, and that Augie's stolen property came from his house."

"That works," he said. "How did she know Garrett was on to her?"

They walked past an on-duty cop. Frankie lowered her voice. "Dunsford came in and read my statement about the evidence. I gather he phoned Garrett and questioned him about Dominique and the evidence box. The guy manning the shelter's reception desk must have told Garrett that Dominique had run off last night.

"It looks like Garrett put two and two together, because he sent his goons to rough up the kitchen help. They wanted to know where Dominique was hiding. When they didn't get an answer, they went into a rage and swore Dominique would get what she deserves."

"How could she know this?" he asked.

"The Jamaican guy called her back and told her."

"But the bodyguards could've beaten the crap out of him and found out about the meeting at the library."

Frankie pushed open the front entrance door. "I told Dominique that, but she wouldn't listen. That's why we're in a hurry."

Chapter 52

They took off in the Jeep, weaving in and out of heavy traffic. "Tell me what happened at the ground-breaking," Frankie said.

He described the confrontation, then ran through a short version of Pryce's story.

"We had it right except for the most important thing—the kid in the photograph," he concluded. "I'm convinced Red approached Garrett and demanded money for the photo of Carter. Garrett sent Dominique to scare them out of town. When they died, Garrett must have felt safe.

"Now here's a piece of the puzzle I witnessed without realizing it. At the funeral home, Augie must have told Garrett about the manuscript. I walked in as he was showing Garrett the photo of himself as a kid talking to Grant. Garrett had kept the secret buried all this time, but now he knew a journalist was digging into the story and that he'd be exposed as an informant right along with Carter. The world would know he played a part in his brother's murder. He'd be held in contempt or, even worse, pitied, something his ego couldn't tolerate."

Frankie shook her head. "The guilt must have eaten him up.

Damn it," she shouted. She slammed on the brakes, and hit the horn.

The old pickup in front of them had skidded to a stop to avoid running a yellow light. Tires behind them screeched. Billy looked back to see a Mazda inches from their bumper.

Frankie smacked the steering wheel. "We're stuck. This is a long light."

He pointed at the library's large parking lot on the right. "Take it easy, we're almost there."

Half a block up stood the ultramodern, glass-and-steel library. Fronting the library was a plaza with five monolithic pillars, twelve feet tall, each with words and symbols etched in their sides, meant to represent printing rollers. Two laid on the ground. Three stood on end.

Frankie blew out a breath. "Dominique said she'd be waiting in the ladies' room just inside the door. I'll go in after her. You switch to the backseat. When we come out, I'll put her in the back where you can keep an eye on her while I drive. She's so nervous, she might try to jump out at a light."

"Yeah, well . . ." He nodded at the library. "Look at that third pillar. There's a woman standing near it—black dress, same colored bandanna as the one she had on in the bus station. That's Dominique."

Frankie craned her neck. "And the short guy walking across the plaza with the box—that's her friend. She's lost her mind. Why go outside when she's terrified Garrett will find her?"

"I guarantee the bodyguards scared her friend into flushing her out in the open. Look at that."

He pointed at a black Cadillac coming from the opposite direction. It slowed and turned into the long driveway that fronted the library. "That's Garrett. Get us out of here," he shouted.

Frankie racked the transmission into reverse. The Jeep's rear bumper slammed into the Mazda so hard it made enough room to clear the pickup in front. She stomped on the gas and powered into the outer lane, right into the path of a lumbering UPS truck. The truck crumpled Billy's door inward, the impact shoving the Jeep into the side of the pickup. The Mazda driver began honking furiously.

Frankie looked at him, wide eyed. "What now?"

"Leave it. We're outta here."

She flung open the door and hit the pavement running. With his door crushed, he had to scramble behind her over the center console. They dodged traffic, both running flat out across the library parking lot packed with cars.

He could see the black Cadillac rolling up the drive, but SUVs and vans in the parking lot blocked his view of Dominique. Running hard, he passed Frankie and drew away, catching a glimpse of Dominique standing in front of one of the pillars. The short guy was handing a box to her, but her attention was on the Cadillac. It turned for her, and accelerated.

"Run," Billy shouted at Dominique. "Get inside!"

The guy took off for the parking lot. Dominique froze. She started across the driveway, but then saw that the Caddy was coming too fast. She reversed and stumbled, the box clutched to her chest making her clumsy. She ran back across the plaza full of people toward the library.

"No, no, no," Frankie screamed from behind Billy.

The Caddy driver jerked the wheel to change course. Parents grabbed their kids and scrambled out of the way. The car jumped the curb and headed for Dominique, the engine roaring as it struck her. The force threw her onto the hood, carrying her along, the knives flying out of the box like pickup sticks.

Directly ahead of the Caddy stood the third stone pillar. The driver braked, tires squealed. A second before the Caddy struck the pillar, Dominique slid down the hood toward the front. The massive bumper smashed the stone with a sickening thud, Dominique in between.

The plaza went still as if it were drawing a breath, then the screams began. People picked up their kids and ran. One man ran toward the car and Dominique, phone already in hand, but Billy knew there was no hope in that.

The Caddy's back door sprang open. Garrett emerged. He fell to his knees, struggled up, and limped toward the library entrance, picking up speed until he disappeared through the automatic door. Billy swerved to follow Garrett just as the front passenger door opened. One of the bodyguards tumbled out, covered in air-bag dust, to lie facedown on the concrete.

"Get Garrett," Frankie shouted, coming up fast behind him.

Now the driver's door opened. The second bodyguard lurched toward the back of the car, his hand to a nose that had been bloodied by the air bag. Billy wanted to go after Garrett, but he couldn't leave Frankie to handle both men.

"Police," he yelled. They split, and he took the driver, who was still on his feet.

"Hands on your head," he yelled. "On the ground, on the ground."

The man collapsed to his knees beside the rear wheel, blood dripping from his chin, his eyes unfocused. Billy holstered his gun, pushed him on his belly and cuffed him, watching Frankie as she approached the second bodyguard. The guy had come to and was pushing himself off the ground. Billy saw a flash of metal in his right hand. Frankie saw it too and stepped in fast, clubbing him on the neck with the butt of her gun. He hit the concrete, dead weight. She kicked his gun, sent it skittering across the concrete, and cuffed his limp arms. When she backed away, her eyes were glittering, her teeth gritted.

They turned to stare at Dominique, pinned between the hood and the pillar. She was upended, her legs splayed, the trunk of her body trapped between the Caddy and stone. One arm could be seen dangling below the bumper. A stream of blood pooled beneath the Caddy's front tire. The green watchband circled her wrist.

Frankie looked back at him, cocked her head toward the library. "I've got this. Go."

He took off across the plaza. Garrett's dash into the library had amazed him, desperation making the man agile and even more dangerous. He could be hiding anywhere in the library, in the stacks or even holding a hostage. Billy's edge was that Garrett had no idea he was coming right behind him.

The automatic door slid open. He drew his weapon and pressed along the foyer wall. Scanning the open atrium, he saw a group of people who were staring at the top of the escalators that ran to the library's second-floor mezzanine.

He stepped into the atrium, barrel pointed skyward. "Police," he said, just loud enough for the bystanders to hear.

They turned. He put his finger to his lips. "Where's the man who ran in?"

A woman pointed to the escalator. "He just went up."

"Is he armed?"

"He might be," the man closest to him said. "He wrestled with a security guard at the top."

A woman's scream rang out from somewhere on the mezzanine. The people in the atrium scattered as Billy bounded up the escalator steps, crouching as he reached the top. He scanned the space then quickly took cover behind a book cart.

Except for a few people peeking out from among the stacks, the mezzanine appeared to be empty. Directly across from the escalator, a woman stood up from behind the information desk, her hands pressed to her mouth. On the floor in front of the desk, a uniformed guard lay sprawled with one knee rising up.

Billy waved to get the woman's attention. "Police. Where did the man go?" he whispered.

She pointed toward a metal door on the back wall twenty feet behind her.

He moved to kneel beside the guard, a man in his sixties. Blood leaked from a gash in his scalp. Billy looked up at the woman behind the desk.

"Where does that door lead?"

"It's the old wing—a hallway with a meeting room and two storage rooms. It ends in a balcony. No one works back there."

He was familiar with the balcony she was talking about. He could see the back of the library from the barge.

"Call 911," he said. "Tell dispatch there are additional injuries at the scene."

The guard opened his eyes and looked around. "Where's that old fucker?"

"Down the hall," Billy said.

"He got my gun, a .357."

"Is it loaded?"

"Empty chamber, and one bullet. I'm not here to shoot up the place." The guard was shaken, groggy.

"Are you sure about the bullets?" he asked.

The guard nodded.

He squeezed the man's arm and ran to the metal door through which Garrett had just disappeared. Garrett would never allow himself to be locked up for murder. Billy wanted to catch the son of a bitch, but if the guard was right, going after Garrett meant risking one shot in order to take him alive.

He cracked open the door to peer around the frame. The hall ran straight back about seventy-five feet, with tall windows on the left and three doors on the right. At the end of the hall, an exterior door was just swinging shut, which meant Garrett was now standing outside, two stories up on a balcony about six feet wide with a waist-high railing. Below him was a steep, grassy slope held in place by a fifteen-foot-high retaining wall. At the base of the wall ran the train tracks, then the road, then the river.

Billy made a split-second decision. He pushed through the door and sprinted toward the first meeting room on the right. Ten feet into the hall he saw a flash of sunlight as the balcony door swung open. Garrett limped inside, the guard's gun tucked in his waistband. Momentum carried him three steps before he saw Billy coming.

"Drop it," Billy shouted, pointing his SIG at Garrett. Garrett's eyes flared with recognition.

He could shoot Garrett, but under these circumstances, he'd have a hard time proving it wasn't a revenge kill. It was a gamble, but he raced the last few steps to the meeting room doorway. As he cleared the opening, he heard the click of the .357's empty chamber. He hit the floor and rolled. A second later a slug caromed off the door frame, exploding the wood into splinters. He came up on the far side of a conference table, his weapon trained on the opening. If Garrett came through that door, he was a dead man. Billy waited, breathing hard in the silence. He heard footsteps going back down the hall. Then the exterior door slammed shut. Garrett was on the balcony again.

Billy raced for the exterior door, factoring in the possibility that the guard had been confused about the number of bullets loaded. He'd have to sucker Garrett into taking another shot to find out. He stopped at the door, brought up his knee, placed his foot on the door's panic bar, and shoved as hard as he could. The door crashed into the outside wall. He crouched, his SIG before him, and peered around the frame.

Garrett was in the corner, wild eyed, standing with his back against the railing. His face was bleached white, and he was mumbling, the muzzle of the .357 pressed to his temple.

"I'm sorry, Robert, sorry, Robert, sorry, Robert." Garrett closed his eyes and pulled the trigger. *Click.* He pulled again. Another dry click. Garrett looked at Billy with huge, empty eyes.

Billy rose from his stance. "Drop the gun. Let's do this right."

Garrett came suddenly to life. He hurled the gun at Billy and heaved his body on top of the railing. Billy was on Garrett fast, grabbing for a handhold, but Garrett twisted and smashed an elbow into his jaw. Billy's head snapped back and he stumbled, his grip on Garrett broken. Garrett launched himself over the rail. Billy dove for the rail in time to see him roll down the slope and then pitch airborne over the edge of the retaining wall. Garrett landed on his back, angled across the first set of tracks, his head resting against a rail. One hand rose and dropped. Then he lay, inert.

He stared down at Garrett. Sirens yowled from three directions, cruisers and first responders making the scene. Red and Little Man. Augie and Dominique and Pryce—all victims of Garrett's pride. *Let the ditch doctors scrape the bastard off the tracks,* he thought. *I'm done.*

He'd pulled out his mobile to alert dispatch of Garrett's location when another sound came to him, a single horn blast. He knew instantly what it meant. Living on the barge, he'd learned to count down the seconds before a train's dual engines powered past. The engineer wouldn't see Garrett in time to stop.

He stared down the slope, knowing that if he jumped he could wind up in the same shape as Garrett. The horn blew louder. He owed the son of a bitch nothing, certainly not his life. At the street corner, the crossing gates came alive, bells sounding and lights flashing.

No one would blame him for not risking it. But if he didn't move now, right now, Garrett would die. He saw Augie's face before him, the warrior's face in the painting behind the catcher's mask. Augie's eyes smiled at him.

He knew what he had to do. "This one's for you, buddy."

He swung over the railing, lowered himself to hang from the bottom edge of the balcony, and let go. The impact with the slope knocked him breathless. He skidded out of control, the grassy slope slicker than he'd imagined. Sliding down toward the edge of the retaining wall, he grabbed a handful of brush at the last moment. The brush tore away but slowed his drop. He hit the gravel bed below, somehow staying on his feet.

The bells rang. The horn blew nonstop. Garrett, who was lying twenty feet away, raised his head to see the black locomotive bearing down. His head fell back.

The engineer must have finally spotted Garrett, because the wheels locked in a high-pitched scream, sparks flying off the rails. Billy raced for the tracks, planning to grab Garrett's belt and haul him to safety.

The locomotive pounded down on him as he reached the rocky strip of ballast. He strained forward. Seconds left. Almost there. Then Garrett kicked out, connecting with Billy's shin. The ballast shifted, and his feet slid out from under him. He went down hard on a creosote tie, his face even with Garrett's, staring straight into the man's eyes.

"You can go to hell," Garrett whispered.

The wheels hit with a furnace blast of hot metal and sound. Billy smelled grease and fire and the blood of damnation.

He rolled away.

Chapter 53

The next day, iPhone videos of the events at the library appeared on YouTube. The videos immediately went viral. A German tourist on the gangplank of the *Memphis Queen II* captured the struggle on the balcony and Garrett's fall. His subsequent beheading by the locomotive was clearly visible.

Because of the sensational videos, the case was red-hot. The footage Jasmine Cooper taped of Billy's accusation at the ground-breaking connected Garrett to Augie's murder. The resulting firestorm compelled Middlebrook to arrange a media briefing at the CJC the next morning. He asked Billy and Frankie to stand on the dais behind him while he addressed reporters. They weren't expected to answer questions, only to make a good showing for the department, then disappear before anyone could corner them.

After the briefing, Billy and Frankie walked the half block west to the downtown First Presbyterian Church. They sat in the back while a church lady walked the rows of pews and placed hymnals in their slots. She kept her eyes averted but wore a secret smile, probably spinning young-lover stories to herself.

Billy liked the sanctuary's old-wood smell and the fragile, clean light coming through the east-facing windows. He'd been raised in church, but in the last year had fallen away after he'd discovered what Lou had done to little Rebecca Jane. Hearing a preacher go on about Jesus' good and faithful servants made him uncomfortable.

Who was good? Who was faithful? He didn't know anymore.

"I saw the train-track video," Frankie said. "Close call."

"I considered standing back, but I couldn't do it."

She nodded. "Guys like you are always looking for someone to save."

"That's not true. I had an opportunity to take Garrett down in the hallway. I wanted to. Payback, you know?" He stared at his shoes, a small smile coming to his face. "I decided against it. Too much paperwork."

She rolled her eyes. "You couldn't live with yourself if you'd shot Garrett."

"I don't know," he said. "Guess it's a moot point. I caught the video of you whacking the guy in the head and kicking his gun. You're one tough chick; *48 Hours* will be calling."

"Oh, shut up." She leaned forward, rested her chin on the heel of her hand. "That was nothing. I was a lot more nervous at the briefing. All those cameras. What happens next?"

"You go back to work. I wait to see if the review board is going to give me the ax."

She gave him a sidelong look. There wasn't much she could say about that.

"Middlebrook met with me this morning," he said.

"And?"

"He said you're the one who broke the Poston case when you

spotted Augie's watch on Dominique. He knows we were poking around in Red's investigation, but we can't be penalized for that. The case was closed."

"Besides, we were right," she said.

"They don't care. It's about procedure and regulations. I told you it would work out. With that video, you're a free ad campaign for the MPD. They'd be fools not to bump you up to an investigative squad."

"Did Middlebrook say that?"

He shrugged. "We didn't talk about much except Garrett and the review board."

She sat back in the pew, frowning. Her toes were doing a little tap dance on the carpet. "You've got to get through this."

"Middlebrook says he'll back me. His statement to the board will have to include my interview with Pryce at his house. He warned that there would be repercussions."

"But not dismissal," she said. "They're not crazy."

"Probably not. I'm not worried."

He rested his arm on the pew, tipped his head back, and studied the walnut ceiling. His casual front was for her benefit. He was worried as hell. Now that he was on the chopping block, he wanted back on the force more than anything.

"They found the phone, laptop, and the missing photo," she said. "Garrett had them locked up in his desk at home. If he'd locked up the watches and manuscript, he would've gotten away with it."

"Pryce is out of the ICU. He talked to Dunsford, told him Garrett was supposed to be at his house around the time of the attack, so I'm off the hook for that."

Frankie nodded. "Will Dunsford try to shoot you down at the hearing?"

"He won't want the board to look too deeply into how he mishandled those cases. And he'd be an idiot to start up with me. As it stands, he'll close four cases at once. He'll retire with the best stats in the squad."

"That's okay with you?"

"No, but he'll be gone. He won't do any more damage. I may be gone, too. Or they may take away my stripes. Or try to move me out of homicide. But I'll be damned if I'll spend the rest of my career chasing down stolen lawn mowers."

"That won't happen."

"On the plus side, my paycheck is already built into the budget. For that reason alone, I may get a pass."

She gave him a broad smile.

He slapped his thigh and stood. "It's been a pleasure, Mz. Police Goddess, but I have to go. I've got business that needs tending to."

Chapter 54

He drove to the Peabody where he found Theda Jones seated on a plush velvet sofa in the middle of the hotel's sumptuous lobby. She was flipping through a copy of *Vogue*, the automated baby grand plinking softly behind her. She wore a tailored jacket and jeans with her black hair coiled in a loose bun that exposed the elegant length of her neck.

"Miss Jones," he said, noticing the carry-on bag tucked next to her feet as he approached. She'd asked for a one P.M. meeting, explaining that she was about to leave for Boston.

"Detective." She stood and tilted her head toward the player baby grand. "That machine is butchering 'Clair de Lune.' But we're not here to talk music."

For privacy, they moved to a small table some distance away from the lobby bar.

"First, thank you for coming. I apologize for getting upset and leaving you so abruptly the other day." She pulled an envelope from her pocket and removed the letter. "I wanted you to read Red's last letter."

It was written out on the same staff paper he'd seen in Red's room and in the same hand that had made notations on "Old Fool Love."

> *Dear Theda,*
>
> *I trust you to keep this package safe. Do not open it, baby girl, because what's inside might put you in danger. I'll write in a few weeks to say where to send it.*
>
> *We·played a club at Tunica last night and had luck at the black jack table. I've enclosed part of the winnings. Go pick out yourself a pretty dress.*
>
> *Remember. You've got what money can't buy. Talent. Don't let nobody stand in your way. If anything happens, carry on for me and Little Man. He said to tell you hello. Remember, we love you, sweet girl.*
>
> *Daddy Davis*
>
> *P.S. I'm working up a new song. "Old Fool Love." It's going to be a hit.*

Billy slipped the letter back in the envelope. "How much money did Red send?"

She rested her elbows on the table and peered at him from behind her interlaced fingers. "Two money orders of a thousand each."

Her gaze drifted away, drifted back. "People have used me all my life, everyone but Red Davis. He was the father I never had."

Behind Theda's eyes, he glimpsed the little girl who'd come from a sordid background and been caught in a trap, yet she possessed an artless aura of confidence and privilege. Theda had talent and beauty, but like everyone else, what she really wanted was someone to love her.

"You don't know about me," she said. "In New Orleans, I got involved in the kind of trouble a lady doesn't like to talk about. Then I met Red and Little Man. I was so desperate for a chance to get out, I believed the scholarship in Boston was true. I didn't know Cool Willy would go after them for helping me."

She pressed her fingertips to her eyelids to stop the tears. "After you told me Willy had hurt them, I had to find out if he'd been involved in their deaths. I called friends in New Orleans, working ladies." She looked up at him, embarrassed. "I asked if he'd ever talked about going after Red and Little Man, hurting them again. They said all he talked about was me. He loved me, wanted me back. I was the only one. Ridiculous, romantic stuff. Willy wants to build a new image. *William* wants to be classy. I'm part of that.

"The ladies said Willy didn't know where Red and Little Man had gone until the *Times-Picayune* reported Red's death. He left for Memphis Tuesday night. Said he thought he'd find me here."

"Cool Willy didn't kill Davis and Lacy," Billy said. "It was the man who died on the tracks."

"I thought that might be the case." She nodded, wiped her cheek. "I have to leave in a few minutes, and we still have the package to discuss. I no longer need you to sell what's inside."

"Why's that?"

She cocked her chin toward the bar. "Check out the guy in the cashmere T-shirt, the one scrolling through his iPhone."

"I spotted Cool Willy when I walked in," he said.

"He paid for my last school semester. He thinks I'll come back to New Orleans to play in his piano bar after I graduate. That I'll be his girl, maybe his wife."

"What about the competition?"

A slow smile crossed her face. "William Cooley is pussy-whipped for the first time in his life. I plan to keep it that way. I'm going to win that competition. I'm going to be a star. He'll fall in line once he gets the bigger picture. He's all about prestige."

"And the package?"

"It's at the concierge's desk in your name. I didn't want Willy . . . William to see me pass it to you. He's bad about sticking his nose in my business."

She stood and gave Cool Willy a wave. He threw some bills on the bar and stood. "Good luck, Detective. Thanks for doing the right thing by Red and Little Man. I plan to do the same."

After Theda left, he went to the concierge desk and collected a box with a Boston address written on the side. He returned to the table. Inside the box were a stack of photos and a yellowed envelope that held a letter written on a piece of stationery with a Federal Bureau of Investigation letterhead.

To Whomever Opens This Envelope:

I don't know Calvin Carter's reasons for becoming a paid FBI informant. I do know he was angry when he discovered that covert surveillance photos had been taken of him. He knew they could be used as coercion if he ever tried to stop being useful to the Bureau.

Carter turned the tables. He followed our agents and took his own covert photos. In mid-April of 1968, he gave me copies of the photos saying, "If your guys threaten me, I'll expose your agents and everyone they're talking to."

Among the photos was one of an agent I knew out

of Washington. He was talking with a man I didn't recognize at the time. When I looked through the photos five years later, I recognized the man as James Earl Ray.

It's been documented that Ray stayed at the New Rebel Motel in the days leading up to Martin Luther King's assassination. This photo was taken at the Rebel Restaurant. Carter must have locked up his copies of the photos and never looked at them again. Or maybe he recognized Ray and decided to destroy his copy for his own reasons.

I can't reconcile the reason one of our agents was meeting with Ray prior to the assassination. After what had been said about Director Hoover's hatred of Dr. King and the multitude of conspiracy theories, I couldn't make the photo public without irrevocably tarnishing the reputation of the agency. But neither could I bring myself to destroy evidence.

That's why I've put the decision in the hands of fate. Like a note in a bottle, I've sewn photos into the pockets of my favorite jacket. When I'm gone, someone may find them. Whoever reads this letter will have to make their own decision.

May God guide you.
Agent Leland Grant, FBI

The photo Grant referred to was on the top. Two men sitting in a booth, staring at menus with the name "Rebel Restaurant" printed on the front. One of the men was James Earl Ray. No doubt.

Billy read the letter a second time. A server stopped by his table and asked if she could bring him anything. He ordered a double shot of Jack. Then he called her back and made it coffee.

He remembered the two inner pockets in Red's Goodwill jacket. Both pockets had clipped threads that curled against the silk lining. One pocket had held the stack of photos with Carter and Garrett talking to Grant. The other pocket must have held this letter and the second set of photos, taken by Carter, with this picture of an FBI agent talking to James Earl Ray.

Red Davis must have sat for a very long time after he'd found the photos, trying to decide what to do with them. He'd been right about the jacket. It was cursed. The photos of Sid Garrett and Carter got Red and a lot of other people killed. The photo of James Earl Ray was potentially even more dangerous.

Billy understood Agent Grant's dilemma. He'd wanted to be loyal to the Bureau, but as a good agent he couldn't destroy evidence of what was potentially the biggest cover-up in U.S. history. So he'd left the decision to chance.

Now it was his responsibility. Should he deliver the letter and photo to the Memphis FBI field office and hope they bumped it up to D.C. for investigation? Should he make an appointment with the state attorney general, or confide in a congressman or senator?

Whatever he decided, he couldn't make a move before he was cleared of allegations that he'd murdered Augie. There would be a lot of questions asked. Events of the past week had knocked the hell out of his credibility.

One thing was for sure, the decision Leland Grant had ducked was now the blue monkey sitting squarely on Billy back.

Chapter 55

James Freeman had hired B. B King's Blues Club for the night, the whole damned place, to throw a Celebration of Life for Red Davis, Little Man Lacy, and Augie Poston.

Billy sat beside Freeman at a balcony table with a great view of the stage, watching a house packed with friends drinking and telling stories about the dearly beloved and recently departed. Freeman had brought in the best: Dr. Feelgood Potts, and Mr. Sipp, "the Mississippi Blues Child." Red and blue spots lit the stage. The crowd was clapping and cheering, swaying and moaning, dancing and shouting to the music.

Billy felt good. He was back on track. He knew who he was again. He thought about his job and the people in this city, the blues and the lawless river he lived beside with its power and its secrets. He'd come home and found what he needed. One thing he'd learned, the ability to spot your own happiness takes talent.

Freeman nodded toward Mr. Sipp, smoking up the stage with his electric guitar. "You ever want to play like that?"

"Nope. You come into this world fully loaded like these guys, or it's best to sit home and play albums. How about you?"

"Harmonica's my thing."

"You any good?"

Freeman laughed. "Hell no. I got no soul."

The crowd on the dance floor hooted as Dr. Feelgood joined Mr. Sipp in trading licks on "Dust My Broom."

The band had it cranked. Freeman leaned in so Billy could hear him. "You asked me to find a literary agent to sell Pryce's book. Turns out, because of all the hype around Garrett, execution by train, the manuscript is hot. HarperCollins made a fat offer. I took it to Pryce this morning. By the way, he'll be out of rehab in a couple of days."

"That's good. Pryce deserves a break. And he needs operating capital for his next project."

"Pryce and I talked about the way you dogged those cases until you nabbed Garrett. You're a force of gravity, man. You showed up in Memphis and bodies started dropping through the ceiling. It's ironic. A kid bargains with the FBI to protect his brother then the FBI screws up and the guy gets killed."

Billy shook his head. "No sympathy for the devil from me. Garrett killed four people, almost five, to cover what he'd done fifty years ago."

Freeman raised his beer mug. "You know the saying, 'Up north their stories begin with *Once upon a time.* Down south it's *You ain't gonna believe this shit.*'"

They clinked glasses.

"What's the fallout going to be at Robert House?" Billy asked.

"Minimal. The shelter has a lot of community support. The museum is a different story. Media coverage about Garrett and Carter is going to make it tough, so I've agreed to take over the fund-raising."

Freeman cocked his head toward the club's main entrance. "Look who just walked in wearing red."

Billy saw Frankie at the door, looking dynamite in heels and a strapless dress. Ramos was at her side in a charcoal suit and dark glasses, his hand on her arm. Billy hadn't met him, only seen Frankie's photos from the funeral. In person, Ramos looked like Antonio Banderas. They had agreed that she would bring Ramos to the party, but it gave him a jolt to see her with him.

He watched them weave through the crowd to join a table of people she seemed to know. When Ramos was seated, she spoke with him, then began looking around.

"Who's the stud with Mz. Police Goddess?" Freeman asked.

"Her priest."

"That's funny," Freeman said, leaning in, shouting over the music, "I thought you said he was her *priest*."

"You got it." Billy stood and got Frankie's attention. She smiled at him and crossed the dance floor.

"You're a lucky bastard," Freeman said, standing, too.

As Frankie started up the balcony stairs, Mr. Sipp took the mike and quieted the crowd. "We have someone here tonight who meant a lot to Red and Little Man. Miss Theda Jones is going to perform the last song Red Davis wrote. It's called 'Old Fool Love.'"

The spotlight hit Theda, her long hair swinging, her short, sequined dress shimmering over the tops of her thighs as she crossed the stage. She looked up at the balcony and gave Billy and Freeman a warm smile and a wave. They waved back as the keyboardist turned the piano over to Theda.

"Good idea to bring her in from Boston," Freeman said. "Red would've loved seeing her here."

Frankie joined them at the rail as Theda began to sing.

"Love at the door feeling bad,
'Cause love can't have what it needs to have.
Old fool love.
That old fool . . . love."

When she was finished, the crowd stomped and cheered.

Freeman shook hands with Frankie. "I'm James Freeman."

"Frankie Malone. Thanks for throwing the celebration. I'm sure the guys would love being remembered this way. Billy said you stepped up during the investigation, really went out on a limb. Thanks for that."

Freeman grinned. "May I get you a shooter? A jelly roll? Wang dang doodle? A voodoo child?"

"Club soda for now. Thanks."

As soon as Freeman headed for the bar, Frankie turned to Billy. "Theda Jones seemed happy to see you."

"Yeah, and it looks like you and Ramos are pretty tight."

"Sergio's a nice man. He's helping me work through those anxiety issues I told you about a couple of weeks ago."

Her hips moved to the music. She looked relaxed for the first time since that night at Central Station.

"Great. Has he sacrificed any chickens lately?"

She looked startled. Then that knowing look came over her, the one that says, *Oh, buddy. Have I ever got your number.*

He felt like a dolt. Maybe it was the red dress. She was definitely showing some cleavage.

"You sure seem interested in what I'm doing with Sergio," she said.

"That's how it is with partners."

She squinted at him as applause drowned out his words. "Sorry. What did you say?"

"I remember thinking when we first met that plainclothes duty would suit you better than uniform."

She shook her head, still perplexed.

"I've been cleared by the board. I'll be back with the squad in a couple of days. And there's something else. Before Augie died and things got screwed up, I talked with the chief about my reinstatement. I agreed to sign on only if I had the right to choose my partner."

"The chief would never go for that. It's not policy," she said.

He spoke up this time to be certain she could hear him. "The chief asked me to tell you to come by his office tomorrow, Detective Malone."

"Oh, my God. That's great." She hugged him.

"You free tomorrow afternoon, partner?" he asked.

"Absolutely, partner. You want to celebrate?"

"You know the photo and letter from the jacket I've been holding on to?"

"Of course. Have you decided what to do?"

"Tomorrow you and I are going to visit Walker Pryce. We'll hand over his next investigative project."

Outside, a train whistle blew. Theda and Mr. Sipp stepped up to share the mike for a duet: "Old Fool Love."

Acknowledgments

My special thanks to:

Linda Kichline: publisher, author, and mentor; and Lieutenant James B. Flatter, (Ret.) Monroe County Sheriff's Office, Key West, Florida. Their brilliant minds and gracious hearts helped to make this book possible.

Rob Sangster, fellow author, for sharing his creativity, his unflagging attention to detail, and his love for me and the written word.

Tessa Woodward, for her support and superb editor's eye.

Robert Gottlieb, for his belief in my writing.

I also thank the following law enforcement professionals, attorneys, and others for their knowledge and amazing stories. Debra Dixon; Debra Heaton; Will Heaton, Esq.; Linda Orsburn, Marc Perrusquia, investigative journalist; Police Officer Jeanette Roycraft, (Ret.); Irvin Salky, Esq.; Bill Selby; Teri Selby BSN, RN; Deborah Smith.